THE SOLOMON SIGIL

TEMPLARS AND THE SHAMIR

DAVID S. BRODY

Eyes That See Publishing

The Solomon Sigil: Templars and the Shamir

Copyright © 2022 by David S. Brody

Eyes That See Publishing

Newburyport, Massachusetts

ISBN 979-8-9851618-2-3

Cover by Kimberly Scott and Renee Brody

Printed in USA

PRAISE FOR BOOKS IN THIS SERIES

"Brody does a terrific job of wrapping his research in a fast-paced thrill ride."
—PUBLISHERS WEEKLY

"Rich in scope and vividly engrossing."
—MIDWEST BOOK REVIEW

"A comparison to *The Da Vinci Code* and *National Treasure* is inevitable....The story rips the reader into a fast-paced adventure."
—FRESH FICTION

"A treat to read....If you are a fan of Templar history you will find this book very pleasing."
—KNIGHT TEMPLAR MAGAZINE

"An excellent historical conspiracy thriller. It builds on its most famous predecessor, *The Da Vinci Code*, and takes it one step farther—and across the Atlantic."
—MYSTERY BOOK NEWS

"A rousing adventure. Highly recommended to all Dan Brown and Michael Crichton fans."
  —READERS' FAVORITE BOOK REVIEW

"The year is early, but this book will be hard to beat; it's already on my 'Best of' list."
  —BARYON REVIEW

ABOUT THE AUTHOR

David S. Brody is a 10-time Amazon #1 Bestselling fiction writer named Boston's Best Local Author by the *Boston Phoenix* newspaper. His children call him a "rock nerd" because of the time he spends studying ancient stone structures which he believes evidence exploration of America before Columbus. He has served as a Director of the New England Antiquities Research Association (NEARA) and has appeared as a guest expert on documentaries airing on History Channel, Travel Channel, PBS and Discovery Channel. A graduate of Tufts University and Georgetown Law School, he resides in Newburyport, MA with his wife, sculptor Kimberly Scott.

The Solomon Sigil is his 18th novel.

For more information, please visit DavidBrodyBooks.com

ALSO BY THE AUTHOR

DEDICATION

To those brave souls who, with courage and dignity, did their best to do the right thing during the ugly years of the Holocaust

NOTE TO READERS

1. **Though this story is fiction, the artifacts, sites and works of art pictured are real. See Author's Note at end of book for more detailed information.**
2. **This is a stand-alone story. Readers who have not read the first thirteen books in the series should feel free to jump right in. The summary below provides some basic background for new readers:**

Cameron Thorne, age 48, is an attorney/historian whose passion is researching sites and artifacts which indicate the presence in America of European explorers prior to Columbus. His wife, Amanda Spencer-Gunn, died a couple of years ago; she had moved to the U.S. from England and was an expert on the medieval Knights Templar. Cam and Amanda adopted Astarte, who is of Native American descent, when she was a young girl. Astarte is now attending college in Montana. Cam resides in the Massachusetts suburbs.

"The world is full of magical things, patiently waiting for our senses to grow sharper."

- W.B. Yeats

INTRODUCTION

From *The Secret Teachings of All Ages,* by Manly P. Hall:

"The Talmud contains a legend concerning the remarkable [object] called the Shamir with which King Solomon tried and trued the stones for the Temple. The Shamir was the magical 'worm' used by Aaron to cut the stones for the breastplate of the High Priest. Solomon, when ordered to build the Temple without the sound of hammers, could not cut the stones in the ordinary manner, but by laying the Shamir against the side of the rock the stones instantly and noiselessly separated according to any desired pattern."

CHAPTER 1

New England
March, Present Day

Cameron Thorne thought about letting voicemail take the call. But he had heard too many stories of lawyers burned by leaving the office early —in this case, meaning 4:30—on a Friday afternoon. It was a favorite tactic of cutthroat attorneys to serve time-sensitive court documents at 5:00 on Fridays, especially on long weekends, just to force their opposing counsel to work over the weekend. Often the service of these documents was accompanied by a "courtesy" phone call that would allow the serving attorney to explain to the judge, "But, your Honor, he had seventy-two hours to prepare a reply."

Gulping, Cam answered. "Cameron Thorne."

"Hi, it's Shelby."

He smiled. A double bonus. He wouldn't have to work over the weekend, plus Shelby Baskin was one of his oldest friends in Boston's legal community. He dropped into a leather chair and spun to look out over the Westford town common, complete with requisite bandstand and cast-iron cannon.

"Surprised to catch you still in the office," she said. When Cam had first joined a Boston law firm as a young attorney, Shelby—a senior associate at the time—had been his mentor. Now she worked at one of the largest downtown firms, splitting her time between practicing law and managing the local Big Sister organization. It was an arrangement most firms would never agree to, but Shelby was such a talented litigator that the firm decided to take what it could get. Shelby possessed an uncanny ability to connect with a jury—as the saying went, women wanted to *be* her, and men wanted to be *with* her. To this latter point, Rivka was convinced Cam was one of those men. "You two have such a connection," she said. "There's an energy flow between you." Cam didn't know about that. It was true, however, that he had a crush on her when they first met.

He returned to the present. "Why would you be surprised to catch me at 4:30?" He feigned being offended.

"Cam. I *know* you."

He chuckled. "Fair enough. Truth is, I was just about to cut out. One of the perks of being a sole practitioner."

"Can I bounce something off you first?"

He pulled out a legal pad. "Of course."

She explained that she was part of a team working to resolve old Holocaust victim cases involving European banks. "Most of the big banks in the large cities have already settled. But there are hundreds of smaller banks that have basically ignored this issue for the past eighty years. Old bank accounts, not to mention safe deposit boxes. But, of course, the paperwork has been lost."

"Let me guess. The banks won't release the assets without proper documentation."

"Yeah, big surprise. Because of course people shipped off to concentration camps kept their bank records and safe deposit box keys with them. Not to mention death certificates. So we come in and threaten to make a fuss. If they're smart, the banks do the right thing and let us try to find the rightful owners without having to bring a lawsuit."

Cam knew that Shelby's uncle Abraham had been involved in fighting for Holocaust victims' rights—sometimes aggressively so—before he died. He guessed that was how Shelby got involved.

She continued, "We've been going through a bunch of safe deposit boxes from a bank in Rouen, in northern France. About two dozen of them. One box has something really, well, odd in it. I thought you might help me figure out what it is." She paused. "Or what it means."

"Sure. Shoot."

"It's a lead box, about the size of a paperback book. Inside, it's stuffed with rough white wool, like it was just shorn from a sheep. We dug through it, thinking there might be jewels inside or something. But it was empty. The only other clue is that on the outside of the box, carved on the lid, there's a Hebrew word, *Shamir*."

"Is that a name? Wasn't he a prime minister of Israel?"

"Yes. Yitzhak Shamir. But we couldn't find any Shamir relatives with any connections to Rouen or even anywhere in northern France. Most people with the Shamir surname are from southern Asia and aren't even Jewish. In fact, Shamir wasn't even Yitzhak Shamir's real name. He changed it when he moved to Israel after the Holocaust—Shamir means a thorn, or a rock that cuts metal. Anyway, the point is, we're not sure it's even a name. It might have another meaning. I'm hoping you can help."

"I'll try. But what makes you think I can figure it out?"

"Because there's one other thing carved onto the lid of the box." She paused. "Next to the word *Shamir*, there's a Templar cross."

His eyes widened. "Oh."

She laughed lightly. "Now do you understand why I called you?"

Hanging up with Shelby, Cam checked his watch. Almost five. Mind still on the mysterious lead box, he flicked off the office lights and locked up. He had another mystery to investigate, one that required a 300-mile drive to Pennsylvania. He phoned Astarte as he walked to his car. She was home from Montana for spring break. "I'm on my way to that pickleball tournament. Should be over by eight, then I'll be home, then we can leave."

"I'll expect you by seven, Dad. I mean, you've never really played before."

Cam and Rivka had been roped into registering for a charity event at a local indoor facility. They had taken a quick lesson earlier in the week, but only played a couple of games. "But I've played a lot of racquetball. And Rivka's an amazing athlete." Before becoming a Mossad operative, Rivka had a short career as a professional volleyball player. With a smile, he added, "It might be later than eight, if the trophy celebration runs long."

"Bye, Dad. And don't hurt yourself."

Five minutes later he pulled into the parking lot of an old warehouse which had been converted into a massive indoor sports facility in the Forge Village section of Westford. He changed quickly in a locker room and found Rivka—tall, tan and fit—warming up on one of the courts. Not surprisingly, she was surrounded by an admiring group of middle-aged men.

"Cameron," she said, trotting over to greet him with a smile and a kiss. When she was excited, her Israeli accent became more pronounced. "Come on, let's warm you up. Our first game is in ten minutes."

"You're in an especially good mood." Which was saying something, because Rivka never seemed to have a bad day.

"It's been a while since I was on an athletic court. I've missed it." She leaned in and whispered, "Let's kick some ass."

She served to open the match, low and hard. The return came floating over the net. Cam charged in and hit it out of the air, a slam that landed just inside the back line for a winner. "Fault," the umpire called.

"What?" Cam said, perplexed.

"You need to let it bounce first on the return of serve," Rivka reminded him.

"Damn." Cam shook his head, smiling. "I got a little overexcited there."

They settled in, managing to defeat more experienced opponents largely because of Rivka's net coverage and elite athleticism. In the semifinals, they lost to a team of sixty-somethings adept at dinks, lobs and spins.

"My gosh," Cam said as they stepped off the court. "That was like being sliced open with a surgeon's scalpel."

Rivka looked at her watch. "I need to run." She had received word this morning that she needed to be packed and ready to leave on a mission tonight.

"Do you have any idea where you're going? Or when you'll be back?"

They trotted down the hallway toward the locker rooms. "No on both counts." She sighed. "I know, it sucks. But part of the whole spy thing is, well, keeping things secret."

After a quick check to make sure they were alone in the hallway, she slipped her arm around his waist, pulled him close, and kissed him eagerly. She tasted sweet and warm and a bit salty, all of which Cam found intoxicating. After five seconds, she pulled away abruptly, took his hand, and led him into a dark utility closet. She closed the door, nibbled on his ear, cupped his crotch, and breathed, "What was it you said on the court about being overly excited?"

She didn't wait for him to answer.

Ten minutes later, they were back in the hallway, their faces as flushed as when they had first come off the court.

She leaned into him and smiled. "Third place is pretty good for our first tournament. I'm glad we had a chance for a quick celebration."

"Wow," he said with a grin. "What would the celebration have been like if we came in first?"

She pulled him closer, her face flush. "Speaking of celebrating, I feel pretty lucky." She blinked. "With you."

"Thanks. Me, too."

She bit her lip the way she did when she was nervous. But she didn't say anything.

"What?" he asked.

"It's just ... well, never mind."

"Tell me."

She seemed to make a decision. "Not now." She kissed him quickly. "When we're alone."

They showered, then shared a long kiss goodbye in the parking lot. "Be safe," he said, squeezing her hand.

At just after eight, Cam was in his SUV driving across town, his hair still wet. He phoned Astarte again. "On my way. Can you be ready to leave in ten?"

"Sure. I just walked Venus. And the bags are packed."

"Cooler also?"

She laughed. "Yes, Dad. Don't worry, I didn't forget your ice cream sandwich." She paused. "You know, you're going to need to eat it fast, before it melts."

He smiled. "That's the plan." Many people thought that diabetics shouldn't eat things like ice cream; the reality was, it was fine if done in moderation. "Then we can stop later for a real dinner."

"You do know that most normal people eat dessert *after* the meal, right?"

"What's normal for the spider is chaos for the fly," he replied, happy with himself for recalling the quote. He made a turn. "Speaking of bugs, remind me to tell you about a call I got this afternoon."

By eight-thirty, they were on the darkened highway headed southwest, Venus on her hind legs in the middle of the back seat hoping Cam would give her the last bite of his ice cream.

Astarte asked about the pickleball tourney, then, glancing at her phone, said, "Estimated arrival is just after one in the morning." Since Amanda's death, Astarte had become Cam's primary research companion, cheerfully jumping in the car with him to go explore strange rock formations and historical mysteries. Being Native American by birth, she was especially interested in research involving Indian sites.

"Sorry to leave so late," Cam replied, "but I wanted to play in that tourney. And traffic will be better now." He smiled. "I'm guessing one isn't so late for you, anyway."

"No, but sunrise wake-up will be like jet lag."

They had made arrangements to view a series of mountaintop boulders arranged to align with the equinox sunrise in eastern Pennsylvania not far from Wilkes-Barre, about a hundred miles west of New York City. A local historical group believed the site—which they had named Council Rocks—had been a ceremonial gathering spot for the native tribes in the region.

"Hotel is twenty minutes from the site. And it's a bit of a hike. So wake-up is actually at five, assuming you want breakfast."

She smiled, her white teeth contrasting with her chestnut skin and jet-black hair. She had always been a pretty girl with cobalt eyes and high cheekbones; now she had grown into a strikingly beautiful young woman. "Friday night bedtime at college."

"I know. I was your age once."

She deadpanned, "Back when the buffalo roamed the plains."

He chuckled as he changed lanes. Astarte shared Amanda's sardonic wit. "It's good to have you home, honey."

She looked at him sideways. "Thanks. Still not sure about that beard, though."

He rubbed his hand across his chin. He had grown what was called a circle beard—a goatee with a mustache, "encircling" the mouth, with nothing on the cheeks. "Me either. Thought I would try it out. Makes me look tough."

"Or makes you look like you're trying to cover up a double chin."

He laughed again. "Like I said, good to have you home."

They drove in silence for a few seconds. "So what's this about the bugs you wanted to tell me?" she asked.

He told her about Shelby Baskin and her work with Holocaust-era bank deposits. "Nothing in the lead box but wool."

"Maybe someone went to the bank in a rush and emptied it, but just left the box behind. Jewels or something."

"Could be. But why have wool in a jewelry box? And why lead?"

Astarte tapped at her phone. "I just Googled it. The only lead boxes I could find are for storing radioactive stuff. I agree, it's weird." She sat back. "But maybe it just happened to be the only box they had lying around."

He looked sideways at her. "One more thing. There was a Templar cross carved on the lid."

She lifted her chin. "Um, maybe you should have mentioned that *first?*"

"I knew this would be a long ride." He turned his palm up and shrugged. "I didn't want to waste all my good stuff too early."

Astarte rolled her eyes. "I'm guessing there must have been Templars in Rouen?"

"Yup. In fact, they had a commandery there. It was one of the first places the Templars were arrested and put on trial back in the early 1300s."

"So they called you and asked for your help." She smiled sardonically. "Cameron Thorne, Mr. Templar."

"Have tunic, will travel."

"Just don't expect me to get on the back of a horse with you."

He nodded, appreciating her reference to the Templar custom of having two knights share a single horse, a reflection of their supposed modest means—their full name was The Poor Fellow-Soldiers of Christ and of the Temple of Solomon. The truth was, they were anything but poor, the order being one of the wealthiest entities in Christendom during the 12th and 13th centuries. The source of that sudden and massive wealth? Nobody knew for certain. History recounted how nine French noblemen traveled to Jerusalem in the early 1100s to found the order and that while there they excavated under the ruins of King Solomon's Temple (hence the name, *Templars*). Within a decade or two they had returned to Europe with power and prestige rivaling the leading royal families of the time. Common sense led to the conclusion that they found something of great and grave importance while excavating but, again, nobody knew for certain what that was. Some speculated it was the Holy Grail or the Ark of the Covenant. Others believed the Templars had uncovered secret writing revealing teachings of Jesus which were at odds with Church dogma, perhaps evidencing a marriage between Jesus and Mary Magdalene. Others suggested they had uncovered ancient knowledge lost to Europe during the Dark Ages which gave them a technological and economic advantage upon returning. And, of course, many believed in the simplest possibility of all: They found King Solomon's lost treasure. Whatever it was that they uncovered, Cam believed the discovery eventually led to the Templar downfall in 1307, the Church apparently feeling threatened by either the strength and power of the monastic fighting force or by whatever secrets the knights were harboring. Cam had spent the past fifteen years researching the Templars, trying to figure out what it was that made them both so powerful and such a threat to the Church. He was fairly certain—based on numerous medieval artifacts and sites found in and around New England—that protecting their secrets spurred the Templars to travel to America before Columbus, in search of a safe haven. But he had been unable to put his finger on their original discovery. Was the lead box a clue?

Realizing he had been lost in thought for a few minutes, he smiled at Astarte. "Anyway, sorry to drag you on another road trip."

"But this trip tonight has nothing to do with the lead box, right? You said the site was Indian. Lenape."

"Right."

"So no need to thank me. I'm psyched to see it." According to centuries-old Native American prophecies, Astarte—the fortieth female in her line—was destined to be a transcendent spiritual leader for the American Indians. As such, she took every opportunity to learn more about, and make connections with, the various tribes around the country. Even if it meant skipping spring break on the Gulf Coast with her friends and being stuck in the car with her dad.

"Of course." He smiled. "But I do appreciate your company."

Since early childhood, since even before Cam and Amanda had adopted her, Astarte had been living under the prophecy's shadow and bearing its weight. Cam sometimes wondered if it had stolen her childhood.

"You know," he said, glancing at her, "you can just walk away if you want. You don't have to try to fulfil this prophecy. You can go be an astronaut or something if you want." He smiled. "Or help manage my pickleball career."

She gave him another eye roll, then stared out the window, taking a few seconds to respond. These were the times Cam most missed Amanda. She had a special bond with Astarte, not to mention being better at understanding and relating to the psychology of a young woman.

"You say that," Astarte finally replied, "but it's not that easy. This is who I am. Who I've always been. It's like if someone told you that you didn't have to research history anymore. Sure, you could walk away if you really had to. But you'd feel empty, incomplete. It's your passion. At least partially, it defines you." She shrugged. "I feel like I have to at least *try* to do this. If nobody listens to me, or they all just laugh, well, then, I can go be an astronaut."

Perhaps trying to end the conversation, she turned on the radio and began quietly to sing along. Cam cruised the middle lane, in no rush. After about ten minutes, he broke the silence. "Knowledge is knowing a tomato is a fruit. Wisdom is not putting it in a fruit salad. Philosophy is wondering if that means ketchup is a smoothie."

She made a face. "Wait, what?"

"Just trying to make conversation. It's a long ride."

"Oh my gosh, Dad. We can talk about anything you want. Just no more … whatever that was."

"Okay. How's Matthias?"

A smile illuminated her face, which he took as a good sign. "Great. He's starting to hear back from law schools. He got into Georgetown and Columbia. Waitlisted at Stanford. Still waiting to hear from Harvard and Northwestern."

"What's his first choice?"

"I think whoever gives him the most money."

Cam nodded. He and Amanda had saved enough for Astarte's college tuition, but graduate school would be a stretch, like it was for most families. "Tuition costs are crazy."

"The thing is, for the work he wants to do, working for the tribes, he's not going to make a lot of money. So he can't take on big loans."

"What's he doing for break?"

"Working at the firm in Bozeman he clerked at over the summer. They give him hours whenever he asks for them."

"Speaking of doing legal work for the tribes, this site we're going to see has an interesting history."

"How so?"

"Apparently, the landowner wants to strip-mine it. The local tribe didn't even know about the site until recently. Now, they want to preserve it. But he won't sell. He's holding out for big bucks."

"The owner is giving us access?"

Cam angled his head. "Unclear. My contact was vague about that. I think they're hoping that, early in the morning, nobody will care."

"Great," she said. "Just what we need. Another one of your adventures."

An hour after hanging up from her conversation with Cameron Thorne, Shelby Baskin descended the staircase to the basement of her brick Tudor home in Brookline, just outside of Boston's Kenmore Square. She had inherited the sprawling home from her uncle Abraham—it was much larger than she needed, so she carved out a handful of rooms, including a suite in the basement, for use as temporary apartments for women on the run from abusive spouses. Incorporated in the suite was a windowless, steel-doored room her uncle had fortified as a safe room. It made a perfect spot—much more secure than anything her law firm could offer —to store the dozens of safe deposit boxes the bank in France had crated up and turned over to her team. She pressed her eye up against an optical scanner mounted on the wall next to the door and waited as the lock whirred and released.

Bruce looked up as she entered. "Thought you'd forgotten about me," he said with a smile.

Thirty years, and he still smiled at her like a kid seeing a rainbow for the first time. All the shitty things he'd done, all the heartbreak, all the lies—but she never doubted his love when he beamed at her like a smitten schoolboy. Which was why here they were, three decades later, somehow still together.

"I thought you might want to take a break."

He looked at his watch. "Wow, I had no idea it was so late." He rubbed his face. "This room is like being in a time capsule."

She kissed him lightly, his fresh, citrusy aftershave overcoming the stale smell of the closed room. It had not been an easy decision to trust Bruce—an accomplished art thief—with the contents of the safe deposit boxes. Obviously, if something went missing, fingers would point at her. But he had shaken his head and said, simply, "You know I don't steal from the innocent or vulnerable." It was a code he lived by, an odd— some would say perverse—moral compass he used to navigate his way through life and, more importantly, rationalize his crimes. He had spread his hands. "And who's more innocent and vulnerable than victims of the Holocaust?"

They left the safe room, locked up, and went upstairs to the wood-paneled, chandeliered living area. Shelby had updated the kitchen, bathrooms and electrical and plumbing systems of the century-old house but left much of the original architectural and design features intact. Seated in a cushioned window seat overlooking the gardens behind the house, she ordered a pizza and opened a bottle of Pinot Grigio. She had long ago accepted that their days of eating in restaurants were over. Four years earlier, Bruce had scammed a mob boss in a real estate deal and been forced to stage his own death to avoid it being arranged for real. For most of the time since, he had lived off the grid in North Carolina under a fake name, occasionally visiting Shelby in Boston but never going out in public in the New England area. Avoiding restaurants was a small price to pay to keep him safe—for a few heart-wrenching weeks, Shelby had actually believed his death had been real.

She poured the wine. "So, any cool finds?" she asked. Bruce, who spoke French, had volunteered to take a closer look and summarize the personal effects left in the boxes after things like cash and bonds had been removed and placed in the firm's vault.

He sipped from his glass, rubbing her stockinged feet with his free hand. "Not cool so much as sad. Letters. Keepsakes. Photos. Personal records." He grimaced. "These were things people thought they'd come back for. There's not a single one with a happy ending."

She sighed. "Not happy. But maybe we can give some of these families a few bucks and some memories."

"And some closure."

"Right." It struck her that, as much as she had never liked her uncle Abraham and his draconian ways, his passion had rubbed off on her. He had devoted his life to fighting for Holocaust victims and their families. And now she was doing the same. The only difference was that she insisted on doing so through legal channels, while he had often resorted to vigilante justice.

"Did you speak to Cam about the lead box?" Bruce asked, bringing her back to the present.

"He's going to look into it for us." She smiled. "I mean, for me."

Bruce nodded. "Yeah, probably smart not to tell him it's a favor for me." On two separate occasions, Bruce had used Cam as a pawn in scams he was running. "I think Cam would like to put *me* in a lead box."

⬦✝⬟

Cam cruised the middle lane at seventy, the traffic light as they cruised west through New York State toward Pennsylvania, passing north of the City. As a Genesis song ended, Astarte turned down the radio volume. "I'm taking an interesting philosophy course this semester. We've been talking about something called simulation theory. Ever hear of it?"

"I don't think so."

"Basically, it suggests that we are living in a computer simulation designed to make us believe this is the real world."

"You mean like that movie, *The Matrix*?"

"Exactly." She shrugged. "It sounds crazy, I know. But the more the professor explained it, the more it sort of made sense."

"I'm all ears. We got another couple of hours." Road trips like this always seemed to lead to interesting conversations with Astarte, which was one of the reasons Cam liked them so much. Too bad Amanda wasn't here to participate. She had died, ironically, on a road trip two years earlier.

Astarte shifted in her seat, turning toward him. "Okay, so the theory postulates that there are only three possibilities. It's a trilemma. One possibility is that we—that is, society—will destroy ourselves before we become sophisticated enough to create a massive, universal simulation.

The second is that we are able to create one, but we choose not to. And if neither of these first two is true, it's very likely that we are in a simulation now."

Cam nodded. "Okay. Interesting. And I bet you're going to say the second possibility is very unlikely. Humans rarely choose not to do something technologically that we are able to do."

"Right. So let's look at the first possibility, that we destroy ourselves before we are able to create the simulation. That might be the case, but for it to be true, that assumes we are in something called *base reality*. In other words, we are the first humans, and we just haven't gotten to the level of scientific knowledge yet to be able to produce a simulation. But really, what are the odds of that? It's safe to assume that any simulation would be a reproduction of the same species that created it, but at an earlier time. That is, humans would create a simulation populated by earlier humans. So, while it's possible that we are at base reality, it's also possible that we are a creation of an advanced version of ourselves who made a primitive simulation."

Cam tried to follow this. "I think what you're saying is that it's possible we are the biggest of the Russian nesting dolls, but it's more likely—just based on statistics—that we are one of the dozen smaller ones that fit inside."

She smiled. "That's a good way of putting it. Another way to think of it is watching a TV show of someone watching a TV show of someone watching a TV show, and so on. We *might* be at the very head of the conga line, but the odds are that we are someplace in the middle. Just one of the people in the show. We just don't know. But if we assume that, *eventually*, we'll get technologically advanced enough to create a simulation of humanity, then we also have to acknowledge that the chances are pretty remote that it hasn't happened yet, pretty remote that we're not version ten or twenty or one thousand."

"Okay," he said, intrigued.

"Here's another way to look at it. Whatever your belief about creation—Big Bang or God—there's still the question, what was there before that happened? Who created God? What was in the universe before the Big Bang?"

Cam nodded. "This simulation answers that. An advanced version of ourselves was here before us. *They* created us. *They* are God or the Big Bang."

"Right. *They* booted up a program, with all the laws of physics and chemistry and biology already programmed in."

Cam went along. "Okay, so let's say we are living in some kind of artificial reality. Is there a way to prove it?"

"Sort of," she replied. "Like I said, I was skeptical at first, but the more I think about it, the more it makes sense." She shifted again. "One way to prove it is something called the Mandela Effect. If the theory is true, there should be dozens or even hundreds of simulations running at the same time. Sometimes they overlap or bleed into each other. Remember that show you made me watch, *The Man in the High Castle*?"

Cam nodded.

"It's like that, with lots of parallel universes. The Mandela Effect is when lots of people share the same memories, which are actually false. It's named after Nelson Mandela. Apparently, millions of people have a memory of him dying in prison, but he didn't. One possibility is that the false memories bleed over from another reality. Here's another example: Lots of people in your generation swear that they ate Jiffy peanut butter as kids."

"I did. Almost every day, a peanut butter and jelly sandwich."

"Are you sure it was Jiffy?"

"Positive."

"You're wrong. It was Jif, not Jiffy." She punched at her phone and showed him an image of the label. *Jif.*

"I'll be damned."

"How about the little guy on the Monopoly board. Do you remember his monocle?"

"Sure. Top hat, cane and monocle. I used to play all the time." He smiled. "While I ate my peanut butter sandwich."

"Wrong again. No monocle." She flashed another image.

"Damn."

"One more. Remember when Darth Vader said, 'Luke, I am your father'?"

"I do."

"No, you don't. He never said that. He actually said, '*No*, I am your father.' But people all remember him using Luke's name."

"Okay. But I'm not sure that's enough to prove your case."

"Agreed. Another example is déjà vu. People swear by it. Maybe because it's true. It might happen when the simulation is changed, like someone called 'cut' and did another take."

"Again, could be."

"That's what I thought. But then the professor made one final argument. He said that, statistically, there should be millions of other life forms in our universe. So why haven't we encountered any yet?" She paused for effect. "The answer is, because the simulation didn't include them. It only included us."

Cam grinned. "Good one. That's the argument I would use to try to convince a jury."

He drove in silence for half a minute, contemplating what Astarte had just proposed. "I have two rebuttals. First, this theory presupposes that a simulation can create conscious beings."

"True. But we are close to producing artificial intelligence, so that doesn't seem like too much of a stretch to me."

He nodded. "Second, is there enough computer power to run a simulation involving billions of organisms like we have on Earth? I mean, all those synapses firing in all those brains and all those cells and, well, just *everything*."

"Fair question. But think how realistic video games have become, just since I was a kid."

"We had a game called Pong. Two vertical lines for paddles and a square dot for a ball. It was the rage. And that was only forty years ago."

"That's my point. Computer power multiplies exponentially. It stands to reason that, eventually, we'll produce enough power for a planet-wide simulation. And, by the way, it's not universe-wide, only planet-wide, because the designers of the simulation made it impossible for us to make contact with any alien life forms."

Cam tapped the steering wheel with both hands. "Okay. You make a good argument. Though it is disconcerting to think I'm not real. Or, if I am, I'm just a lab rat in some experiment. I mean, why bother saving for retirement?"

"That's actually one of the problems with the theory. Why do anything good? Why donate to charity? Why have kids, if they're not real? Why floss? Why love?"

"All good questions." He glanced over, smiled, and squeezed her hand. "But I will say this. The things I felt for your mother. What I feel for you. What I'm guessing you feel for Matthias. If those feelings are part of a simulation, it's a damn good one."

Bruce Arrujo sat back, feet up, Shelby on the couch next to him as they watched the final scene of *The Sting* in Shelby's Victorian-styled living room. She had rolled her eyes when he suggested it. "Again? You must have seen that movie ten times."

"You eat sushi once a week, but you still love it," he had replied, knowing it was a weak rebuttal. The truth was, ten times was a vast undercount. For large parts of his adult life, he had lived on a sailboat, with only a black-and-white TV, an old VCR player, and a handful of movies for video entertainment.

As the credits ran, she stood. "Finally," she breathed, "it's over."

He eyed her toned figure, as smitten by her now as when he first saw her at Harvard Law School, watching as she merrily skipped her way across campus like Gene Kelly in *Singin' in the Rain*. It was finals week, the law students tense and grumpy and sleep deprived. Yet somehow Shelby squeezed joy from the dark, stormy night. Perhaps, he had mused, she could find a way to squeeze love from him as well.

She leaned down to kiss him. "That," she said, "is a thank you for all your work on the French bank stuff."

He smiled. "Maybe I can do more work on it tomorrow. Assuming I get the same kind of thanks."

She turned. Over her shoulder, she said, "I thought you were going to that pow-wow tomorrow."

"I decided against it. I doubt there'll be anyone there who'd recognize me. I mean, not many Indians join the Mob. But still, why risk it?"

From the kitchen, she said, "I agree. It just takes one. You yourself told me there are hardly any pure-blooded Wampanoag walking around. Some of the tribe members might have Mob connections."

He nodded. He himself was only one-eighth Indian, his Portuguese grandfather—who basically raised him—having been half Wampanoag. And who knew who some of his crazy relatives had married?

Shelby returned with a glass of water. "But on the other hand, you can't hide forever." He knew she was beginning to tire of this lifestyle, of him basically being under house arrest. "It's been four years," she continued. "And I know the tribe is important to you."

That was the issue. Anyone looking for him—*really* looking for him—would, like Shelby, know about his ties to the tribe. Would they be at the pow-wow? Not likely, but also not impossible. He exhaled. "It's one thing to do some legal work for them." He had been informally advising a few tribes in and around New England on legal matters, mostly involving real estate and tribal land claims. "But I don't use my real name, and very few of them see my face."

"Um, you're disbarred, Bruce."

He smiled. "But I work cheap. As in, free." Technically, he shouldn't be representing anyone, *pro bono* or not. "You'd be amazed at the demand for free legal advice. My phone won't stop ringing."

She nodded. "Funny. Everyone hates lawyers. But they sure do love free legal advice."

CHAPTER 2

Cam's alarm went off just before five, one of the rare times he was not awakened by Venus licking his face. Rolling onto his side in the hotel bed, he repaid the dog by kissing her on the nose. Her brown eyes opened and she lifted her head, then she yawned and flopped back onto the pillow.

"Sorry, girl, time for a walk. Then we're going to leave you alone for a while." He had secured a room with an outdoor balcony so she wouldn't be cooped up.

Ten minutes later, he returned and awakened Astarte, asleep on the couch in the suite's living room. She stretched and mumbled, "Is it true that people who work actually get up this early *every* day?"

"But only for forty years, until they retire."

"Ugh," she said, kicking off her sheets. "I never want to graduate."

An hour later, they were parked on the side of a country road at the base of a forested slope. He could just make out a narrow path running upward between the trees in the morning mist.

"Remember," Astarte said. "No fanny pack."

He smiled. It was an old joke between them. "But I'll feel naked."

"Deal with it, Dad. You promised. Wear a real backpack or else carry everything in your pockets."

Even though it was only going to be a short hike, he stuffed a few granola bars and water bottles—along with rope, a flashlight, matches, and a first aid kit—into his pack. "Seems like a waste, when everything would have fit fine in the fanny pack."

"These are the sacrifices we make for fashion, Dad."

In the purple light of dawn, a new-model Subaru Outback approached from the opposite direction and slowed. "That must be Anita and Sue," Cam said. "They're going to show us the site."

"They're not the owners, right?"

Cam shook his head. "No. But they're friends with the local tribe members. The Lenape."

"But you said the Lenape don't own it yet."

He smiled. "Right. Not anymore, at least. Five hundred years ago, yes. Today, some guy named Pomeroy owns it. Him and his brother."

"So is he meeting us?"

Cam shook his head again and gestured toward the path, a large "No Trespassing" sign stapled to a tree. "I got an email late last night with more info about this. Pomeroy doesn't want anyone on his property. He's the one who wants to strip-mine it. His brother gave us permission, but he lives down in North Carolina." The Subaru did a U-turn and parked behind them. Cam opened the door. "Hopefully it's early enough so Pomeroy doesn't notice."

Astarte stepped out. "Hope isn't a plan, Dad."

"But when you stop hoping, you start settling. Come on. I'll introduce you."

Large-boned and with a full head of curly gray hair, Anita strode toward them through the dew-covered wild grass with a toothy grin. She embraced Cam. "I've spoken to you so many times that I feel like I know you." She then wrapped her long arms around Astarte, who did her best not to act surprised. "And you, you must be Astarte." She pronounced it correctly, with the accent on the middle syllable. "It's so encouraging to see the younger generation take an interest in these historical sites."

Sue, who had been unloading gear from the Subaru, shuffled forward. Tall like her partner but rail-thin, she mumbled a hello, barely making eye contact. They applied bug spray and then Sue, eyeing the glow on the eastern horizon, said, "We should head up. Watch your step. It's not much of a trail." The women belonged to a couple of local historical groups, including the Pennsylvania chapter of the New England Antiquities Research Association, a group that studied and preserved ancient stone sites not just in New England but in the Mid-Atlantic states as well, which is how Cam first met Anita.

Wearing his backpack, Cam fell in behind Sue, allowing Astarte to chat with Anita as they followed the deer path through the trees, each of them carrying a flashlight and the two women using walking sticks. The morning mosquitoes were out, and Cam was already beginning to sweat from the humidity. He tried to make conversation with Sue, a trained archeologist, but had little luck until he asked about the site.

She spoke over her shoulder, still not making eye contact. He got the sense that she was not comfortable around men. "This area is on the border between the Lenape tribe—most Americans know them as the Delaware tribe—to the east and the Iroquois to the west. One theory is that it was a ceremonial meeting spot for the tribes." She pointed toward the ridgeline, barely visible through the trees. "We're going to the top. There are a bunch of boulders up there that mark the solstices and equinoxes." He knew that but let her continue. "To the ancient people, the passing of the seasons was a cause for celebration. Sort of the way we celebrate New Year's Eve today."

"So the site is Native American?" Cam asked. As a lawyer, he knew it was often helpful to ask questions you thought you already knew the answer to.

For the first time, she turned to look at him. Around fifty, she had large brown eyes and classical features—attractive, as long as she wasn't scowling or tucking her chin into her chest. "Yes. But maybe other things as well. That's one of the mysteries. Why Anita called you."

The trail began to thin and the slope decrease, and within a few minutes they reached the crest of the hill. "Look at those views," Astarte said, peering west over a valley to another line of mountain peaks beyond.

Anita pointed in the opposite direction from where Astarte was looking. "The sun will come up over that hill in about fifteen minutes," she said.

Anita, a recently retired geology professor, led them along the ridge-line to a clearing on the slope of the hill. Cam studied the site. Four boulders dominated the clearing, three in a line and the fourth off to the side, the arrangement making a backward letter L. The largest was about the size of a storage shed; the smallest, at the point of the L, the size of a refrigerator. One of them had split, the top half sliding to the ground where it now rested against its mate.

"This is an overhead shot we took with a drone," Anita said, showing Cam and Astarte her phone.

Council Rocks, Four Boulders

"These were placed here by human hands," Anita said. "See how the largest one, at the end of the L, sits on a bed of smaller stones?"

"Wait, they were *moved* here?" Astarte asked. "How much do they weigh?"

"Between ten and thirty tons."

"So how did they move them?"

Anita smiled, showing a full mouth of teeth and gums. "As a scientist, I can say: with great difficulty."

"But how do you even know they were moved?"

"First of all, like I said, one of them is nestled on smaller rocks. Second, all four are less than ten meters apart from their neighbors—the next closest boulder is 300 meters away. The odds of a cluster like that occurring naturally are, like, 200 million to one. Third, the alignments themselves. They mark the sunrise and sunset on the equinoxes and solstices. As you shall soon witness."

Cam nodded. It was a lot of coincidence.

Astarte asked another question. "What makes you think there was another culture involved here, beyond Lenape and Iroquois?"

The eastern sky was continuing to brighten. "Let's get ready," Anita said. "I'll let you watch the alignment, then answer Astarte's question."

Anita positioned them behind the largest boulder, at the "top" of the letter L. The boulder featured a notch cut away from its lower part. Anita crouched behind the notch and looked toward the fourth boulder, the one forming the short stem of the L. "If you position yourself correctly, the boulder in the distance fits right into the notch area, almost perfectly," she said. "As if it was designed that way."

Cam traded spots with her and snapped a shot with his phone.

Council Rocks, Notch View

He then moved aside so Astarte could see.

"Okay," she said, a bit skeptically. "What happens next?"

Anita grinned. "Just wait for the sun to rise. See that small triangle of light where the notch meets the boulder? The gap? The sun should squeeze right in there."

Cam and Astarte sat side-by-side. The sun peeked over the hill and slowly climbed. Sure enough, after about half an hour, at just after eight, the sun filled the triangle of light and burst through.

Council Rocks, Notch View

"Wow," Astarte breathed. "That's pretty cool."

They sat in silence for a few minutes until the sun climbed higher and disappeared behind the boulder.

Standing, Astarte asked another question. "But today is March 17. Shouldn't the alignment be off a little, since we're a few days from the actual equinox?"

Sue answered. "It has to do with how we measure the equinox. Our calendar date of March 21 is when the middle of the sun crosses the horizon at the equator. But since the rim of the sun comes up earlier and sets later, we actually gain a few minutes of daylight at either end. So if we wanted to be technical about it, if we wanted a real *equinox* with equal parts day and night, we'd mark the day where the rim of the sun crested and the last vestige dipped twelve hours later. That's the way the Indians did it. At this latitude, that date is March 17. Today."

Astarte looked at Cam. "Did you know that?"

"No. I've always used the traditional dates. But what Sue said makes perfect sense. That's what *equinox* means, after all—*equal night*."

Sue's eyes gleamed. Cam didn't know her well, but he recognized when someone was pleased with themselves. "It gets better," she said simply.

Removing a folder from her backpack, she showed Cam and Astarte a photo. "This is a virtual image, generated by Stellarium software. I picked the 2010 date randomly, but it's the same every year, so ignore that." She waited while they studied the image. "Obviously, same boulders, same notch. The sun squeezes into the corner of the notch on March 17, just like today. But look at the other sunrise, at the very bottom of the notch, just cresting the horizon. That's March 6."

Council Rocks, Notch View, 2 Sunrises

"That's an eleven-day difference," Astarte said. "Is that meaningful?"

Sue replied. "We think it might be. The March 17 date, the equinox, is important, obviously. But not all the ancient cultures used a solar calendar. Lots of them used a lunar one. Some still do—in much of the Arab world, for example. That's why Muslim holidays like Ramadan bounce around the calendar. A lunar year—that is, twelve full moons of 29.5 days each—is 354 days, eleven days fewer than a solar year. But when cultures meet and mix, and one culture uses solar and the other uses lunar, you need to somehow reconcile the two calendars. One way is to make an adjustment for the eleven days, which is called intercalation. A good example is Easter. It's based on the lunar calendar, but it doesn't bounce all around the year like Ramadan because of intercalation. The eleven days are added back in to keep the two calendars in sync."

"I get it," Astarte said. "If you don't have intercalation, you end up with the same problem as the Julian and Gregorian calendars drifting further and further apart."

"Right," Sue said. "Getting back to this alignment, that's what this alignment is doing. It's marking not only the equinox on the solar calendar, but it tracks it on the lunar calendar also. The alignment marries the two calendars together by recording the eleven-day difference. One has the sunrise at the top of the notch, the other at the bottom."

They all stared at the image for a few seconds, contemplating the importance of what they were viewing. Cam and Astarte exchanged a quick look. "Very cool," Astarte whispered.

"So," Anita said. "That's one of the reasons we think this site may be more than just Native American. The tribes mostly used a lunar calendar. But this indicates they thought the solar calendar was important also."

Cam finished her thought. "Maybe because they had important visitors who used it."

"Exactly. That's one reason. Here's another." Anita stepped forward, toward the notch, and ran her hand along the horizontal edge as Cam, Astarte and Sue stood a few feet away. "As a geologist, this really jumped out at me." She cleared her throat, taking on the demeanor of a college professor. "The notch feature consists of two very linear sides at a nearly perfect right angle to one another, not uncommon in breaks along natural strata. What is remarkable about this notch is that its edges are oblique to the rock strata by approximately fifty degrees and are instead parallel and perpendicular to the ground plane. Also notable, they are not connected to any natural fracture lines, many of which are visible on the stone." She smiled. "In simple terms, what I'm saying is that there's no way the rock should have broken like that. The notch was manmade. And this rock is quartzite, very hard, which means the cut would have to have been made with metal tools, which the Indians didn't have. No metal tools, no notch."

Sue muttered to herself, "Unless the Shamir did it."

Cam's ears perked. Did he hear that correctly? Shamir? Shear? Smear? Spear? "Wait, what did you say?"

She looked down and muttered, "Nothing."

"I thought I heard you say, *Shamir*?" Not that he could fathom what a mountaintop ceremonial site had to do with a lead box from a French bank. And it was entirely possible he was hearing things.

"Just forget it." She looked to her partner. "Sorry to interrupt, Anita."

Anita continued before Cam could follow up. But he made a mental note to do so. "I also want you to look at the weathering on this face," Anita said. "Where the notch was removed. It's much less weathered, much less smooth, than the surfaces of any of the other boulders at this site." She rubbed her hand on the rock above the notch. "See how rough this is? What that means, again, is that the notch was cut away at some later date, after the boulder's formation."

Astarte asked, "Can you tell from the weathering how long ago the notch was cut?"

"Not exactly. It's not a fresh cut, but it's also not as smooth as the other faces, like I said. I'd say many centuries, at least."

"So, pre-contact?" Cam asked.

"Almost certainly. And I see what you're getting at. If it was post-contact, that could explain where the metal tools came from. But the weathering is much older than that. If I had to make a guess, I'd say the notch was cut around three thousand years ago. Right at the beginning of the Iron Age." She paused for effect. "But fortunately, I don't have to guess."

Cam bit. "Why not?"

"Because we have science. Last year we did something called optically stimulated luminescence—or OSL—testing." She shifted to her geology professor voice and gave a formal definition. "OSL is a highly sophisticated technique for dating rock and soil samples by measuring residual radioactivity captured in quartz grains from the time they were last exposed to light."

She looked at Cam and Astarte, who both nodded. "Got it," Cam said.

Anita continued. "The idea is to take a rock sample from under the boulder, something which has not been exposed to sunlight, and test it to see the last time it was exposed to the sun. That would, obviously, be the date the boulder was put in place on top of it."

Cam and Astarte both nodded again.

Anita pointed. "See that broken boulder out there? And this one right here, as part of our 'L' cluster? We think they were part of the original equinox alignment. But when the boulders broke, they erected a new equinox alignment, parallel to it. That's the alignment we've been looking at, with the notch."

She continued. "So, back to the OSL testing. We dug down beneath the boulders and took one of the small rocks from underneath—remember, I said the boulders were placed on beds of smaller rocks. The tests came back as four thousand years ago for some boulders, and about three thousand years ago for others, including the ones that are part of the new alignment, with the notch." She shrugged. "Doesn't tell us who placed the boulder here, but tells us when."

"What more can you tell us about the original configuration?" Cam asked. "Do the other boulders align to anything?"

"Great question. See the long part of the 'L'? Those three boulders are in a straight line that aligns almost perfectly with the summer solstice sunrise and winter solstice sunset. I say 'almost perfectly' because, unlike the equinox, which stays fixed, the solstice line drifts over time due to Earth wobbling on its axis like a slowing top. Currently, the alignment is half a degree off from where it would be if built today. However, according to computer modeling, it lines up perfectly with the solstices from four thousand years ago, the date indicated by the earlier OSL dates."

"Amazing," Cam replied. "There's a site up in New Hampshire,

America's Stonehenge, which has similar alignments. They're also off by, like, half a degree, for the same reason. And," he added, "that site dates back to the same time period, about three or four thousand years ago."

Anita rested her eyes on the boulders. "This is a fascinating site. Even more so when you consider the extraordinary efforts someone went to in order to repair the equinox line after that middle boulder split. I mean, they had to find or invent or even steal some kind of advanced technology to make precision cuts in a thirty-ton boulder, probably thousands of miles from home." She smiled. "It's almost screaming at us, saying, 'Pay attention to me!'"

Cam nodded, twice this time. His neck tingled, his body's way of telling him he was on the verge of something significant. Three thousand years ago, the time the notch was cut, would be around the time which Cam believed that Phoenician merchant ships—the Phoenicians being the preeminent seafarers of the ancient world—crossed the Atlantic to mine and trade for copper in North America. In fact, a growing list of historians believed that the New Hampshire America's Stonehenge site to which Cam just alluded—consisting of standing stones arranged calendar-like to mark the passing of the seasons—served as a base for Phoenician copper trade in America. Though rudimentary iron tools existed at that time, there was still a healthy demand for bronze artifacts, tools and decorative items, all of which required both copper and tin in the ratio of 88:12. It was widely accepted that the Phoenicians acquired tin along the southern coast of England; had they continued across the Atlantic to acquire the mountains of copper needed as well? Intriguingly, from what Cam had read, the Phoenicians used a lunisolar calendar, similar to the modern Hebrew calendar. A lunisolar calendar essentially was a lunar calendar with an intercalation—that is, an addition of days— made to bring it into sync with the solar calendar. In other words, a calendar similar to the notched boulder. It was entirely possible—based on the dates and the calendar usage—that the Phoenicians had a hand in designing the second, notched alignment at this ceremonial site.

"One more thing I want to show you," Anita said, beginning to walk away. "Right over—"

A gunshot rang out. Cam grabbed Astarte's arm and dove behind the notched boulder, dragging her with him. Anita and Sue likewise took cover, behind the next boulder in line.

"Shit," hissed Anita in a whisper. "Must be Pomeroy."

Cam scanned the ridge, the morning sun now high enough to fully light the day. "There. Near the top. Two guys with rifles."

"They can't shoot us for trespassing, can they?" Astarte asked.

"No," Cam replied. "But they could say they thought we were deer."

"Did anyone see which way they were shooting?" Cam asked in a hushed tone. Maybe the men really were hunters, and by hiding the four of them were making themselves appear more like prey.

A call from the ridge answered Cam's question. "We know you're there," a man wearing a cowboy hat said in a slow drawl. "Come out so we can see you."

"That's Pomeroy," Anita said. "Best do as he says."

Cam stepped out first, shielding Astarte. Anita and Sue followed.

"We're here to observe the equinox sunrise," Anita yelled.

The two men loped down the ridge like they had done so a thousand times, rifles hanging by their sides. "Figured as much," the older man, Pomeroy, replied. Tall and clean-shaven with a weathered visage, he looked to be about sixty. His younger companion, shorter with a pock-marked face and close-set, angry eyes, stayed a step behind. "I told you last time, and the time before, this here is private property." Pomeroy turned away politely to spit out a stream of tobacco juice.

"Your brother gave us permission," Anita replied. "I wrote to him weeks ago and told him about Mr. Thorne's visit." She gestured to Cam. "He was fine with it. And he says he's the half-owner."

Pomeroy shook his head and let out a long sigh. "My brother's a weasel. More to the point, he's not here. And even if he was, my lawyer says that when two people own a property, it needs to be unanimous if one wants to burden that property in any way." He paused. "And I'm beginning to find these intrusions of yours a real burden."

"I understand your concerns," Anita replied. "Truly. But I hope you can understand that this site is of great cultural significance. It needs to be studied by experts like Mr. Thorne. And preserved."

"I don't know anything about that. What I do know is that this land has been in my family for decades." He reached down, plucked a few berries from a bush, and tossed them in his mouth, as if to prove the point. "I played on those boulders when I was a boy, and my grandkids do the same today. So, yes, you are correct, they are *significant*." His eyes narrowed. "Otherwise, I'd dynamite the damn things and be done with all this silliness."

Anita stepped forward. "Please. Don't even say that in jest."

Pomeroy turned to the younger man, who looked to be about Astarte's age. "Jason, did it sound to you like I was jesting?"

"No, sir."

He turned back to Anita. "In fact, those boulders are in the way."

"Of what?" she asked, eyes wide.

"Strip-mining. This land is full of minerals."

"But it's *sacred*."

"The only thing I hold sacred, honey, is the almighty dollar. That's what built this great country." With his gun, he pointed at Cam. "You say this Thorne fellow is some kind of expert?" He snickered. "A thorn in my side is more like it."

Anita answered, her voice tight and controlled as if addressing a disruptive student. "Mr. Thorne is a historian. We are trying to determine who constructed this site. We suspect the Native Americans might have had some assistance."

Pomeroy eyed Cam. "Mr. Historian, let me ask you a question. Do you do a lot of reading in your line of work?"

Cam held his eyes. "I do."

"I figured." He spat again, this time the juice splashing onto Cam's boots. "So how is it that you didn't read my 'No Trespassing' signs?"

Cam shifted, not sure if the question was rhetorical or not. And he didn't want to further antagonize the armed landowner, not with Astarte by his side. "As Anita said, it was my understanding that we had permission. We came to view the sunrise. We didn't think we were doing any harm."

"That may be. But you still have not answered my question about the signs. Brother or not, the signs are clear."

"Look, I suppose the best solution is for us to just leave. To get off your property."

Pomeroy nodded. "Now we're finally making some progress." He raised his gun a few inches, then also his voice. "All of you, scoot! Off my land!"

Cam put his hand on Astarte's back and turned, taking a few steps back toward the path. A second gunshot froze them. "Not *that* way," Pomeroy said. He pointed in the opposite direction, toward the valley below. "Hundred feet in that direction, the edge of the clearing, is the border of my land. I'll give you thirty seconds to get there."

Anita replied. "But there's no way back to the cars from there."

"Twenty-five seconds," he snarled.

"Come on," Cam said. "We'll figure it out."

Jogging, the four of them loped down the slope, seeking shelter as the meadow morphed back into a wooded area. Shielded by a copse of trees, they stopped to regroup.

"Sorry about that," Anita said, breathing hard. Cam figured she was pushing seventy. "Is he right about the brother giving permission?"

Cam nodded. "Probably. When people own property together, generally decisions need to be unanimous. Simple example is that if you and I owned a house together, I wouldn't be allowed to bring in a roommate without your permission."

Sue's perpetual scowl deepened. "But walking on someone's land's not the same as bringing in a roommate."

"Unfortunately, legally, it sort of is."

"And can he really strip-mine the land?" Anita asked with a shudder.

"I think so," Cam said. "There's nothing in the law to stop him."

They stood in silence for a few seconds, contemplating the desecration of the ceremonial site. Finally, Astarte looked around and said, "There's nothing we can do about it now. How do we get down?"

Anita gathered herself and replied, "If we keep going this way, it's going to take the better part of the day."

"Can't we cut across?" Cam asked.

She shook her head. "It's too steep, almost like a cliff face." She gave him a half-smile. "Great views, but not great for hiking. That path we came up is really the only easy way down."

Cam nodded. "So we take the road less traveled by. Is there a map we can pull up online?"

Anita shook her head again. "No coverage up here, unfortunately. But I have a general idea of where we need to go."

A movement back up the slope caught Cam's eye. He lowered his voice. "I think we have company."

Anita let out a long breath. "Pomeroy's too smart to follow us down and make trouble and get his hands dirty. But that doesn't mean he didn't send his ranch hand. Jason."

Cam grabbed a thick branch to use as a walking stick as Sue led the way down. He didn't like this—two older women, no weapons, an unmarked trail, only a few basic provisions. No way were they prepared to spend the night in the woods if they got lost. Assuming the henchman let them get that far.

He took up the rear, occasionally angling his body to glance behind him. Pomeroy's ranch hand had been wearing a camouflage jacket, so Cam guessed he'd be tough to spot from a distance. The hike itself was treacherous, the narrow path steep and still wet from a storm the day before. Mosquitoes swarmed in the thick, still air, and both women were panting from exertion. And the heat was beginning to rise.

After fifteen minutes, he whispered to Astarte, "I still see him back there." The steep descent, it turned out, might be the least of their problems. "At first, I thought he was just going to make sure we left. Now I'm questioning that."

"You think he's going to do something?"

Cam nodded. "Can't think of another reason he'd still be there."

"How about, I circle around to see what he's doing?"

"How about, no way?"

"I'm not a little girl anymore, Dad."

"No. But he has a gun. What if he hears you and decides to take a shot?"

"So you have another plan?"

Cam bit his lip. He didn't.

They walked in silence for a few seconds. "Well, I do," Astarte said.

Cam pushed a branch away. "I'm listening."

"Matthias taught me how to make a snare trap. I could use that twine you have in your pack; it's thick enough. All I need is a sapling and a couple of wooden spikes and trigger I can make with my army knife."

Cam mulled it over. "How would you get him into the trap?" With an animal, a trapper used bait of some kind.

"You have a couple of twenties? We could leave them by the trail, make it look like we dropped them. He walks over to grab them, then zing."

"But a snare trap isn't going to hold him for long. They're designed for small animals like rabbits, right?"

"Right. But it'll flip him into the air. I'm guessing he'll drop his rifle."

Cam nodded. "Might work. And he's not a big guy."

He moved forward to consult with Sue and Anita. They concurred. As a cover, they would stop for a rest. Astarte, in a loud voice, announced she was going to look for berries like the ones Pomeroy ate. Instead, she would push ahead another fifty feet to begin her preparations.

"Give me half an hour," she said, her voice lowered. Then, with a smile, "Oh, and a couple of twenties."

"Half an hour seems long," Cam replied, handing the cash over. "He might get suspicious."

"Not if I sprain my ankle," Anita replied with a smile. "I can be quite a hypochondriac."

They staged the injury—with Anita wailing in pain—while Astarte moved down the trail. Twenty-five minutes later, Astarte scampered back. She pretended to pass around some of the berries she had picked, assuming the ranch hand was watching, to keep up the ruse. "All set," she whispered. "Hopefully, it'll work."

"If not, you owe me forty bucks."

They set off, Anita—limping and with her ankle wrapped—playing her part. Astarte led them, Cam noticing the cash on the side of the trail but not seeing the snare trap. "You disguised it well," he said.

"I covered the twine with leaves."

They ambled along, not even certain their tail was still with them. It was possible he had turned back. But Astarte, who had been spending more and more time in the woods with Matthias and was in tune with the rhythms of the forest, sensed his presence.

Slowing a little, they continued on, now fifty feet past the snare. "He should be there by now," Astarte said in a low voice.

"Maybe he didn't see the money," Cam replied.

"Or," Sue added, "he didn't fall for the trap."

As if in response, a man yelled in anguish.

"Got him," Astarte said with a grin. "Come on."

She and Cam crept back, staying low in case Jason still had his gun or had somehow gotten free. But the trap held. The sapling wasn't strong enough to lift him totally off the ground, but the recoiling tree had flipped Pomeroy's ranch hand onto his head, one of his legs straight up in the air while his body rested on his shoulder blades. The rifle lay a few feet away, not far from the cash. Cam raced forward and snatched it.

"You're going to pay for this," Jason snarled, grasping his leg. Apparently, the trap had wrenched his knee.

Cam studied him. The snare was tight around his ankle and the sapling showed no sign of snapping. He'd be there for quite a while if left alone. With an injured knee, he wouldn't have the leg strength to pull the sapling back down to create slack in the twine to untie it. The best he could hope for would be to use his stomach muscles to do a sit-up in the air and hold it long enough to free the snare from his ankle. But that would require the strength and agility of a gymnast, which Cam guessed the man didn't have. "You're not exactly in a position to make threats."

Jason thrashed, his face red from either exertion or anger. Probably both.

"Let me down," he demanded.

"Not sure you're in the position to issue orders, either." Cam stepped closer and picked up the man's walk-talkie, which had fallen from his pocket. "I assume this talks to Pomeroy?"

Jason spat. "Of course."

"Okay. I'll call him."

Carrying the rifle, Cam turned, and he and Astarte began to lope away. He tucked the walkie-talkie into his back pocket.

"Wait, what about calling Pomeroy?" Jason yelled.

"I will," Cam said, over his shoulder. "Just as soon as we get close to the bottom."

Bruce Arrujo awoke early, jumped on his bike, covered his face with a bandana and sunglasses, and, in the morning light, pedaled three miles along the Storrow Drive Esplanade before winding his way across the Charles River to the marina in Boston's Charlestown neighborhood. He didn't have a driver's license—he was supposed to be dead, after all. No credit cards, either. But he did have a sailboat. A thirty-foot Sabre daysailer. Other than Shelby, it was his one joy in life. In fact, he had gone through the cumbersome and expensive ruse of sailing the boat to North Carolina and then "selling" it to himself as a way to retain owner-ship when he went underground. Then he sailed it back to Boston last summer. If push came to shove, he could live on the boat indefinitely. Not that Shelby would ever go for that.

He chained his bike to a rack and jogged toward the docks. Head down, baseball hat pulled low, and still wearing his bandana across the lower half of his face, he ignored the smattering of other boaters—one of the reasons he got here so early was to avoid having to fraternize. A healthy breeze blew from the west as it normally did in Boston when the weather was fair. Home plate to left field at Fenway Park, Red Sox fans knew. Not that he was a baseball fan. But he knew things, random things, trivial things. Things that might keep you alive. Like which way the bills would blow if someone released a garbage bag full of anthrax-contami-nated cash at a ballgame. That had been, what, seventeen years ago? He shook his head. All the stupid things he had done, all the assholes he had run with, all the enemies he had made. He had no right to still be alive. Alive he was, however, and never more so than when sailing.

As a young man, he had developed a way to look at the world, a methodology to analyze and understand people. Some people were like the land, rational and grounded and steady. They were usually boring. Others were like the sea, turbulent and emotional. They were often volcanic and creative, but unreliable. A few, the really successful ones, were like sailboats, coupling the passion and power of the sea with the stability and permanence of the land. Those were the people who did great things. Or he was beginning to realize as he hit middle age, they at least *tried* to.

Aboard the boat, he removed the sail covers, started the engine, and untied the lines. Somehow, despite all the crime, he found himself almost broke. His last score—a three-million-dollar real estate play—should have set him up for life. But what does someone without a social security number do with three million bucks? Bruce had put the lion's share of it into bitcoin, the market for which had recently tanked, shrinking his lion to the size of a house cat. He didn't care about the money, really. He did care about Shelby, however. He wanted her to retire, and implicit in that decision was that they would be able to travel and enjoy theater and concerts and fine restaurants—and to do so without needing to sell the Brookline home, which Shelby wanted to continue to maintain as a safe house for victims of domestic abuse. The problem was that things like travel cost considerably more when everything needed to be done off the grid.

In fact, his only hard assets were the sailboat, a duffel bag in the back of his closet with $100,000 in cash, and a sleeve of fifty gold coins worth another hundred grand which he kept buried in Shelby's backyard. He wasn't going to starve, and his day-to-day needs were few. But being dead meant he couldn't claim any Social Security or Medicare benefits, and two hundred grand and a forty-year-old sailboat—pristine though it was—were not nearly enough to retire on.

Still under motor power, he angled toward the mouth of the harbor, the cool morning breeze on his cheek. The ice had recently cleared, but water temperatures made it feel ten degrees cooler here than at the docks. His thoughts turned to the safe deposit boxes. Of course, he had no intention of stealing anything from the French bank. He'd never be stupid enough to risk losing Shelby with such a betrayal and, in any event, he never victimized the innocent. He tried not to victimize anyone, in fact.

Why bother? The best crimes—the ones with the least chance of getting caught—were the victimless ones. Stealing a rare painting and replacing it with a skilled forgery, the art gallery never suspecting a thing, for example. Or, in the guise of giving legal advice, convincing a bank that a piece of real estate was worth $100,000 rather than $300,000 due to environmental contamination, and then using a straw to purchase the property. Or, after shorting an alarm-company stock, making an anonymous online post instructing hackers how to bypass its security protocols, causing its stock price to plunge.

Finally in open water, he spun the bow so that it pointed into the wind and raised the sails. The boat swung as the sails filled, and he was underway, the Sabre slicing through the blue-brown harbor waters. He let out a long breath, one hand on the tiller and the other on the main sail sheet. The stability and permanence of the land; the power and passion of the sea. Nothing attested to the depths of his love for Shelby more than the fact that, at some point today, he'd take one last long look at the horizon, come about, and reluctantly return to port.

But being on land cost money. So he needed a score. A big one.

Cam, along with Astarte and Sue, continued to tail Anita as she led the group down the mountain. They had found a stream and decided to follow it. "It must lead to a larger river, which we can follow back to civilization," Astarte said. Cam nodded. She—under Matthias' guidance —was becoming an accomplished outdoorswoman.

But the hike had taken most of the day, and the older women were tiring. The problem was that the ascent had begun two-thirds of the way up the mountain, where they parked on an access road. This journey down the backside would require that they descend all the way to the valley below.

Astarte, who could see the older women dragging, called out. "Hey, I still have a bunch of those berries I picked earlier. They're just like the ones Pomeroy ate. I think they're elderberries." She tasted one. "A little bitter, but better than nothing. And I can easily find more." For lunch, the four of them had shared a couple of granola bars Cam carried in his pack along with a small bag of trail mix Anita had brought.

"Let's take ten minutes for a break," Cam suggested. "We could all use it."

They sipped from their water bottles while Astarte gathered more of the greenish-purple berries—clustered on a red stem like a bunch of grapes—and Anita and Sue rested. Cam said to Sue, "You said something earlier. I thought maybe you said the *Shamir* cut the rock?"

She eyed him. She had not exactly turned warm and friendly, but the shared peril had caused her to drop her defenses a bit. "I did. It was a joke."

He felt a tingle run up his back, his body's way of telling him to pay extra close attention. "I've never heard the word before. At least, not until yesterday. Then you used it again. Can I ask what it means?"

"It comes from the Talmud."

Cam nodded. He knew that the Talmud contained the accumulated teachings of Judaism's leading rabbis, spanning centuries. Essentially, it was a compilation of Jewish knowledge. "Okay," he said.

"I'm not Jewish, but I study ancient religions and texts, including the Talmud. One of the passages in the Talmud discusses the construction of King Solomon's Temple." She pulled out her phone. "Here, let me read something to you from a book I downloaded. This is from Manly P. Hall, *The Secret Teachings of All Ages*. It's a good summary." She cleared her throat.

The Talmud contains a legend concerning the remarkable object called the Shamir with which King Solomon tried and trued the stones for the Temple. The Shamir was the magical "worm" used by Aaron to cut the stones for the breastplate of the High Priest. Solomon, when ordered to build the Temple without the sound of hammers, could not cut the stones in the ordinary manner, but by laying the Shamir against the side of the rock the stones instantly and noiselessly separated according to any desired pattern.

Sue looked up and continued. "According to the Talmud, and I quote,

'The Shamir was, without doubt, an extraordinary object as it possessed the ability to alter stone, iron, and diamond.'"

Cam smiled. "So that's why you said the notch was carved by the Shamir. It was a joke."

Sue shrugged. "A nerd joke. Only, like, a couple dozen people in the country would get it. We call the Shamir 'God's Exacto Knife.'"

Cam chuckled. "I like that."

"Anyway, yes, I was referring to the otherwise unexplainable cut in the rock."

Cam asked, "When they say *worm*, is that a metaphor? Or is it a real worm?"

"Nobody knows for sure. I've heard some people suggest it was a laser or something. But most Biblical scholars think, yes, it was some kind of magical green worm, created by God on the sixth day of Creation, right before the Sabbath. That's when he created supernatural things like the Rod of Aaron and manna and demons."

Cam turned to Astarte, her lips purple from the berries. "You ever hear this before?"

"No. But it's pretty cool. A magical green worm." She turned to Sue. "But go back a second. Why did Solomon need the worm in the first place? Why not just cut the stone the same way they did for all the other buildings?"

"Apparently God told Solomon that he couldn't use metal tools, because this was a temple of peace, and it was possible some of the tools might have been reconfigured from old weapons."

"So what happened to the worm?" Cam asked, his mind still on the lead box.

"That's another interesting story, but a bit convoluted. I'll read more from Manly Hall. This picks up the story where Solomon is trying to find the Shamir." Again, Sue read from her phone.

In order to learn the whereabouts of the Shamir, Solomon invoked the spirits, who told him that Asmodeus, the great king of the demons, could give him the desired information. Solomon thereupon sent his faithful general, Benaihu, to capture Asmodeus.

From Asmodeus, Solomon learned that the Ruler of the Sea had entrusted the Shamir to a wild rooster, from which Solomon speedily secured the stone.

Asmodeus was held captive by Solomon until the completion of the Temple, when that great demon affected his liberation in the following crafty manner; Solomon, becoming curious as to the magical powers of Asmodeus, questioned him. The king of the demons replied that if Solomon would remove the chains bearing the name of God and lend him the signet ring he wore he would then demonstrate his supernatural powers. Solomon complied with the request, and the demon, picking up the King, cast him four hundred miles into a distant country and, after taking upon himself the figure and appearance of King Solomon, ruled Israel in his stead. A sadder but wiser man, Solomon regained his throne after many adventures. Asmodeus, spreading his wings, ascended to his own throne in the spirit world.

"And the worm?" Cam asked.

She shrugged. "Nobody knows. Never been seen since. Some scholars believe that Asmodeus took it back to the spirit world. But it's also possible that Solomon hid it somewhere. It could be part of his treasure."

Now we're talking, Cam thought. The location of King Solomon's treasure—whatever it was—was one of history's great unsolved mysteries. Many scholars believed the Templars uncovered the treasure while excavating under Solomon's Temple in Jerusalem in the 12th century. *And the lead box had a Templar cross on it.*

Anita brought the discussion to a close. "Unless you want to spend the night in the woods, I'm afraid this history lesson is over for now." She stood. "Come on, troops."

Astarte, who never was one to let a good conversation flame out from lack of oxygen, fell in behind Sue and asked, "So what were the other supernatural things God created on the sixth day?"

Sue seemed to appreciate the girl's interest in her studies. "According to the Talmud, there were fourteen of them. These are the things that defy the laws of nature. Things that are otherwise unexplainable, because, well, there are *laws* of nature, created by God, that these don't follow. So to reconcile this metaphysical conundrum, the Talmud concludes they were created in the 'in-between time,' after Creation but before the day of rest. They don't violate the laws of nature because God created them for special, supernatural purposes."

Cam chimed in. "They break the laws, but it's okay because they have a note from home. Signed by God."

Sue offered a rare smile. "Something like that. Anyway, to answer your question, let's see if I can remember them all." She looked up to the sky, as if for guidance. "There were three mouths: the mouth of the earth, which swallowed Korah and his followers after they rebelled against Moses; the mouth of the well, which gave the Israelites water in the desert; and the mouth of the donkey, through which God spoke to Balaam, who was a wicked prophet. The fourth thing was a rainbow, which was a gift from God to Noah. Also, manna to feed the Israelites in the desert. And the staff of Moses. And the Shamir. That makes seven, right?"

Astarte nodded.

"The next three are all sort of the same, relating to the Ten Commandments. One is the letters used to write the Commandments—in other words, written language. Another is that the Commandments could be seen from all four sides. And another is the Commandments them-selves. Even though Moses carved the second set after smashing the first, God made the original ones. So that makes ten."

"Okay," Astarte said, helping Anita over a fallen tree on the trail.

"Demons is number eleven. They frequently appear in the Old Testa-ment. Twelve is the grave of Moses. Since nobody was there for his burial, and he obviously couldn't bury himself, the rabbis concluded that God must have dug his grave. The thirteenth is the ram which appeared to Abraham so that he could sacrifice it instead of sacrificing Isaac. And the last one is the first set of tongs. You can't forge tongs in fire without first having a pair of tongs to hold them." She shrugged. "So God must have created them."

It was an odd list, Cam thought. A strange combination of the mundane—such as the tongs and Moses' grave—combined with extraordinary creations like the Shamir and demons and manna from heaven. However, the list, interesting as it was, offered no more insights on the Shamir, and Shelby's mysterious lead box, unfortunately.

They hiked in silence for a few seconds as they navigated an especially treacherous decline. "Mind if I pick your lawyer brain as we walk?" Anita asked as they emerged into a flatter area.

"Pick away."

"One solution to all this craziness is to buy this land from Pomeroy. Then we could preserve it and freely come view the alignments."

"Has he given you an asking price?"

"No. But we got the tax assessment records. The parcel is landlocked, other than that path we climbed up on. It has a three-foot right of way, an easement, but pedestrian only. No motorized vehicles allowed."

"That really suppresses the value, which is good news for you guys. Not only can you not drive onto the property, but it becomes really hard to build anything on it. You have to carry things in by hand." Cam paused. "Or land a helicopter." He swatted a mosquito. "And another thing. I'm guessing the easement won't allow for water or electrical lines. So no utilities."

"The problem is, it's been in Pomeroy's family for generations. Like he said, his grandkids play on the boulders."

"Hey," Astarte said, interrupting. "I think I hear cars. A road."

Anita looked around. "Makes sense. We must be close. We've been hiking for hours."

Stopping to lean against a tree, Cam took out the henchman's walkie-talkie. "I guess it's time to reach out to Pomeroy and tell him where his man is." He held down the transmit button. "Hey, Pomeroy, your man Jason got a bit hung up. He's about a half-hour hike, straight down from the top." Cam emptied the rifle's magazine and tossed the gun into a deep pool formed where the stream turned. "But he'll need a new rifle."

Static for a couple of seconds, then, "You made a mistake. You don't want to make an enemy of me."

Cam shook his head. "Strange words from a man who put innocent people in danger and then sent a henchman after them to finish the job."

"Just protecting my property rights. Next time, maybe you'll think twice before trespassing." He paused. "By the way, you have less than an hour."

Cam's chest tightened. "For what?"

As if in response, Astarte stumbled, barely catching herself before falling. She turned, a puzzled look on her face. "Dad, I don't feel so great." She lowered her head and vomited out a purplish stream of bile.

"Those berries the girl picked ain't edible. They're pokeberries. Toxic. Jason saw her picking them. Lots of people not from around here make the same mistake. Pokeberries in this area look like elderberries, like I was eating up here on the ridge. But, like I said, they ain't."

Cam's heart raced. Astarte had eaten more of the berries than anyone else and she was the smallest of the group. "What do you mean, we have one hour?"

"Depending on how many she ate, her blood pressure is going to continue to drop. Those berries can be lethal."

Cam swallowed. "Lethal?"

"Like I said, it depends on how many she ate. Hopefully, not more than ten."

Cam glanced over at Astarte, bent over. Between retches, she said, "Maybe twenty-five."

"Shit," Cam hissed.

"Milk might help," Pomeroy said. "Or ipecac."

"We don't have either," Cam growled.

"I don't imagine you do." He chuckled. "But what you do have, is a problem."

Astarte knelt by the edge of the stream, vomiting purple liquid onto the waterway's banks. Her gut felt like it had been tied in a knot with wild horses pulling on its two ends. So much for being a capable outdoorswoman. No way would Matthias have made such a stupid mistake.

Cam, hovering over her, must have read her mind. "Not your fault. Like Pomeroy said, both berries look the same."

Her response was to retch again. This time, with her stomach empty, nothing came out.

"Can you walk? We need to get you some medical attention."

"I can barely kneel at the moment." A spasm hit her and she gasped. "Give me a second."

She saw Cam glance up at the western horizon, where the sun had dropped below the treetops. He made a decision.

"Anita and Sue, you guys should go ahead. Just keep walking until you hit the road. I'll stay here with Astarte."

After arguing the point for a minute, the women, exhausted, trudged away. "We'll send help as soon as we can," Anita said over her shoulder.

Cam handed Astarte the last of his water. "You have to drink to avoid dehydration. Small sips, so it stays down."

She moaned. "These. Are. The. Worst. Cramps. Ever." Staggering, she made her way behind a tree and squatted. "You have any paper?" she called, too sick to be embarrassed.

Cam brought her some napkins from his pack. "The vomiting and defecating probably helps. Gets it out of your system."

She teetered out from behind the tree, gagged again, then spat. Clenching her fists, she raised herself up to her full height. "All right. Let's go."

"Go where?"

"Down this bloody mountain."

Cam bit back a smile at the use of Amanda's favorite adjective. "You sure?" he asked.

"I can be sick as I trudge along just as easily as I can be sick bent over."

"Okay, then. Walk behind me. Keep your hand on my back. And use this." He handed her his walking stick.

"I'm sick, not an old geezer like you," she replied with a brave smile.

"Sassy. Good. You must be feeling better."

But it was a temporary reprieve. Another spasm hit, ripping at her guts. She dropped to one knee after only a few strides. She teetered there for a couple of seconds, then her world turned dark.

Astarte had barely hit the ground before Cam lifted her back up. Fighting a rising sense of panic, he spun his backpack around to his chest and hoisted her onto his shoulders in a fireman's carry, then began to trudge down the mountain. The slope was steep and slick and uneven. He staggered often and stumbled occasionally, always careful to cushion Astarte's fall with his own body. Every hundred steps, he stopped and lowered her to the ground, both to check to make sure she was still breathing and to give his body a quick reprieve. It was all he could do to hear her faint respiration over his panting. The pattern became rhythmic: counting to one hundred, setting her down, resting, then setting off again. He let his mind go numb, ignoring the fatigue and the pain in his knees and elbows from his falls and the throbbing in his head from overexertion.

He completed the sixth rotation of one-hundred steps just as sweat, already drenching his clothes, dripped into his eyes, blinding him. He eased Astarte to the ground, rinsed his eyes in the stream, filled his water bottle, and—not caring if the unpurified water made him sick, his only goal being to get Astarte to a hospital—gulped ravenously. He angled his head, trying to catch the sound of a roadway below, but all he could hear was the ringing in his ears. He checked his watch. Almost seven. It was already darkening here in the woods. Soon the sun would set, making his descent even more hazardous.

But what choice did he have? She had not reawakened, and her breathing was growing weaker. She would die, he feared, without medical care. With a primal scream, he dumped the remainder of the water from his bottle over his head and trudged back to Astarte. For the seventh time, he lifted her. For the seventh time, he trudged forward, head down, eyes on the ground a few feet in front of him, one foot in front of the other, losing himself in the numbing throb of exertion.

He stumbled again, dropping to a knee, pain shooting up his leg.

Gathering his strength, he staggered to his feet, the effort causing his head to spin and circles of light to dance in his field of vision. He had run a marathon once and knew his body's limitations. He was beyond them. His senses were shutting down, hence the ringing in his ears and the orbs of oscillating light.

Still he trudged onward, the dancing lights now growing to the point where he could barely focus on the terrain in front of him. Had he hit his head during one of his falls, the lights being a sign of a concussion? It was possible—he had a history of concussions which, in the past, had resulted in pinpricks of light, smaller than what he was seeing now, impeding his vision.

The lights continued to grow, as if automobile traffic was steadily moving toward him. Cam tried to blink them away but, in so doing, lost sight of the path and stumbled over a root. Face first, he fell, willing himself not to brace his fall with his hands lest he drop Astarte. *Hold on.* He managed to partially break his fall with his elbow, but the combined weight of the two bodies—almost three hundred pounds—sent darts of unbearably sharp pain up his arm. The last thing he remembered was hearing the crack of bone, then his world—even the dancing orbs of light —went completely dark.

Jason Goodrich seethed as his Uncle Pomeroy stood over him, taking his own sweet time cutting him down from the snare.

"That girlie sure got you good," the old man said, chuckling. "Tied you up like a calf in a rodeo."

Dizzy from all the blood rushing to his head, Jason spat. "How you know it was her?"

"When you called in, you said she's the one who went up ahead."

Jason cursed. "Just wait. I'll tie *her* up next time. Then see what I do."

Pomeroy cut the line, sending the sapling springing upward and releasing Jason to flop to the ground. "Big talk for such a little man. That the only way you can get a girl? By forcing her?"

"No," Jason said, sitting on the dirt and rubbing his knee. He looked away. "I've had girls before." He never should have agreed to spend the summer at the ranch.

His uncle laughed. "Sure you have."

The truth was, the only girl he'd ever been with was a fat girl who he took advantage of after she passed out at a New Year's Eve party. That was part of the reason he was here—the judge had agreed to community service without jail time if Jason kept his record clean for six months, and his mother thought being on the ranch with Pomeroy would keep him out of trouble.

Pomeroy spat some tobacco. "That rifle cost two hundred bucks. I'll be deducting it from your wages."

Shit. He was only making four hundred a week. And Jason needed to save up for a truck. That was the main reason he had agreed to this nightmare. It was either that or work at Wendy's back in Indiana again, and that sure as hell wasn't happening. Not after the way the other workers treated him, especially the girls. Just his luck that the fat girl was friends with the assistant manager, who turned everyone against him. It was like he was the only one to blame. *She* was really drunk, and *he* was really drunk, so why did the blame fall entirely on *him*?

"You hear me about the rifle, boy?"

"Wasn't my fault," he said, rubbing his nose on his sleeve.

"Wasn't your fault? Some girlie springs a snare trap on you and it's not your fault?" He shook his head. "Boy, this is going to be a long six months if you don't get your head on straight."

It was already a long six months, and he was only two weeks into it. He wondered if jail would have been better.

His uncle continued. "Now get up off that ground. We got ourselves a bit of a hike before nightfall. And I don't want to hear anything about your knee hurting you. Your momma asked me to toughen you up. And that's what I intend to do."

They walked in silence for a few minutes, descending, Jason limping and favoring one leg. Apparently, Pomeroy had gone back down the original trail to his truck and driven around the mountain, then hiked up to find Jason.

"Say," Pomeroy said, "what is an *incel*?"

Jason looked down. Had his uncle and aunt been checking his internet usage? Jason had been spending time in a Reddit incel chat room. He'd need to be more careful. Spend more time playing *World of Warcraft* instead. "It's just a word," Jason replied.

"I know it's a *word*. I'm asking you what it *means*?"

This seemed like one of those times where adults knew the answer but wanted to lord it over you. "It means a guy who is *in*voluntarily *cel*ibate." But he didn't want his uncle to think he was a total loser. "I have some friends who go there. So I just went on to chat with them."

"But you're not an incel yourself?"

Jason shook his head. "No. Like I said, I've had girls before."

"Well, it looks like they were saying some pretty nasty things on that chat room. Talking about raping and killing women."

The words came out before Jason could stop them. "Most of them deserve it."

Pomeroy stopped and turned, his eyes shining in the fading light. He looked down on Jason, who stood at only five-foot-six even with the generous heel of his boots. "Your mother is a woman, Jason. Does she deserve it?"

Jason felt his face flush. "No. Of course not. I was talking about women my age. You know, the bitchy ones. The entitled ones. The Stacys."

Pomeroy began walking again. "Stacys?"

"The pretty girls. The ones who go out with Chads."

"Let me guess. The popular guys."

Jason nodded. He guessed his uncle, when he had been younger, was a Chad. Tall, handsome, well-spoken, an easy smile. Just the kinds of superficial things that Stacys liked.

"And you're not a Chad, Jason?"

This time, Jason shook his head. "But I could be. If I had my own truck. And a few bucks in my pocket." He swallowed. "Once girls got to know me."

His uncle chewed on a toothpick for a few seconds, as if doubting Jason's words. Hell, Jason wasn't sure even he believed them himself.

But he did know that having the truck, and having a few bucks, was better than not.

"I tell you what, Jason. You stay off that incel website, and you work real hard all summer, and you stay out of trouble, and I'll help you buy that truck."

◈✛⊛

Cam awoke, jostled by movement. He felt a rubber oxygen mask on his face and saw a round light—a single orb, now, rather than many—above him. He blinked, his mind slowly processing that he was out of the woods. Literally.

"Astarte?" he slurred.

A young Asian female in uniform—a paramedic, he deduced—smiled down on him. "If you mean the girl, she's in another ambulance. Good thing you brought her as far as you did. I think we got to her just in time. She's in the ambulance ahead of us. They've stabilized her."

He let out a long breath and looked up at her, not caring that she saw him tear up. "How did … you find me?"

"You practically stumbled into us. We were only about fifty feet away when you fell and passed out."

Aha. The orbs of lights were actually flashlights. So not a concussion after all.

"Looks like you banged your elbow pretty bad," she said. "It's already swollen. May be broken."

His right arm was immobilized in a splint by his side. He licked his lips. The truth was, he didn't care, as long as Astarte was safe. "There were two women with us. They went ahead."

The paramedic nodded. "They brought us to you. They're exhausted, but fine." She laughed softly. "They were already talking about going back up the mountain tomorrow."

He lifted his head a bit. "Tomorrow? Really?"

"There were four guys with them. I think Native American, based on how they were dressed and the things they were saying." She shrugged. "But I might have that wrong."

Anita must have called them when she got close to the bottom, with cell coverage. Through the fog in his brain, Cam tried to puzzle it out. Why would they be going back up tomorrow? "Did they seem angry? The men, I mean?"

"Pretty heated, yeah."

Cam nodded and settled back in. It was one thing for Pomeroy to scare off a few amateur historians. But the local Lenape would not take kindly to being chased off their ancestral lands. He tested his right arm, moving it an inch or two to the side. Sure would be fun to join the Lenape on that climb tomorrow.

CHAPTER 3

Astarte unsuccessfully tried to stifle a yawn as she sat in the Minneapolis airport waiting for her connecting flight to Bozeman. Her body still felt feeble from all the vomiting, her stomach continued to do somersaults from the berries, and a fog clouded her brain from lack of sleep. After many hours of observation, she had been released from the hospital late Saturday night. Her dad had offered to pay for a later flight, but she missed Matthias and wanted to get back to school. So they raced back to Boston from Pennsylvania—Cam driving one-handed most of the night —to catch her morning departure. It actually wasn't such a bad day to waste in airports. She felt so wrung out that she likely wouldn't have accomplished much anyway.

She made a call. "Hi, Dad. I just landed in Minnesota."

"How you feeling?"

She tried to sound chipper. "Better, thanks. But I skipped the blue-berry muffin they served for breakfast." The truth was, she barely got down a couple of bites of bread. "Anyway, I was thinking about something on the flight. About simulation theory and the Shamir."

"I'm listening."

"If we really are in a simulation, then there's no reason the Shamir can't be real. I mean, the programmers could program anything they want. Unicorns, giants, fairies, magic green worms, demons, anything."

"Okay. But that's a big if. Maybe we're not in a simulation. Maybe this is the only reality."

"I agree, that's possible. But then we're back to the question of how we got here. Big Bang or God."

"No way to know the answer to that one. Most people would say God. I read that eighty-one percent of Americans believe in God. And three-quarters believe in the Bible."

"Okay, let's go with that. It's the same argument as the simulation: If you believe God created the universe, then why couldn't he—or she—create the Shamir and demons and whatever else he wanted to create?"

She was right. No reason why an omnipotent God couldn't create whatever he or she wanted.

Astarte continued. "Another point. Let's focus on the three-quarters for a minute, the people who believe in the Bible. Most of them would probably have no problem believing in the Shamir, assuming it was explained to them by the rabbis and priests, like in the Talmud. I mean, they believe in parting of the seas and virgin births and Jonah in the whale's belly, so why not a magic green worm? Again, assuming their religious leaders explained it to them."

"Okay. I think that's fair."

"So, here's my point. You always tell me that it doesn't matter what's true or not. What matters is what people believe, since beliefs are what motivate behavior."

He chuckled. "I had no idea you were listening."

"Usually, not. But you said it so often…"

"Ouch."

"Anyway, my point is, I think you need to treat this Shamir as if it was real. And you also need to assume people are going to hear about it and want to use it to their advantage. I mean, we've seen this movie before, right?"

She was correct. His research, which often started out as theoretical and abstract, had a way of blowing up in his face.

Astarte continued. "Word is going to leak out. It always does. People who are religious are probably going to have no problem believing in the Shamir, believing it has magical powers. That's what faith is. And if they believe it, they're also going to realize how important, how powerful, it is. Which means they're going to want it, like I said." She paused. "Dad, we've been talking about the Shamir like it was some kind of theoretical, imaginary object. I think you need to start thinking about it like it's a ticking time bomb."

Cameron sipped his twelve-dollar beer as the scoreboard above center ice flashed and blasted music, trying to pump energy into an otherwise-lethargic Boston Bruins crowd. Cam hated being gouged, especially by someone as wealthy as the owner of the Bruins. At least the team was playing an exciting brand of hockey this season. To help offset the cost of his beverage, he had brought his own bag of peanuts to the stadium. The problem was, with his injured right elbow throbbing and immobi-lized in a splint, he was having trouble shelling the nuts.

His friend, Alex Trevino, filled the void. He shifted his girth and reaching into the bag. "Thanks," Trevino said, effortlessly cracking a shell and tossing a pair of nuts into his mouth.

Cam smiled at his old college roommate. He had always been a loyal and enthusiastic companion, if sometimes a bit self-absorbed. "You get the tickets, I buy the beer and snacks," Cam replied.

"Sorry all I could get was nosebleed seats."

"Don't be. I like it up here." Cam paused as they watched a Bruins forward race up ice and clang a shot off the goalpost as the crowd first roared and then groaned. Despite the action, Cam swallowed a yawn. It had been a long night. After this beer, he would switch to Diet Coke for the caffeine. "This is where the real fans sit. Bird's-eye view."

"Remember our freshman year? We were at the old Garden practi-cally every night."

Cam nodded. "And then Fenway Park once baseball season started." He and Trevino had graduated from Boston College together twenty-six years ago. The time had passed in a flash, but at a glacial pace. Cam shook his head and smiled at his friend. "We had it all wrong back then. We thought that the Red Sox would never win and that we would never get old."

Trevino grunted. "I'm a fat slob with hardly any hair. But you don't look like you've aged much."

Cam deflected the compliment. "A fat slob with his own business, a beach house on the Cape, and a Beemer," Cam replied. The truth was, Trevino, a software engineer, had let himself go. A hockey player in college, he now spent much of his free time at Masonic events, most of which seemed to include copious amounts of eating and drinking. "Not to mention a hot wife," Cam added.

Trevino turned to look Cam in the eye. "Speaking of hot wives, how you doing? It's been two years now, right?"

"Okay, I guess. People said time will help, that I'd get used to her being gone. I thought they were crazy. But, in a way, it's true. I still think about her a lot, but I'm past the stage where I expect her to be there when I get home or when I roll over in bed."

Trevino gave him a half smile. "Good thing. Not sure there's room in that bed for Amanda *and* Rivka."

A couple of players pawed at each other in a scrum in front of the net, but the linesmen broke it up. Back in the day, most scrums like that resulted in brawls. It made Cam wonder about the details of what had transpired at the Council Rocks site this morning. He had had a brief conversation with Anita, who told him that a dozen Lenape had marched up the mountain to confront Pomeroy, who had promptly called police to have them removed. At one point, before the police arrived, Pomeroy actually aimed his gun at the Lenape, apparently fearing for his safety, then fired a shot over their heads to keep them from advancing. "I think he actually was right to be afraid," Anita had said. "I thought they were going to rip his head off and feed it to the vultures." Someone had videoed the entire encounter; Anita was waiting to get a copy and promised to share it with Cam.

The tussle on the ice over, Cam replied, "Actually, I think Amanda would be fine with me dating again. I used to talk to her a lot. In my head. I still do, but not as much. Anyway, I think she would want me to get on with my life. And Rivka's pretty cool. Astarte likes her. So, like I said, I think Amanda would be fine with it."

"You and Rivka getting serious?"

Cam shrugged. "She works for some international conglomerate," he lied. He couldn't really go around telling people his girlfriend was an Israeli spy. "Half the time, I don't even know where she is." The truth was, half the time, Cam didn't even know if she was alive. "So it's tough to think long term. Which, actually, is fine."

They watched as the Bruins successfully killed a penalty. "So," Cam said, "I got an interesting call on Friday from an old lawyer friend." Cam likely would have skipped the game and gone home to flop onto the couch after the weekend he had, but he really wanted to pick Trevino's brain.

"And?"

"And I was hoping you could help. Ever hear of a thing called the Shamir?" Trevino was the Senior Warden—second in command—at a sizeable Masonic lodge in the Boston suburbs. King Solomon and the construction of his Temple played key roles in the Masonic degree rituals. It seemed reasonable that the Shamir might factor into those rituals as well.

Trevino grabbed another handful of peanuts and popped one into his mouth. He chewed, then swallowed and turned to face Cam. "I need to be careful. I can't reveal certain secrets."

Cam nodded. "I know, under penalty of having your throat cut across, your tongue torn out, and your body buried in the rough sands of the sea." He smiled. "From the Masonic initiation oath."

Trevino laughed. "Almost the exact words."

"Not hard to find this stuff on the internet."

Cam's point, which he hoped he did not need to verbalize, was that so many Masonic secrets were now available on the web that Trevino would not be violating any confidences by telling Cam what he knew about the Shamir; rather, he'd merely be saving Cam the time of digging the information out.

Trevino sipped his beer and lowered his voice as the players skated off the ice for intermission. "Okay, here's what I know." He summarized the story of Hiram Abiff, the architect in charge of building Solomon's Temple. Abiff was murdered inside the Temple by three ruffians after he refused to divulge to them the secret passwords, reserved for master craftsmen, which would give them a higher wage and better work. "There's a really important ritual in Masonry, presented to all candidates as they go through their initiation ceremony." He leaned closer, Cam able to smell both the beer and the peanuts on his friend's breath. "But here's something interesting. These rituals have been around for a couple of hundred years, right? And you know how Freemasons are—we love our rituals. So oftentimes a senior guy will write a treatise on the different rituals, going back through all the old historic sources to offer commentary and explanations. This one guy, Finch was his name, did a whole treatise in England back in the early 1800s. He was a bit of an eccentric, and not everyone agreed with everything he said, but nobody doubted that he knew his shit when it came to Freemasonry. I only know about him because I happened to stumble onto this old book a few months ago in our library. Anyway, he said that the ruffians didn't kill Hiram Abiff because they wanted the passwords." Trevino paused. "They killed him because they wanted the magic worm. The Shamir."

Cam's eyes widened. "Wait, so Freemasons believe this whole Shamir story?"

Trevino nodded. "We do. At least those of us who've educated ourselves. That's how Solomon was able to build his Temple without metal tools."

"Holy shit," Cam muttered. Maybe "God's Exacto Knife" was an accurate description. Until now—or at least until his conversation today with Astarte—he had been progressing under the assumption that the Shamir thing was a legend, a myth. Sure, people believed the Shamir story fifteen hundred years ago, when the Talmud was written. But they believed in all sorts of things they couldn't otherwise explain back then, before modern science shed light on so many of life's mysteries. Most modern Freemasons, however, were educated, many of them leaders in the fields of science and medicine. That they believed in the Shamir was surprising. And telling.

The evidence was mounting that Cam needed to open his mind to the possibility as well.

Driving one-handed, Cam sat in traffic trying to wind his way to the Route 93 onramp from the TD Garden arena. The Bruins had made a spirited comeback, erasing a two-goal deficit to tie the game and then win it in overtime. Cam was pleased with the result, though it left him stuck in traffic as his car clock flipped to 10:00. At least the Shamir mystery gave him something to keep his mind occupied.

He turned the radio to a classic rock station and thought about what he had learned over the past few days. He didn't generally believe in coincidences, so the fact that the date of the construction of Solomon's Temple—around 960 BC—was contemporaneous with the date of the placement of the Council Rock boulders—approximately 3,000 years ago, or on either side of 980 BC—intrigued him. And both events seemed tied to the Phoenicians, Hiram Abiff being a Phoenician builder hired by King Solomon and the Phoenicians being the leading candidate to have constructed—or to have assisted the Lenape in constructing—the Council Rock site. His mind settled on one obvious possibility: Had the Shamir, which according to Masonic legend had been stolen from Hiram Abiff, been used to make the neat right-angle cut in the Council Rocks boulder? The cut would have been a difficult one to make with the rudimentary tools of the day, going against the natural fracture lines of the rock. Difficult, that is, for a stonemason. But not necessarily for a magic, rock-cutting worm serving as God's Exacto Knife.

Cam's mind continued to make connections. Many authorities, including Cam, believed that Freemasonry evolved from the outlawed Knights Templars. Not surprisingly, therefore, much of Masonic ritual derived from Templar teachings, discoveries and doctrine. If the Masons believed in the Shamir, chances were that the Templars did as well. Which made Cam wonder: Had the Templars discovered something while excavating beneath King Solomon's Temple in the early 12th century? Perhaps the Shamir itself? And had they then used the magic stone-cutting worm to aid them in erecting the massive Gothic cathedrals —including Notre Dame and Chartres—which sprang up under their direction all over Europe during that time period?

Inching along in traffic, Cam realized he needed to slow his musings as well. It was one thing to play games of what-if and connect-the-dots. But he was getting ahead of himself. Way ahead. There was no evidence the Shamir was anything more than a legend. Plenty of stories in the Bible—and, by extension, the Talmud—were either mythical in their entirety or sensationalized well beyond any factual basis. And even if the story of the Shamir turned out to be true, there was no hard evidence the worm had made its way to America with Phoenician seafarers and/or been discovered by the Templars while in Jerusalem.

Yet the worm would not leave his thoughts. With an ironic smile, Cam turned off the radio and sat in silence for a few seconds. An earworm had gotten stuck in his head, on continuous replay. But this earworm was not a song. It was a worm itself.

Cam finally broke free of postgame traffic, pulling into his Westford driveway well after 11:00 Sunday night. He hadn't slept much the night before, driving late into the night and then again early the next morning to get Astarte to the airport for her flight. So he was planning on calling it a night after walking Venus. Then his email pinged. The video from Anita.

His elbow still throbbing, he opened a can of seltzer water, swallowed an Advil, and sat in an oversized chair looking out at the moonlight glistening off the lake behind his house, most of the winter ice having melted in the March sun.

The encounter in the video pretty much matched what Anita had described. But what she had not communicated was the level of anger and outrage expressed by the dozen Lenape protestors. Cam understood. This had been their land. *Sacred* land. And now they were being told they could not visit it to observe the ancient ceremonial alignments built into its lithic features. It was like telling Jewish people they couldn't worship at the Western Wall. The problem—similar to what was happening in the Middle East—was that things had turned personal. One of the young Lenape men had spat at Pomeroy's feet. Pomeroy, in turn, had lifted his shotgun menacingly. When they didn't back down, Pomeroy fired his weapon, aiming a few feet over their heads. Fortunately, the police, who had been alerted to a possible confrontation, arrived to defuse things. But only temporarily, Cam guessed. There would be another alignment at the site in June for the summer solstice, and no doubt the Lenape—not to mention Anita and Sue and their history-buff cohorts—would want to view that phenomenon as well. At some point, the combination of a loaded shotgun, a steadfast Pomeroy, and an irate group of Lenape would ignite.

So what was the solution?

Cam typed out an email to Anita. *Has anyone approached Pomeroy again about purchasing the land?* Cam knew of many occasions when civic groups, taking advantage of tax breaks, raised money to purchase land to keep it from being developed.

After going upstairs and washing for bed, Cam checked his email a final time. He was hoping for something from Rivka, the memory of their rushed coupling after the pickleball tourney still fresh in his mind, as well as on his lips. Instead, he got a response from Anita:

Where to start? We've made him an offer, but Pomeroy says he has no interest in selling. Land has been in his family for generations. 48 acres. But my sense is that he would sell at the right number, like we discussed. Problem is that the property is landlocked. As you know, there's an easement to walk up there—the one we used. But no motorized vehicles allowed. So you would need to build solar power and use well water. In other words, it's not worth much on the open market. Tax assessment has valuation of $260,000. But it's worth a lot to Pomeroy—both for sentimental reasons and because he thinks it's rich in minerals he can extract. And it's worth a lot to the Lenape. My guess is you might need to pay 3x or even 4x the assessment to get his attention.

Cam replied immediately, asking how much money the Lenape had. He knew that many tribes had struck it rich with casino money over the past few decades. But he doubted they had an extra million to spare. Again, she replied quickly.

It gets complicated. Most of the Lenape were kicked off their land and ended up in Oklahoma. Some are still in the area, but they don't have much. No casino. A couple of decades ago, the tribes were swimming in cash and could have funded something like this, but COVID really hurt the casinos. And, before you ask, no way do any of the historical groups have that kind of money.

Cam ended the exchange and flicked off the light. It was a shame that the ceremonial site was in the hands of a redneck. Cam would need to do more research, but it was entirely possible that the site could prove the existence of ancient explorers crossing the Atlantic three thousand years ago, thereby rewriting American history. But if the site was strip-mined and the boulders destroyed, all evidence would be lost. He scratched Venus behind the ears. "If only we were rich, girl."

CHAPTER 4

Cam got up at six on Monday morning, walked Venus, and went for a slow-paced, three-mile run with his arm tucked by his side. It was one of those mornings where the rising sun crested the horizon below a canopy of thick clouds, then faded behind them as it ascended. So the day actually darkened as it brightened. Cam hoped it wasn't a metaphor for his week.

Returning home, he cycled through a couple of sets of one-armed bench presses and curls on dumbbell weights he kept in the basement. He was between sets, wiping his face with a hand towel, when a CNN video froze him in place.

"The landowner," said the breathless anchor, "fired a gunshot only feet over the head of the Lenape tribe members. The tribe is calling for criminal charges to be brought, while the landowner is claiming he was acting in self-defense."

The station ran a chunk of the video, then interviewed a tribal spokeswoman about the ceremonial importance of the site. Cam was thrilled to hear her say, "Not only is Council Rocks important to the Lenape, but there is growing evidence that the site might have been constructed as some kind of joint effort between the Lenape and a visiting group of Mediterranean-based seafarers." Looking straight at the camera, the Lenape spokeswoman added, "Much of our oral history has been lost, torn from us by genocide and forced relocation and cultural indoctrination. But the evidence at this site and others tells the story of olive-skinned seafarers who came to mine and trade for copper. These *People of the Giant Canoes* worshiped the sun god and wore bright purple garments."

The story ended there, abruptly, the network apparently needing to move on to the latest political scuffle. Cam smiled at the television. The spokeswoman had been adept—she had said nothing, but conveyed much, adding to the mystique of the site. She never actually said that the Lenape oral history told of visitation by the *People of the Giant Canoes,* but most people would walk away from the interview thinking she did. Such a visitation was possible, of course. The ancient Phoenicians built boats twice the size of those sailed by Columbus and the name *Phoenicia* itself meant, "Land of Purple." Cam shook his head. Two days earlier, when he had visited the Council Rocks hilltop, the site was an obscure footnote in history. Then the angry encounter with Pomeroy, followed by Astarte snaring the ranch hand, then Astarte's near-death experience and his own collapse, and finally yesterday's shotgun blast to scare off the Lenape. Now it was featured on the national news. It had been quite a forty-eight hours. Amanda had always said that Cam attracted trouble like shit attracted flies. Apparently, this was another example.

An hour later, just before eight, he was seated at his desk in his office overlooking the Westford town common. Opening his email, he found a message from Trevino. "Found this online, so OK to share with you." Pasted below the message was the exact quote from the Masonic historian Finch, from the year 1804, regarding the Shamir:

What was the real secret our Grand Master Hiram Abiff was slain for not revealing? Not the sign, token and word of a Master Mason, as is erroneously believed, but the wonderful properties of that noble insect called the Shamir, which cut and shaped all the sacred utensils and holy vessels in King Solomon's Temple.

Cam read it a second time. *Cut and shaped,* like an Exacto Knife.

The statement was straightforward and clear. No hedging, no qualifiers, no equivocation. This was a bold statement of fact, made even more brazen in light of the fact that it contradicted accepted Masonic teachings. The historian, Finch, whoever he was and whatever his faults, seemed like a man confident of the ground on which he stood: Hiram Abiff was killed over the Shamir.

It had been less than three days since Shelby called to ask Cam to look into the lead box. She had sent over a photo of the box, but it didn't provide any additional clues—like she said, a simple box filled with rough, off-white wool, with the word Shamir carved on the lid and a Templar cross next to it. Cam decided to take an hour now, before the office got busy, to do a deep dive to see what else he could learn about the mysterious green worm.

With a yellow legal pad in front of him, Cam opened his internet browser. Right away, he could see the problem he was going to have: *Shamir* was also the name both of an American pop star and a company which produced optical lenses. He would need to combine his search with other words, such as "worm" or "Solomon." Eventually he narrowed the search enough to find some relevant information, but much of it was basic and repetitive. Most authorities agreed that the Shamir was some kind of maggot-sized worm or salamander which could cut through even the hardest elements, such as diamonds. Other sources opined that it was a glowing, jade-colored stone able to cut like a laser, perhaps because it was radioactive. All authorities, however, agreed that the Shamir, whatever it was, was kept in a lead box, wrapped in wool. This made Cam sit up, of course. *A lead box, wrapped in wool.*

Nobody, it seemed, had ever actually seen the Shamir. At least not since the time of King Solomon. Or so Cam believed until he stumbled onto the obscure writings of a German author from the year 1683. The author recounted the reports of a monk living in the Normandy region of France who discovered an odd-looking, Shamir-like worm *eating through a rock wall* in his monastery. Based on the description provided by the monk, the author drew a depiction of the worm biting into stone.

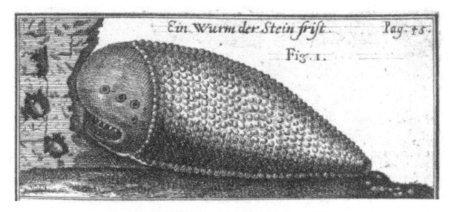

Shamir-Like Worm, German Book, 1683

Cam studied the worm, then shrugged. Who knew if this was an accurate depiction of the Shamir? What intrigued him was the fact that the monk lived in a monastery in Normandy. The largest city in Normandy was Rouen, which could have just been an odd coincidence. Except Cam had long ago learned not to believe in coincidences, ascribing to the old adage that "coincidence" was the word people used when they couldn't see the levers and pulleys.

Cam sat back and looked at his notes: a possible Shamir sighting, in Normandy, approximately 260 years before the lead box was deposited in a bank, also in Normandy, with the word "Shamir" etched on it along with a Templar cross. Cam let his mind race. Rouen had been a Templar stronghold during medieval times. Could the Templars have somehow found the Shamir in Jerusalem while excavating under King Solomon's Temple and brought the object back to France? Then, later, after the Templars were outlawed in the early 1300s, could the Shamir have been passed down to another monastic order living in the Rouen area and held by them for safe keeping, where it was rediscovered by a monk in the 1680s? To continue the thought, was the Shamir then deposited into a safe deposit box at the dawn of World War II, its caretakers—whether Jewish or Christian—not wanting such a powerful and magical object to fall into Nazi hands?

It was a lot of conjecture, and there was not a ton of evidence to support it, but the story held together. That didn't make it true, of course. But Cam's neck was tingling. The game was afoot.

Shelby balanced on the elliptical trainer in an alcove off her master bedroom, sweat dripping from her face as she completed a one-hour workout. The news played, a story about an altercation in Pennsylvania at a Native American ceremonial site.

"Hey, did you see this?" she asked Bruce as he made the bed.

He strolled over and watched with her. "I've heard of this Council Rocks site," he said. "There was a whole debate during a Zoom call I was on about it. Most elders agree it was probably influenced by an outside culture. Maybe Phoenician. But a lot of the tribal leaders don't want to admit it, because they say it makes it seem like the Indians were inferior. Like we couldn't figure out how to line boulders up with the sunrise on our own."

Shelby wiped her face as she stepped off the machine. "What do you think?"

"Personally, I'm not threatened by it. Just because we *didn't* do it doesn't mean we *couldn't* have. Maybe we had no reason to align the boulders with the sunset. Maybe we had other ways to mark the passing of the seasons. That doesn't make us inferior, just different."

Shelby pointed at the screen. "You know what, this story has been updated since I saw it an hour ago. They've added information about a GoFundMe page. They're trying to raise money to buy the land."

Bruce smiled. "The tribes have gotten really savvy lately with their public relations. I'm guessing they fed this story to the networks, spun it just the right way, and then were ready with the GoFundMe page to capitalize on all the ugly publicity."

"Well," Shelby said, glancing at her phone, "it's working. The Atlanta Braves baseball team just contributed fifty grand."

Bruce sniffed. "Not nearly enough for all those obnoxious tomahawk chop celebrations. But at least they're making a gesture."

"A pretty sizable gesture, in fact," Shelby replied. "If all the teams did that, well, you have the Chiefs in football, plus the Redskins, even though they just changed their name."

"Indians in baseball, also just changed their name."

She nodded. "Blackhawks in hockey. Plus some of the big college teams, like Florida State Seminoles."

"I don't think college teams, at least public schools, can give money. But I see your point. Snap your fingers and you could be at $250,000 just from the pro teams."

As if making her point, and also affirming Bruce's observation that the tribes had become adept at PR, someone tagged the other pro sports teams, challenging them to match the Braves' contribution. In addition, a couple of celebrities with Indian heritage had jumped in with donations. The GoFundMe page was on the verge of going viral.

Shelby checked her watch. Just past nine. "Hey, you're supposed to be at work. Those safe deposit boxes aren't going to catalog themselves. I don't pay you to lollygag around."

He smiled. "You don't pay me at all."

"Not my fault you don't have a Social Security number." She tossed her towel at him. "Maybe you should set up a GoFundMe page of your own."

Jason tapped at the family computer in his Uncle Pomeroy's house, about ten miles from the mountain with the boulders. His uncle and aunt had gone to some Bible study class, leaving him alone at the kitchen table. They had tried to wake him to join them, but if God could take Sunday off, then Jason could take Monday off. Besides, he had it coming to him. He was supposed to get the day off Sunday, but instead he had gone back up the hill and watched his uncle almost shoot one of those screaming Indians between the eyes. Jason couldn't believe the guy hadn't soiled his pants. Things were getting crazy up there. Jason was beginning to think it might be time to head back home. It was one thing to bust his ass working on the ranch. But nobody said anything about getting scalped.

An ice pack on his stiff knee and a can of Mountain Dew next to him,

Jason clicked at the keyboard, searching the internet. His uncle had told him to stay off the incel chatrooms, but that didn't mean he couldn't do other surfing. In fact, it was one of his best skills; the other kids in school used to ask him to help them search for things on the web, like where to get fake IDs or the best way to score roofies or even how to get someone beat up. What he was looking for now wasn't nearly as scandalous. He just wanted to understand more about these dumb boulders up on the mountain. They just looked like rocks to him. But those Indians sure were pissed.

Hard as he looked, he could only find one short article about the site. Like that historical woman had said, the boulders lined up to mark the equinox. Yippy shit. That's what they made calendars for. The article said the site was maybe 3,000 years old. Same thing that Lenape woman on the news said when she talked about the *People of the Giant Canoes*. Three thousand years was pretty old but, again, yippy shit. Plenty of things in Europe and the Middle East—like Stonehenge and the Pyramids—were way older than that.

Jason sat back. The way he saw it, neither his uncle nor the Indians really cared about the stupid rocks. They both just wanted the land. Wanted to be able to say it was *theirs*. Like dogs pissing on trees. Like dogs, both wanted to be the alpha. It likely wouldn't resolve itself without one of them getting the other by the throat.

That's where Jason could help. To continue the analogy, he was the runt of the litter. He knew better than to try to fight the big dogs. Instead, he got other dogs to fight for him. Or he tricked the big dogs, beating them with guile and deceit.

His uncle wanted him to prove himself. Said he would buy him a truck if he did. Well, maybe those Indians were just the way to do it.

Cam spent the morning preparing for a couple of closings, then just before lunch Anita called. "You have a minute?"

"Sure."

She told him that the GoFundMe page set up for the Council Rocks land purchase had raised over $100,000 already. "The issue is, some people are asking about the Phoenician connection. It's one thing for this to be an Indian ceremonial site, but the fact that it might be more than that is pretty intriguing. I just don't know enough about the Phoenicians to explain why they were here, or if they were even here at all. Can you send me some talking points?"

"It's all circumstantial, but there's a decent amount of evidence. I'll put something together for you this afternoon."

"Great. The more we can say to convey the importance of this site, the better."

"Do you really think you can raise enough to get Pomeroy to sell?"

"If you asked me yesterday—which," she laughed, "I think you did— I would have said no way. But this GoFundMe thing is magic." She chuckled. "Like printing money. It's gone up another couple of thousand just since we've been on the phone."

"Yeah, I read that the George Floyd page raised like seven million dollars in the first four days. Obviously, this is not as compelling. But if you capture the public's attention, it can add up quick."

"And we don't have to raise it all this week. If we get, say, halfway, it'll make it a lot easier to raise the rest."

"Okay, I'll get those talking points to you."

Even before he hung up, Astarte clicked in. "I was thinking about something," she said. "Actually, it was Matthias who thought of it."

"I'm listening."

"He went backpacking in the Andes during winter break his freshman year. They spent a day at the Pumapunku site."

Cam knew of it. Built around 500 AD, on a summit 12,000 feet above sea level, the site consisted of a series of plazas and ramps leading to a terraced platform with a ceremonial structure atop it. For the Incas, it was believed to be the place where the world was created.

"It's famous for the precision of its stonework, right?" Cam said. He pulled up a picture of one of the decorated walls while they spoke.

Wall, Pumapunku, Bolivia

"Exactly. Matthias said it was amazing. Otherworldly. You couldn't even slip a playing card into the seams between the stones. Here," she said, "let me read something from an article I found. These are the findings from two architectural historians who studied the site."

To obtain the smooth finishes, the perfectly planar faces and exact interior and exterior right angles on the finely dressed stones, they resorted to techniques unknown to the Incas and to us at this time. No matter how fine the hammerstone's point, it could never produce the crisp right interior angles seen on the stonework. Tools have never in history been excavated or identified that were used in the construction of Pumapunku. Experiments showed that the Pumapunku artisans may have possessed additional tools which facilitated the creation of exact geometric cuts and forms and of which archeology has no record at this time.

As Astarte read, Cam found an example of Pumapunku stonework with precise right angles and perfectly flat, smooth finishes.

Ruins, Pumapunku, Bolivia

Cam took a second to mull over the ramifications of what the article, supported by the images, was conveying. "Basically, they're saying it should have been impossible to build the site based on the technology and tools available at that time."

"Bingo," Astarte said. "One of the archeologists working at the site told Matthias that the cuts were so precise that they must have been done by something like a laser."

"But obviously they didn't have lasers back then."

"But maybe they had something better. I don't know, Dad. Maybe they had a little green worm."

Cam was about to step out of his office to grab a sandwich for lunch when Alex Trevino pushed through the front door. "Glad I caught you," he said. He was unshaven and disheveled, his shirttails out and his hair uncombed.

"You okay?" Cam asked.

"No. You're driving me fucking crazy with this Shamir stuff. I've been up all night. Then spent an hour on the phone this morning with a lodge brother who's really into the esoteric side of Freemasonry." He motioned toward the door. "Come on, walk with me. I need to clear my head."

"Aren't you working today?"

Trevino shrugged. "Supposed to be. But, like I said, I'm too deep down this rabbit hole to concentrate."

"Okay, then, let's walk." Cam threw a windbreaker over his golf shirt and khakis, gently pulling the jacket over his injured elbow. Trevino, bare-armed, didn't seem to notice the fifty-degree temperature.

"Here's the thing. You're all fixated on the Shamir. And I get that. But think for a second about the rest of the story." They were walking along the perimeter of the town common, a few dirty snowbanks still covering the sidewalk in the shaded areas. "The way Solomon got the worm was by conjuring up demons. He had a magic ring he used to command the demons and jinn to do his bidding. Jinn, by the way, are sort of like invisible spirits; that's where the word *genie* comes from. Anyway, that's how Solomon found the Shamir—he ordered the king of the demons, Asmodeus, to tell him where it was hidden. For some reason, Asmodeus is able to find it." He stopped and grabbed Cam's uninjured arm. "The Shamir is cool. It can cut through rock. But talk about burying the lead. If you can find Solomon's ring, you can order the jinn to do *anything you want.* Solomon even left a manuscript, translated as *Ars Goetia*, describing how to call forth the seventy-two demons he commanded. We're talking three wishes from the genie in the bottle, Cam." He paused. "And we're talking seventy-two genies."

Cam still wasn't quite sure why Trevino was so spun up. "That would be amazing, I agree. But we don't have a lead box that might have held the magic ring. At best, we have a lead box that held the Shamir."

"That's the point, Cam. If you read the stories, read the Talmud, it makes it clear: After Solomon finished building the Temple, Asmodeus, the king of the demons, tricked Solomon into giving him the magic ring. Then Asmodeus took Solomon's throne by using magic to send Solomon far away and then cloning himself to look just like Solomon."

"Okay," Cam replied, still not getting it.

"The Talmud talks about all the ugly things Asmodeus did when he took Solomon's throne. Having sex with his own mother, Bathsheba, who was really Solomon's mother, of course. Being drunk all day long. Worshiping idols. Overall, just being a tyrant. Eventually, Solomon returned and somehow regained his throne." Trevino paused again to show Cam an image on his phone. "Here, this is a painting showing Solomon retaking the throne and his soldiers leading Asmodeus away. This is before Asmodeus breaks free and escapes."

Asmodeus Removed From Solomon's Throne

"Okay," Cam said again.

Trevino took a deep breath, apparently now, finally, getting to the point. "The only way for Solomon to regain his throne was first to recapture the magic ring—"

Cam cut him off, finally getting it. "Right. And the only way to get the Shamir is to use the magic ring to order Asmodeus to tell you where it's hidden. So, if, later on, the Templars ended up with the Shamir, as we think they did, they must have also had the magic ring. No ring, no Asmodeus; and no Asmodeus, no Shamir."

Trevino flopped onto a park bench, spent. "Exactly. That's my point. If we believe *any* of this—which, I think, we have to, based on the lead box—then we have to believe *all* of it. Magic rings and demons and genies and all."

Cam joined his friend on the bench. "So where could the ring be?"

"I assume it wasn't in the box?" Trevino asked, peering intently at Cam.

"Um, I'm guessing Shelby would have mentioned that."

"Right. Of course."

A thought popped into Cam's head. Shelby had said that Bruce was cataloging the contents of the safe deposit boxes for her. Bruce wouldn't have known enough about ancient Jewish history to pay attention to a small worm, if one had happened to have been in the lead box. But if he had seen a fancy ring just lying there? Might he have pocketed it? Cam shook the thought away—he had no evidence to suspect Bruce. *Other than Bruce's history as an art thief and con artist…*

"The ring is probably close by," Trevino continued. "From what we know, you need the ring to summon Asmodeus to help find the Shamir. So, it makes no sense to separate the ring *from* the Shamir. You might keep a key far away from a lock, but chances are they'd be close together."

"So someplace near Rouen," Cam said.

"I bet you can narrow it down more than that," Trevino said. "I'm thinking it might be in one of those other safe deposit boxes."

An hour after his conversation on the park bench with Trevino, Cam parked on the street outside a wrought iron gate fronting Shelby's brick Tudor home in Brookline. The property was tucked within a brick oasis of luxury homes in an eight-block square between the Massachusetts Turnpike and Beacon Street.

Cam had phoned ahead, and Shelby came out to unlock the gate and greet him with a warm hug. She reached up and touched his beard. "A few gray highlights. Distinguished. I like it."

Dressed in a charcoal gray skirt which showed off her toned legs and a sky-blue silk blouse which did the same for her breasts and also brought out her eyes, she looked as alluring as she had twenty-five years ago when he first met her. Many people said she resembled a young Katie Couric, and she possessed the same perky, playful intelligence as well. "How is it that you never seem to age?" he asked.

She took him by the arm—his good one—and guided him along a shaded, winding path toward the front door. "I just got a membership offer from the AARP, Cam. So you don't know how sweet it is to hear you say that."

Cam did the math in his head. She was four years older than him, so fifty-two. She could easily pass for forty. As a young attorney, he—like many of the men in their law firm—had thought about dating her. Especially after she stayed up one night playing poker and smoking cigars with Cam and a group of young associates—and cleaning them out, while she was at it. But it had always seemed to Cam that she had built a wall around herself. Sometimes she would gaze out at him from behind it, as if sad that she could not invite him in. But the barriers seemed impenetrable. That wall, of course, was Bruce Arrujo. For whatever reason—and it did not seem that even she understood it fully—Bruce had won her heart. Cam had asked Amanda about it once. "What do you think Shelby sees in him?"

"His inaccessibility. He's a loner. Doesn't need anyone or anything. Would rather spend all his time alone on his bloody sailboat. No friends, no family. But, despite all that, he wants *her*. Every girl likes to feel like Cinderella. Of all the damsels in the land, Bruce chose her. Nobody else would do."

Cam had nodded. "That makes sense, I guess."

"Plus he's damaged. Vulnerable. Parents neglected him, from what I recall. Women like to be nurturing. Like to be needed."

"That makes sense, also."

With a laugh, Amanda had added, "And it doesn't hurt that he looks like something chiseled by an Italian sculptor."

As if reading his thoughts, Shelby said, "By the way, Bruce went out for a sail."

Cam knew Bruce didn't like to be around people. Which was fine with Cam—he didn't like to be around Bruce, either.

Shelby surprised him by saying, "You know, it was his idea to call you. When he saw the Templar cross. He knows you're an expert on the Templars."

"So, how's it going?" Cam asked. "With you two."

Wide blue-green eyes on him, she sighed. "Okay, I guess. But it's hard. He's naturally a loner. On top of that, now he can't go out in public, especially in Boston. And I don't want to leave my life here and move away. So he's almost under house arrest. Other than going out on his boat, he pretty much never leaves the property except when we're traveling. I miss the little things like grabbing a bite to eat or catching a movie or even going for a walk along the river." She forced a smile. "But I'm not complaining. For a few weeks there, I thought he really *was* dead." To pull off his scam, Bruce had not told even Shelby of his plan to stage his own death. "A fake death isn't nearly as bad as a real one."

She turned to him and held his eyes. "I mean, you know that more than anyone. Here I am whining when I should be asking about you. How are you doing? You still seeing that Israeli woman?"

Cam nodded. He wanted to tell Shelby that he and Rivka had some of the same issues as her and Bruce. There were certain things Rivka simply couldn't do, certain places she couldn't go to because she needed to keep a low profile. On the other hand, they had the opposite problem—while Bruce seemed always to be around, Cam would go weeks without seeing Rivka and have no idea, like now, even what continent she was on. Instead, he said, simply, "She travels a lot for work. Which is fine for now. But it sort of puts a limitation on how serious we can get."

"Do you want it to get serious?" she asked lightly as they passed a gargoyle fountain.

"Truly, I don't think about it."

"Well, that says a lot right there. Either you're not ready, or she's not the one."

It was a good point. With Amanda, he had known almost immediately that he wanted to spend the rest of his life with her. He didn't have those feelings with Rivka, but how realistic was it to catch lightning in a bottle twice? He gave a noncommittal answer. "It's only been two years since I lost Amanda. I have fun with Rivka when she's around." He shrugged. "For now, that's enough."

Shelby squeezed his arm. "Well, any woman would be lucky to have you. If she's smart, she'll cut back on those business trips before someone swoops in and steals you away from her."

She seemed to hold his eyes for an extra beat as she said it. For a fleeting moment, he wondered if he should have made more of an effort to pursue Shelby when they first met. Or even after Amanda died. He let the thought die on the vine.

"Speaking of swooping in," he said, "sorry to rush down here with so little notice. But I really want to see that safe deposit box."

"Don't be silly." She pushed open the ornately carved front door, stepping aside so he could pass in front of her. She smelled fresh and floral, her scent and her eyes and her words reminding him of the first time she had ushered him into her office as a young, nervous associate. "Don't be silly," she had said to him then, eyes dancing, in response to him asking if he should call her Ms. Baskin rather than Shelby.

He brushed by her, careful not to get too close. "I have a hunch about something," he said.

She smiled. "You always had good instincts." She led him through a foyer into the kitchen. With a key, she unlocked a thick door next to a broom closet. "So, what's this hunch of yours?"

As they descended a well-lit staircase, and then stood outside another locked door at the bottom of the stairs, Cam explained what he had learned about the Shamir, its use in building King Solomon's Temple, and his suspicion that the Templars may have found it while in Jerusalem in the early 12th century. He answered a few questions she had about the Shamir, then continued, "My Masonic friend thinks that if they found the Shamir, chances are they did so after first finding Solomon's ring.

Solomon used the ring to summon the demons who helped find the Shamir."

"So he thinks that the Templars would have needed the ring to find the Shamir, just like what Solomon did. No ring, no Shamir," she said. "Logical."

"Right. And he thinks that, once they found the Shamir, they'd probably keep the ring nearby, with it." He shrugged. "They sort of belong together."

"And you think the ring might be in one of the safe deposit boxes."

"Honestly, I don't know. But it's definitely worth a look."

She stepped toward the door and put her eye up to a retinal scanner. A whirring sound followed, and then the sound of a deadbolt sliding back. She pushed through a steel door into a carpeted, bedroom-sized room. A double bed and dresser were tucked into one corner, but the room was otherwise filled with metal safe deposit boxes haphazardly stacked on folding tables.

"Sorry," she said, marching over to the unmade bed to pull the comforter up. "Just washed the sheets and forgot to make this up." She shrugged. "My grandmother used to say, 'If you want to change the world, start off by making your bed every morning.'"

He smiled. "But it's not actually *your* bed."

"Thank you, counselor." She met his smile. "But I'd advise you against crossing my grandmother. She was a tough old bird."

Straightening herself, she pointed at a single safe deposit box sitting on the desk. "Anyway, that's the one," she said.

"Do you know anything about the family who owned it?"

"*Owns* it. Still does."

"Right. Sorry."

"All we have so far is a name. Aaron Kahn. No address."

"I'm guessing there are thousands of people with that name."

"Right. And, of course, during the war most of the records were lost. My uncle's organization has close ties with a bunch of Jewish groups. They've agreed to look through their databases. If we can find his descendants, or get more info about his life, we might learn something about him that is useful. But most people don't work over the weekend, so nothing yet."

Cam examined the container. Like Shelby said during their first phone call, inside the metal box sat another lead box filled with rough, off-white wool. On the lid, the word *Shamir* was carved in Hebrew, along with a Templar cross next to it. Despite what the Talmud said, and despite Astarte's simulation theory, Sue said some scholars were skeptical that the Shamir was an actual worm; "worm" was likely a metaphor for something otherwise unexplainable, they believed. But what? Cam examined the wool, pulling at it to see if anything was hidden inside. He also examined the box, looking for niches or hidden compartments. Nothing. Which meant the Shamir must somehow have been removed from the box, putting aside the possibility it was a real worm and actually, well, crawled away on its own and was now curled up in a moist corner someplace, just chilling out. But who would take the worm and not the box? From what Cam had read, the worm could cut or eat its way through any metal or stone or wood carrying case, other than lead. Which meant that if it had been taken, whoever took it knew how to handle it.

His musings were interrupted by Shelby turning on a laptop resting on the corner of the desk. She quickly opened a spreadsheet. "For all his faults," she said, "Bruce is very organized. He inventories almost all the boxes, then does research on all the personal items to try to get values and also clues as to who might own them."

Cam was surprised Shelby allowed Bruce access to the boxes. He wasn't exactly Mr. Trustworthy.

As if reading his thoughts, Shelby commented, "A lot of the work we did, especially in the early days, was recovering artwork stolen by the Nazis. Bruce was really helpful." She smiled ruefully. "He knows a lot about stolen art." She held his eyes. "And—at least working on the Nazi stuff over the years with my uncle Abraham's team—he's never once done anything to make me or anyone else question his honesty. As you know, he's supposed to be dead, so he can't exactly be out there chasing down stolen art anymore." Gesturing toward the safe deposit boxes, she said, "But this, here, he can do. And he's good at it."

Cam nodded. "Understood." *He* wouldn't trust Bruce, but it wasn't his call. And Bruce, devoted as he was to Shelby, and knowing how important her work was to her, was surely smart enough not to risk losing her by double-crossing her.

"So," she said, "what kind of ring are we looking for?"

"Nobody knows for certain." Cam held up his phone. "But this is a pretty good guess as to its design." Trevino had texted it to him after consulting sources discussing ritual from esoteric groups who had broken off from orthodox Masonry.

Design of Solomon's Magic Ring

After studying the image of the ring, Shelby said, "Well, let's get started." She examined Bruce's spreadsheet, Cam moving closer to do the same. Their elbows touched, but neither pulled away.

He cleared his throat. "There are, like, eight or ten boxes that have rings."

"Come on, let's look." She smiled. "It reminds me of when I was a kid and went to the dentist. After the appointment, I got to open a jewelry box and pick out a ring."

"I always chose the Superball," Cam replied.

She laughed lightly. "Of course you did."

Shelby jotted down the numbers of the boxes holding rings, and one by one they opened the lids and sorted through them carefully. Standing side-by-side with Shelby, their bodies close as they leaned over the long, narrow, metal containers filled with mysterious items, Cam sensed that anything was possible. Shelby always had been one of those people who success followed around; Cam actually attributed her luck to that old saying about good fortune being the residue of hard work and careful preparation. He felt his hands getting sweaty, noticed his pulse rate climbing. *King Solomon's magic ring?* Could it really be under the lid of one of these boxes?

Ten minutes later, he sat back, an empty feeling in his gut. They had found many rings, some of them valuable, but nothing that looked remotely like the image on his phone. And no Templar or Masonic symbols on rings, either. In short, nothing that might tie back to Solomon.

"It must be somewhere else," Cam lamented, his sense of giddiness evaporated like the morning dew. He didn't voice a gnawing suspicion that perhaps Bruce had pocketed it.

"We need to go through these boxes again, more carefully. Maybe we missed something." She paused. "Also, the bank only turned over, like, one-third of the boxes. Only the dormant ones. Maybe the ring was in one of the others." Shelby chewed on her bottom lip, then reached for her phone. "It's six-thirty in France, five hours ahead. Maybe we'll get lucky." In French, she asked to speak to a Mademoiselle Belanger. She covered the phone. "She's my contact at the Rouen bank, a vice-president. Maybe she can let us take a peek into the other boxes." As a French woman spoke, Shelby's face suddenly clouded. Cam didn't catch the rest of the conversation, but Shelby was clearly distressed.

She hung up. "She's missing. Her apartment's been ransacked. They think a kidnapping."

"The banker?"

"Yup."

"That's horrible," Cam muttered. "Did you know her well?"

"Not well. I flew over there a few weeks ago to work through the details of the transfer. A pleasant woman. Very bright." She paused. "But there was something odd about her. At the beginning, she was very methodical. Resistant to turning the boxes over to us, as most banks are when we come in. That's part of my job, to convince them that us taking the problem off their hands will save them from embarrassment and bad publicity. Then, near the end of the process, something changed. It was like she couldn't wait to get rid of the boxes. She practically crated them up for me herself."

"Do you think she knew anything about the Shamir?"

"Maybe. I have to believe they went through the boxes before letting us take them. And presumably she made a phone call to a local rabbi, or," she added with a smile, "even the French version of Cameron Thorne, and asked the same questions I asked you."

"And he told her that the box was a hot potato and to get rid of it as soon as possible."

"It adds up," she replied. "Or, I'm just being paranoid and this was just a headache she wanted off her desk."

"Assuming you're not being paranoid, the next logical question is, could the Shamir have anything to do with her abduction? Maybe the French version of myself, or the rabbi, made a phone call to a friend in the Mossad?"

The comment hung in the air, interrupted by a wailing sound coming from outside the closed door.

Shelby turned. "What's that?" Cam asked.

"The alarm. Somebody breaking in."

"Could it be just an animal set it off or something?"

She shook her head, her jaw set. "No. My uncle designed the system.

It's state-of-the-art. Hidden cameras all around the house, monitored remotely. Somebody is here."

Shelby crossed the room to a bank of monitors mounted on the wall. "Look," she said, "two men in black, just outside the back window. And another pair in the bushes there, in the side yard. They must be coming for the Shamir."

Cam's heart thumped. "But in the middle of the day?"

"Probably figure our guard will be down." She scowled. "And they're right. I didn't lock the front gate or the doors before we came down here. Plus Bruce is gone. So, four against two."

Cam held up his injured arm. "Actually, one and a half. And we're not trained operatives, obviously."

"I'm not advocating we *fight* them. But we can outsmart them. Or outmaneuver them."

"Back up a second. Are you sure they're here for the Shamir? Couldn't it be something else?"

She shook her head. "There's some jewelry in the boxes, but nothing special." She looked up at him. "Other than maybe Solomon's ring. I think we have to assume that they've been questioning Mademoiselle Belanger, which led them here." She glanced again at the monitors. "And those guys look like pros."

"Pros don't waste their time on small stuff."

"Right. That's why my money's on the Shamir and the ring. Not that it changes anything. I'm not letting them in. This stuff is too important."

"All right, so what's the plan?"

She pushed the door closed and entered a code on a keypad mounted nearby on the wall. A series of whirs announced the setting of deadbolts. "My uncle designed this as a safe room. They might get in, but it'll take them a while. And we don't need much time." She pulled a white plastic bag from an office trash can, dumped the garbage on the floor in the corner, and said to Cam, "Help me. All the contents of the safe deposit boxes into the bag. But not the Shamir box. Let's keep that separate."

Within thirty seconds, the bag was half full. Using his good arm, Cam twisted it and bound it with a bread tie, then tossed it over his shoulder. "What next?"

Shelby grabbed the Shamir box, crossed the room, and reached around to the back of a bookcase. She released some kind of lever, and the bookshelf swung open. She flicked on a light to reveal a hidden room about the size of a butler's pantry. A metal pole extended up through a hole in the floor. She smiled. "Ever wanted to use the Batpole?"

"Where does it go?"

"The Batcave, of course." She pulled the bookcase closed and, with an impish smile, tucked the Shamir box under an arm, wrapped her ankles around the pole, and slid down. She called up to Cam, "Slide the deadbolt on the bookcase, then follow."

Cam did so, landing on a foam mat after descending about eight feet into a stone chamber of some sort.

"This used to be for coal storage. Then my uncle made some improvements." She pointed at a steel door set into the far wall. "That tunnel brings us out into the basement of an apartment building half a block away. My uncle was pretty paranoid."

Cam strode toward the door, plastic bag over his shoulder. "It's not paranoia if they really are after—"

An explosion from above cut his sentence short.

"Shit," Shelby said, glancing at another monitor. "I see smoke. Some kind of detonation." She watched for another couple of seconds. "They're into the safe room."

"Already?"

"They must be pros, like you said. Come on."

Shelby spun a bank-vault dial, then pulled open the steel door. A rush of dank, earthen air wafted over them. Cam's eyes adjusted and he was able to make out a brick-walled, dirt-floored tunnel extending into the dark. "Not a good day to wear a skirt," Shelby said. "But at least I didn't go with heels." Cam was glad that, having no meetings today, he had gone casual with tennis shoes with his khakis. Shelby grabbed a flashlight from a shelf, took Cam's hand, and led him into the passageway. The light reflected off a half dozen pairs of rodent eyes. "I hate rats," she said.

Setting down the plastic bag, Cam picked up a broken brick off the ground with his left hand and tossed it forward, temporarily scattering them. "Me too. But I prefer rats over trained operatives." They began to maneuver through the narrow tunnel, Shelby's floral scent offering a welcome relief against the stale air.

A pair of thumps from behind them announced the arrival of two operatives descending the pole from the butler's pantry.

"Shit," she whispered. "How did they find us so quickly?"

"Probably some kind of thermal imaging. They read the heat of our bodies." It occurred to Cam that they should have closed the vault door, though doing so ran the risk of locking themselves in this dungeon if the far side of the tunnel turned out to be blocked. "Come on. These people mean business."

Crouching, they trudged forward, navigating the uneven ground, Shelby lighting the path. "Damn," she called out.

"What?"

"I caught my blouse on a nail or something. Ripped the buttons right off."

Cam could see her breasts tumbling out above an immodest black bra. She worked for a couple of seconds to cover herself with her damaged shirt, finally saying, "Screw it. Come on."

At a bend in the tunnel, Cam glanced back. A pair of bodies were silhouetted against the glow of the coal storage room.

"How far does this go?" he asked.

"Another hundred feet."

"Then what?"

"Out a bulkhead door to a car in the alley."

"You keep a car there permanently?"

"Like I said, my uncle was paranoid. In his will, he left money for all his security precautions to be maintained."

A gunshot rang out. Then a voice, echoing in the tunnel. "Stop where you are." A man with some kind of foreign accent. "That was a warning shot. The next one won't be. We won't hurt you. We just want the box."

Shelby gritted her teeth. "People who don't want to hurt you usually don't shoot bullets in your direction."

"Agreed."

Cam noticed water dripping into the tunnel. Reaching up, he grabbed at some crumbling mortar and dug his fingers in, hoping to extract a brick to use as a weapon.

"Careful. It'll come down on our heads."

He stopped. "Any other ideas?"

"Yes. Let's move faster."

The bend in the tunnel would protect them from a direct shot for a few seconds, at least. Still grasping the lead box, her blouse hanging open, Shelby increased her pace, bent at the waist in the short-ceilinged passageway.

"One of them looked tall," Cam said, based on how much they needed to crouch.

"Good. And hopefully the other is claustrophobic."

Ahead, her light reflected off another steel door.

"That one locks from this side," she said. "A deadbolt. To keep people from the apartment building from coming this way."

"There's no chance someone put a lock on the other side?" Cam asked.

"My uncle paid a lot of people a lot of money to make sure stuff like that doesn't happen." She scowled. "But he's been dead seven years."

Cam set down the plastic bag again, reached forward and, with effort, forced the dead bolt open with his left hand. He tugged on the door, pain shooting up his injured right arm. Mercifully, it budged, swinging toward them an inch or two with a sharp groan. "Come on," he said, yanking harder, the sound of footsteps echoing behind them.

Light flooded the tunnel as the door swung open. Cam lifted the bag as Shelby took his hand again and guided him across the threshold, blinking as their eyes adjusted to the brightness.

Suddenly, a female voice carried down the tunnel. "Cameron? What's going on?" In the dim light, twenty feet away, a tall, masked form dropped to one knee, a gun drawn.

He froze. He recognized her voice, her body shape, her eyes. "Rivka?" *What was she doing here?* Her tone wasn't hostile as much as surprised. Even hurt. He looked down, his hand in Shelby's and her blouse hanging open. *Oh shit.* He began to stammer a reply.

Shelby didn't share Cam's inclination to explain things. She jerked him forward before he could form his words, then reached for the door and slammed it closed.

"Damn it," she said. "No lock on this side."

Without asking, she handed him the lead box, reached toward his crotch, undid his belt, and quickly pulled it through the loops. She wound it through a handle on the door, then around a nearby metal storage rack, and cinched it.

"That'll hold them for a few seconds," she said, retaking the box. From the tunnel side, someone gave the door a sharp tug. Shelby began to move. "Hopefully that's all we need." She turned. "That was *the* Rivka, I take it."

Numbly, he nodded. *Was the Mossad after the Shamir?*

"Well, at least we know who the bad guys are." She tugged him along. "Come on. And hold onto your pants." She smiled over her shoulder as they pushed through the bulkhead door. "If Rivka didn't like the sight of us holding hands, she's definitely not going to like the sight of your pants around your ankles."

✦✝⛤

Rivka, on one knee, remained frozen in place in the dark tunnel, the memory of Cameron hand-in-hand with the pretty, perky, half-naked blonde emblazoned onto her retina. And what about that unmade bed in the safe room? Rivka always suspected—perhaps feared was a better word—that there was a special bond between Cameron and Shelby...

"Rivka, come on," Menachem shouted. "They're getting away."

She tried to rally, swallowing back the bile rising in her throat. But her body felt heavy, like she was advancing through chest-high water. And she couldn't seem to get her lungs to fill with air. *Stop it!* She was being silly, emotional, irrational. Acting like a teenager. He was allowed to have female friends. It was probably all innocent. Maybe work-related. So why did she feel like vomiting?

She watched as Menachem rushed for the steel door, gun drawn. A wave of fear broke through the numbness as her eyes locked onto the Glock. *Don't shoot Cameron.* "No," she said, leaping to her feet and taking a step forward. The thick underground air caught in her lungs and she slumped back to one knee. Her world narrowing, she focused on a pair of black rat's eyes sizing her up from the edge of the tunnel...

"Rivka, get up." Menachem's voice. Angry.

She turned her head to his voice and dug her fingers into the dirt to try to keep her world from spinning.

With a scowl, he shook a water bottle at her, splashing her face. Menachem had never been known for his bedside manner.

She blinked, then spat. "Don't be an asshole."

"Good," he said curtly. "Anger usually helps. But I never took you to be so weak. Come on, get up."

Her chest throbbed and the taste of her own bile soured her mouth. Menachem was right. She was being weak. Maybe because, while watching the sun rise over the Atlantic this morning, she had contemplated telling Cameron she loved him the next time they were together. Fortune favored the bold, and all that. But even in the warmth of the rising sun, the thought of it had made her want to crawl under her bed. What if he didn't reciprocate? What if he smiled politely and thanked her? What if he told her he loved another? Someone blond and perky...

Menachem took a step toward her, jarring her back to the moment. He pulled her to her feet. His face so close to hers that she could smell the salami on his breath, he said, "This is an urgent mission. You must put your personal feelings aside."

She turned away from him, again close to vomiting. "Okay," she murmured. "I'm fine."

"Now, pull that door open as far as you can."

Moving mechanically, Rivka did so. Menachem slipped a knife between the door and the frame and sliced through the leather belt. Tension released, the door flew toward Rivka as she continued to pull on it, sending her tumbling against the tunnel wall.

"Shit," she exclaimed, rubbing the back of her head. But the jolt seemed to do her good, to jar her back to the present.

Menachem didn't wait to check on her this time. "Come on," he said, racing through the doorway. Light streamed in from around the bulkhead, and Menachem scampered across the room to it. As he pushed the bulkhead door open, the sound of a car engine met her ears. Tires squealed, then Menachem cursed. He raised a radio to his mouth. "Do you see them? They just left the alley. Black Lexus sedan."

Static, then a reply. "They just raced past us. Sorry, but they're gone."

Menachem smashed his fist against the basement wall. Seething, he turned on Rivka. "You had a chance to stop them."

She swallowed. "No. I had a chance to *shoot* them." To shoot *Cameron*. She held his glare. "You can ask a lot of me, Menachem. But you can't ask that."

Cam peered in the side-view mirror as Shelby sped through the side streets of Brookline. "I don't see them."

Shelby slapped the steering wheel. "Dammit. I should have seen this coming. The Israeli embassy reached out over the weekend and asked to see the safe deposit boxes, and I said no. Said they weren't mine to share."

"The Israelis don't usually take no for an answer."

She slowed. "That's Storrow Drive right up at the next light."

"If I were them, that's where I'd be looking. The highways. Maybe we should stay local."

She nodded. "Okay."

Rather than taking the on-ramp, she drove onto the Boston University Bridge, crossing into Cambridge, navigating through the early part of the afternoon rush. Halfway across the bridge, she handed him her phone. "Throw it into the river. Yours also. They can be traced, even when they're off."

"Good point." He emailed himself a picture of the seal on Solomon's ring, then, one at a time, flung the phones over the bridge rail. Fortunately, he regularly backed up his contents.

Shelby said, "We could head over to Charlestown, get on the boat with Bruce. Then figure things out from there."

Cam's initial reaction was to reject the suggestion. But was that just his personal feelings talking? "I think that limits our options too much. If they find us, we'll just be sitting ducks. Literally." Who knew what kind of resources and technology the Mossad had? "I think we need to ditch this car and then get out of the city."

She nodded, turning east on side streets paralleling the river. "We have an old van we use for Big Sister events. It's parked at the Somerville YMCA. I have a key. We could ditch this car in a parking garage, then walk over to the Y and take the van."

Cam nodded. "I like it." *And no Bruce.*

"Check under your seat. There should be a leather satchel."

Cam unzipped it, rifling through its contents. Ten bank envelopes, each with a thousand dollars in twenty-dollar bills. A stack of gift cards from Target and Walmart and CVS. Four burner phones with internet access. A pair of fake passports, one with Shelby's picture and the other with Bruce's, and driver's licenses to match. "Not sure I look like him," Cam said.

"Not to mention the five-inch height difference." Bruce was a few inches north of six feet. "There's a suitcase in the trunk filled with supplies and clothes, not that they'll fit you."

"I can roll up the pant legs and sleeves." He smiled. "Make a fashion statement."

She returned his smile with a rueful one herself. "I've been dreading this day for years. Having to run on short notice." She touched his arm. "But I always thought it would be with Bruce."

"What fun would life be without a few curveballs?"

"I've had enough curveballs, thank you very much."

Cam didn't know how to respond to the curveball comment, so he didn't. He knew she had lost her entire family—parents and brother—to a drunk driver. Then she and Bruce lost a baby during childbirth about fifteen years ago, just after Cam and Amanda adopted Astarte. Shelby and Cam never talked about that loss, other than she told him once that they would never be able to have children and that Bruce refused to adopt. Shelby always did her best to appear cheery and bright, but Cam noticed the melancholy in her eyes whenever she asked about Astarte. Which reminded him, he needed to call her.

"Are you going to try to contact Bruce?" he asked.

"He knows, already. The alarm system is synced with his phone. So he's seen the video."

"Do you guys have a plan where to meet?"

She shook her head. "We have *elaborate* plans. But they all are based on the assumption that someone is chasing *Bruce*. He goes to a certain spot, sends me notice if and when it's safe, and I pick him up. But we never arranged it to work in reverse." She sighed and, at a stop light, held Cam's eyes. "And we never expected to be fleeing the Mossad."

"I'm guessing I wasn't in your plans, either," he said with a wry smile.

"No. But I'm not complaining about *that*."

Twenty minutes later—the Lexus tucked into the dark corner of a parking garage—they climbed into the velour-covered bucket seats of an orange, fifteen-passenger, 1997 Chevy Express van.

"Um, could we be any more conspicuous?" Cam asked as he dropped the plastic bag onto the floor at his feet and tossed the suitcase into the back seat.

"I know. I always thought this thing looked like a giant carrot on wheels." She shrugged. "But they're looking for a black sedan. Maybe we can hide in plain sight."

"Nobody'll report it stolen?"

"No. Half the youth workers in Boston have a key. People take it all the time to buy supplies or bring the kids to the park. It'll be days before anyone realizes it's gone."

Shelby turned the key, and the engine coughed to life.

"How many miles does this thing have on it?" Cam asked.

"Almost three hundred thousand," she said, exiting the parking lot.

He swallowed. "That's comforting."

"It is, in a way. That means it's reliable. But see that gum on the floor at your feet?"

"Yeah."

"Don't pick at it. It's holding the chassis together."

He chuckled. He liked that she was so calm under duress. Panic led to tunnel vision which, of course, led to mistakes. She accelerated. "So, Cam, where to?"

He glanced in the side-view mirror again. "I think job one is to find someplace safe to hole up. Then we need to reexamine the stuff in the plastic bag."

"Okay, agreed. I have a house on the Cape, but they'll probably look there."

He held up the leather case. "All this, but no safe house?"

"There should be a key in there."

Cam found it in a side pocket. "What's it to?"

She bit her lip as she rolled through a yellow light, seemingly comfortable navigating the oversized vehicle even in Boston's rush hour traffic. "That's the thing. This is for if *Bruce* needs to run. We never thought it would be me. I have no idea what that key is for. I could call Bruce—"

"Too dangerous," he replied, perhaps a bit too curtly. He exhaled. "I have a condo up in New Hampshire. It's owned by a trust. Can't trace it back to me."

"Does Rivka know about it?"

A pang of guilt shot through him as he pictured the look of hurt on Rivka's face in the tunnel. "No."

"Okay," she said, angling toward Route 93. "We go north."

Cam helped her navigate out of the city, then she moved to the right lane, the van rattling and shaking, and cruised at fifty-five. "So," he said, "what do we know?"

She looked at him sideways. "We know you broke that woman's heart."

Cam squirmed. He didn't want to talk about Rivka with Shelby. Which was odd—an hour ago, he had done so gladly. "Besides that. What do we know about the Shamir?"

"I think it's safe to say that the Mossad didn't find what they were looking for in Rouen, which is why they abducted Mademoiselle Belanger. If they had, they wouldn't have needed to come looking here."

"Agreed."

"I also think it's logical that they wouldn't be going to all this trouble if they didn't believe the legend of the Shamir was true."

"Agreed, again," Cam replied. "And I'll take it one step further. They probably also believe in Solomon's magic ring, since one is tied to the other."

"That actually brings me to my third point," Shelby said. "The Shamir is fascinating from a historical perspective. Also from a religious one. But the mission of the Mossad, as I understand it, is to protect Israel's *security*. Not its culture or history or religion." She glanced at Cam. "Which makes me think you may be right about Solomon's ring. The Shamir itself is not enough to get the Mossad involved—"

Cam cut in. "But a magic ring that summons demons and genies granting three wishes, well, that could be useful. For *either* side in the Middle East."

She glanced down at the garbage bag on the floor at his feet. Shelby had handed him the lead box, which he had closed up and stuffed into the bag with the other safe deposit box items. She slowed and smiled. "I better drive extra careful. Get into an accident, and someone's likely to toss that bag into a dumpster."

Cam was actually worried *they* might end up getting tossed into a dumpster. On the one hand, the Mossad didn't go around randomly torturing and killing American citizens. But, on the other, he had no doubt that Menachem would do what he needed to complete his mission, even if Rivka might balk at taking out her lover. Or was it former lover? And that mission, apparently, involved retrieving the Shamir and possibly also Solomon's ring.

Using a burner phone, he called Astarte. She knew enough not to ignore strange numbers. "Hello?" she said tentatively.

"Hi honey, it's me. Don't worry, I'm fine."

"If that was true, you'd be using your own phone."

"Good point." He explained the situation. "So, we're running from the Mossad."

"That usually doesn't end well, Dad. Be careful."

"I will. I'm guessing they won't come looking for you." It was one of the benefits of her being at school two thousand miles away. "But, just in case, you might want to stay with Matthias' family for a few days." They should be safe at the reservation.

"Okay. Can I do anything to help?"

"Call Brandon and ask him to watch Venus."

"Okay." She paused. "Um, you want me to text Rivka?"

This was awkward. When your girlfriend was a spy who caught you with a woman she was trying to abduct, was it proper protocol for your daughter to reach out to try to mend fences? "Don't text because it might be traced. But send an email from the school library. Just tell her I'm sorry and we can talk when, well, this is all over."

"That's sort of lame, Dad."

Astarte didn't know about the handholding. And Cam didn't know if it meant anything. Or even if he wanted it to. "I know. But, for now, lame is the best I got."

Shelby gave him an inquiring look but remained silent. They crossed the border into New Hampshire, the traffic heavy but steady.

"No transponder in this van, is there?" Cam asked. They were approaching a tollbooth.

She shook her head. "No. Most people know better than to take this thing on the highway."

But they had managed to put fifty miles between themselves and Boston, with no mechanical problems and no sign of the Mossad team. Still, as they drove, Cam pictured Menachem and his army of techies, their tentacles spreading around New England, monitoring cell phone towers and credit card transactions and satellite imagery and land records and security cameras. Not to mention their vast network of informants, both Jews and Christians, friendly to the state of Israel. It was only a matter of time—and not much of it—before Menachem caught their scent. A generation ago, a person could go off the grid and have a decent chance of staying there. But in today's digital world, as Shelby had learned with Bruce, it was next to impossible. Especially at a moment's notice.

"I'm rethinking the condo decision," Cam said. "We can stay there for one night, but then I think we need to move on." When he had set up the blind trust a decade ago, he hadn't expected the Mossad to be the ones trying to peer through the fog. He doubted any kind of trust would be completely blind to them. And he had witnessed the Mossad's brutal interrogation tactics—walking away blinded, and nothing worse, might be considered a fortunate outcome for him and Shelby if they got caught.

"Should we try to cross into Canada?" she asked.

It was tempting to put as much distance as they could between themselves and Menachem's team. But, again, acting out of panic was not generally a wise strategy. "Like you said, I don't look anything like Bruce. And I don't see what we gain. The Mossad can cross also." He shifted in his seat. "I think what we need to do is figure out if we have the ring or not. If we do, then we can try to negotiate with the Mossad. And if we don't, well, we can try to convince them to believe us."

"There is a third option."

"What's that?"

"We go public with it."

He smiled. "That would work, if we could get the magic ring to actually, you know, do magic. Card tricks, maybe saw a lady in half."

"How about a flying carpet?"

Cam turned. Something about Shelby's comment rang a bell deep in his memories. Turning on a burner phone, he did a quick internet search, waiting as the phone slowly searched the web. "Bingo," he said. "There it is. The flying carpet."

"What?"

"The *Arabian Nights* stories. They had a flying carpet, of course. And that's where the idea of a genie in the bottle, giving three wishes, comes from. But here's the thing. In the *Arabian Nights* stories, it's a fisherman who first finds the bottle and lets the genie out. The genie's name is Asmodeus. The stories say he was locked in a copper jar with the seal of Solomon on it."

Shelby gave him a quick look. "Isn't Asmodeus the name of the demon who first gave Solomon the Shamir and then took his throne?"

"It is. What's interesting about all this is that the Shamir story, as far as I could find, is all based on Jewish sources. This Asmodeus-in-the-bottle stuff is from Arab stories that go back to the Middle Ages." He paused. "And the stories specifically mention Solomon and his magic ring."

She chewed her lip. "I see where your mind is going with this. But these are just fables. They don't really prove anything."

"They don't, I agree. But legends are almost always based in fact. And when you have two separate cultures sharing similar legends going back a couple of thousand years, chances are there's a lot of truth in them."

She nodded. "Okay. Fair enough."

"What it means is that this magic ring might actually exist. Might actually work."

"All we need to do now is find it."

He looked out Shelby's window at the cars passing on their left. He couldn't wait to go through the contents of the garbage bag again. "Any chance we can go any faster?"

She glanced at him sideways. "Only if you can get that genie of yours to change this rolling carrot into a magic carpet."

CHAPTER 5

Astarte darted around her dorm room, haphazardly packing an overnight bag. She had just hung up with her dad. Not exactly what she wanted to do the day after getting back from spring break. But, whatever. As Matthias liked to say, having to relocate for the night was a First World problem. Many people on the planet would be sleeping tonight on the street, or worse.

Matthias texted. *Got your message. Just leaving class. Meet u at car and we can head to reservation.*

She had hoped for a few nights alone with him after being apart for ten days. But, again, a First World problem. They would have to wait a few days before fooling around. She smiled to herself. Or maybe just figure out a way to keep things quiet at his parents' place.

Her dad had given her his old SUV for college. He said it was so he could get a new one for himself. The reality was he didn't want her on the back of Matthias' motorcycle. They each were happy in their own truths.

Ten minutes later, she met Matthias at the parking lot near her dorm. He loped over, dark and broad-shouldered, his ponytail swinging, a big smile on his dimple-chinned face. He leaned down to kiss her, his lips somehow both firm and supple.

"You want me to drive?" he asked.

"I will." She was still nauseous from the berry poisoning. "Driving makes me less carsick."

"If you're going to get that sick, you might as well take peyote."

"True." She had been experimenting with the mind-altering cactus root as a way to conjure up both visions of the future and past memories of her ancestors. "At least with peyote, I usually learn something."

Matthias grinned. "Sounds like you learned something this time, also: Don't eat wild berries."

She cuffed him on the shoulder and hopped into the driver's seat. Ten minutes into the drive, after sharing a few details about their days, Matthias said, "So, tell me more about this site in Pennsylvania."

The night before, after landing, she had told him about the encounter with the landowner and also her berry poisoning, but not much about the boulder alignments or the mysterious notch. She did so now. "My dad thinks the Phoenicians may have been involved."

Matthias nodded. Astarte knew that he was familiar, and comfortable, with the theory that the Phoenicians had traveled to America to mine and trade for copper, using the America's Stonehenge ceremonial site in New Hampshire as a base of operations. The Phoenicians, being sun worshipers, chose the site in New Hampshire not only because of its location on a hilltop close to the Atlantic coastline, but because it aligned with the Stonehenge site in England. On the summer solstice, the most important day of the year for a sun-worshiping society, an observer viewing the sunrise from the center of the America's Stonehenge site would see the sun rise on the northeast horizon and sit atop a standing stone like a golf ball on a tee. If extended, the imaginary line formed by these three points—the center of the site, the standing stone and the sun—would cross the Atlantic and pass through the main stone arch of the Stonehenge site in England.

She handed Matthias her phone. "You've seen these alignment images, Stonehenge to Stonehenge, right?"

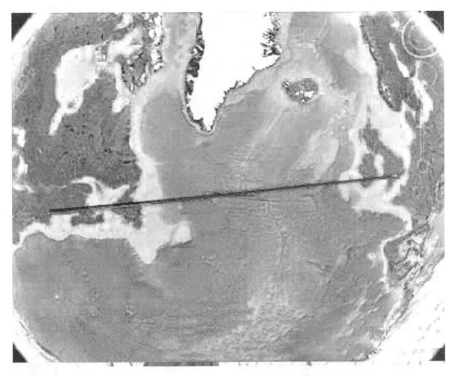

Summer Solstice Sunrise Line - America's Stonehenge to Stonehenge

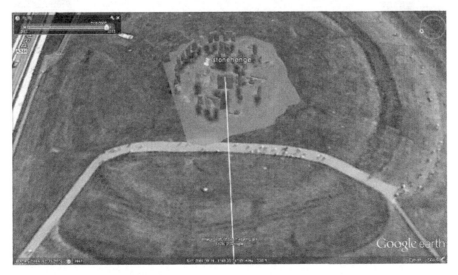

Summer Solstice Sunrise Line - America's Stonehenge to Stonehenge

He nodded again. "Hell of a coincidence."

"Especially when you add in the Israeli site," she replied.

What she was referring to was that this imaginary great circle arc, if continued, would pass within one-sixth of one degree of a site in the Golan Heights of Israel, formerly part of the Phoenician homeland, called Gilgal Refaim, the Wheel of Giants, also known as Israeli Stonehenge.

Summer Solstice Sunrise Line - America's Stonehenge to Stonehenge
to Israeli Stonehenge

This ancient series of stone circles in northern Israel, dating back to Phoenician times, marked the solar alignments and served as an ancient calendar, like its namesakes. The site, the size of a soccer stadium, consisted of over 40,000 rocks and boasted a center mound which rose up fifteen feet off the ground and outer walls standing nine feet in height.

Israeli Stonehenge, Golan Heights

Astarte let out a long breath. Somehow these ancient Phoenician voyagers—experts at navigation and seafaring—had been able to reverse-engineer the site in New Hampshire to align with sacred sites both in England and their Phoenician homeland on the summer solstice, their most sacred day. Six thousand miles away, and only off by one-sixth of one degree. Impossible to imagine. Yet also impossible to imagine as a coincidence.

They drove in silence for a few minutes.

"You're still thinking about the Stonehenge alignments, aren't you?" Matthias asked with a smile.

"How did you know?"

"You always get this faraway look in your eye, as if you were trying to actually look across the Atlantic." He smiled again. "Then you shake your head in amazement."

"Amazement, and also frustration. Up until about a year ago, the state archeologist from New Hampshire had never even visited the America's Stonehenge site. And he's lived there his whole life. Can you say close-minded?" She gritted her teeth. "I mean, why will nobody in academia even *look* at this stuff?"

Matthias lowered his voice. "You know the answer to that. They're afraid of what they might find."

"And it's not just the New Hampshire site." She and Matthias were familiar with research establishing that oral history of the tribes in the Great Lakes region spoke of mining conducted by "fair-haired marine men" and that carbon-dating of artifacts found in the ancient Great Lakes copper mines dated back to the Phoenician era, approximately 1,000 BC. Phoenicians would have made the long trip to America because of the abundance of American copper, its purity, and the fact that other supplies had dried up. She directed Matthias to another image on her phone, a petroglyph of a Phoenician ship found on the shores of Lake Superior in Michigan's Upper Peninsula. "Check it out."

Ship Petroglyph, Copper Harbor, Michigan

He nodded. "Looks Phoenician. Definitely not Indian. And definitely not Colonial era."

"The story holds together," she replied. "The Phoenicians definitely went up to England, to Cornwall, to trade for tin. But nobody knows where all the copper came from to mix with the tin to make bronze, which is, like, eighty-eight percent copper. A lot of copper came from Cyprus, but eventually those mines ran out. Then they found that arrowhead in Cornwall and did a metallurgy test on it. The copper came from Michigan." She shrugged. "Connect the dots. The Phoenicians went from Cornwall to the Great Lakes, stopping off in New Hampshire, to get copper to mix with the tin."

He rested his hand on her leg and smiled. "Now you're letting evidence cloud your judgment."

She knew she sounded like her father, but she couldn't help it sometimes. "It's just frustrating. The evidence is there, but, like I said, most of the historians just ignore it. I mean, just look at that Uluburun shipwreck off the coast of Turkey." The Uluburun, she had learned from her research, was a Phoenician ship dating back to 1300 BC. Preliminary testing indicated that the copper ingots were of a purity only found in the Great Lakes. But, for some reason, in what was becoming a pattern, they didn't test any further.

"Hey, you don't need to convince me. The Indian legends agree with you."

"It's not just the legends. What about those Hamsa hands in the Alabama mounds? They're at least a thousand years old. Definitely pre-contact."

"Yup." He poked at his phone. "Like this?" He pulled up a decorative plate with a human hand—with an eye looking out from its palm—in the center. The symbol was a common one in ancient Phoenicia.

Hamsa Hand, Alabama Burial Mound

"That's it. Some shapes are pretty common. But this is a hand with an eye in the palm. What are the odds of it being invented on both sides of the Atlantic?"

He nodded. "I agree. More likely, one group invented it and shared it with the other."

"And since there are, like, a gazillion of them in the Middle East and only a handful here—pun intended—chances are it came across *to* America rather than *from*. Brought by the Phoenicians."

"Okay, I'm with you."

She had other examples to give, but realized she risked becoming a bore—or had already crossed the line. And she was curious if Matthias might be able to shed some light on the Shamir mystery. "I told my dad about your trip to Pumapunku and the stonework. But we were wondering, are there other sites, other examples of precision cuts?"

He nodded. "One of my professors has been studying this. He says there are dozens of ancient sites, mostly in Central and South America, which show the Indians exhibited advanced technology in their stonework." He poked at his phone. "Here's a picture of a wall in Cusco, in Peru. An Incan site, about a thousand years old."

Cusco Stone Wall, Peru

"One of the Spanish conquistadors, Pedro Pizarro, wrote about it in the 1500s. This is what he said:"

In the lower part of this wall there were stones so large and thick that it seemed impossible that human hands could have set them in place...they were so close together, and so well fitted, that the point of a pin could not have been inserted in one of the joints.

Matthias continued. "It's a UNESCO World Heritage site today. But nobody can figure out how they cut the stones so precisely." He angled his phone toward her again. "Here's another picture. Same place, different wall. This is called the Twelve Angle Stone because, obviously, it has twelve different angles, all designed to interlock with the rocks next to it."

Cusco Twelve Angle Stone, Peru

"Listen to this description," he said:

The perfectionist Inca stonework is remarkable. This is because they laid the stones so precisely that the use of mortar to hold them together was not necessary. In fact, so perfectly the stones fit, that a piece of paper would not fit between them. As a result, their constructions were also so stable, that they would simply "dance" and then resettle in the event of an earthquake.

"God's Exacto Knife," Astarte replied in a whisper.

"What?"

"Nothing. Just something my dad told me."

Matthias continued, "Machu Picchu is another Incan site my professor's been studying. Again, amazing walls, with the stones precisely fit together, but no iron tools. Nobody's quite sure how they managed it." He shrugged as he showed her yet another image on his phone.

Machu Picchu Wall, Peru

She quickly glanced at it before refocusing on the highway. "Wow. Like you said, precision work." She took a deep breath. "Do you think there's any possibility that the Incas somehow got their hands on the Shamir?"

Matthias shrugged. "Some people say some advanced alien civilization flew in and built Machu Picchu. Which is not as outlandish as you think, if you look carefully at the construction. For most of the walls, the really sophisticated work is at the bottom, the base. Then there are layers of looser rocks just piled on top. It's almost as if the original builders had advanced technology which was later lost." He smiled. "Could have been that the aliens flew away and went home. Or could have been the green worm died. One's no crazier than the other."

"Maybe the aliens took the green worm with them when they left," Astarte offered with a half-smile.

Matthias shrugged again. "The point is, like I said, the Incas would have needed some kind of advanced technology to build all these amazing sites. The Shamir is as good a theory as any as to what that technology was."

Astarte drove in silence for a few minutes, chewing on what Matthias said. "Just playing connect-the-dots for a minute. I remember my dad saying something about the Phoenicians getting blown off course and ending up in South America. They carved a stone, which later disappeared, called the Paraiba Stone."

Matthias poked at his phone. "Right. Discovered in the late 1800s in Brazil. Says here that a professor from Brandeis, Cyrus Gordon, the head of the Department of Mediterranean Studies, translated it in 1967. He thought it was authentic." Matthias paused, reading. "The inscription talks about being blown off course, about living during the time of King Hiram, about sacrificing a youth to their god, Baal, and about praying for salvation. The carving was lost, but here's what it would have looked like."

Paraiba Stone (Brazil) Reproduction

She nodded. "That's it. And King Hiram—different guy from Hiram Abiff—was a contemporary of King Solomon. So, if the Shamir really was stolen from Hiram Abiff by some of the stone workers and then brought back to the Phoenician homeland, maybe it made its way to South America with the ship that got blown off course."

"It's possible. Like you said, the dates work."

"And we think the Phoenicians were here."

Matthias continued to work his phone. "Not just *we*. Apparently, there are at least a few academic types who agree. An Austrian professor who wrote a book about the ancient history of Brazil. Also a Dutch scholar considered the father of Brazilian archeology. They both made the assertion that Phoenician explorers crossed the Atlantic to Brazil." He looked up. "And if the Phoenicians were in Brazil, no reason they couldn't have also been in Peru."

Astarte stared at the road ahead. "And if they were, no reason they couldn't have brought the Shamir with them."

Shelby and Cam chatted as they cruised north on Route 93, the temperature dropping about ten degrees and the wind buffeting the orange van as they climbed into the White Mountains in the fading daylight.

"You're pretty good at driving this thing," Cam said.

"You'd be amazed at the skills I've picked up running the Big Sister organization. Nurse. Short-order cook. Therapist. Banker. Seamstress. Hypnotist."

"Hypnotist?"

She nodded. "A lot of the kids have mental health issues. Mostly anxiety and depression. So we brought in a hypnotherapist. It was really helpful. But also expensive." She shrugged. "So I took a couple of courses. I'm certified."

"Very cool. And it works?"

"Usually." She smiled. "Bruce was a bit skeeved out by it." She glanced his way and smiled again. "I think he was afraid I was going to turn him into my sex slave or something."

Cam met her smile and angled his head. "And that frightened him?"

She rolled her eyes. "Very funny. Bruce is a bit of a control freak. So, yes, afraid."

They took the Lincoln exit and followed a local highway to a complex of townhouse condos set on a hillside opposite the Loon Mountain ski area.

Cam hopped out as Shelby pulled up to the garage door. "Give me a second to make room for this beast," he said. "It's one thing to drive it. It's another to leave it out in plain sight where people can gawk at it." Entering through the condo's main door, he quickly tossed aside the garbage cans and snow tubes piled at the end of the garage, then ushered Shelby in and closed the door behind her.

He let out a long breath. "Finally." It had been almost four hours since they fled Brookline. "I think we're safe. For now."

She stepped out of the van and stretched. "I'm going to need some clothes. It's cold up here. And a lady in a skirt at a ski resort stands out almost as much as an orange van."

He glanced at his watch. "Let's do this. It's five o'clock. A couple of the shops stay open until six, to give people a chance to swing by after getting off the slopes. Let's walk into town, keep the van hidden. Get some clothes and other supplies, then grab some dinner."

She smiled. "And maybe a bottle of wine also? I'm not used to people pointing guns at me."

"Sure."

To be safe, they decided to get dinner to go. And they made it two bottles of wine, since it was still early. "But we don't open the second one until we finish looking through that bag," Cam said, paying cash at the liquor store.

"By the time we get to the second one, *I'll* be in the bag," Shelby replied.

After walking back, they ate quickly at the butcher-block table in the dining area, sharing chicken wings and a tossed salad.

"I try to eat healthy," Shelby said, reaching for a third wing. "But on days like today, it just feels stupid. I mean, we almost got shot, so what difference does an extra few calories make?"

"I had this discussion with Rivka once. She looks at it just the opposite. In her mind, staying in shape is what keeps her *from* getting shot."

Shelby stopped mid-bite. "Hmm. I see her point." She tossed the wing down and reached for her fork, stabbing at some lettuce. "You're not going to tell me she skips dessert, are you?"

Cam smiled. "No. Chocolate after every meal. But only a small piece. She says that some things are worth getting shot over."

Shelby laughed lightly. "Honestly, she sounds like a keeper, Cam."

Another pang of guilt hit Cam. She was. Just maybe not for him. Either way, she deserved better than seeing her boyfriend hand-in-hand with another woman. Would the incident motivate her to want to stay on the mission, to hunt down Cam as some sort of revenge? Or, instead, would she bow out, ask for a leave? Or, as a third choice, would Menachem simply relieve her as unfit for duty? Not that it really mattered. Menachem had a team of trained operatives, with or without Rivka. Cam and Shelby would need to act quickly.

Cam pushed his plate aside. "Let's dive into that bag."

Shelby nodded. "Agreed."

He retrieved the white plastic garbage bag, which he had deposited on the couch. Shelby looked forlorn, so he resisted making a ho-ho-ho joke. "I really wanted to return all this to the families," she said. "Now it's all a jumble."

He saw the pain in her face. She had always been that way, even as a young lawyer—passionate about protecting the rights of the beleaguered and oppressed. That's what made her such an effective attorney. "We can go through it later," he said, squeezing her hand. "We have Bruce's cataloging. But for now, we need to figure out if Solomon's ring is here."

She let out a long sigh. "Okay."

He pulled out his new burner phone and found the email he had sent himself. "I showed you this already." He angled the phone so she could see it. "This is one version of what experts think Solomon's ring might have looked like. Solomon's seal. Some people call it a sigil. In magical terms, the symbols on it prove to the spirits that he has Yahweh on his side. The symbols, along with magical incantations bestowed onto the ring, are what gives the ring its power. So this is what we're looking for."

Design of Solomon's Magic Ring

"Okay," Shelby replied, rallying. "Let's take out all the jewelry first."

"Agreed. We think we're looking for a ring, but maybe it got turned into a broach or something."

Using his good arm, Cam emptied the plastic bag onto the carpeted floor. Seated side-by-side on couch cushions, each with their second glass of white wine next to them, they went through the pile, removing items of jewelry and putting them in a cereal bowl on the coffee table nearby.

Shelby smiled sadly. "Before my grandmother died, she gathered the whole family. She took all her jewelry and keepsakes and dumped them onto her bed, then told us all to tell her what we wanted." She reached under her blouse and pulled out a teardrop-shaped blue topaz pendant. "I chose this. It's my birthstone. I remember she smiled at me and said,

'Good choice, it matches your eyes.'" She looked up at Cam. "I wear it all the time because it reminds me of her." With a sigh, she gestured at the pile. "But all this. Nobody had a chance to claim it." Her voice dropped. "These people have no keepsakes. No memories. Nothing from grandma that matches their eyes."

He touched her arm. "Like I said, we'll organize it later. Make sure it gets back to the families. But we can't do that if the Mossad has us locked up in some interrogation room. So, for now, we need to focus on finding that ring."

"Then what?"

"Good question. What's that old joke? When a genie gives you three wishes, one of them should be to ask for ten more."

That got a smile from her, and they worked in silence for a few minutes, continuing to separate the jewelry.

Cam said, "One thing I don't get. Your uncle was a fighter for Jewish causes. Why didn't the Mossad just ask for the safe deposit box instead of coming in guns blazing?"

"First, they probably knew I wouldn't give it to them. And Uncle Abraham didn't have great relations with the Israeli government. He exacted vengeance on people who attacked Jews. He was a vigilante. Most Jewish groups opposed him."

"Who are the Israelis to complain about vigilantism? The Mossad does the same thing. They killed all those terrorists from the Munich Olympic massacre. Not that they didn't deserve it. But it was still vigilante justice."

She nodded. "True. They called it Operation Wrath of God. But that was the government acting, not a private group. There's a difference. At least to the Israelis."

"So the Israelis thought, if they asked you, you wouldn't give them the Shamir?"

She looked up from her task. "They're probably right. The stuff in these boxes is private property. I work for the families. In this case, the descendants of Aaron Kahn, whoever and wherever they might be. If they want to donate things to the State of Israel, that's their business. But I can't make that decision for them."

"So the Mossad decided to just come take it."

She smiled. "You mean, *try* to take it. They didn't count on a couple of kick-ass attorneys."

Cam grinned. "If they had caught us, we could have tried to argue them to death."

After a few seconds, she asked, "How are you feeling about Rivka?"

He wanted to reply, "How you feeling about Bruce?" but thought better of it. "Guilty. Sad. I'd like to at least explain to her that it wasn't what it looked like, but I can't even do that."

"We were just holding hands. It's not like I had my tongue down your throat."

He wondered if Shelby would have made such a brash comment absent the wine, and also absent the danger of the day. On the other hand, he did recall that she had a raunchy sense of humor, which had on more than one occasion shocked some of the older attorneys at the firm. "I know," he replied. "But we were alone, in your house. Then the hands. Not to mention your shirt hanging open. If nothing else, she must have been shocked. I mean, who knows what Menachem told her about you? You were a target. As far as she knows, maybe even a terrorist."

Shelby nodded. "You're a sweet guy, Cam. Understanding her side of it."

It was an odd response to being called a terrorist, but Cam let it go and moved the conversation to safer ground. They had nearly filled the cereal bowl with jewelry. "All right. Let's see what we have."

One by one, they removed rings and bracelets and broaches and earrings and other metal objects, looking for something adorned with Solomon's sigil. After ten minutes of sorting, Shelby sighed. "Nothing. The ring must be back in France."

But that didn't make sense. "The Mossad doesn't agree with you. They thought it was in the boxes you had in Brookline."

She tilted her head and smiled. "You saying you trust the Mossad more than you trust me?"

"Silly of me, I know. Especially when my own lying eyes tell me you're right."

She reached over and took Cam's phone, studying the image of Solomon's sigil again. "What if this is wrong?"

Cam shrugged. "If it's wrong, it's not off by much. As I understand it, in magic every spirit has a sigil that allows them to be summoned and controlled. Solomon had the power with his ring, which had a powerful sigil on it, to actually do the summoning. Either way, all the sigils have the same basic shapes and patterns and elements." He gestured toward the bowl of jewelry. "Most of these don't have any markings at all."

She chewed her lip. "Maybe we're looking at this the wrong way. If the idea was to be secretive, why wear the markings in plain sight?"

"So maybe it's hidden away, inside something?"

"That makes more sense than on the face of a ring."

Together, kneeling in front of the coffee table, they began to reexamine the bowl of jewelry.

"Look for anything with a hinge," Shelby said.

"What about this?" Cam asked, holding up a silver locket.

Shelby took it from him and undid the clasp. Inside, a photo of two cherub-faced children stared back at them. Odds were, they had not survived the war. She looked behind the photo. Nothing. "A treasure of its own kind," she said sadly. "But not the one we're looking for."

Cam pawed at the pile, catching his finger on a sharp edge. "Ow," he said, pulling out a brass cigar cutter. "The bugger got me."

He began to toss it aside, but the ornate pattern—squiggly lines and asymmetrical shapes—surrounding the hole into which the cigar tip was to be inserted caught his eye. "Hey, do these designs look familiar?"

Shelby leaned closer, her forehead near his. "Maybe. Pull up that image on your phone again."

His breath caught in his throat as he did so. "Holy shit. They match. Those designs are the same ones as in the outer ring of Solomon's seal."

She grinned. "They cut the middle part out of the ring and repurposed the rest of it as a cigar cutter. Brilliant. Now we just have to find the missing part, the center."

Still kneeling in front of the coffee table, they divided the bowl of jewelry and examined each piece. "We're looking for something the exact size of that hole," Cam said. "About three-quarters of an inch in diameter, the size of a penny."

After fifteen minutes, Shelby sat back with a loud sigh. "Damn. I thought we had it. Maybe it's back in France."

Cam studied the jewelry, then let his eyes drift toward the pile of other personal items dumped onto the floor from the trash bag. "Maybe it's not jewelry."

She nodded. "Okay. I like it."

They scooched over to the pile and began to examine its contents. Papers, letters, books, diaries, legal documents, photographs.

"Hey," Shelby said. "Look at the clasp on that leather book. That's the right size."

Cam leaned closer as she held it up for him to see. The brass clasp itself was circular; a metal hook had been added to one side to allow it to attach to an eyelet on the cover of the book. Cam undid the clasp and turned it over. "Bingo," he said. With the clasp closed, the designs were hidden. But, once opened, the obverse side of the clasp, with the designs, became exposed. There was no doubt: The etchings exactly matched the inner portion of the seal.

"So that's it," Shelby said. "You combine the cigar cutter and the book clasp and you get the entire sigil. What used to be Solomon's magic ring."

"Pretty damn cool," Cam replied with a grin.

Using his folding knife, Cam pried the clasp away from the leather book and snapped off the thin metal hook. He then placed the round clasp over the hole in the center of the cigar cutter, rotated it so that the designs on the cigar cutter and the clasp lined up in a way that matched the image on his phone, and snapped the clasp into place.

"Voila," he said, holding the cigar cutter up by one end. "The seal is complete. Given that there were two dozen safe deposit boxes, my guess is that the two halves were kept separate. Or I suppose they could have come from the same box, with the objects kept by different family members. Either way, one person kept the cigar cutter, another the book. You would need both of them to complete the seal. So no one individual had the power."

"Sort of like the nuclear suitcase," Shelby replied with a half-smile.

"Same idea. It was too important, too much power, to leave in one person's hands."

"Now that you mention it, there was a second safe deposit box with the Kahn last name. Probably belonged to a relative." She sat back. "So, quite possibly, we have King Solomon's magic ring in our hot little hands. But now what do we do with it?"

Cam shrugged. "I see your point. Sort of like the dog who caught the mail truck."

She took a sip of her wine. After a few seconds pause, she asked, "I don't suppose you know anyone who dabbles in black magic?"

A smile crept onto Cam's face. In fact, he did.

Rivka stared out the window of the airport hotel, watching as jets took off and landed in the glow of a full moon. The immense machines were majestic. Defiant, even, as they roared and soared in rebellion against the laws of nature. The hubris of humankind on full display.

And she couldn't even get a guy to commit to her. And least she had waited before telling him she was in love with him....

Menachem marched into the conference room, fury in every step, the long scar on his cheek pulsating in concert with his frustration level. For a man weighing 150 pounds, he sure filled the room. "Anything, yet?" he barked at Esther, the Mossad team's analyst. The team used a suite of secure conference rooms at one of the Logan Airport hotels as a base of operations, living in a block of rooms on an upper floor when not out on a mission.

"Sorry, no. We tracked the car into Cambridge. That's the last sighting. I'm guessing they ducked into a parking garage and changed vehicles. I've been working on it all day."

That was not entirely true. For half an hour this afternoon, Esther had consoled Rivka. Despite being almost total opposites, Esther and Rivka were close. Rivka was dark and buxom and athletic, while Esther was fair and slight and bookish. Yet they shared a snarky nature and had bonded over Harry Potter books. And, it turned out, bad luck with men.

"It could have been innocent," Esther had argued.

Rivka had replied, "It wasn't just the way they were holding hands. They were *together*. A team." The opposite team, as Menachem was making clear.

Menachem replied to Esther. "Well, they couldn't have disappeared off the face of the earth." He looked around. "Their capture is our top priority."

Rivka came to the defense of her friend. "Cameron knows what he's doing. They're not going to just use her credit card at a gas station or book a hotel room under his name."

Menachem turned on her. "And you say you don't know anything about this Shelby Baskin?"

"I met her once or twice. Cameron used to work with her." *And stands too close when they speak.* "She's a lawyer. But that's all I know." She resisted adding, "If you had given me all the details of the mission beforehand, I could have gotten more information on her. Maybe even kept us from screwing up." *And maybe done something to keep Cameron away from her.* But Menachem was already pissed at her for her inaction in the tunnel, so she swallowed her words. Instead, she said, "Did Tzion find anything?" Tzion was the munitions expert who had set the charge allowing them to access the safe room. He and another agent had remained at the Brookline mansion, searching the premises.

"Nothing. Whatever was there, they took it with them."

"Or it was never there to begin with."

Menachem shook his head. "We're pretty sure it was in that bank in Rouen. The woman banker we abducted confirmed there were rumors in the bank about something mysterious in the boxes. And she also confirmed that everything in that box was shipped here to Brookline. We got there too late, unfortunately. So, unless the little worm crawled out of its box and fell into the Atlantic, it must be with Thorne and the attorney. The question is, where are *they*?"

Esther looked up. Until now, Menachem had not shared with her the target of their search. "We're looking for a *worm*?"

Menachem let out a long breath. "Yes, a worm." He tossed a manila folder onto her desk. "You can read about it here." He turned to Rivka and pulled her into an adjoining room. "And from you, I need an answer. Now. Can I trust you to stay on this mission?"

She swallowed. "Of course."

"Don't say 'of course' like it's a stupid question. You froze back there. You had a shot and did not take it. I need to know that won't happen again."

"I didn't *freeze*. I made the choice not to shoot my lover." Or perhaps ex-lover. Who knew? It all could have been innocent—the handholding, the open blouse, the unmade bed. But there was no denying the energy flowing between them. Innocent or not, the chemistry was real. And that was worse than anything that might have happened in that unmade bed.

"And I understand that," Menachem replied. "It was an impossible choice, with no time to weigh the options. But now you've had time. If the choice presents itself again, what will you choose? Cameron, or your country?"

The truth was, she didn't know. But she did know that she didn't want to leave Cameron's fate up to some random agent who might replace her. So she lied. "My country, of course. I've told Cameron from the beginning that I would always be loyal to him, second only to Israel. He knows that. I know that."

Menachem studied her, his eyes trying to bore into her soul. She could tell he still doubted her. But it would take at least a day to get another agent in from Tel Aviv, and Menachem hated breaking in new team members.

She held his eyes and spoke. "I read something once that has always stayed with me. Saint Thomas Aquinas said, 'There are three things in life: what you desire, what you believe, and what you know you have to do.' What I desire and what I believe are irrelevant. If we meet up with Cameron again, I know what I have to do."

Menachem nodded slowly. "Thomas Aquinas was one of the few medieval theologians who was friendly to the Jewish people. You are wise to cite his teachings." He leaned closer. "Be sure you do not fail to heed his words."

☆✛⊗

Shelby sat on a bed in one of the guest rooms at Cam's ski condo. Her family used to ski regularly but, since the death of her parents and brother, she had lost her passion for the sport. Being here, so close to the mountain, had ignited a bit of the old spark. Too bad Bruce didn't ski. Maybe she and Cameron could come back once things were safe for a day of spring skiing.

Before jumping in the shower, she pulled a slip of paper from the leather satchel Cam found hidden under the Lexus' seat and, using her burner phone, dialed the number on it. Perhaps a hundred miles away, Bruce answered the call on a burner phone of his own.

As they had agreed, he answered in code, indicating he was able to talk freely. "In skating over thin ice…," he said, his voice tight.

"…Our safety is our speed," she replied, completing the Ralph Waldo Emerson aphorism.

His tone turned breathless. "Shelby, are you okay?"

"Yes. We're on the run. You saw what happened at the house."

"*We*? Who are you with?"

"Cameron, of course." Maybe Bruce only saw the security footage from outside the safe room and didn't realize she was not alone.

Bruce's tone changed. "Why are you with him?"

"Um, because he was helping me figure out the Shamir when the Mossad attacked. Was I supposed to just leave him there?"

Instead of focusing on the Mossad part, which Bruce had no way of knowing about and which was pretty damn important, he remained fixated on Cameron. "That wasn't part of the plan, Shelby. When it came time to run, we were supposed to run alone."

"*None* of this was part of the plan, Bruce. Cam and I were attacked. Almost killed. Now we're trying to stay alive." She wanted to add, "If you hadn't been so antisocial and ducked out before Cam arrived, you'd be with us now." But she bit the words back.

"Well, where are you?"

"I'm not going to say over the phone, Bruce. You know that."

A few seconds of silence ensued.

"Then tell me where you're headed. I deserve that."

She wasn't sure what it had to do with *deserving* anything, but she didn't want to argue. She recalled a boat trip she and Bruce had taken once to the Isle of Shoals, off the coast of Portsmouth. One of the islands supposedly was the site of Blackbeard the pirate's honeymoon. "Where a pirate might take his bride," she said, not wanting to be too specific.

Another pause. "Okay. Got it." But still no warmth.

"Are you okay?" she asked. He knew how to stay in the shadows. But she felt like she needed to show her concern by at least asking the question.

"Fine," he replied curtly.

Well, this was going swimmingly. Once in a while, Bruce's jealous side surfaced—fueled, of course, by insecurity. Frankly, she didn't feel the urge to try to placate him. Partly because he was being a baby. But partly, she realized with a pang of guilt, because she wasn't entirely certain he had nothing to feel jealous about.

"I have to run," she said. "Stay safe. I'll call tomorrow." Hopefully he'd shake himself out of his funk.

"Okay. Bye."

The line went dead. She sighed. "Love you, too."

Under a moonlit sky, and buffeted by a cool breeze, Menachem paced the mostly abandoned roof of the airport parking garage, his haphazard thoughts punctuated by the sporadic roar of jet engines. Something wasn't right. But he couldn't put his finger on just what it was.

At nine, he had sent Esther and Rivka home for the night. Which, he guessed, meant that they had headed for one of the airport pubs. That was fine. Rivka needed it. He hoped she would bounce back. But women were so hard to figure. One of his close friends coached basketball in Tel Aviv. He used to coach the men, then switched to women. He said the biggest difference was that men felt good when they played good, while women played good when they felt good. There were exceptions, of course, but it was often the same, Menachem had learned, with his agents. If a woman broke up with a man, the man would likely dive into his work and try to build himself back up by besting his opponent on his mission. Women, on the other hand, seemed to be more effective workers when the rest of their lives was in order. During times of crisis or instability, such as what Rivka was experiencing now, they sometimes became less effective at their job. Not all, but a trend. Hopefully, Rivka would buck it.

But Rivka's emotional state was not the main source of Menachem's angst. He reached the far end of the garage roof and pivoted as a jet roared overhead. It seemed like, for this entire mission, he was always one step behind. The tip had come in, anonymously, about the Shamir perhaps being in a safe deposit box in Rouen. By the time Menachem could send a team, the safe deposit box was on a flight to Boston. So they abducted the bank officer in charge in order to question her. Even under sodium pentothal, she claimed to have no knowledge of the Shamir, other than vague rumors she had heard at the bank. Then, when they tracked the safe deposit box to Brookline, the Baskin woman—accompanied by Cameron Thorne, of all people—needed only seconds to make it to an escape tunnel. Menachem and Rivka caught their quarry, yet they still managed to slip away. Now, the car they were driving had vanished as well.

Menachem knew better than to expect every mission to go off without a glitch. But he was not used to his team suffering failure after failure like some hopeless crew of *schlemiels* and *schlimazels*.

The run of ineptitude was inexplicable. And inexplicable things always made Menachem nervous.

Cam sat at the kitchen table, using the laptop he kept at the ski condo. He made sure his email tracking blocker was functioning, then checked his messages while Shelby grabbed a shower.

"Hmm," he mumbled. A long email from Anita, in reply to his inquiry. He had asked if there were any cuts in the boulders—other than the notch marking the equinox—which struck her as noteworthy in any way. Obviously, he was looking for more evidence of the Shamir. She had replied:

Funny you should ask. The boulder with the notch on it used to be rounded, but then someone cleaved off one entire face, making it almost perfectly flat. I don't think that could have been done with Bronze Age tools.

She attached a picture of the boulder's flat side, facing to the left.

Council Rocks Boulder, Flat Face

I've been wrestling with the mystery as to why this was done, and I think we've figured it out. Sue and I went back and looked through the pictures we took last year, before Pomeroy decided to militarize the site. We focused on the shadows. I'm pretty sure the face was cut so that there would be a flat surface—like a viewing screen—to observe and track shadows moving across the boulder during the days before the equinox. Those shadows would instruct where the notch needed to be cut. Secondarily, this is the side of the boulder perpendicular to the side where the notch was cut. Having a flat surface there also made it easier to precisely cut the notch.

P.S. The GoFundMe page is up over $200,000!

Cam was happy to hear about the fundraising, but he was much more focused on the rock cut. This cleaved face, like the right-angle notch, didn't prove that the Shamir was used to cut the Council Rocks boulders. But it was additional evidence that cuts were made to the boulders using some kind of technology that should not have been available at the time the work was done. He had a sense that, whatever it might take to purchase the site, it would be money wisely spent.

Shelby strolled into the kitchen, her hair wet, wearing sweatpants and a T-shirt she just purchased. "It wasn't so much that I was physically dirty. But I just felt like I needed to *cleanse* myself."

"I get it." He tugged at a silver chain around his neck, revealing to her that he had hung the cigar cutter on it; he had found the chain in a drawer. "Not much of a fashion statement. But it's sturdy, so at least I won't lose the ring." He angled his head. "Unless you want to keep it."

"You hold it for now. I'm more of a gold choker kind of girl."

From the leather satchel, she took the gift cards and cash. "If we buy a car, that will be most of our money."

He nodded. "But we can live off of the gift cards. And, hopefully, we're only talking a couple of days."

"Why do you say that? How does this all end?"

"Either we figure out the Shamir mystery, and maybe Solomon's ring also, or we don't. If we do, well, I guess we go public with it. Try to find the owners." He offered a half-smile. "And if we don't, well, there aren't a lot of good options." He closed the laptop. "It's past ten. We should probably get some sleep. Early start tomorrow. You still okay with our plan?"

She nodded. They had weighed the pros and cons of continuing with the orange van, purchasing a new vehicle, taking public transportation, using an Uber, or staying holed up at the ski condo. They both agreed that moving was preferable to staying put. And that it was time to ditch the carrot on wheels. On the off chance that they were tracked here, Cam didn't want to buy a used car in Lincoln—how hard would it be to sniff out a cash-paying vehicle purchase in a small town? And the only daily bus leaving Lincoln departed early in the afternoon, which was too late to get started. So, almost by default, they decided to take an early Uber to Manchester, purchase a used car, and drive it to Portsmouth.

"But what do we do when we get to Portsmouth?" Shelby asked. Cam had left this last part of the plan vague. "I mean, why there? And then what?"

Cam's first priority was to stay one step ahead of the Mossad. But Shelby, of course, was right: They needed some kind of way to figure out the ring. Which was why he had made a call while Shelby showered.

"You asked before if I knew anyone who did black magic. A few months ago, I met a guy, a musician, who was playing at this club in Portsmouth. He was playing some of his own stuff, and this one song was really haunting. I went up to him during a break to say hi and we started chatting."

Shelby smiled. "Was Rivka with you?"

He grinned. "All right, you got me. I sent Rivka up to chat with him first."

"Right. No guy is going to walk away from *her*."

"So, like I said, we became friendly. I bought his CD and we exchanged numbers. The more I listened to the lyrics, the more I realized he was talking, or singing, about magic and casting spells and demons and stuff." Cam reopened his laptop. "Here. This is one of the songs. It's called 'Babes in the Abyss.'"

A guitar intro played, then lyrics, then the chorus, which is what Cam wanted Shelby to hear:

We are but dwellers on the threshold,
Babes in the abyss.
We seldom see what's coming,
Until it can't be missed.

Cam explained, "The 'dwellers in the threshold' and 'babes in the abyss' lines are references to Aleister Crowley. Ever heard of him?"

"I think so. Isn't he the guy they called the wickedest man on earth?"

"Right. Famous in the early 1900s. He was big into magic and the occult. Anyway, the point is, this singer was writing songs about Crowley because he's into magic himself."

"So *that's* why we're going to Portsmouth. To see him."

"Right." Cam offered a one-shoulder shrug. "I'm hoping he can help us figure out how to use this cigar cutter. You know, find the 'on' switch to the magic ring."

"Cam, you don't really think we're going to be able to perform magic, do you? I mean, genies in a bottle? Really?"

"Do I think so? No." He shook his head. "But the Mossad was ready to put a bullet in my brain because, apparently, *they* think so. So that makes me wonder if it's at least worth a shot."

"Okay, I guess. It's better than any plan I have."

"Then we're off to Portsmouth. On the way, we should also pick up some cigars."

"Cigars?"

"Just in case the magic thing doesn't work." He smiled. "I remember you like cigars. No reason to let that cutter go to waste."

⬦✛⊕

Rivka glanced up, her eyes focused on the hockey game on the airport bar's television set but her mind was far away. She had long feared her job would come between Cameron and her. The travel, the danger, the secrecy, the uncertainty. But she had never suspected he was seeing anyone else. Much less a person of interest in one of her missions. How was she supposed to deal with that?

And, to be fair, things sucked for Cameron, as well. He was running for his life, and she was one of the people doing the chasing. Sure, he deserved to be punished. But not killed. She allowed herself a sad smile. A castration was probably sufficient....

Or was it all innocent?

"Hey?" Esther called out. "Come back to earth."

"Sorry." She turned back to her friend, whose laptop sat on the cocktail table next to a plate of nachos. "I know I'm not much company."

Esther smiled. "Why do you think my laptop's open?"

"Because you're compulsive?"

Esther pursed her lips. "Well, there is that."

"You finding anything?"

"Cam is too smart to leave a trail. So I'm looking at Shelby's boyfriend." Rivka had actually crossed paths with Bruce—and even interrogated him using sodium pentothal—while visiting Cameron in North Carolina last winter. Using Rivka's intel, Esther was trying to pick up his trail. "What a piece of work this guy is. Like you said, faked his death and went off the grid a few years ago. Moved back to live with Shelby Baskin a year ago. Very careful, but he left one clue. He bought back his old sailboat. I tracked it to a marina downtown." She pointed through the bar window across the harbor to the Boston skyline. "In fact, that marina right there, in Charlestown. My guess is, he's hiding out on his boat."

"Did you tell Menachem?"

"I'm about to call him." Esther reached across and took Rivka's glass of wine out of her friend's hand. "And enough of that. You have work to do."

Cam sat at the kitchen table of the ski condo, working at his laptop as Shelby puttered around the living room. He was checking bus schedules and searching for hotels in Portsmouth that would take cash. She was, well, he wasn't sure why she was still up. It was almost 11:00. They should be in bed. Neither seemed to be in a rush to call it a night.

It occurred to Cam that, as long as he had known Shelby, they had never really spent time alone together. Meetings at the firm. Group lunches with other attorneys. Double dates. Today, on the other hand, had been a crash course in togetherness. Ten hours, under a lot of stress and pressure. But no awkwardness, and definitely no squabbling.

"Sorry," she said, peering over his shoulder, smelling clean and fresh from her shower. He couldn't help but notice the outline of her breasts under her T-shirt. "I'm too wired for sleep."

He turned to look up at her. "Same here."

Their eyes locked. Cam exhaled as he recalled what it was like to be single. Were this a date, this would be the time he might make a move. But it was not a date. They were on the run. If you made a move on a date and got rebuffed, you skulked back to the car and sang along loudly to the music. If you made a move while on the run and things turned awkward, you might end up with people singing loudly at your funeral.

His cell rang, perhaps saving him from doing something stupid. Astarte, on her burner phone.

"You awake still?" she asked.

"Yup. Making plans for tomorrow."

"Before you ask, I'm safe."

"Good. Me, too."

"So I spent a few hours tonight diving down the Shamir rabbit hole. Thought I would share what I found."

"I'm guessing there's a worm down there?"

"Funny." She took a breath. "There's actually not a lot out there. And what there is … is shrouded, I guess you'd say. It's like nobody wants to talk about it openly."

Cam nodded. One of the things that most surprised him in doing his research was how salacious and outlandish and bizarre many of the stories of the Old Testament—and, by extension, the Talmud—were. It was as if all the religious authorities had agreed they would only talk about and teach, say, twenty percent of the Bible, and just ignore the other stuff because it was too incendiary. Maybe that was why the Church conducted Mass in Latin for all those centuries.

"So, two things," Astarte said. "First, Rosslyn Chapel."

Cam chuckled. "Of course." If there was a Mount Rushmore of Templar-related sites, Rosslyn Chapel would definitely be featured on it.

"You know the Apprentice Pillar."

It was one of the most famous aspects of the chapel, and one that inspired Freemasons from around the world to visit the site in droves. There were many versions of the story of the murder of Hiram Abiff, including the one Trevino had shared with Cam in which the architect was slain by workers—jealous of his power and prestige—in order to obtain the magical Shamir. A parallel to that story could be found in the legend of the Rosslyn Chapel Apprentice Pillar. According to the legend, the ornate pillar was carved by a young apprentice in the 15th century, his work so exquisite that it enraged his jealous master, who killed him with a mallet. "I know that Freemasons think the story of the jealous master murdering his apprentice is a parallel to the story of the jealous workers murdering Hiram Abiff," Cam said.

"Right. But here's the thing. There are eight worms, linked together, carved around the base of the Apprentice Pillar. Look it up on the internet."

Cam did. "Could be worms. Could be snakes."

Base of Apprentice Pillar, Rosslyn Chapel

She replied, "It's weird to find worms *or* snakes carved in a chapel."

"Unless they're symbolic of something."

"Exactly. If this pillar is meant to symbolize the murder of Hiram Abiff, and he was killed over the Shamir, then the worms would make perfect sense."

"Good work. I like it."

"But you don't have to take my word for it. Here, let me read something to you, from a book I found." She read aloud:

The eight serpents writhing at the foot of the Apprentice Pillar enshrined the legend of the Shamir, a mysterious worm-like creature whose touch split and shaped stone, and whose magic powers enabled Solomon to build the Temple without iron tools. This was a secret jealously kept by Hiram, the architect of the Temple, whose face also appears on the pillar.

"Nice, Astarte. It's pretty subtle, like you said. Just below the surface. But, once you focus on those worms, it's hard to ignore the symbolism."

She took another breath. "Okay. Item number two. I know you know the story of Rennes-le-Chateau."

"I do." The small town in southern France near the coast of Spain received thousands of visitors every year, drawn by rumors of a treasure found, and later reburied, in the late 1800s by a local priest, Father Sauniere. The priest became inordinately wealthy after a mysterious visit to the Vatican, leading conspiracy theorists to believe that he had discovered some kind of amazing secret and had blackmailed the Holy See into buying his silence.

Astarte explained, "With all the money Sauniere got from the Vatican, he renovated the church. Near the entrance, he installed a statue to hold up the basin of holy water. But here's the weird thing. The statue is a demon. I'll wait while you look it up."

Cam did so. "Got it." He chuckled. "Handsome devil. Literally."

Asmodeus Statue at Rennes-le-Chateau

"Not the devil, actually. But you don't recognize him?" she asked.

"I don't think so."

"You should. It's our friend, Asmodeus."

"Wait, what?"

"Yup. The demon who Solomon got the Shamir from, the guy who later stole Solomon's throne."

"Holy shit." Cam stared at the image. Why would a priest install a statue of Asmodeus in a church? And, even more to the point, why further glorify him by having him support the basin of holy water, so everyone had to focus on him as they entered the sanctuary?

Cam's mind raced. Was Father Sauniere making the claim that *he* had found the Shamir? Had he agreed to keep the find quiet at the behest of the Church, which viewed the Shamir story—with its sordid ties to demons and black magic—as too incendiary for its parishioners? Cam speculated further. The priest was rumored to have had a longtime affair with his housekeeper. Had she inherited the Shamir after his death and brought it north to Paris, where she was known to frequent? From there, it would have been a short journey to Rouen before World War II.

He laid out his case to Astarte. "I know the evidence is speculative. Flimsy, even."

"Honestly, it is pretty flimsy, Dad. You're the lawyer, but it sounds like there has to be more to this story."

"That's fair. Who knows what kind of deal Sauniere cut with the Vatican? But all the researchers agree that he *did* cut some kind of deal that made him incredibly wealthy. He must have discovered something pretty explosive, then been smart enough to protect himself." Cam paused. "It's one thing to discover a worm. It's another to end up sleeping with them."

"Fair point."

Cam rubbed his face. "It keeps coming back to that statue of Asmodeus. It screams out for some kind of explanation. I mean, why did Sauniere choose Asmodeus? What was he trying to tell us?"

"It tells *me* that you're neck-deep in it. Again. So be careful, Dad. Whatever the truth behind this magic worm, it's clearly important to the Mossad. It's not worth dying over. If they track you down, just give it to them."

On the off chance the call was somehow being monitored, Cam lied. "Good advice, except for one thing: We don't have it." Technically, it wasn't even a lie. They really didn't have the Shamir, though it looked like they did have Solomon's ring.

Cam reminded her to be careful, then he thanked her, and they hung up. By that time, Shelby had gone to her room. Cam could see a light shining from under the door, and he thought about knocking to say good night. But *good nights* in this situation sometimes led to *good mornings*. Which, paradoxically, often were not so good.

Instead, his head filled with demons and stone-cutting worms and magic rings, he went to bed. At least all the turmoil bouncing around his brain kept him from thinking so much about Shelby.

Dressed in black, Menachem used his night vision goggles to survey the marina. It was a cold night in March as winter took its sweet time warming into spring. The marina was mostly empty—only some die-hard boaters and a handful of people who lived on their vessels year-round. Esther had described Bruce Arrujo's boat, and it didn't take Menachem long to locate it. The marina sat in a small lagoon, its perimeter lined with piers, broken only by a narrow outlet to the harbor. The glow of a small television visible through a cabin window near the outlet told him that Esther's hunch was right, that Arrujo was holed up inside his vessel. Menachem grunted to himself. Good work by Esther. She was of no use in the field, but her skills behind the scenes were top-notch.

As Menachem motioned to Tzion and Rivka to get into position, a pang of anxiety welled up inside him. He hated these kinds of operations. Rushed. Undermanned. Unrehearsed. The kind of scenario where mistakes were made. But he also knew they had no choice. They needed to find the Shamir and Solomon's ring, which meant they needed to find Cameron Thorne, which meant they needed to capture Arrujo to see what he knew about his girlfriend's movements. Which, Menachem guessed, was not insubstantial.

In addition to this being a slipshod operation, the whole idea of leading a mission in pursuit of a magic worm made him feel, frankly, foolish. Really? A magic worm? What was next, fairy dust? A sorcerer's wand? A crystal ball? Yet Tel Aviv had been insistent: The Shamir assignment had been designated *Top Priority—Critical and Crucial*. In his entire career, he had only been on three other missions with the "Critical and Crucial" designation. So there must be something to it. The rabbis must be convinced that the Shamir, or the ring with it, really did have magical powers. That was the problem with living in a Jewish state —people with religious beliefs often controlled the political process.

He looked up at the stars. On the other hand, who was he to say the religious types had it wrong? If there was a God—and Menachem, though not religious, had to admit he had no other explanation for how the universe came into being—then why could it not be that God had also created a magic worm along with all the other miraculous things he had brought to life? And if a magic worm, why not demons also, along with a magic ring to summon them? God was, well, God. He could do what he wanted.

With a long sigh of exasperation, Menachem refocused. If the worm was out there, he'd find the damn thing. Plus whatever ring came with it. And if it turned out not to be magic after all, then he'd grab his fishing pole and use the little bugger as bait.

Tzion, his dark-skinned face barely visible in the dim light, crept toward the boat, using other vessels to hide his position as best he could. It would have been nice if the marina were full; movement and noise would stand out more now than during the summer season. Hopefully Arrujo would be distracted by whatever it was he was watching.

Rivka, in scuba gear, gave a thumbs-up and lowered herself into the water fifty yards away, on the opposite side of the inlet from Arrujo's boat. She would be in position to intercept him in case he dove into the water, or jumped into a dinghy, and tried to make a water escape.

Tzion arrived at Arrujo's sailboat and dropped to a crouched position on the dock under the overhang of the bow. Menachem, staying low, joined him. The two men needed no words. Tzion, an accomplished boxer, led. They moved along the dock, knowing Arrujo would sense the disturbance in his environment as soon as they boarded the boat. Leaning over the cockpit, Tzion gave a hand signal—three, two, one—before reaching for the cabin door and shoving it open. Menachem tossed a flash grenade through the opening. They both turned away and covered their ears; a second later, the device concussed. Bright light filled the night, accompanied by a fireworks-like bang. Menachem would have preferred to be more subtle. But, undermanned as they were, with one member of the team remaining behind to guard the Brookline mansion, he didn't want to take any chances.

The Mossad operatives didn't hesitate, leaping down the stairs into the narrow cabin, ready to apprehend their blinded and disoriented prey. Eyes wide, Menachem scanned the berth. Nothing. "He's not here."

"There!" Tzion yelled, pointing toward the bow and running in that direction.

Menachem retreated to the cockpit and looked to the bow in time to see Arrujo's head pop through the forward hatch. *Damn.* He must have been in the front of the boat—perhaps in the latrine—when the grenade blew. Arrujo was up and through before Tzion could reach him; one leap and he was on the pier and into a full sprint.

Menachem cursed again. He was no longer a young man. Tzion might match their quarry's speed, but Arrujo had a thirty-yard head start. A slap of rubber caught his ear. *Rivka.* She had seen Arrujo's escape attempt and climbed out of the water onto the pier. With a quick motion, she kicked off her fins and dropped her tank. Then she was off, the moisture from her wetsuit glistening in the marina lights.

Rivka and Arrujo raced from opposite directions toward the marina's single exit. Arrujo had a head start, but Rivka's starting point was not as far from the egress as was Arrujo's. Tzion trailed Arrujo, not losing ground but not gaining, either. By Menachem's eye, it was a two-horse race.

Rivka pumped her legs and arms, ignoring the pain of her bare feet on the rough asphalt surface of the marina's wide parking area. Her prey, Bruce Arrujo, was a fast runner. But she was faster. And she could do this all night if necessary—that's what all those forty-mile bike rides were for.

He glanced back, his features stoic. He was too far away to recognize her. Which was probably a good thing—if he knew it was the Mossad chasing him, he'd run even faster.

The gap was now only ten yards. She could see his pace begin to slow. Most humans could only go at a full sprint for about thirty seconds. Normally, in a situation like this, Rivka felt nothing besides adrenaline. It was a task, a job. But tonight she felt anger welling up inside her. He was a good-looking guy. Obviously fit. Why the hell couldn't he keep his woman satisfied? She understood, of course, that it wasn't as simple as that, but her rage and frustration overwhelmed any reasoned analysis....

With a surge, she closed the final gap and lunged, draping her arms over his shoulders and yanking him backward. She stayed atop him, riding him to the ground, using his body to cushion her fall. As they bounced and rolled, she held tight, glad for the layer of rubber covering her body. Their bodies together, she sensed his strength, his vigor. Again, her thoughts veered: Why couldn't he satisfy his woman? He tried to buck her off, but she wrapped one arm around his neck, flipped herself onto her back, and yanked his head back, pressing her free hand on his ear to immobilize his head and crossing her legs in front of his waist so he could not escape by grabbing one of her feet and wrenching her knee. He writhed for a few seconds but then, gurgling as his air flow slowed to a trickle, his body went limp. Furious at his ineptitude, she tightened her hold, squeezing, the frustration of the past two days releasing itself in the power of her hold over him.

"Rivka, enough!" Tzion barked, standing over her. "We can't question him if you break his neck."

She blinked. "Right." She loosened the pressure on his head. "Just waiting for you to get here."

Tzion shook his head. "Well, here I am. Let him breathe." With practiced movements, he bound Arrujo with duct tape and hoisted him to his feet just as Menachem pulled up in a dark minivan.

"Come on," Menachem said, "get in."

Tzion patted Arrujo down and tossed him onto the back seat.

"Rivka, are you coming?" Menachem asked.

"Um," she said, her body shaking. "I should go back and find the scuba gear. You guys can handle this, right?"

Menachem nodded. "Okay. Meet you back at the hotel."

Turning, she trudged back toward the end of the pier. *What was that all about? I could have killed him.* She had said she needed to find her scuba gear. But what she really needed to find was herself.

Bruce Arrujo sat bound and hooded in the backseat of the Mossad's minivan, his body sore from being tackled on the asphalt and then choked and hogtied. But it could have been worse. He had figured the Mossad would make a move on him, and he had tried to make it look good by running. But, the truth was, he knew he had no chance of escaping once they had his scent. And he didn't even really want to evade them, which was why he hadn't put up much of a fight against Rivka.

They wanted to find Shelby and were looking for his help.

Just as he wanted to find Shelby and was looking for theirs.

For some reason, Shelby had decided it was a good idea to go on the run with Cameron Thorne and leave Bruce behind. Was this bank project really that important? More important than their life together? By running, as opposed simply to turning over everything to the Mossad, she had put not only herself, but Bruce also, in danger.

As he mulled it over, the only reason he could come up with for her behavior was that she *wanted* to go on the run with Thorne. Sure, in her mind she may have justified it as loyalty to clients. But no attorney risked his or her life just to deliver the contents of a safe deposit box—no matter how mysterious—to the descendants of long-dead bank customers.

He heard jet engines, then a few minutes later the minivan wound its way up the spiral drive of a parking garage. Obviously, they didn't much care that he knew they were at the airport. Were they going to stuff him on a plane to Tel Aviv? That seemed a bit extreme, given that he really didn't know much. But who knew? This was the Mossad. They lived for extreme.

The big guy, the one they called Tzion, led him to an elevator. They ascended, which made no sense if they were going to a departure terminal. Instead, Tzion pushed him down a carpeted hallway and into what smelled like a freshly cleaned hotel room. He felt the crinkle of plastic on the floor beneath his feet. He swallowed. Probably to catch bodily fluids. *His.*

Tzion pushed him to the floor and removed his hood. The room was dark, other than a light the short guy, Menachem, shined in his face. "You're a smart man, Arrujo. You can tell us what we want to know. Or we can extract it from you." Menachem shrugged. "Either way."

Bruce did his best to look him in the eye, despite the light. "I have nothing to hide. And I've been questioned by you before under sodium pentothal, so I know how this works. The truth is, I want Shelby found as much as you want to find her. Her running was a stupid move. It puts her, and me, in danger."

"So where is she?" Menachem asked.

"If I tell you, do you promise not to hurt her?"

"We have no reason to harm her. We want the contents of those safe deposit boxes. That's all."

"Actually, I think you want more than that. You want what she knows, also."

"True. Another reason why we won't hurt her. I assume she and Thorne have figured out some of this mystery already. It would be nice to not have to start from ground zero."

Bruce sat up. Shelby would be pissed, but at least she'd be safe. And Bruce would avoid some unpleasant interrogation. Then they could get on with their lives, hopefully without Cameron Thorne in the picture. Let him go back to his Gal Gadot lookalike. "I had a quick call with Shelby last night. I'm pretty sure they're heading to Portsmouth, New Hampshire." He shrugged. "You can drug me and beat me and pull out my fingernails, but that's all I know."

Menachem nodded. "If you're lying to us, your fingernails will be the least of your problems."

CHAPTER 6

Cam woke before five, beating his alarm by ten minutes. He ate a banana and frozen waffle, then pounded out three miles jogging through the winding, paved areas of the condo complex. By the time he returned, Shelby was awake and dressed. She had also packed the contents of the safe deposit boxes in a duffel bag she found in a closet. Cam quickly showered, and at 6:15 they took their bags, hiked a half mile down the road to a local resort hotel, and waited outside for their Uber to pick them up and drive them to the airport in Manchester. Just a handsome couple—he with an injured elbow after a nasty fall on the slopes—taking a long weekend for some spring skiing, then rushing back in time to get a full day of work in.

From the airport they took another Uber, this time to the southern part of downtown Manchester, where a handful of used car dealerships were clustered in a gritty part of the old mill city. While Shelby waited in a coffee shop with their bags, Cam scouted the dealers. It was still early, and he pounced as a young car salesman was being dropped off at work by his wife in an older model Toyota sedan, baby in a car seat in the back. "Hey," Cam said, jogging over. "Is your car for sale?"

The young man smiled. "Anything's for sale, at the right price. But there are, like, dozens of other cars on the lot."

"I want yours." Cam didn't have time to get his purchase inspected by a mechanic, and of course he and Shelby couldn't afford to go on the run with a car with mechanical problems. Plus they were limited on funds. But Cam figured there was little chance a young father who worked at an auto dealership would let his wife and baby drive around in a clunker. "Find the Blue Book value, and I'll give you a thousand on top of that. Cash."

The man blinked, then nodded. He motioned for his wife to turn off the vehicle. "Make it fifteen hundred, and you've got yourself a deal."

Shelby sat in the coffee shop, sipping a cup of cold tea and picking at a sad-looking plastic container of fruit salad. Manchester was experiencing a rebirth, but this part of downtown—like Shelby's churlish waitress—was gray and listless, the neighborhood long past its prime and no longer trying to hide it. Shelby had chosen a table in the corner, close to the rear exit in case she needed to make a run for it. Her back hurt from six hours in the old van, and from sleeping on the cheap ski condo mattress, and from the tension of being hunted by the planet's most efficient intelligence agency. By all rights, she should be miserable. But she had to bite her lip to keep the smile off her face.

That Cam had solicited her input on today's plan was one of those small things that spoke volumes. Bruce, too, was good at making plans. But they were always *his* plans. In fact, most things in their lives together belonged to either one or the other of them. Conversations were almost always hers, for example, created and sustained by her questions and observations and commentaries. Bruce was not incapable of deep thought, but he usually kept those thoughts to himself, leaving her to try to fill the silence of their car rides and meals together. By comparison, the conversation flowed freely yesterday during her ten hours together with Cam. Yes, they spent a chunk of it discussing their escape plans, but large blocks of time were also spent chatting about politics and current events and their families. In some ways, she felt like she had shared more with Cam in one day than she had with Bruce in a year. Not her body, of course. But intimacy was not just about sex. And, to be honest with herself, a part of her had hoped he would knock on her door last night.

Part of what she was feeling, she knew, was her psyche reacting to the adrenaline and heightened emotional estate brought on by the encounter with the Mossad—people often developed attractions to one another during times of danger. But she was pretty sure this went beyond that. She had known Cam for decades. That they had bonded over the past twenty-four hours seemed to be a natural extension of their already-close friendship.

She sipped her tea. She wondered if she was having what modern-day psychologists described as an emotional affair. The realization, while liberating, was also deflating. It had never so much as occurred to her to cheat on Bruce. It wasn't her style, plus she would never want to hurt him that way. But here she was. The heart wanted what the heart wanted. And it wasn't like Bruce hadn't played fast and loose with her feelings in the past. He had put her through weeks of hell when he faked his death four years ago. He could have told her beforehand and saved her the heartache, but he was such a control freak that he had kept even her in the dark.

She sighed. She was rationalizing, she knew. What Bruce did was wrong. But that didn't make it right to cheat on him. Cheating was never okay. She knew that. With every synapse and neuron and cell in her brain, she knew that.

But her heart lived south of her brain. In fact, not far from where her blouse had ripped open to reveal her partially bare breasts to Cam. The truth was, she could have done a better job of closing up that blouse. But she hadn't wanted to.

An hour after paying cash for the Toyota, Cam—with Shelby in the passenger seat—exited Route 101 at its terminus in Portsmouth, along the seacoast. New Hampshire had only an 18-mile coastline. Cam hoped they could find everything they needed along it.

"So, where does one conduct a black magic ceremony?" Shelby

asked. "Out in the woods? A haunted house? Do we have to wait for a full moon?"

"Believe it or not, we're going to my buddy's condo. His name is Martin Hall-Perez, by the way. He says he has a spare bedroom he uses for ceremonies."

She smiled. "Come on. No self-respecting demon is going to make an appearance in a *condo*."

Cam laughed. "I know, right? I wonder if he has a treadmill in there he never uses."

The reality was, the condo was on the top floor of an old mill building overlooking the Piscataqua River and featured exposed brick and wooden beams along with hardwood floors, stainless steel appliances, and a sprawling roof deck with panoramic views. "I take it back," Shelby whispered to Cam as they strolled through the unit. "A demon could be very happy here."

Cam nodded. By the looks of things, Martin had a lucrative day job in addition to his evening and weekend music gigs, which perhaps explained why he had rebuffed Cam's offer to pay for the ceremony. "This is a spiritual thing for me. I wouldn't feel right taking money for it," he had said on the phone.

Their host wore a pair of jeans and a light blue oxford shirt. Tall and fit, he had an easy smile and dark eyes in which, Cam guessed, many a young lady had gotten lost while Martin sang on stage. But Cam could see the concern on his face. "You okay?" Cam asked.

Martin swallowed. "I think so. I've been up all night getting this ready." He turned to lead them down a carpeted hallway. "I'm more of a mystic than a mage, so I've only done this a couple of times before. And never with a demon as powerful as Asmodeus. Not to mention using Solomon's ring."

Cam guessed that what he meant to say was, it had never worked before. And, if it worked this time, what were they supposed to do then?

Cam patted him gently on the back as Martin opened the door to a windowless room. "Think about all the great lyrics that might come out of this."

Martin smiled nervously. "I just hope *we* come out of this."

Martin flicked on a ceiling light fitted with a red bulb, bathing the rectangular room in a bloodshot hue. A round, white rug with hand-painted decorations sat in the middle of the room, filling most of it. Cam studied the carpet. A red square had been drawn in the center of the rug. Four yellow, six-pointed stars surrounded the central square, the point of each star touching one of the corners of the square, like a 5 on dice. One of the stars was labeled "Alpha" and another, opposite it, "Omega." A single letter filled each of the six triangles formed at the points of the two other stars—A, D, O, N, A, I. "Adonai," Cam whispered, the Jewish name for God. A snake, also yellow, had been drawn around the perimeter of the rug, encircling the four stars and central square. A string of Hebrew letters had been scribed within the body of the snake; Cam guessed the Hebrew was some kind of incantation.

"This rug is the magic circle," Martin explained. "We'll need to stay inside it, inside the snake, in order to be safe." He then verified Cam's suspicion about the incantation. "The words in Hebrew mean, 'I forbid thee Lucifer and all demons of the underworld from entering within this circle, in the name of the Almighty, blessed be He.'"

Four cup-shaped candles sat on low bases around the rug, also at the four points of the compass. Outside the rug, aligned with the star marked "Alpha," sat a second, smaller, white rug, this one triangular. A black circle filled the center of the triangle. A plain mirror, angled at forty-five degrees, sat within the black circle, resting against a metal stand and facing the middle of the room.

"That's where the spirit will appear. Hopefully. In the mirror," Martin explained. "That's to the east."

"What, exactly, are we going to do?" Shelby asked.

"This is a summoning in the tradition of the *goetia* of Solomon. *Goetia* derives from a Greek word meaning *charm*. We are going to try to evoke a demon. That is different from *invoking* one, which would be when you channel the spirit to speak through one of us, like in voodoo. In an evocation, we are going to call on the spirit, the demon, to appear —like I said—in the mirror."

Martin removed a lighter from his pocket and began to light the four candles. As he did so, Shelby leaned into Cam. "Are we really going to do this, Cam?" He felt her shudder. "I mean, this is crazy."

He nodded. "In all likelihood, nothing will happen, and we can just go grab some lunch after and figure out our next move. But if something does happen, well, how cool would that be?"

She blinked twice. "I guess that depends on what the *something* is."

He chuckled. "Fair point. How do you feel about kissing a frog to turn him back into a lawyer?"

Smiling, she replied, "Why do you suppose *you're* the one being turned into the frog?"

"Ribbit," he replied, the sound barely out of his mouth before she cuffed him and rolled her eyes.

Now finished lighting the candles, Martin also lit a yellow brick-like object Cam had not noticed before which was sitting on the hearth in the fireplace along one wall of the room. The object emitted a rank, rotten-egg smell. Sulfur, Cam guessed. Known as brimstone, it was found deep in the earth's core and was commonly associated with the underworld. This guy was serious.

"Okay," Martin announced. "Almost time to get into positions." He nodded at Shelby. "I'm glad you brought a friend. The ceremony requires an odd number of people." He walked to a corner of the room and lifted the lid on a black steamer trunk. From it he removed a maroon robe which he put on, silently mouthing some kind of prayer as he did so. Reaching in again, he took out a brass bowl and a silver, scalpel-like knife. He then pulled out a forked, wooden wand and handed it to Cam. "Please hold this." Next, he reached into the trunk and lifted a small wire cage. From the cage he removed a brown mouse, holding it by the tail. He proffered it to Shelby. "And you, please, hold this. By the tail."

She recoiled. "Um, I don't think so."

"Why not?" he asked, flustered. "You need to."

"Why do I need to?"

"Well, because it's a female mouse."

"What the hell difference does that make?"

Martin lifted his chin. "In magic, everything makes a difference. The grimoire says it should be a woman."

Shelby put her hands behind her back. "I don't even know what a *grimoire* is. But I'm not holding that mouse."

Cam stepped in. "A grimoire is a book of spells." He handed Shelby the wand. "And I'll hold the mouse."

Martin replied, "But it's supposed—"

Cam cut him off. "I'll put on lipstick. That should fool the demons. It's dark in here."

Martin shrugged. "Okay. But if the evocation doesn't work, don't blame me."

Reaching into the trunk for a fifth time, he removed a leather book and opened it to a page marked by a red feather. This, Cam guessed, was the grimoire.

He turned to Cam. "You have the ring of Solomon?"

Cam reached under his shirt and pulled out the cigar cutter, still hanging from its silver chain. "Got it." Cam had snapped the center disc in place, completing the sigil.

"Good," Martin said, carefully examining it, eyes wide. "Unbelievable," he whispered. He looked up. "You didn't steal this, did you?"

Cam looked at Shelby. They both shook their heads.

"Good," said Martin. "Its power gets negated if the person using it used nefarious means to obtain it."

From inside the leather grimoire book, Martin pulled a glossy sheet of paper and showed it to Cam and Shelby. "This is Asmodeus' sigil." The black and white design featured intersecting straight and curved lines, with what looked like a devil's tail sticking out one side.

Asmodeus Sigil

"What's it for?" Shelby asked.

"It will help conjure Asmodeus," Martin replied. "A sigil is not just a symbol. The sigil itself has magical powers. It's almost like a calling card for otherworldly spirits."

Shelby glanced at the mouse, now squealing. "Oh. Okay." It occurred to Cam that they were a long way from a courtroom.

"All right," Martin said. "Please follow me into the magic circle."

As Cam carried the writhing mouse, Martin led them onto the round carpet. Facing the mirror set on the triangular rug, Martin took the wand from Shelby and lifted it, proclaiming:

My name is Martin Hall-Perez. I have purified my mind and body. I have completed my work within the world. Thus may I enter into the Temple of the Infinite and behold the serpent biting its own tail. This is the prayer of the snake. I invoke the bornless one. Thee that did create the earth and the heavens. Thee that did create the darkness and the light. Thou did make the female and the male. Thou did produce the seed and the fruit. Thou did form men and women to love one another and to hate one another. I invoke thee, the terrible and invisible God who dwells in the void place of the spirit.

Martin set down the wand, lifted the leather book and, reading from it, decreed in a deep and sonorous voice:

I do evocate and conjure the spirit Asmodeus and being with power armed from the Supreme Majesty, I do strongly command thee. I do evoke thee and, by evocating, conjure thee. And by being armed with power from the Supreme Majesty I do strongly command thee by him who spake and it was done, and unto whom all creatures be obedient. Also I, being made after the image of God with power from God and created according unto God's will, do exorcise thee by that most mighty and powerful name of God, strong and wonderful, oh thou spirit Asmodeus.

He paused, rocking back and forth, eyes closed. Cam felt Shelby press up next to him, as if the room were becoming more crowded. The candle flames all rose and flickered, as if a breeze had entered the room, and the smell of sulfur thickened. Martin turned to Cam, his face pale and intent. "Hold up the ring of Solomon, toward the mirror." Martin took a deep breath and continued.

And I command thee by all the names of God lord most high, and also in the name of Solomon, king of the Israelites, oh thou spirit Asmodeus, that thou dost forthwith appear unto me here before the circle in a fair human shape without any deformity. And by this ineffable name, and in the name of King Solomon, I do command thee, at which being heard the elements are overthrown, the air is shaken, the sea runneth back, the fire is quenched, the earth trembleth, and all the hosts of the celestials, terrestrials and infernals do tremble together and are troubled and confounded. Wherefore come thou oh spirit Asmodeus forthwith and without delay from any or all parts of the universe wherever they may be and do all things that I shall command of thee. Come thou peacefully, visibly, and affably, without delay, manifesting that which I shall desire. For thou art controlled by the name of the living and true God. Where- fore fulfill my commands, and come!

The room seemed to hum, and Martin whispered to Cam, "Now, kill the mouse." He pointed to the brass bowl which he had set down on the rug. "Use the knife. Cut off its head."

"Wait, what?"

"It is a sacrifice to the demons. To Asmodeus. Let its blood fill the bowl."

Cam blinked. This might be a bridge too far. After a pause, Cam exhaled and said, "Whatever." At least Martin hadn't told Cam he needed to drink the blood. And he had killed many a mouse before, for causes not nearly as great.

Might as well do it quickly. Hand trembling, Cam dropped to one knee, slapped the mouse into the bowl by the tail to stun him, then quickly slashed its throat, jerking his hand away before blood splattered on it. Shelby, not surprisingly, edged away.

"Now what?" Cam asked.

"We wait. And watch the mirror."

Again, the candles flickered. The hum seemed to grow louder, though Cam wasn't sure if the sound was inside the room or just inside his head.

"Cam," Martin said, "make sure you hold out Solomon's ring, so the spirit can see the sigil. It's very powerful."

Martin did the same with the paper displaying the sigil of Asmodeus, holding it up like a livery driver at the airport awaiting his passenger.

A few seconds passed, then the mirror began to glow. Cam's heart thumped. He whispered to Shelby, "Do you see that?"

"You see it too?" She grabbed his arm. "I thought I was imagining things."

Martin must have seen it also. In a loud but quavering voice, he said, "Come, Asmodeus! Join us. Cross into our realm. Follow my voice, as I have commanded thee."

The mirror's glow grew brighter. Cam took a step closer, Shelby following, careful to stay within the circle. The mouse, dead now for a few minutes, twitched. Cam thought he could see the image of a face begin to appear. *What the fuck?*

Shelby had the same reaction. She actually turned around to make sure there was nothing behind them causing the reflection in the mirror.

Martin, his breathing elevated, continued to implore the spirit. "Yes, come! The Almighty demands it! King Solomon commands it! By all that is holy!"

A voice, distant and deep, replied. "I. Am. Here." The face in the mirror grew more defined, its eyes red, its face greenish brown and its mouth black and cavernous. "But words like *holy* will only serve to send me back to the underworld."

"Holy shit," Cam breathed.

"Don't use that word," Martin shot back.

"Sorry." He thought back to what Astarte had said: If life was merely a computer simulation, then the creators could easily have programmed in demons and magic worms. And if it wasn't, if the universe had been created by an omnipotent God, then the same was true—God could have created demons and magic worms, just as the Talmud said he did.

"What is it you command?" the demon asked. Cam peered closer. It struck him that the image looked not unlike the Asmodeus statue Astarte found in the church in Rennes-le-Chateau.

Martin turned to Cam, waiting for Cam to reply. Cam swallowed. *Now what?* He hadn't expected this to actually work. And from the look on Martin's face, he had no idea how this worked either. Cam studied his new friend. Was it possible this was a setup? But that made no sense. Cam had contacted *him*, asked for *his* help. Cam shook the thought away. For now, he would just go with it, see where things led.

"Um, are you Asmodeus?" Cam asked.

"Some call me by that name. Others use Ashmedai." His image glowed. "But, yes, that is I."

The spirit had used the word *command*. Was this like the genie granting three wishes? "Are you really under our command?"

The spirit's face contorted. "For now. Just as I was at one time subjugated to Solomon. But beware. I bested him and took his wives." The spirit seemed to see Shelby for the first time. Leering, he said, "Perhaps I will do the same to you."

Cam's head was spinning as his heart raced. Was the spirit's power unlimited? Could Cam ask for something incorporeal, like assigning the spirit to safeguard Astarte? "I don't want to subjugate you. We just need your help." He decided to keep it simple, for now. "We are looking for the Shamir, the magic worm. Do you know where it is?"

"Of course I do. And you are not the first to ask."

Cam looked at Shelby. *Not the first?* "Who else is looking for it?"

"Religious figures. Your name for them is the *Rabbinate*."

Shelby whispered, "The Rabbinate is the council of the head rabbis in Israel. But what does he mean that they are looking for it?"

Cam asked the question.

"They have been praying," the demon replied. "Many of them. Just as you evoke me through your incantations, so, too, do the religious leaders. They are, of course, more powerful than you. The rabbis command me invoking the name and power of *Shemhamphorash*."

"What's that?" Cam whispered to Martin.

"*Shemhamphorash* is the mystical name of God, used in the Kabbalah. It is often used during magical ceremonies. As Asmodeus said, the name itself is very powerful."

The demon continued. "The rabbis conjure me by praying to Shemhamphorash. To Yahweh." The demon, perhaps in a sign of disrespect, referred to God by the name—*Yahweh*—which was not supposed to be spoken. "If the prayers become sufficient, Yahweh hears them." His red eyes narrowed. "And then I hear from Yahweh."

Cam realized they should not have been surprised that the Israelis—through whatever means necessary, including prayer—were trying to track down the Shamir and, if they were aware of it, also the ring of Solomon. Part of him was surprised that the whole praying-to-God thing really worked, but he pushed the thought aside for now to focus on the demon in the mirror.

He decided to try something. "I *command* you to tell me where the Shamir is."

The spirit made a face and said, simply, "I refuse."

So much for genies and three wishes. "I thought you were under my command?"

"Normally I am beholden to the incantations made in the name of Yahweh. But in this case Yahweh himself has issued a decree. It is Yahweh's desire that the Rabbinate obtain the Shamir." He scowled. "Not you."

This made no sense to Cam. If God wanted something, couldn't God just make it happen? But maybe it wasn't as simple as that. If it was, God could have just given the Shamir to Solomon in the first place instead of making Solomon work through Asmodeus. Maybe the same thing was happening here. Maybe God for some reason wanted Asmodeus to be involved.

Cam tried another angle. "But the Shamir is still here, on Earth?"

The demon nodded. "And it still has its full powers. The Rabbinate is wise to seek it out."

"Can you give me some kind of hint where it is?"

Chuckling, the demon replied, "Very well, here it is: A wise man does not seek that which he has already found. But perhaps you are not as wise as you think."

With that, the demon began to fade. Before disappearing completely, he spoke one last time, his red eyes focused on Martin. "You, conjurer."

Martin stepped forward. He had been watching the exchange between Cam and Asmodeus like a spectator at a tennis match, his head swinging back and forth. Cam had no doubt he would be sharing this story with his fellow goetia practitioners for years to come. "I am here."

"You insult me with your offering. A mere mouse," he sneered. "Next time, if you expect me to appear, make an appropriate sacrifice."

Martin nodded, swallowing.

The demon disappeared in a puff of smoke. Martin dropped to his knees on the round rug. "Did that really just happen?"

Cam swallowed, his heart still racing. "I think so." He looked around, as if half-expecting a television crew from one of those practical joke programs to march in with a laugh.

Martin didn't seem to know what to do next, so Cam helped him to his feet. Cam extinguished the candles as Martin shrugged off his robe.

"Wow," Martin said, his face pale.

Shelby, staring at the dead mouse, shook her head. "I hate to be a buzz kill. But we're really no closer to finding the Shamir than we were before. Whatever that ... *thing* ... was, it wasn't much help."

"True," Cam said. "But he did confirm the Shamir was here on Earth. And he implied it was findable. Assuming we can trust him, that's important information. We're not just wasting our time."

"That wasn't much of a clue," she replied. 'A wise man does not seek that which he has already found.' What does that mean? We already have it?"

Cam shrugged. "Clearly, we don't."

It was just another mystery to add to the list.

◈✝⊕

Needing to clear their heads, Cam and Shelby sat on a bench in Prescott Park on a sunny but cool midday, overlooking the Piscataqua River not far from Martin Hall-Perez's condominium. The briny smell of low tide wafted over them. They had grabbed hot chocolate and corn muffins, leaving Martin alone after the Asmodeus ceremony.

"Should we have stayed to help him clean up?" Shelby asked. "I mean, what's the proper etiquette for a demon conjuring?"

"He's probably happy to be rid of us," Cam replied. "He looked pretty shaken."

"I think we are all shaken." She fixed her eyes on his. "I mean, what the hell was that?"

Cam stared out at the river, mindlessly fingering Solomon's magic ring draped around his neck. Three-and-a-half centuries earlier, not far from this spot, the Puritans had put a woman healer on trial for witchcraft, accusing her of conjuring up spirits. Had she, Cam wondered, experienced the same kind of thing Cam and Shelby just went through? Or was there some alternate explanation?

He answered her question. "Honestly, I don't know. I know what I saw and what I heard. And you saw and heard the same thing. So I think we have to at least be open to the idea that it was real."

"I've never believed in the paranormal."

"Me neither." He shrugged. "For what it's worth, seventy percent of people say they've experienced some kind of paranormal event. That's a lot of people to be wrong."

"I don't know, Cam. Lots of people believe some pretty stupid stuff."

"True. But it's not just ordinary people. I read an article about how plenty of scientists believe in ghosts also."

Smiling sadly, she let out a long breath. "I guess it's possible. They don't teach this stuff in law school."

They went back and forth for a few minutes, Cam explaining Astarte's argument about simulation theory. "Whichever way you believe —that we live in a computer simulation or that God created the universe —there's no reason to think demons and magic worms couldn't exist. In both cases, the creator is omnipotent."

"What about the Big Bang theory? That's the third option, right?"

He nodded. "Yes. To me, if we're going to believe that intelligent life formed from non-life—from the synthesis of organic molecules in some kind of witch's cauldron of pea soup—then it seems it's plausible that those chemical reactions formed demons and magic worms along with everything else." Cam shrugged. "I mean, the whole thing is a one-in-a-gazillion shot anyway."

Shelby let out a long sigh. "All right. I guess, for now, we just need to trust our own lying eyes. We saw what we saw."

Cam chuckled. "What was it that Reagan said about the Soviets? Trust but verify."

"But who can we really trust, Cam?"

"Good point." Normally he could trust Rivka, but she was on the opposing team now. Plus she was hurt and probably angry. Same with Shelby trusting Bruce. From what she had said, he was behaving a bit like a spurned teenager. Even Martin Perez-Hall was an unknown. Cam watched as Shelby dumped the trash in a barrel. Could he even trust her? They had been friends for more than two decades, but that friendship had never been tested as it was being tested now. She smiled at him as she returned, her face lined with concern. The reality was, things had gone too far. They were in this together.

He stood. "All right. We should keep moving." If there was nobody they could trust, then there was no place that was safe.

"Where to?" she asked.

He made his way toward the car. He didn't really have an answer. But movement from behind a tree caught his eye. A tall black man, turning away. New Hampshire was one of the whitest states in the country. Sure, there were some people of color. But not many. And Cam knew a tall one, for certain, who worked for the Mossad: Tzion.

He put his hand on Shelby's back, guiding her away. "I'm not sure, but we may have a tail. I think the Mossad."

Her jaw tightened. "Why a tail? If it is them, why not just take us?"

"It may have to do with something Martin said about the power of the ring being negated if it's taken by force. That may be why Asmodeus couldn't hold Solomon's throne, even though he had the ring. I'm guessing the Rabbinate told the Mossad to try to convince us to turn the ring over voluntarily."

"*Try* being the operative word. If we don't agree, then what?"

"I'd rather not find out." Looking sideways as they walked toward the edge of the park, he held her eyes. "Maybe we should just give them the ring. Like the demon said." An hour earlier, he would have argued to stay the course. But that was before the Mossad showed up. They were out of their league.

Shelby bit her lip. "I can't do that, Cam. It's not mine to give." She swallowed. "I get it if you want to bail on this. Truly. It's not what you signed up for. And I know it's dangerous. But I can't." She shrugged. "I know it sounds cliché, but I really do take that whole loyalty-to-client stuff seriously. For some reason, eighty-odd years ago, someone decided to hide something very important to them—probably the Shamir—in that safe deposit box. It's my job to find it."

What was he supposed to say to that? *I'm a chicken shit and on top of that I don't really care about a lawyer's responsibility to their clients, so I'm just going to leave you here and head home.* Even if he wasn't developing feelings for her, no self-respecting man could walk away now. Maybe, down the road, he could talk her into giving up the damn ring.

He nodded. "All right then. I have an idea. Come on." He led her toward a freestanding brick theater building at the edge of the park. They slipped in through an open side door. "If someone asks, we're looking for a bathroom," he said.

He guided her down a set of basement stairs and found an unlocked door. Inside, dozens of costumes hung from metal racks. "Jackpot," he said, pointing to a section of Colonial-era clothes. "Find something that fits. It'll look like we work across the street, at the Strawbery Banke museum." At the site, dozens of workers recreated life during Colonial times.

She nodded. "I like it. Just wandered over on our lunch break."

Within minutes, Shelby had changed into a long brown dress with white apron and matching white bonnet. Cam found a Founding Father outfit featuring a dark thigh-length jacket with silver buttons, a matching vest, knickers to his knees, white hose, and black, single-buckled shoes.

She took his uninjured arm. "Would you be so kind as to escort me, kind sir?"

He removed his black tricorn hat and bowed. "It would be my pleasure, madam."

"I assume we're going to try to go back to the car," she said as they climbed back up the stairs.

"That would be best." Most of their supplies, plus the contents of the safe deposit boxes, were inside. "But first, let's try to lose ourselves at Strawbery Banke."

The problem, of course, was that whoever was following them had seen Cam and Shelby duck into the theater and would be watching for them to come out.

"We should go one at a time," Shelby said.

"Agree. Even better if we can mix in with a crowd."

They went upstairs and peered out the window, looking for other workers in costume. "There," Shelby said. "Those two women."

"Go," Cam agreed.

She did so, sauntering across the street and out of the park as if with old friends.

Cam's turn to move. Then a voice.

"Cameron."

He turned slowly. "Rivka."

Eyes wide, arms by her side, feet flat, directly facing him. The body language of someone in a non-adversarial posture. Apparently, she was not here to confront him. At least not physically. Good thing—he stood little chance against her.

"Why?" she asked simply. He had no idea one word could convey so much agony.

He took a small step forward. "You're assuming something is happening." He held her eyes. "I swear, it's not."

"I saw you holding hands."

"We were running through a tunnel together, being chased by people with guns."

She rolled her eyes. "What, does holding hands make the bullets bounce off?"

"No. But it can make you not fall when you trip in the dark."

"Come on, Cameron. I was in that same dark tunnel. You didn't see me holding hands with Menachem."

A law professor had once told Cam that one of the worst things that could happen to a human being was to be wrongly accused. And here he was, defending himself for something he hadn't done. Yet her instincts were correct. There was an attraction—albeit unacted upon—between Shelby and him. "I don't know what to say, Rivka. It was innocent. I'm telling you, nothing happened." He shrugged. "If you don't believe me, don't trust me, then you don't know me as well as I thought you did."

Her eyes narrowed. "Don't throw this back at me, Cameron. *You're* not the victim here."

"No. But neither are you. *Nothing happened*."

But the look in her eyes told him she would never fully believe him. He knew that her previous relationship had ended because of infidelity, so he had touched a raw nerve. Seeing Shelby and him together had opened a door in her imagination, through which all sorts of doubts had come rushing through. It was not unlike seeing the demon from this morning. Real or not, it had made a lasting impression—the mind could not unsee what it had seen.

And now, the floodgates open, she was seeing meaningless things and attaching grave import to them. She focused on the silver chain around his neck. "What, did she give you jewelry also?"

Cam didn't want to explain the cigar cutter, lest she rip it off his neck. "It's not from her."

"I've shared a bed with you, Cameron. I've never known you to wear a necklace." She shook her head, her fists now clenched and her jaw set. Her tears of pain were morphing into tears of rage. "She's pretty efficient, I'll give her that. Has her claws into you after only two days." She lowered her voice. "And only, what, half a day after us having sex? Really?"

"Rivka, please. The necklace is not from her."

"Who's it from, then? Show it to me."

He let out a long sigh and tried to deflect the question. "Would it really matter? You don't believe anything I say anyway."

"Nice try. But you still didn't show it to me." In her mind, that sealed his guilt. Her eyes fired. "I just wish you had been honest with me. That's all I ever asked."

"I never lied to you, Rivka."

"No. Because I never thought to ask if there was someone else. I just assumed you'd tell me if there was." She held his eyes. "Can you swear to me that you're not attracted to her?"

He blinked. "I admit, she's an attractive woman."

"That's not what I asked, Cameron."

They stood facing each other, each trying to control their emotions. After a few seconds, she exhaled and straightened herself, as if she had come to grips with the situation. "You need to give us that ring. Now. Menachem is only going to ask once. Then he's going to kill you if he has to."

"No he's not. The ring loses its power if it's acquired via force."

"*Some* of its power. Half a loaf is better than none."

"If Menachem wanted to take it by force, he could have done so before the conjuring. I'm guessing you didn't just start following us in the last half hour."

"He wanted to see if the ring worked. If the power worked. Now we know it does. So now he's going to take it." She put out her hand. "I'll take the ring." It struck him that, in Rivka's mind, she might have envisioned a different scenario in which a valuable ring went from Cam's hand to hers. This whole situation sucked. He cared for her and had no desire to see her hurting like this.

"Truly, Rivka, I'd like to end this. And try to fix things with you. Now." He shook his head. "But the ring is not mine to give. I'm sorry."

Her face contorted in rage. "Why are you letting her control you like this?"

"I'm not. But the ring is *hers*. Not mine. So even if I give it up voluntarily, *she* didn't. And I'm guessing you need its full power. Not just half. Otherwise, you would have taken it from us already."

Rivka blinked, seeming to concede the point. "So convince her. Convince her to give it up. You know what's at stake. The ring is incredibly powerful. Not to mention the Shamir. If Israel wants to rebuild the Temple, we'll need both to do so according to God's commandments."

"Maybe Israel *shouldn't* rebuild the Temple. Not to mention have the power to call up demons. Maybe that'll just add more fuel to an already-hot fire in the Middle East."

"That's ridiculous, Cameron. You might as well argue that the state of Israel should not exist." She shook her head. "You claim to be working for the Holocaust victims. Well, a strong Israel is the best defense against it happening again. And you're standing in the way by not turning over that ring."

They were going in circles. And he sensed that his time was running out. For all he knew, Menachem was around the corner, listening. He needed to delay. "All right. Let me do this. I'll talk to Shelby. Explain what's at stake. I'll try to convince her. I think she'll listen to me."

Rivka's shoulders slumped and she blinked back tears. "I know she will. That's the problem."

Cam crossed the street and entered the Strawbery Banke historical area. He and Shelby had arranged to meet at the twin-gabled Sherburne House, built in 1695. The face of the old brown home looked out of scale, the windows too few and too small for its wide expanse. Cam wondered how many secrets had been shared within its walls and in its shadows. They were about to add one more.

He found Shelby behind some shrubs, half-hidden.

"You made it," she breathed.

"Only because they let me go." He glanced around. "I don't see them, but they're here."

"Why would they let you go?"

"They want me to talk to you. About giving up the ring. Voluntarily."

She chewed her lip. "It's not mine to give up. We've been over this."

"I get it, Shelby. But they're not really asking. They're going to take it either way. This is the *Mossad.* The only question is, when they rip it off my neck, do they take my head with it."

"You don't think we can make a run for it."

He shook his head. "I think this is it. We gave it a good shot. But even the demon said it's God's will that the Rabbinate gets the ring."

She smiled sadly. "Well, I do sort of like the way your head attaches to your neck." She fingered an evergreen branch. "Is it worth trying to fool them? Give them the wrong ring? By the time they figure it out, we're back on the run."

Cam sniffed. "What happened to liking my head attached to my neck?"

"Seriously, how would they know?"

"Seriously, they're not going to just take our word for it. And I'm sure they know what Solomon's sigil looks like. Where are we going to get a fake ring with the right sigil?"

They stood together in silence for a few seconds until Shelby said, "How about this. We give them half the ring. Tell them we're keeping the other half until we're sure we're safe."

Cam angled his head. That could work. He thought it through, contemplating how it might play out. "Okay. But I have another twist to it." He reached under his Colonial-era white dress shirt and removed the chain. From the cigar cutter, he snapped out the inner insert and handed it to Shelby.

"What am I supposed to do with this?"

"I'm going to walk back across the street. Menachem is practically a legend, but he has a couple of biases I think we can exploit. First, he thinks Americans are soft. Second, he thinks American women are especially soft. And I won't even mention what he thinks about lawyers."

"Charming. I wear the Triple Crown."

"Which means he's going to dismiss you. Underestimate you. When I tell him that you're scared and I talked you into giving up, he'll believe it."

"And Rivka, who would normally point out just how formidable a woman can be, is not going to come rushing to my defense."

"Not likely, no." He paused. "But you're not going to like this next part."

"What?"

"How do you feel about swallowing the inner part of the seal?"

"Swallow it? Can't I just hide it somewhere?" She looked around. "Like, under this bush?"

"We may not be able to get back here to retrieve it."

She blanched. "Can I just hide it in my … private parts?"

He shook his head. "They're used to dealing with smugglers. If they decide to search us, they'll search *all* of us."

"Then why don't you swallow it?"

"Because you're not coming with me. They're definitely going to search me. And remember, Menachem is going to believe that you don't have the stomach for this any longer."

"My stomach is fine now. It's after swallowing that metal seal that I'm worried about."

He smiled. "Anyway, hopefully, you'll be long gone before they can search you."

"So, what, you're going to give Menachem just half the seal?"

"Right. They've never seen the whole thing. I'll tell them this is all we found—the cigar cutter but not the book clasp. That's when they'll probably search me. Maybe even with an X-ray machine. Eventually they might figure out the truth, maybe through Martin, but by then hopefully it'll be too late."

She nodded. "In fact, we *want* them to figure it out. It's the only leverage we have over them. They're going to want the other half of the ring."

"In the meantime, we need insurance that they'll let us go. I'm going to make them sign a contract. I'll give up the seal voluntarily if they agree to let us go free." Normally, a contract wouldn't be worth the paper it was written on, but the Mossad—that is, the Rabbinate advising them—would want to ensure that the power of the seal was not diminished by an involuntary transfer of the ring, so they would abide by its terms.

"Making them sign a contract." She smiled. "You really are a tough guy."

"One more thing. I know how this works because I've seen Rivka in action. They have a drug. A truth serum. Sodium pentothal, injected in my butt."

"And they're going to ask about the other half of the seal."

"Right. I won't be able to lie. But if I honestly *believe* I never found the other half, then this might work."

She nodded, a smile slowly forming on her face. "You want me to hypnotize you."

"How good are you?"

"Good enough to convince teenage girls from broken families that everything is going to be all right."

"Wow. That's good. Compared to that, I should be a pushover."

They found a secluded spot in a garden behind a closed gate and sat on a bench in the dappled sunlight. Shelby led him through some breathing exercises to get him to relax, then spoke to him in a slow, soothing voice. "Let my words wash over you. Everything here is safe, calm, peaceful. Let yourself sink back into the bench, as if you are floating. Your eyes may feel heavy. Let them close. Let your body go, let it float." She removed her watch and held it by one end of the strap, using her body to shield it from view of any prying eyes. It swung slowly back and forth. "Focus on the watch. Listen to my voice. You are feeling calm.

So calm. So peaceful. So relaxed. So comfortable. So light. So free. So tired…"

The next thing he knew, he was awake and sitting on the bench, feeling like he just had a great power nap. "Wow. I feel good." He had a vague memory of asking her to hypnotize him but couldn't remember exactly what for.

"Excellent." She squeezed his hand. "I think it went well."

She reviewed the plan with him again to make sure he was still clear on all the details, which he was.

"One thing," she said. "We never discussed what I should do while you're gone. And how do we meet up after?"

A tour bus pulled up to the curb and a group of older tourists ambled over to board. "Talk your way onto that bus," he said, his mind sharp after the session. "Then let's work our way back to Boston." He smiled. "Remember that pizza place in the North End we used to walk to for lunch?"

"Of course. We still bring the new associates there on their first day."

"Let's plan on six o'clock tonight. I'll be there if I can. If not, we can message on the Words With Friends app." They had a game going; they could access the app with their burner phones. "Okay. I better get moving. Menachem's not known for his patience. I'll try to get back to the car to get our stuff before I come tonight."

She nodded and held his eyes. "The stuff's important. But not as important as you."

"All right, wish me luck."

"Okay, good luck." She kissed him on the cheek, the edge of her lips brushing against his mouth. "But you know the expression. *Luck never made a man wise.* I'd rather you be smart and careful."

Rivka watched as Menachem transformed the basement wardrobe room of the theater to a makeshift interrogation center. Apparently, he had made a call. They expected Cameron to appear any minute.

Tzion loped in. "Thorne is on the way." Two other agents were shadowing him to make sure he didn't run.

"I don't want to be here for this," Rivka said.

Menachem fixed his dark eyes on her. "No. Of course not. You will follow the woman."

"Shelby? Follow her?"

"Yes. We are all assuming Thorne will give us what we need. But we know how resourceful he can be. How cunning. We can't take anything for granted."

"Can't Tzion follow her?"

The black man flashed his white smile. "In case you hadn't noticed, I don't exactly blend in."

"Well, what am I supposed to do with her once I catch her?" Rivka asked. She actually had a couple of ideas of her own.

Tzion answered before Menachem could. "A girls' night out might be entertaining."

Rivka gave him the middle finger, but with a smile. "Nice to have friends I can count on."

He reached out and touched her arm, his eyes on hers. "Yes. You do."

Menachem finally had the opportunity to reply. "Follow her, like I said. Stay close. Be ready to apprehend her at my command."

"Why not just take her now, boss?" Tzion asked. "Just in case."

"Because she and Thorne might have some kind of signal system going. I don't want to spook him by spooking her." He turned to Rivka. "Go. Follow her. Keep me posted."

Rivka turned. "Yes, boss."

"And Rivka. Please don't do anything stupid."

Accompanied by two Mossad agents, Cam descended the theater stairs to the basement wardrobe room. Menachem and Tzion were waiting for him. Menachem dismissed the two escorts and addressed Cam.

"Mr. Thorne. We meet again."

Cam actually got the sense the operative liked him. Not that it mattered. Menachem would deliver his own mother's liver to the butcher if the Mossad needed to make meat pies.

Cam nodded to Menachem, undid his belt, and dropped his trousers to his thighs. "I know the drill. Sodium pentothal. Let's get this over with."

Tzion administered the shot, then guided Cam to a folding chair. Within a few minutes, Cam began to feel loopy, like he was drunk. A couple of minutes later, Tzion leaned over and examined his eyes. "Pupils dilated," he said. "He's ready."

Menachem approached and took a seat opposite Cam. He asked a few simple questions with yes or no answers. These, Cam knew, were tests to see if Cam would be truthful, things that Menachem already knew the answer to. Satisfied, the Mossad agent moved on.

"Did you use this ring earlier today in a ceremony to summon a demon?"

"Yes."

"And did it work?"

"Yes."

"Do you mean to say you actually conjured up a demon?"

"Yes."

"What was the demon's name?"

"Asmodeus."

"What did he say?"

"That it is God's desire that the Rabbinate in Israel find the Shamir, not Shelby and me."

Menachem, seemingly satisfied, nodded. He glanced at Tzion to see if the agent had anything he wanted to ask.

Still standing, Tzion leaned closer. "Have you had sexual relations with Shelby Baskin?" He turned to Menachem. "Sorry," he said in a low voice, "I had to ask. For Rivka's sake."

"No," Cam answered.

Tzion began to ask a follow-up question. "Do you want to have—"

Menachem cut him off. "That's enough, Tzion. We are the Mossad, not a reality dating show."

Rivka climbed the theater's basement stairs two at a time, her body glad to have a physical release from the stress and despondency that had consumed her over the past twenty-four hours.

As she pushed her way out the front door, she saw a tour bus idling a block away, next to the Strawbery Banke tourist site. An older couple carrying gift bags boarded, then a fit, middle-aged woman in a Colonial-era dress hopped on. Rivka saw her profile for a second as she boarded. *Shit. That looked like Shelby.* The bus door closed, the engine roared, and the vehicle began to accelerate into traffic.

Cam had changed into Colonial garb, so it made sense that Shelby had as well. And why would one of the historical site workers board a tourist bus? Rivka pulled out her phone, searching for a website matching the name on the side of the bus. There. She dialed the number.

"Yes, hi," she said in a fake British accent. "I hope you can help me. I was on one of your bus tours, but it just pulled away from the curb without me. In front of Strawbery Banke, in Portsmouth. My fault, I was in the gift shop. But can you tell me the next destination so I can take a taxi and join up again?"

"They are on their way to Boston. An afternoon of walking around Faneuil Hall."

"Splendid. Thanks so much for your help."

At almost a full sprint, she raced to her car, parked a few blocks away. The bus had a head start, but Boston was fifty miles away, so Rivka should have no trouble overtaking it. She started her Honda and plugged her destination into Google Maps. One hour, four minutes. She needed to carve fifteen minutes off that to make sure she had time to park (Menachem made them pay for their own parking tickets) and was waiting when Shelby disembarked.

She smiled. A little adrenaline would do her good. She accelerated out of her parking space and spun an illegal U-turn, then raced for the highway. With a flick, she unbuttoned the top button of her blouse, then quickly applied lipstick and fluffed her hair. There was a decent chance she would be pulled over. But also a decent chance the cop would look down her shirt and let her go with just a warning. And even if she wasn't stopped by the cops, there was no way she wanted to confront Shelby without looking her best.

✦✝✡

Bruce paced around the windowless hotel room, the television blaring in the background, its volume control purposefully disabled and the device somehow hardwired to stay powered-on. He thought about putting his foot through the screen but figured that would not endear himself to his captors. Other than a couple of meals delivered to his room, he had had no contact with anyone since his interrogation by Menachem the night before. At one point, he was so bored he looked down to see himself actually twiddling his thumbs. But at least he wasn't hanging by them.

Without knocking, Menachem pushed open the door and strolled in. "Get out," he said.

Bruce stopped pacing. "That's it? Just leave?"

Menachem nodded. "We found Thorne and the Baskin woman. There's nothing else we need from you."

"Where are they?"

"We just released Thorne, after questioning him. The woman is on the run still, we think headed to Boston."

"Let me guess. You're releasing me because you want me to follow them."

Menachem nodded again. "Very astute. We, of course, will be following as well. But you have the advantage of knowing how the woman thinks."

"If you had Thorne, why are you letting him go?"

"He gave us Solomon's ring. Or at least half of it. He may be going after the rest. Or he may be going after the Shamir." Menachem shrugged. "Or he may simply be going on a tryst."

"A tryst?"

"Yes. Under truth serum, Thorne admitted to having … relations … with the Baskin woman." Menachem held his eyes as Bruce's chest tightened. He reached for the dresser to steady himself. Menachem continued, "I thought, man to man, that you had the right to know."

Bruce swallowed, trying to think rationally. *How could Shelby do that to him?* "Why would you even ask Thorne about something like that?"

"Because he is involved with one of our agents. She, like you, has the right to know."

"Right. Rivka." Bruce's head swam. They wanted him to follow Shelby. But did he even want her back? As hurt as he was, and as angry as he felt, the truth was he didn't know how to live without her. She was, literally, his only human companion. He had no other friends, no family. Bruce's grandfather had once said that he worried about young Bruce. When Bruce asked why, he had replied, "Because you don't need anyone. It's not healthy." Bruce had replied, "Better to have and not need than to need and not have." But his grandpa had merely shaken his head. "No, Bruce. I want you to *live*. What you are describing is nothing more than an *existence*." So Bruce had tried to make a connection with someone besides his grandfather. Had, eventually, given his heart away. Many people thought of Bruce as heartless; if so, it was because the organ no longer resided in his body.

Bruce looked at Menachem and sighed. If Grandpa could only see him now. "So you want me to report back to you. To rat on Shelby."

"Yes."

"But she won't be hurt?"

"As I told you last night, we have no reason to harm her. We just want to recover the ring and also the Shamir."

"And you don't know where they're going?"

Menachem shrugged. "They had some kind of séance or something. Wherever the spirits told them to go."

Bruce walked to the far side of the room and stared at a seascape hanging on the wall, allowing his mind to search for answers in the painting's stormy tumult. So far, his plan was working. Well, not the infidelity part—that was a disastrous case of collateral damage. But the rest of it. He needed to get back to puppeteering. Which meant he needed to get out of this hotel room. Which meant he needed to agree to the Mossad's terms.

Turning toward Menachem, he nodded. "Okay. I'll do it. But you'll need to help me get a rental car."

In the fading daylight, the smell of tomato sauce and garlic in the air, Cam stood beneath the red awning of a brick building sporting a neon "Regina's Pizza" sign. The façade of the building was elliptical-shaped, nestled into the curve of the meandering streets of Boston's historic North End. As the legend went, the streets tracked the old cow paths. True or not, it was a good story.

A few pigeons waddled by. Cam knew that, in a few hours, they'd be replaced by rats. Too many people, too many restaurants, too much garbage. But at least no cow dung.

After leaving his interrogation with the Mossad, he had recovered their Toyota and driven south into Boston, calling Astarte on the way to update her.

"So Menachem let you go?" Astarte had asked.

"Yup."

"Until he captures you the next time."

"Probably."

"Maybe he should just put you on the payroll."

"I don't think Rivka would be too happy about that."

Cam had no delusions about Menachem's reason for letting him go: He figured Cam still might lead them to something important. The truth was, Cam had no idea what his next move would be. Other than mushroom pizza, that was.

Shelby strolled toward him with a smile. "Howdy, sailor. You on shore leave?"

She greeted him with a tight hug, her cheek warm against his. As always, she smelled delicious.

He searched desperately for a witty reply, but all he ended up doing was grinning back at her with a stupid look on his face. Hopefully, she would think the truth serum hadn't worn off yet.

The truth was, he had no idea what Shelby was thinking. Her greeting was warm and effusive. But, in the end, it was only a hug. Entirely innocent. The same as their earlier brush of lips. Not to overanalyze things, but was the sailor comment just meaningless banter? Or did it elevate to actual flirtation? Or even more, to some kind of implicit solicitation?

All he knew was that he, in fact, really was behaving like a lonely sailor on leave. Maybe it was because he felt like he had achieved some kind of closure with Rivka back in Portsmouth. Or maybe the sodium pentothal really was making him loopy.

They ordered pizza and a couple of beers, then took a table by the window. "So," she said, "what's our next step?"

"I've been thinking about what the demon said. The hint he gave us."

She smiled. "Those are words I never thought I'd hear. Much less actually listen to."

"I know, right? Part of me thinks it's crazy to take him ... or it ... seriously. But I don't have another explanation for what happened. I don't think we were drugged or hallucinating—I mean, we both saw the same thing. And there's no reason for Martin to have set up some kind of elaborate ruse. What does he have to gain?"

"And nobody else even knew we were going to Martin's condo."

"Could the Mossad have somehow figured it out?"

She leaned forward. "If so, they would want to *stop* us from conjuring the demon. The demon convinced us *more* of the power of the ring. If anything, the Mossad would want us to think the ring was worthless so we'd turn it over to them."

Cam nodded. As usual, her analysis was spot on. "Okay. So I think we need to keep an open mind about this."

"Me too. And here's another thing: It seems like the Israelis believe in the demon also. Not just the rabbis, but the government as well." She blinked. "You can say a lot of things about the Israelis. But you can't say they're stupid."

"Agreed. So, like I said, I'm keeping an open mind. Which leads me to the hint the demon gave us: 'A wise man does not seek that which he has already found.' At first I thought he meant we already have the

Shamir. But he didn't use the word *have*. He used the word *found*. To me, there's a difference. It sort of implies we no longer possess it."

She nodded. "I guess that's fair." Then a smile. "Assuming the demon went to law school."

"Half of my graduating class was demonic," he replied. "And the other half aspired to be."

She chuckled and raised her beer. "Mine too."

Cam wondered if that's what drew Shelby to Bruce—by comparison, Bruce didn't seem all that bad. He, at least, had a moral code, twisted as it might be. But Cam steered clear of that conversation.

He continued. "Also, he said *wise man*. Not woman. That implies it's something I found, not you."

"Or he's just a sexist demon, using the male pronoun to refer to everyone."

"Could be. But, at least, I think it means I was there also. So something I found, or something we found together."

"Agreed. Not something I found without you."

"So not something in the safe deposit boxes you examined before I got there."

"Okay."

He took a bite of his slice. He hadn't realized how much he had missed authentic Italian-style pizza. He began to speak again, but Shelby interrupted by reaching across with her napkin and wiping some sauce off his cheek. "Thanks," he stammered.

"Don't mention it. I'm sure, by the time I'm finished, it'll be all over my face and in my hair." She smiled as she lifted her slice to her mouth. "Just keep talking while I make a pig of myself."

He cleared his throat. "You may be right about the *wise man* thing. But it had me thinking about what I've been doing without you. And the answer is, not much. Other than one thing: a trip to Pennsylvania."

"Right. You told me about that. Some cool boulders marking the equinox. You said you think they may have been carved using the Shamir."

"It's just speculation. Playing connect-the-dots. The Phoenicians *may* have ended up with the Shamir after building Solomon's Temple. And the Phoenicians *may* have come to America around that time to trade and mine for copper. And the Phoenicians *may* have brought the Shamir with them. And while they were here, they *may* have carved the Council Rocks boulder." He held her eyes. "And, if you interpret Asmodeus' hint in a certain way, they *may* have left the Shamir someplace at the site."

"Did you look around while you were there? Dig?"

He shook his head. "We were more interested in the alignments. Then, the owner showed up and kicked us out."

"But the demon implied you found it."

"Right. But maybe I didn't know it. Maybe it was there and we just didn't notice. Remember he said I might not be as wise as I thought I was? Maybe that's what he meant. I should have found it, but I didn't."

She nodded and then sipped her beer. "Let me guess. We're going on another road trip."

"If you're up for it, yeah." He knew she was feeling guilty about Bruce. But the truth was, Bruce hadn't done anything to mend fences with her, either.

She sighed, then seemed to reach a decision. "Up for it? It's not like I need to rush home to anything. Finish your pizza and let's get going."

Peering through a monocular from the entryway of a closed office building half a block away, Bruce watched Shelby and Thorne share a pizza. Objectively, there was nothing intimate about the meal. No kissing, no handholding. But Bruce knew Shelby, knew her body language. Eyes wide. Leaning forward. Quick to laugh. A toss of her hair.

He sighed and lowered the monocular, his heart heavy. If she was thinking at all about Bruce, it was only to try to figure out a way to get rid of him.

Okay then. He was a big boy. He hadn't exactly behaved blamelessly, ratting her out to the Mossad. But that had been because he suspected something was going on with her and Thorne. Which, Menachem just verified, was accurate.

So what were his options? He wanted her back; he was sure of that.

She was allowed one indiscretion in thirty years. One possibility was to *win* her back, like in the movies. But he really had no idea how to do that. Flowers? Poetry? Grand gestures? No, for someone like Bruce, the best way to win a game like this was to cheat. To eliminate the competition. No Thorne, no problem.

He raised the monocular again. Thorne was paying the check. Like on a date. Shelby didn't even offer to chip in. She'd make her contribution later, perhaps in bed. Bruce shook the thought away. Don't let the emotions of the situation cloud your judgment. Stay rational. Stay grounded. Follow the plan.

Seated in a real estate office a block away from the pizzeria where Cameron and Shelby were eating, Rivka cursed. It was bad enough that she had to watch her lover dine with another woman. But she was hungry herself, not having eaten since breakfast. She popped another breath mint into her mouth. Pure sugar, the sweetness contrasting sharply with her mood.

She couldn't even conduct this surveillance from her car, because Cameron would recognize it. So she had paid some rental broker fifty bucks to let her use his internet connection and sit in his vestibule. The office window offered a good view of the restaurant and also Bruce Arrujo in the doorway across from it.

His presence was a complication she had not anticipated. She guessed that Menachem—who trusted no one and loved nothing more than a good failsafe—had tasked Bruce with tailing Shelby. Why leave it up to one spurned lover when you could have two? Even so, she resented the implication she was not up to the job. Or maybe he questioned her commitment to it, guessing she still had feelings for Cameron.

Probably not a bad guess. She was just not sure what those feelings were.

Sitting around the dinner table on Tuesday night, Uncle Pomeroy made a point of coming right after Jason. "We know you got a delivery today. Your aunt saw the FedEx truck. You going to tell me what it was?"

"No," Jason mumbled, sticking his fork in some mashed potatoes. His aunt was a gossipy bitch, but at least she could cook.

"You're living under my roof. I have a right to know."

Jason looked up. "It's private. I'm an adult." He guessed his uncle thought it was drug paraphernalia or something. Maybe porn. "Nothing illegal, if that's what you're worried about."

"Is that why you made that excuse to get out of working today? Because you wanted to be here when the package arrived?"

"No. My knee is all stiff, like I told you." He sipped from his Mountain Dew can. "Besides, I did work. I weeded the vegetable garden."

Pomeroy shook his head and muttered, "Women's work."

Jason bit back a retort. At this point, if his uncle wanted to shit on him, whatever. It would be worth it in the end, when he got that truck.

"You know, you're already on thin ice. Not telling me what's in that package only makes it worse."

Jason pushed back his chair and stood. "I'm not hungry anymore."

"We could search your room."

Jason shook his head and began to walk away. *Jeez, let it go already.*

"Jason, did you hear me?"

Jason turned and rolled his eyes. "Whatever." The crazy thing was, he was actually trying to *help* his stupid uncle.

✧☩⊕

Back in the Toyota, Cam and Shelby headed southwest toward Pennsylvania, mirroring the trip he and Astarte had taken only four days earlier. *Four days.* Things sure had changed in his life.

"Should we try to get a different vehicle so they can't follow us?" Shelby asked.

"I'm not sure it matters. We did that whole song and dance up in Manchester, and they still found us. My guess is that they're going to try out the ring. If it doesn't work, they'll circle back to us. So they're probably tracking or following us now, but letting us run."

"Like a fish on a line," she replied.

"Yup."

She squeezed his hand. "Sorry to have dragged you into this. You thought you were just giving me advice on the Templars. Not stepping into a real life *Bourne Identity* adventure." She looked at him sideways. "Though I've always thought you look a bit like Matt Damon. Especially with the beard."

"Um, he almost dies in that movie, right?"

She smiled. "Almost." She shifted. "But hopefully now that the Mossad has the ring, it should be smooth sailing for a while." She paused. "But once they talk to Martin Hall-Perez, they're going to realize we duped them. He saw the entire ring. Not sure it was such a great idea to get the Mossad pissed at us."

Cam turned. "What do you mean, the *entire* ring?"

She grinned. "You still don't remember? I told you it was okay to remember the truth once the Mossad interrogation was over."

"Remember what? What truth?"

She laughed lightly. "I hypnotized you before you went in to be interrogated. Made you forget we actually have the other half of the ring."

"Really?" He looked at her with wide eyes. "We do? Is there anything else I should know?"

She laughed again. "No. You've been a perfect gentleman."

"So where is it?"

"Um, you don't want to know."

"Yes, I do."

"Let's just say you'd need an X-ray to find it."

He mulled that over, then swallowed, feeling a little queasy. "Are you saying it's in my digestive tract?"

She shook her head. "Worse. Mine."

"Wow, you are a trooper."

"Tell me about it." She shifted. "Anyway, like I said, they're going to be pissed when they find out we have it. Which they will."

"There's a chance that all of this is moot. It may be that half the ring, along with all those rabbis, is powerful enough to conjure up the demon. So they might not even need the half we kept."

"That would suck. Hate to go through all this and still have them find the Shamir before we do."

He glanced over. "I have to say, your devotion to your clients goes above and beyond. I mean, they don't even *know* what it is they don't have." He smiled. "And they'd probably just laugh at you if you told them the safe deposit box had some kind of magic worm in it."

She sighed. "I know it sounds crazy. But these families lost everything during the Holocaust. And nobody did anything to help them. Not the governments, not the institutions, not the people. And now the Mossad comes along and wants to screw them over again. I mean, maybe Aaron Kahn's family will happily hand the Shamir over to the Israelis. But it would be nice if someone asked first."

"Do you even know if there are any descendants?"

She shook her head. "That was going to be Bruce's next project. After he catalogued everything. Trying to find the living relatives of Aaron Kahn and all the other families." She stared out the window. "Someone else will have to do it now, probably."

"He hasn't called today?"

"Nope. I tried once. Straight to voicemail."

Cam thought it best to change the subject. "Back to the ring. To be clear, you still have it?"

"If by *have* it you mean, is it working its way through my digestive tract, then yes."

"Well, let me know if we need to make a stop."

"I'm hoping we make it to the hotel. Not sure I want to do this in a public restroom."

He accelerated and shifted to the left lane. "I hear you. ETA is four hours."

They drove in silence for a few minutes, Cam humming along to a Bob Seger song. Out of the blue, Shelby said, "Bruce doesn't like listening to music in the car."

This was the second time she had brought him up. "Why not?"

"He says it's unproductive. Thinks we should be listening to a podcast or the news or maybe a book on tape."

"I suppose he has a point."

"Up to a point, he has a point. But, come on. It's okay to relax a little."

It seemed to Cam that Shelby was working through the idea of life without Bruce. Which made him realize he was not thinking nearly so much about Rivka. He felt remorse because he had hurt her. And sadness that she may no longer be part of his life. But no real heartache. Which was not all that surprising. They had been dating for a year and a half. But between her traveling and him dealing with the loss of Amanda, only recently had things turned serious. And even that was a relative term—he had never told her he loved her, even after she had hinted at having those feelings for him.

Shelby seemed to be waiting for Cam to reply, so he said with a small smile, "That's a long time for no music. Are you still stuck in the nineties with 'Achy Breaky Heart' on a cassette tape?"

She grinned. "Yes, in fact we do the Macarena before bed every night.'"

"I'm having trouble picturing Bruce doing the Macarena."

"He's actually not a bad dancer. He's just never in the mood."

That was criticism number three. But who was counting?

Shelby may have sensed that her complaining about her old lover to her potential new one was inappropriate, because she changed the subject. Or maybe she just had something else she wanted to talk about.

"You know that expression, *You look like you saw a ghost*? That's how I feel. I can't get that demon's face out of my mind." She shuddered. "Green face, red eyes, black mouth."

"Sort of like an alligator at night. Their eyes shine red."

"I could do without both of them. I have a feeling I'm going to have nightmares tonight."

Cam paused. Is this where she wanted to direct the conversation? To her nightmares? He hadn't thought about their sleeping arrangements at the hotel. The safe thing would be to get two beds and then let things play out as they might, with or without the influence of nightmares. He moved the conversation along. "This'll be quite a story to tell someday. We conjure up a demon but instead of getting three wishes, he laughs in my face. Like the Soup Nazi. *No wishes for you.*"

"Seriously, what would you wish for?" She paused and lowered her voice. "Other than Amanda coming back."

He swallowed. "Can it be anything, like ending world hunger? Or does it need to be more tangible?"

"Let's make it something specific to you."

"Okay." He mulled it over, still in the left lane. "I've always wanted to manage the Red Sox."

She smiled. "Everyone in New England thinks they'd be good at that job. But no yacht or a mansion?"

He smiled. "I wouldn't say no to a Porsche. What about you?"

"When my uncle died, I inherited a chunk of money. But I didn't really buy anything for myself."

"You used the money to renovate your house, putting in those suites for battered women, right?"

She nodded. "I guess, if I had a wish, I'd build more shelters like that."

"Sorry to be such a stickler, but you said it had to be for yourself."

She shifted in her seat. "All right. Don't laugh. I've always wanted to play Eponine in *Les Miserables.* I really think I'd be perfect for it." She smiled. "Other than the fact I can't sing and can't act."

Cam chuckled. "That's what the wish is for. I just hope the Red Sox aren't playing that night. I'd hate to miss your show."

Why Eponine? From what Cam recalled of the play, her love went unrequited. And she was a criminal. Odd choice for an accomplished lawyer with a devoted, albeit flawed, life partner. Was this some kind of hint, that Shelby harbored feelings for Cam that had gone unrequited? He shook the thought away. Don't overanalyze things. It was just a play. Shelby had probably seen it as a girl and become enthralled with the part.

"Hey," she said. "You there?"

"Sorry." He looked sideways and smiled. "Just making out the batting order in my head."

She held up her phone and turned off the radio. "You shouldn't have got me going about Eponine. Now I'm going to make you listen to her song."

A haunting rendition of *On My Own* wafted across the front seat. At one point, Shelby brushed a tear away. "Sorry. I'm just a bit emotional."

"I get it," Cam replied. He touched her gently on the arm. "Lots going on."

When the song ended, she put the radio back on and they drove in silence. An hour and a half into their drive, as they approached Hartford, Connecticut, Cam said, "Just about three and a half hours to go. How you doing?"

"If you mean my digestive tract, I'm fine. If you mean my emotional state, I'm a bit frazzled."

Before Cam could reply, his phone rang. He recognized Menachem's number and put the call on speaker. "Hello."

"What kind of asshole ignores a demon?"

Cam glanced at Shelby and shrugged. "What do you mean?"

"The demon told you that God preferred that the Rabbinate find the Shamir. Yet you continue to pursue it."

"So I'm really ignoring God, not the demon." Cam had learned that the best way to deal with Menachem was to stand up to him.

"Even worse, then."

"If God really wants the Shamir, I don't think anything I do is going to matter."

Menachem exhaled. "I would be inclined to agree with you. But the demon—and, by the way, also the Rabbinate—seems to think you are an important player in all this."

"How do you even know what the demon said to me?"

"Please, Cameron. Don't insult me. Did you think we would not question your conjurer friend?"

Cam glanced at Shelby. "Right."

"In any event, you gave us only half the ring, and the rabbis tell me it is not enough. They have tried to conjure Asmodeus again, but no luck. Either he is being stubborn, or the magic is not strong enough. We need the rest of the ring."

Cam took a breath. "This is where you tell me we can do this the easy way or the hard way, right?"

"Well, there is no easy way. You had your chance and blew it. Now we are left with different levels of hard."

"You're not exactly selling me on this."

"You're a big boy, Cameron. You know how this works. Eventually, one way or another, we *will* have that ring. The only question is what happens between now and then."

Eyes wide, Shelby looked at Cam. This was her first experience dealing with people like Menachem. Practicing law could be incredibly confrontational and adversarial, but it was rarely physically dangerous. She swallowed, then shook her head. She was nothing if not resolute. Cam nodded to her and replied to Menachem.

"Sorry. Normally I wouldn't doubt your threats of violence. But we know that the ring loses its power if you take it from us by force."

"Some of the experts say that, yes. But, Cameron, what do we have to lose by trying? As it stands now, we cannot conjure the demon. If we take the ring by force, and still cannot conjure him, we are no worse off."

"Except that you lose the chance forever of us turning it over voluntarily."

"Are you saying that is a possibility?"

Cam looked at Shelby, who shrugged as if to say she had no better idea.

"It is. Give us twenty-four hours."

Menachem mulled it over. "Okay. Twenty-four hours. Not a minute more." He ended the call.

Shelby looked at Cam. "Why twenty-four hours?"

He smiled. "Because I didn't think he'd give us forty-eight."

"So you don't have a plan?"

He shrugged. "Other than stalling for time, no."

Menachem phoned Rivka. "Are you with them?" He was back at the airport hotel, in the conference center they used as a war room.

"Yes. They're three or four cars ahead of me. Not far from crossing into New York State. Luckily, it's night so Cameron doesn't recognize my car."

"Don't do anything. Just observe. I think they have a plan. I want to know what it is."

"Roger that."

"We just questioned the conjurer friend of Thorne's. Turns out Thorne was lying. He did have the other half of the ring."

She grunted a reply.

"And Rivka?"

"Yes."

"How are you doing?" He didn't like to see any of his agents hurting. It affected their performance. And, the truth was, he had grown fond of her. Not that he would ever tell her that.

She let out a long breath. "Not great. But I have a job to do, and I'll do it."

"For what it's worth, when we had Thorne under sodium pentothal we, um, asked him and, well, I don't think he has been intimate with the Baskin woman." Esther had insisted Menachem mention this to Rivka.

"Yeah, well, somehow he fooled you into believing he didn't have the other half of the ring, so I'm not sure how reliable your questioning is."

Menachem shook his head. He still wasn't sure how Thorne had deceived them while under sodium pentothal.

Menachem changed the subject. "One more thing. Don't be surprised to see Bruce Arrujo. He's following Shelby."

"I saw him. It's a regular convoy."

Esther motioned for Menachem's attention. "Hold on one second." Esther handed him a note. He read aloud. "Esther says that, if Arrujo is cute, it's okay to jump his bones." Menachem glanced at Esther to make sure he got that right. He read on. "And if you don't want him, at least get his number for her."

Menachem was surprised that the comment elicited a short laugh. He would have thought things were still too raw. But what did he know?

"Anything else?" Rivka asked.

"I've given Thorne twenty-four hours. He has a plan. But I'm not sure what it is."

"So don't do anything until tomorrow night?"

"Not necessarily. I told him we'd wait until then. But you know I'm not above changing my mind."

Ignoring the agreement he made with Menachem, Bruce drove northeast out of downtown Boston, toward the airport, even as Shelby and Thorne drove southwest. Bruce had attached a tracking device to the underside of the wheel well of their Toyota while they were eating in the North End. But, at this point, he was pretty sure where they were going even without the tracker. The question was, why?

The more Bruce thought about it, the more he thought that answers could be found in Portsmouth. Shelby and Thorne had driven there for a reason. Then, something happened that caused the Mossad to jump into action. Whatever that something was, it had sent Shelby and Thorne racing out of town, presumably back to the Council Rocks site. The thing about the Mossad, like most good intelligence operations, was that there was really no way to predict what they might do. They were simply too careful, too skilled. But, once something happened, they often weren't so careful about cleaning up after themselves. Bruce was hoping that was the case here.

He came up out of the Callahan Tunnel and stayed right at the airport exit. He was almost certain the Mossad had taken him to the central parking garage, so he followed the signs and entered the hulking, six-story structure. He had counted while blindfolded: into the garage, then up the spiral ramp two times, then a quick turn to the right, then another turn to the right after six or seven seconds, then backing into a parking space. He repeated the steps in his rental car, looking for a minivan. There. Dark blue Chrysler Pacifica. Facing out.

Bruce parked a few spots away. He hoped he wasn't too late. Whatever had gone down in Portsmouth had occurred late morning or early afternoon, before Menachem released him. It was possible an agent had already been sent out to clean up any mess. But, more likely, the cleanup would be an afterthought.

He waited forty-five minutes, beginning to think this was a waste of time. Then a young man carrying a duffle bag, a cigarette in his mouth, stepped from the elevator and sauntered toward the minivan. Bruce slouched low in his seat. The young man checked many boxes—fit, with an arrogance to his walk, carrying what could be cleaning supplies. And Bruce recalled that the minivan had smelled like cigarette smoke. With a key fob, the man Bruce suspected was a junior Mossad operative unlocked the minivan's doors.

The agent pulled out, and Bruce followed. The minivan headed north on Route 1, Bruce guessed toward Portsmouth. He checked his watch. Shelby and Thorne now had almost a two-hour head start. And every mile Bruce drove put him two miles further away from them as they moved south. At some point he'd need to pull a U-turn. Hopefully, that would be after he had some answers.

Fifty miles north of Boston, now on Route 95, the minivan took the downtown Portsmouth off-ramp. Bruce followed. It was eight at night now on a Tuesday, and the agent double-parked in front of an old mill building along the river. Bruce did the same further down the block and jogged back in time to see the agent, carrying the duffel bag, get buzzed in and push through the front door. Bruce followed before the door could close behind him. Sloppy. But, again, the precisely choreographed theatrics were over—this was merely the night crew coming in to clean up. No precision necessary.

Bruce watched the agent push the "4" button on the elevator and edged by him to the stairs, where he raced up. A door at the end of the hall marked 404 opened, and the agent stepped in. Bruce followed. He waited in the hallway for a few seconds until he could hear voices fading away from inside the unit, then tried the unit door. It opened. Bruce slipped in, ducking into a bathroom.

"I'll give you a hand with that stuff," a man's voice said from a few rooms away.

The agent replied with an Israeli accent. "No need. I have it."

"Well, I need to bring some stuff down to the storage unit in the basement anyway."

Half a minute passed, then Bruce peered out as he heard the two men approaching from down the hall. The agent carried a medicine-cabinet-sized wall mirror along with a couple of rolled-up electrical cords while the unit resident struggled with a black steamer trunk. They exited the unit and headed down the hallway.

Bruce began his search. He wasn't sure exactly what he was looking for, but he didn't find it in the living room or master bedroom. On his way toward a closed door at the end of the hall, a voice rang out. "Hey! What are you doing here?"

The unit owner. Tall and fit. But confused. Bruce smiled and took a step toward him. "Sorry, I'm looking for Barry."

"Barry?"

"Yeah, is this 304?"

"No. This is 404."

Bruce shook his head. "My bad." He stepped forward as if to exit the unit, then spun and snapped off a quick right cross, nailing the owner on the jaw. Bruce caught him as he crumbled, barely conscious, and dragged him to a hallway closet. He stuffed him inside, wedged the door closed with a fireplace poker, and returned to his search.

The door at the end of the hall opened to an empty, windowless room. The pungent smell of sulfur greeted him as he entered. A round red carpet covered the middle of the room, next to which sat a white triangular area rug. Candles surrounded them. Bruce crouched, examining both rugs. Odd symbols, perhaps satanic. A dark discoloration in the smaller rug caught his eye. A hole, penny sized. Bruce lifted the rug and found a couple of electrical wires beneath. *What the?*

He examined the larger rug, lifting it as well, but found nothing underneath. What had been going on in here? Menachem had mentioned something about spirits and a séance. Was that what was happening? Were Shelby and Thorne following clues given to them by some paranormal spirit?

Bruce reexamined the power cords. One was a standard electrical cord, the other a cable wire. *Just like for a television set.* Using his phone, he did a Google search for "mirror" and "TV set." Immediately, an image of a sleek Samsung mirror television appeared. Still crouching, he scrolled through more images. Apparently, when powered off, the thin display screen didn't look like a television screen at all. It looked like a simple hanging mirror. Bruce sat back. *A framed wall mirror.*

"Well-played, Menachem," Bruce said aloud, shaking his head. "And it looks like they bought it."

Cam looked longingly at the roadside Hampton Inn as they cruised by in the Toyota. He would have liked nothing better than to pull in, take a hot shower, and see how the whole two-beds-and-nightmares thing played out with Shelby. But the fates had dealt him a different hand for tonight: The bright full moon and warmish temperature and possibility of Pomeroy patrolling his property in the daylight had augured for a night-time climb to the Council Rocks sites.

After Cam's phone call with Menachem, still two hours outside of Wilkes-Barre, Cam and Shelby had picked up hiking supplies along with flashlights and a shovel at a Home Depot just before it closed at ten. Now, as midnight approached, Cam asked, "You sure you're up for this?" He half-hoped Shelby would talk him out of it.

She smiled. "Sure. Sounds like a fun adventure."

Despite the late hour, Cam had reached out to Anita and Sue. If they found something at Council Rocks, Cam wanted there to be reputable witnesses to the discovery, and both Anita and Sue were respected professionals. Surprisingly, they had agreed to the moonlit climb. "Let me get out of my footie pajamas and throw on some jeans," Anita had said with a laugh. "We'll meet you at the trail in an hour."

It was almost one in the morning when Cam parked at the foot of the easement trail. Crickets chirped, the sound carrying in the still, cool air. Cam thought about pulling the Toyota into the brush to hide it but was worried he might not be able to get back out. Instead, after unloading the supplies, he drove it a quarter mile up the road, parked on the shoulder, and jogged back.

The jog invigorated him. "Glad you're still here," he said to Shelby. "Where else would I go?"

"Thought maybe you'd climb up without me, find the Shamir, and be on your way."

She took his arm with a knowing smile and held his eyes. "No you didn't."

He laughed, the warmth of her hand sending a tingle up his arm.

Cam considered that this might be a good time for a first kiss, but approaching headlights ruined the mood. Anita pulled over; Cam made quick introductions and then drove Anita's car in the opposite direction from his vehicle and again jogged back.

"Shelby is darling," Anita whispered to Cam when he returned. "Are you two an item?"

Cam felt himself blushing. "Unclear. Maybe."

Anita took Sue's hand. "Be bold. Love is worth the risk."

They began the climb, Anita, wearing a headlamp, in the lead and Cam bringing up the rear, a walking stick in his left hand. "So," she said over her shoulder to Cam, "what are we looking for?"

Cam liked Anita and Sue, but he didn't really know them well enough to tell them that he and Shelby had conjured a demon using Solomon's magic ring and the demon had hinted that the mystical Shamir worm might be hidden at Council Rocks. Instead, he kept it simple. "We need to find more evidence tying this site to the Phoenicians. When we were here last time, Pomeroy chased us off before we could really look around."

Sue turned to look at Cam, skepticism on her face. She sensed there was more to the story. "You know that you can't dig, right?" Sue said.

Cam nodded. "Of course." Though, with Sue being a trained archeologist, Cam hoped she would agree that it would be okay to move some dirt around if the situation called for it.

They climbed in silence for half a minute. Sue turned again, her perpetual scowl back. "There's something you're not telling us, right? I mean, nobody drives five hours to climb a mountain in the middle of the night without a good reason."

Shelby replied. "You're right, Sue. I'm bound by attorney-client privilege not to divulge details, but we have good reason to believe that we might find something tonight."

Cam smiled to himself. Well-played by Shelby. Playing the attorney-client privilege card always worked; it was like a magic wand that, when you waved it, put an end to any discussion you didn't want to continue, no questions asked. Laypeople didn't really understand what the privilege entailed, but they knew that lawyers and judges always spoke of it reverentially, in hushed tones, like it was some kind of foundational cornerstone to our democratic way of life.

"Oh, okay," Sue muttered.

They took things slowly, but the trail was well-marked, and Anita found her way with no problem. Forty-five minutes after starting, they reached the ridge.

"Okay," Anita said. "We are officially trespassing."

They turned off their headlamps in the moonlight and, descending a hundred feet, easily found the Council Rocks boulders. It was breezier and a few degrees colder at elevation—Cam guessed in the low forties—which made things a bit uncomfortable but kept the mosquitoes away. Cam took five minutes to pull Shelby aside to explain the astronomical alignments, then showed her the right-angle cuts on the largest boulder. "I think there's a good chance that cut was made by the Shamir," he said in a low voice.

Shelby asked a few questions, then they made their way back to Anita and Sue.

"So," Sue said, her arms crossed in either a sign of skepticism or an attempt to keep warm, "what are we looking for?"

"I'm not sure, exactly," said Cam. "But it sure would be nice to find something that proves the Phoenicians were here."

Sue sniffed. "Whatever falafel they might have left behind, the animals already made off with it."

Cam smiled good-naturedly. She was right to be skeptical, especially since he and Shelby weren't divulging much information. "I guess, ideally, we would find some kind of carving with Phoenician script." Actually, ideally, they would find a little magic worm wearing a "Shamir" nametag, but Cam knew that wasn't likely to happen. Instead, he held up a bottle of water and a flashlight. "One of the reasons I wanted to come up here at night was because rock carvings are easier to see in indirect light, while wet. The direct sunlight during the day tends to wash them out. So, like I said, let's look for carvings."

Sue, partly mollified, nodded. "And I suppose it doesn't have to be a script. Could be a carving of Tanit or something."

"Right," Cam replied. He dropped to one knee and began to examine the first boulder with his light. "After thousands of years, it might have faded. But hopefully not so much that it's gone entirely."

Anita commented, "These rocks are hard. They'll hold a carving for many millennia."

Sue nudged her. "Go ahead. Tell them what you found."

Anita pursed her lips. "I don't know."

"Look, now's the time," Sue said.

"What?" asked Cam.

"You're going to think I'm off my rocker."

"Believe me," Shelby replied, "after what we've been through and seen the past couple of days, nothing would surprise us."

Anita took out her phone. "Okay. This is from last year. I was staring at the boulder with the notch in it, wondering what it could be. And this face kept popping out. Looking back at me. Two faces, actually. Every time I looked at the rock, I saw them."

Sue rolled her eyes. "She even had dreams about them."

"So, anyway, I took a picture. Then I drew on what I thought I saw." She held up the images on her phone for everyone to see. "Eyes, nose, mouth, curly hair. I wouldn't bother mentioning it to you, but you specifically said to look for any carvings. Here, let me zoom in so you can see what I'm talking about.

Two pictures. Just the rock, then with the faces drawn in."

Council Rocks "Face" Carvings

Shelby said, "I guess I see the faces."

Cam nodded. "Could be." The truth was, sometimes the pits and cracks and crevices of a rock were just that.

Anita let out a long breath. "I know you're skeptical. As you should be. Sue is also. But as a geologist I think there's a decent chance these markings are manmade. And here's another thing. I did some research on how Baal was depicted by the ancient Phoenicians in their artwork. He was almost always depicted with large round eyes, an open mouth, and curly hair."

Cam angled his head, this time studying the actual boulder face. "Really?"

"I know, right?" she replied.

Cam splashed some water on the rock face, dabbed off the excess with a cloth, then used his flashlight to examine it at a low angle. "Could be," he said for the second time. But a "could be" didn't seem to be enough: Asmodeus had implied that it was something Cam had found, or at least *could* have found had he had the time to look or been more observant. Cam was not sure if, given a month to wander the site, he ever would have noticed the face carvings. Even so, he snapped a couple of pictures and asked Anita to forward hers to him as well.

"I vote we keep looking," Shelby said. "Maybe something else will catch our eye."

They split up, shining lights on rock faces. "Hold the lights at a low angle, not straight on," Cam advised. "And if you see something, dab some water on it, like I did."

Forty-five minutes later, all of them now chilled, they had examined every face of every boulder in the cluster. "Maybe it's not a carving," Shelby offered.

"Well, if you're looking for an artifact, you can't dig for it," Sue said for the second time, her hands now stuffed in her pockets.

Cam turned to Shelby and spoke in a low voice. "I don't get the sense we were supposed to dig, do you?"

"No. The demon said *found*, like it was something you had already seen or stumbled upon. Or *should* have seen."

Cam smiled. "Right. Had I been wiser. I get it. Asmodeus thinks I'm a lightweight."

She fluffed her hair playfully. "Well, he did say he might make a move on your woman."

Cam grinned, not sure how to respond. She had referred to herself as *his* woman. Or was she just repeating back what the demon had said?

Rather than standing there like a love-struck eighth-grader, Cam regathered himself. "Let's see if we can find something around or under the boulders." The notched boulder sat on a bed of smaller rocks, so there were cavities underneath. "Maybe in a crevice." He glanced at the split boulder. "Or in the gap between the two split pieces."

He dropped to his belly to peer under the notched boulder with his flashlight. Shelby joined him while Anita and Sue crawled around the split boulder. Less than five minutes had passed when Sue exclaimed, "Wait. I think I see something."

Cam jumped to his feet and strolled over.

On her belly, Sue shined her light into the gap between the two halves of the boulder, one of which laid propped against the other. "I think I see something cylindrical in there. I poked at it with a stick and it seemed to roll. But I can't reach it. The gap is too narrow."

Cam joined her on the ground. She shined her light. "It's there, where the light is hitting. See the dark object? But I think I pushed it deeper into the crevice."

Cam took his folding knife from his pocket, found a long, straight stick in the woods, opened the metal hook tool on the knife, secured the knife to the stick with some duct tape, and returned to the split boulder. With Sue holding the light and guiding him, and Anita taking video on her phone, he fished around with his left arm for the cylindrical object. After a minute or so, he hooked something. "Okay. I'm pulling something out. Be ready to reach in and grab it."

Wishing he had the use of his right arm, he tugged slowly and steadily, not wanting to damage the object or tug so hard that it rolled free. In less than thirty seconds, he had pulled it close. Sue reached in and extracted it. "Oh my God," she exclaimed, raising herself to her knees. "It's ceramic. I think I see a face." She rubbed the dirt off a six-inch figurine and proclaimed breathlessly, "I'm pretty sure it's Tanit."

Anita, still recording with her phone, voiced what was on everyone's mind. "She's a Phoenician goddess. A mother figure, the consort to Baal."

Cam nodded, recalling that the site was, in fact, believed to be constructed to honor Baal. And this discovery would help prove it. He said in a clear voice, "Just what you'd expect to find at a site dedicated to the sun god."

Bruce cruised the middle lane of the interstate under a bright full moon. He was a good four or five hours behind Shelby and Thorne. Except for the fact that he was ahead of them.

He dialed a number.

"Pomeroy here."

"It's Bruce. I'm headed your way."

"Why?"

"It seems that all roads lead to Council Rocks."

"I'm not sure I understand." Pomeroy spoke slowly in a Southern drawl, which made some people underestimate his intelligence. Not Bruce.

"I'm not sure I understand either," he lied. And then added, "But I'm following Thorne and Shelby." Bruce left out the part about the Mossad. Pomeroy was his partner, but that didn't mean Bruce had to tell him everything.

"You think they're going to the site?"

"I'm betting they're already there. They must think the Shamir is there. Or something else that will lead them to it."

"You want me to go up and scare them off again?"

"No. Give them space. Let's see what they find."

"This might all be too soon."

"I know. What's the GoFundMe up to?"

"About $350,000. And no sign of slowing down. Plus, we may have a foundation that will do a dollar-for-dollar match. So $700,000. Like I said, we could use more time. Let it keep growing."

Bruce exhaled. *More time.* That was the problem with puppeteering actual people. Sometimes the puppets snapped their strings.

Shelby watched as Cam, Sue and Anita excitedly examined the Tanit figurine under the silvery-blue moonlight. It occurred to her that Cam, his eyes wide with excitement, saw the world as a great adventure; Bruce, on the other hand, saw it as a looming adversary.

She, too, was excited—the statuette apparently was the object the demon had hinted at them finding. But the lawyer in her knew it soon would be time to play defense.

"Anita," she said, "please keep the video going."

"Okay. It is."

"And please give the exact time and date."

"Two-thirty-eight AM, on March 21."

"And could you state where we are and what time we arrived."

"We are at a site called Council Rocks, outside Wilkes-Barre, Pennsylvania. We met Shelby and Cameron at the base of the trail at quarter to one. I recall the exact time because the deejay on the radio announced it as we pulled up."

Shelby turned to Cam. "You and I purchased hiking supplies at a Home Depot in Newburgh, New York, almost a two-hour drive from Wilkes-Barre. Can you show the camera that receipt and specifically note the time stamped on it?"

Cam pulled the receipt from his wallet. "Receipt shows we paid at ten-nineteen PM." Cam smiled. "I'm sure they'd remember us. They weren't happy they had to keep the register open for us after closing time."

Shelby continued. "And then we stopped for gas when we got off the highway in Wilkes-Barre. Can you show that receipt?"

Cam did. "Timestamp is twelve-eighteen AM." He smiled at her, encouraging her to proceed.

Shelby nodded. For most of their time on the run, Cam had been the one solving problems and formulating strategy. It felt good to be contributing. "Okay. So that timeline makes sense. We leave the Home Depot, load the car, get back on the highway, drive to Wilkes-Barre, get off the highway, and buy gas. That takes almost two full hours. Then we drive to the base of the trail, which takes another fifteen minutes."

"Right," Cam said. "In fact, we arrived at the base of the trail just after twelve-thirty."

Shelby turned back to Anita. "And how long does it take to hike up to the Council Rocks site?"

"About forty-five minutes. You could do it in thirty-five if you really hustled."

"And the descent?"

"Thirty-five minutes, twenty-five if you jogged. Not that you could in the dark."

"Okay. I just wanted to get the timeline clear. Based on all this, is there any way Cam and I could have arrived at Council Rocks early, climbed the mountain, planted the Tanit figurine, come back down, and been there waiting when you arrived at quarter to one?"

Anita did the calculations and shook her head. "If those receipts are real, then no. No way."

"Thank you," Shelby said. "And, for the record, no doubt there are security cameras showing Cam and me at the Home Depot and gas station which confirm the timestamps on the receipts."

Shelby turned now to Sue. "During the time we have been here at Council Rocks tonight, has there ever been an opportunity for Cameron or myself to somehow deposit the Tanit figurine in the crevice between those two boulders?"

"No," Sue replied. "Prior to the discovery, we had divided up and were looking for carvings on the face of the boulders. Anita and I inspected the split boulder. You and Cam were inspecting other boulders. You were never even in close proximity to the split boulder."

Shelby nodded, her cross-examination complete. Someone might question the legitimacy of their find. But the timeline Shelby had just established made it almost bulletproof.

CHAPTER 7

Cam sat in a mostly empty diner with Shelby, digging into a stack of pancakes smothered in butter and syrup. He felt like he deserved it after their big find at Council Rocks. "I might even have a piece of pie for dessert," he said as he finished chewing.

Shelby sipped her coffee and smiled. "Nice to see you so cheerful at five in the morning." She leaned in. "Most guys only eat like that after sex."

He laughed. "Most guys don't get to discover something that will rewrite the history books. Assuming the figurine is legit, it's conclusive proof linking the Phoenicians to America."

It had been almost four in the morning by the time they descended the trail and made it back to their cars. Too wired to sleep, they had said their goodbyes to Anita and Sue and found an all-night breakfast place. After taking photographs, Anita and Sue had graciously offered to let Cam retain custody of the Tanit figurine. But Cam had refused.

"You're the archeologist," he had said to Sue. "It should stay with you. Chain of custody."

Sue had flashed a rare smile, then rolled her eyes. "Great. Just what I need. Not like there'll be any controversy attached to it."

Sue and Anita had, in fact, already reached out to an associate at a lab to have the ceramic figurine undergo optically stimulated luminescence testing, a methodology that would determine when the clay from inside the statuette was last exposed to sunlight—that date being the date the figurine was shaped.

"So," Shelby said, taking a spoonful of yogurt, "what's next?" She smiled. "I mean, after your pie."

He lowered his fork. "Good question. We came down here because Asmodeus said we missed something the first time. And now we found it. But I'm not sure the Tanit figurine gets us any closer to finding the Shamir." He had been so excited by the Tanit discovery that only now was he focusing on the reality that, as pertaining to the magic worm, the figurine had not really moved the ball down the field.

"That's my point. I'm not sure that we found what Asmodeus was referring to. Like you said, it doesn't get us any closer to the Shamir. And that's the whole point of this … quest, I guess you'd call it."

Cam nodded. While he was contemplating pie, Shelby was dipping her spoon in vanilla yogurt. She seemed happy for him, for his discovery. But she still had no magic worm to turn over to the Aaron Kahn family.

"I'm wondering," she asked, "did we miss something? Did we get so excited about the figurine that we missed the Shamir?"

"I don't see how. We looked pretty much everywhere." He sat back. "In fact, I don't see why it should be in Pennsylvania. It was in France eighty years ago. Even if someone removed it from the safe deposit box before the war, how would it end up on a mountaintop in America? Maybe it was here three thousand years ago when the Phoenicians helped build Council Rocks. But it didn't stay here."

"Maybe that's what Asmodeus meant when he said you'd already found it. You found evidence of the Shamir with the notch cut from the boulder. Maybe we made it more complicated than it needed to be."

Cam thought about that. "What I found, specifically, was evidence that the Phoenicians possessed the Shamir and brought it to Pennsylvania."

"Right. But how does that help us find it today?"

"Maybe it means the Phoenicians still have it."

"How could that be? There are no Phoenicians, or Lebanese, in northern France. At least not many."

Cam dropped his hands onto the table. "Clearly, we're missing something."

"Or the demon is screwing with us. I think I read someplace that Asmodeus, in particular, was known for being mischievous."

"Well, we're running out of time. Menachem gave us twenty-four hours. Until seven-thirty tonight."

She swallowed a yawn. "I guess that means no nap, huh?"

Cam paid the bill, but they made no move to leave. Mostly because they had no idea where to go next.

Cam leaned forward. "Okay, let's think about this methodically." He turned the paper placemat over, took out a pen, and began listing dates, reading them out as he did so. "The first time we hear about the Shamir is around 960 BC, when Solomon is building his Temple. Then, according to that Masonic historian, Finch, some workers, ruffians, killed the architect Hiram Abiff and stole the Shamir."

"And, presumably, brought it back to the Phoenician homeland," Shelby said, "because after that it disappears from Jewish history."

"Okay." Cam nodded. "Then, possibly, around 950 BC, it makes its way to Council Rocks with Phoenician explorers. Maybe one of the ruffians got caught, and the king ended up with the Shamir, and he gave it to the sea captain. Or maybe one of the ruffians was on the boat. It doesn't really matter."

"That's lots of maybes."

"It is. But even though the Shamir seems to have disappeared, it keeps getting written about, all the way up to the Middle Ages."

She smiled. "When you say, 'Middle Ages,' the veins on your fore-head pop out in the shape of a Templar cross."

He laughed aloud. "That must be quite a look."

"Even the nuns begin to pant and disrobe."

They were both laughing now, the joy of their discovery and the fatigue of the night and the tension of being on the run and the energy between them causing a kind of spontaneous giddiness to wash over them. Then the laughter dissolved into grins, their eyes locked.

Cam reached over slowly and took her hand. "This has been quite an adventure."

She nodded, stroking his wrist with her thumb. "Frightened as I've been, I almost don't want it to end."

He nodded. But he knew better than to have this discussion now. They were too, well, joyful and fatigued and tense and energized and giddy to make good decisions.

She seemed to have reached the same conclusion. Slowly, gently, she untangled her fingers and pulled away.

"Well," she said with a sigh. "To be continued."

"Yes. Definitely."

"But, for now, back to the job at hand."

"Yes. Disrobing those panting nuns."

Grinning, she cuffed his uninjured arm. "Jerk."

"You brought it up."

"Pick up that pen and keep writing."

He did so. "So, we're up to medieval times. The Templars go to Jerusalem in the early 1100s and find something amazing while excavating under King Solomon's Temple. Something that makes them incredibly wealthy and incredibly powerful."

"You think they might have found the Shamir. And/or the magic ring."

"Definitely." He paused and smiled. "Definitely they *might* have."

She rolled her eyes. "Jeez. Hold a guy's hand and right away he turns into a jerk."

"Sorry. It makes sense that they did. And it also makes sense they found Solomon's summoning rituals which made their way to Europe in medieval times." He explained, "I'm talking about a book of spells used to summon demons. Like Martin used. It's called the *Key of Solomon* and, like I said, it appeared in Europe at the same time as the Templars. Lots of people dabbled in magic back then."

"I'm sure the Church loved that."

Cam smiled. "Just another thing the Templars did to piss them off. Anyway, it's still all circumstantial. We really have no evidence to support the theory that the Templars found the Shamir and the magic ring." He paused and angled his head. "Other than they went back to Europe and built massive stone cathedrals never before seen in the history of the world."

"The Shamir would help with that. So would a magic ring. But, like you said, it's just circumstantial." She paused, chewing her lip. "Here's a question. How would the Shamir have made its way from the Phoenicians back to Solomon's Temple for the Templars to find it?"

"Good question." He smiled. "I agree, it didn't crawl all that way." He sat back. "You know, maybe I'm wrong, maybe the Templars didn't find it while digging under the Temple. I read how, when the Templars got to the Middle East, they were surrounded by Muslims. The only allies they had were a small group of Lebanese Christians. They used them as guides and translators, then later brought a lot of them into their order."

"So you think maybe the Shamir was passed down through the generations by the ancient Phoenicians to their descendants in Lebanon, and then the locals decided to give it—or maybe sell it—to the Templars?"

Cam was going to say, "Definitely they *might* have," again, but didn't want to push his luck. Instead, he said, "It's very possible."

"So we have two possible ways the Templars might have found the Shamir. And we think they did, because of the Templar cross on the lead box."

"Right. Going forward, the next time we hear anything about the Shamir is just before World War II, in Rouen, in your safe deposit box. The Templars were very active in Rouen until they were outlawed in 1307." He shrugged. "Maybe one of the Templar leaders brought it to Rouen for safekeeping and then it just stayed hidden."

"But that's over six hundred years, Cam. Not exactly a tight timeline."

"Oops, wait. I'm forgetting that monastery in Normandy. The monk found a rock-eating worm in the wall. That was the late 1600s. Close to Rouen."

"Fair point. It would make sense for the Templars to bring the Shamir to a monastery for safekeeping after they were outlawed."

"And don't forget Solomon's ring," he said. "The ring and the Shamir are linked. The fact that we have the ring tells me we're close to the Shamir. Like Trevino said, where one is, you'll likely find the other."

She nodded. "But we haven't. Found the other."

He exhaled. "Honestly, I don't know where else to look."

She leaned forward. "For me, it keeps coming back to this, Cam: The Mossad has better things to do than chase myths. That means someone in Israel, high up, believes the Shamir is real. And that, at one point, it was in the safe deposit box. With the ring. And it didn't just disappear. We just have to pick up its trail. And the only clue left that we really haven't followed is the name Aaron Kahn. I haven't checked in with any of the groups going through their databases since Monday morning. Maybe one of them found something."

Cam nodded. "Good idea." He stood. "We should get moving." He wasn't sure if Shelby's idea would lead to anything, but one thing was certain: The Shamir wasn't going to crawl out from under what was left of his stack of pancakes.

Menachem rubbed his face in the hotel war room as the sun crested over the horizon beyond the airport runway. He had been up all night, getting reports from Rivka, none of them encouraging. He had been hoping Thorne's little drive to Pennsylvania would be the last glow of a dying ember, a final attempt to find the elusive Shamir. Instead, seemingly miraculously, he and the Baskin woman had discovered some kind of historical artifact which only served to propel them onward on their quest.

Tzion walked in, a perfect target for Menachem's morning wrath. "That stupid riddle of yours is costing us Solomon's ring."

"Sorry, boss," Tzion muttered, his tongue still black from yesterday's makeup. He set a box of pastries down on the conference room table and sipped his coffee. "I didn't mean anything specific by it." He shrugged. "Who would hear, 'A wise man does not seek that which he has already found,' and think they need to drive to Pennsylvania?"

"Thorne, that's who," Menachem growled. "And now they've found something on the mountain, which makes them think they're still hot on the trail of the Shamir, which means they're not even close to being ready to give up the other half of the ring."

Tzion rubbed his face, his cheeks still exhibiting a faint green tint. "I'm a field operative, not an improv actor."

"Yes, and as an operative you are supposed to possess a quick mind."

Menachem turned away and cursed. *"Zayin ba'ayin." A dick in your eye.* It was always the stupid little details that tripped you up. The operation in Portsmouth had gone off without a hitch. The technology had worked flawlessly, the Samsung mirrored television—which really did look like a simple mirror resting on the carpet—fooling Thorne and the woman. And the young conjurer, Martin Hall-Perez, had done a remarkable job selling the whole charade, convinced by Menachem—with the help of the local police chief—that Thorne was planning to sell the Shamir and magic ring to an international crime syndicate and that the blood of thousands would be on his hands if he did not help. Even Tzion had done a credible job impersonating the imperious Asmodeus. Until the stupid riddle.

Menachem checked his watch. Thirteen hours. That's how long he had given Thorne to turn the ring over. But what then? Menachem's hands were tied—Tel Aviv, heeding the advice of the Rabbinate, was insisting that the ring not be retrieved using violence or force. Hello? How was he supposed to do that? He was a Mossad agent, not a bloody sorcerer.

Esther stuck her head through the doorway. Menachem, out of the corner of his eye, saw Tzion shake his head as if to warn her away. Menachem ignored the insolence, knowing he probably deserved it. "What is it?" he said with a sigh.

"I might have something, boss."

Cam drove northeast back toward Boston in light, mid-morning traffic. There was no reason for them to stick around Wilkes-Barre, and they both agreed it didn't make sense to run from the Mossad indefinitely. As the expression went, sometimes you get the bear, and sometimes the bear gets you. The Mossad was a big, nasty, grizzly. It was best to get the hell out of the woods.

Shelby had signed into her email account to check to see if any information had come in regarding the descendants of Aaron Kahn, but so far, nothing conclusive. "The best lead seems to be a Gabrielle Kahn living in West Hartford, Connecticut, age eighty-eight," she said. "Aaron had a young daughter named Gabrielle. The ages match up. But who knows? It's a fairly common name."

"And she probably would have changed her name if she got married."

"Still, we're going that way, so it's worth a stop."

"Agreed." He glanced over. "What would you do if she wanted to turn the ring over to the Israelis, just give it to them?"

Shelby sniffed. "Grab a hot shower and a long nap."

"Really? You wouldn't be disappointed?"

"A little, I suppose. But only because I don't really trust the Israelis not to try to weaponize it." She shrugged. "I would try to talk them out of it, but if that's what the owners want, so be it."

He glanced over. "Really? All this work and time and trauma, and in the end there's nothing to show for it?"

She smiled, reached over, and squeezed his arm. "Nothing? I wouldn't say that."

While Cam drove northeast through New York and then Connecticut, Shelby worked the phone. She found a number for Gabrielle Kahn and left a message on her machine. An hour later, the eighty-eight-year-old woman called back.

"Who's this?" she demanded in a thick New York accent.

Shelby explained as much as she could. "I am an attorney working to return property to the families of people lost during the Holocaust. We found a safe deposit box owned by a Mr. Aaron Kahn in Rouen, France. He had a daughter named Gabrielle who would be eighty-eight

now. We were thinking that you might be the Gabrielle we are looking
for."

"What if I am?"

"Well, like I said, we have some property that may belong to you."

"You mean like a condominium? In France?"

Shelby smiled at Cam. "No. Personal property. Things from a safe
deposit box."

"I don't know anything about any safe deposit box. But I was born in
Rouen."

Shelby raised an eyebrow. "We are driving up through Connecticut
now. Maybe we could take you to lunch?"

After almost an hour of back-and-forth, it was finally decided that
Gabrielle's daughter, who lived in the Hartford suburbs, would pick up
her mother and they would meet for a late lunch at Rein's Deli in Vernon,
outside Hartford, at two o'clock.

With a sigh, Shelby hung up. "I think the Geneva Convention was
easier to negotiate than that lunch."

"I'll buy you a knish."

She turned. "You asked earlier how I would feel if I had nothing to
show for all this work." She smiled. "Well, I happen to love knishes. So,
either way, it's a win."

Bruce's phone rang as he drove north, still on the trail of Shelby and
Thorne. It was getting a little silly, to be honest. He had followed them
south for three hundred miles, and now he was following them north for
three hundred more. At least he didn't have to see them check into a
hotel room together and let his imagination torment him.

Pomeroy skipped the pleasantries. "I just heard something."

"Tell me."

"My wife was on Facebook. She monitors the local historical society
page." He chuckled. "Mostly because she's a busybody. That woman, the
geologist, just posted something about a big find at Council Rocks. Some
kind of figurine. A goddess."

"Tanit?"

"Yeah, that's it. They're getting it tested, then they're going to turn it over to the tribes. They think it's three thousand years old. Bastards were trespassing again, just like you said." He paused. "I may bring charges. She stole that off my land."

Bruce sniffed. "You really think they're going to prosecute a seventy-year-old woman for turning an ancient artifact over to the indigenous people who used to live on the land?" In fact, she was probably hoping Pomeroy did something stupid like press charges, just to get more publicity.

"So you think I shouldn't do anything?"

"Just sit tight. The find is actually a good thing." A few miles ahead, just east of Hartford, Shelby and Thorne took a highway exit. Probably getting lunch. "The more people who know about the site, the better."

"I don't know. All those academic types make me nervous. I read about some guy, he found Indian pottery on his land and the government came in and wouldn't let him build an addition. I don't want a bunch of eggheads running around on my property telling me what I can and can't do."

"I'll handle all that. Don't worry."

Pomeroy exhaled. "Okay."

"So do you think that figurine is legit?" Bruce asked.

"The timing is a bit convenient, just when everyone has started paying attention to the site—"

Bruce interjected. "Well, that could explain *why* they found it. You know, people are paying attention to the site, so more researchers are spending time there, looking for clues."

"Suppose so. Anyway, it could be a problem. It's going to convince Thorne that this site really is Phoenician. And that the worm thing is here. Or was here. Like I said, this is starting to get messy. Complicated."

Bruce smiled. "Messy and complicated are good, my friend." He recalled something his grandfather used to say. "Chaos is nothing but a well-disguised opportunity."

◬✝✡

Cam pulled into the crowded strip mall parking lot just off the highway outside of Hartford. Even on a weekday, Shelby could see a line stretching out the door of Rein's Deli.

"Good thing we got here early," she said, getting out of the car. "I'll go put our names in for a table while you get gas. Wouldn't want Mrs. Kahn to have to wait."

"You just want to get your order in for those knishes," he said with a smile.

"Two days, and you already know all my secrets," she said with mock dismay.

Twenty minutes later, a thin young woman with glasses led an elderly, gray-haired version of herself into the restaurant by the arm. Shelby studied them. "If this checks out, that would be Aaron's daughter and granddaughter," Shelby said, standing to greet them as a hostess led them over.

Before introductions, Gabrielle announced in a New York accent, "You'll have to talk loud. I forgot my hearing aids." Gabrielle dropped into the chair next to Cam, leaving her daughter, Jodi, to sit between Gabrielle and Shelby at the round table.

Jodi smiled. "Okay, mom. I'll make sure you can hear everything."

Fortunately, their table was off in a corner, and the diner was loud, so there was little risk of someone eavesdropping. Shelby began by explaining the work she did. "This property belongs to the families," she said. "It's my job to make sure they get it." Shelby gave more details, then the waitress came to take their order.

"So," Shelby concluded. "We found some property that we think might belong to you."

Jodi, who looked to be around sixty, took her mother's hand. "My grandparents didn't survive the concentration camps," she said. "They sent my mother into the countryside to live with relatives, and luckily, she made it out. But we don't have anything to remember them by."

Gabrielle cut her off. "I don't want another condominium. The monthly fees are high enough on the one I have now."

Jodi smiled. "It's okay, mom. I don't think Attorney Baskin is talking about any condominiums."

"She said 'property,' right?"

Jodi looked inquisitively at Shelby. "What *are* we talking about, by the way?"

The waitress brought chicken soup with matzo balls for everyone, then Shelby explained how the safe deposit boxes had sat dormant for almost eighty years. She looked at Gabrielle and enunciated clearly, knowing that doing so would help the woman understand. "Based on documentation found inside, we think two of the boxes belonged to your father, Aaron Kahn."

The old woman, her mouth only an inch or two from her soup bowl, looked back at Shelby noncommittally through thick glasses, but her daughter replied, "Obviously, we'd like to have whatever you found."

Suddenly, Cam yelled out and jumped to his feet as something crashed to the floor. Shelby, who had been looking at

Jodi, turned her head in time to see a puddle of soup on the table and a wet stain in Cam's lap.

"Mom!"

Gabrielle waved her hands as Cam hopped around in pain, holding a napkin to his crotch. "I'm sorry," Gabrielle said. "I ... someone ... knocked over my soup bowl."

Cam, his face red, took a deep breath. "It's okay. It just, um, surprised me. It's fine."

A waitress came over to help clean up and give Gabrielle more soup while Cam went to the men's room to tend to himself. Gabrielle, embarrassed by the accident, said to Shelby, "I hope that doesn't mean you won't give me my property."

Shelby laughed lightly. "No, of course not. I'm sure Cam is fine." She looked up to see him strolling over with a wry smile, a napkin hanging from his waistband. "Anyway," she said as Cam sat, "like I was saying, we have a little paperwork to fill out, nothing complicated, and then the safe deposit box and its contents are yours. But first, if I may, I do have a couple of questions just to make sure we have the right family."

Jodi nodded.

"Mrs. Kahn, do you happen to recall your father's birthday?"

She nodded. "March 14. But I don't know the year."

Shelby nodded. "That's fine." The date matched what Shelby had been able to learn about Aaron.

One more question. "Obviously, Mrs. Kahn, you have a child. Why is it you still have the Kahn name? I would think, if you were married, you would have taken your husband's name?" Shelby spread her palms. "I'm sure you understand, we need to be certain we have the right person."

Gabrielle's face flushed, but otherwise she looked around the restaurant as if she hadn't heard the question. Jodi leaned in. "She gave birth to me out of wedlock. No big deal today, but quite a scandal back then. She doesn't like to talk about it."

Shelby nodded, satisfied. "Okay." She took a deep breath. "One more thing. Does the word *Shamir* mean anything to you?"

Jodi shrugged, but Gabrielle blanched. She blinked and took a sip of her water before responding. "My father spoke of this often," she said in a shaky voice. "The Shamir. He said it was our family legacy. Since I was an only child, it would be my job to keep it safe." Her eyes began to pool. "I haven't thought about that in many, many years."

Shelby leaned closer. Gabrielle may have been hard of hearing and a bit infirm and clumsy, but she seemed to have all her faculties. "Do you know anything about it? Can you tell us what the Shamir is?"

Gabrielle shook her head. "I was only a little girl. Six years old when the Nazis came. My father told me our family had been guarding it for hundreds of years. I was the twenty-sixth in line. He said the Shamir was a tool for peace and that the great rabbis would come for it when the time was right. At that time, we would need to say a special prayer and the Shamir would appear. But I don't know what the Shamir is. Just that my father kept it in a metal box."

Cam leaned in and whispered to Shelby, "Kahn is one of the names of the class of high priests in Judaism. Makes sense they would be tasked with guarding this."

She whispered back, "And that's why we can't find it. You need a prayer, an incantation, to make it appear. It's probably still in that lead box, invisible, just waiting to be, well, activated."

Shelby addressed Gabrielle again. "Do you know the prayer, by any chance?"

Gabrielle looked out the window, focusing on some spot far in the past. "Yes. Yes, I think I do. My father made me memorize it. Every night, before bed, he would ask me to recite it back to him." She turned back to Shelby, her voice stern as if repeating her father's words aloud. "But I must not share it with anyone."

"No. We wouldn't ask you to. As you said, it is your family's legacy."

As her daughter patted her hand and listened with wide eyes, Gabrielle continued, "It was our job to take care of the Shamir, to guard it." She held Shelby's eyes. "But, of course, I never did. I never had the chance."

Shelby sat back and smiled. "Well, I think that's about to change."

Bruce had no idea who Shelby and Thorne were having lunch with, but it gave him time to get some gas and grab a bite to eat himself. And do some thinking.

After making quick work of a turkey sandwich, he phoned Pomeroy. "First of all, send me a link to that Facebook post, the one talking about the goddess figurine."

"Okay."

"Also, how quickly can you get a Bobcat and drive it up the trail to the site?"

"Like, right away. Maybe a couple of hours. But that'd be a violation of the terms of the easement."

"And?"

"Well, the neighbors would probably try to get some kind of injunction or something."

"Bullshit. They'll complain first, tell you not to do it again."

Pomeroy paused. "All right. Maybe. But what am I supposed to do with a Bobcat up there?"

"Push some dirt around. Park it next to a boulder. Maybe get a crate, write 'Plastic Explosives' on it, and set it down nearby where everyone can see it."

Pomeroy laughed. "Got it. You think it's time to create some urgency?"

"I do."

"What was it you said? Chaos is opportunity?"

"Something like that."

"All right then. I'll get that Bobcat up there and make some chaos."

Cam and Shelby stood in the parking lot outside of Rein's Deli, having just said goodbye to Gabrielle Kahn and her daughter. With a big smile, Shelby opened her arms for a hug. "We did it," she said.

"*You* did it," Cam responded, turning his body so the wet soup stain didn't soil Shelby.

She pulled away so she could look him in the eye, still holding his arms. "Don't be ridiculous. This was a total team effort. I did the work, while you made the old lady feel guilty for scalding you."

Cam smiled. "Always willing to take one for the team."

Shelby had made the decision that they should not drive all the way back to Boston. "Let's get a hotel. I can draft and print out the documents there and give the ring to Mrs. Kahn—I guess it's actually Ms. Kahn—this evening. Then we can ship the rest of the stuff to her when we get back tomorrow."

Cam had smiled. "Can't wait to get rid of that ring, huh?"

"Regarding the ring, and without going into too many details, let's just say I need that hotel room for another reason also. As they say, *this too shall pass.*"

Cam laughed as they walked to the car. "I was thinking," he said. "Gabrielle said she was the twenty-sixth person in her family to serve as custodian. Figuring twenty-five years per generation, that takes us back to around the year 1300."

"A long legacy."

He nodded. "And one that makes sense historically. That's around the time when the Templars were outlawed, in 1307. I'm thinking the Templars in Rouen had the Shamir, which is why there's a Templar cross on the box. But then they had to quickly pass it along before their commandery was raided. So they brought it to the local synagogue—"

Shelby finished the thought. "Where someone from the priestly families was chosen to safeguard it. And the Kahn family has had it ever since."

"Right," Cam said. They got into the car. "So, do you think there really is some magic incantation that makes the Shamir appear and disappear?"

She shrugged. "We're talking about a magic worm created by God on the night of the sixth day that noiselessly cuts stone and metal. The fact that it might appear and disappear is probably the easiest part of the story to believe."

He smiled. "Good point."

They found a Holiday Inn a few hundred yards up the road from the deli and checked in, Cam stashing the safe deposit box in the back of the closet under some dirty clothes. After he changed into a clean pair of pants, Shelby asked for some privacy alone in the room, so Cam found a quiet corner in the hotel lobby and phoned Menachem.

"I assume you have someone following us," Cam said, "so you already know we're in Connecticut."

"Any chance you'd go back to Rein's for me?" Menachem asked. "I love their matzo ball soup. They serve it nice and hot."

"Very funny. But I do have some news for you."

"I assume regarding the women you lunched with?"

"Yes. I won't give you their names, but they are the rightful owners of the safe deposit box. I think, if you don't come on too strong, they would be open to turning the Shamir over to you. With the ring. As I understand it, the ring is needed as part of some incantation which makes the Shamir appear. Otherwise, it's invisible."

Menachem grunted a response. Cam continued, recounting what he knew about the Kahn family and their custodianship of the Shamir. "Apparently, they are supposed to hold onto it until the great rabbis came to retrieve it. That's the good news. The bad news is that the Shamir cannot be weaponized. It is a tool of peace, to be used only for rebuilding the Temple."

Menachem was silent for a few seconds. "And you think they are ready to turn the Shamir and the ring over to us?"

"I do. To the Rabbinate, probably. But, like I said, don't come on too strong. Stress that the Shamir will be used to rebuild the Temple. Show your good faith by offering to return the other half of the ring if that's what they choose. Thank them for their service. Be kind and courteous." Then he added, not able to resist a final jab, "Maybe you should have someone else handle the negotiations."

Menachem actually laughed aloud at that. "You may have a point there, Thorne. I will consult with Tel Aviv and get back to you."

Cam returned to their room and knocked softly. A few seconds passed, then Shelby pulled the door open. She dangled a Ziploc plastic bag in the air, containing the inner half of Solomon's ring. She held up an open hand. "Don't. Ask."

He smiled "Okay." He couldn't help himself. "But did everything come out okay?"

"Asshole."

"Yes, that's what I was asking about."

She rolled her eyes, strolled to the desk, and popped open her laptop. "The adults need to do some work now. You can watch cartoons if you'd like, but no talking."

Cam stepped out of the shower in the Holiday Inn hotel room. Shelby had been working on the legal documents needed to formalize the transfer of the contents of the safe deposit box to Gabrielle Kahn. Cam, rather than watching cartoons, had gone for a mid-afternoon run.

"That feels good," Cam said, standing in a T-shirt and sweatpants.

"What? The shower or the exercise?"

"Both." The truth was, the hot soup had given him what looked to be first-degree burns around his crotch area, forcing him to cut the run short.

He had applied aloe lotion and chose the sweatpants over tighter-fitting jeans.

She held up a stack of papers. "Done. My turn for the shower."

It was still unclear to Cam whether they planned to stay the night in Connecticut. He tried not to think about the fact that the room had only a single king bed. Or about the fact that his burns might make the whole bed thing irrelevant.

"I assume you made those documents pretty basic?" he asked.

"Yes. But if thcy want to have their attorney look at them, that's fine."

"So we may be here for a day or two."

"Maybe." She smiled. "Which is why I need that shower."

As she closed the bathroom door, Menachem called back. "Okay," he said. "We'll do this your way. Don't come on too strong, as you said."

Cam was surprised. He guessed Menachem would have handled things differently. But what was he going to do, kidnap an elderly Jewish Holocaust survivor and pressure her into turning over her family bequest? There were some things even the Mossad couldn't do, at least on American soil. "Okay," Cam replied. "Good. Once we hand the safe deposit box over to them, I'll ask them if it's okay to give you their contact information. I'm just going to tell them the truth, that the Israeli government is interested in obtaining the Shamir and ring."

"In fact, you can tell them that we'll make a generous offer for it."

"Honestly, I'm not sure that's necessary."

"I know. But it never hurts to throw a few bucks around to get people feeling happy. At some point, we may need their future cooperation."

"Okay. I have no objection to the Kahn family getting a few bucks for their trouble."

"As a show of good faith, I have an agent driving the other half of the ring down to you now. He should be there within the hour."

"We're at the Holiday Inn."

"Yes. I know."

Of course he did. He probably also knew the room number. "Havc your agent call me when he arrives. After he drops off the ring, he can run up the road to get that matzo ball soup for you. My treat."

Menachem sniffed. "Hardly seems like a fair trade. But, as I said, we'll do this your way."

◇✝⊕

Cam sat in the hotel lobby, catching up on emails. He had left the hotel room to give Shelby some privacy after her shower, then phoned Astarte to update her before she ran off to class. It looked like this adventure would soon be over, and he would need to refocus on the rest of his life. He checked his watch. Almost five o'clock. The longer the day went, the less likely it would be that could complete the transfer of property to the Kahn family this afternoon. Which meant a night in the hotel, perhaps after a celebratory dinner.

His phone rang. Menachem's agent, calling from the parking lot. The man strode into the hotel lobby, identified Cam, and, unsmiling, handed over a small jewelry box. Cam peeked inside, confirming the outer part of the ring he had given Menachem back in Portsmouth was there. Of course, there was no way to verify it was the same ring.

"You want me to sign for this or anything?" Cam asked.

The man's eyes narrowed. "That will not be necessary. We know where to find you if there is a problem."

Cam handed the agent a twenty-dollar bill. "This is for Menachem's soup. Get him a cookie to go with it."

As the agent left, Shelby stepped from the elevator. Cam held up the jewelry box with a smile.

"And I didn't get you anything," she said with mock dismay.

"For the girl who has everything," he replied, handing it over.

"I just heard from Jodi. They are at their lawyer's office. The lawyer asked for a couple of small changes, but otherwise the documents are all set. So we can do the transfer now. They're waiting for us."

Cam nodded. Oh well. There would be other king beds. Hopefully.

Cam changed into a loose-fitting pair of khakis and grabbed the safe deposit box from the back of the closet. They drove ten minutes to a suburban office park where Gabrielle Kahn and her daughter waited with their attorney.

"I think I'll just wait in the car," Cam said as he pulled into the parking lot just after 5:30.

"Really? Why?"

"I'm running out of clean pants."

She cuffed him. "Come on. Be brave."

The law office was almost empty at this hour, but a short, balding, male attorney in a dark blue suit met them in the reception area and guided them to a conference room overlooking the highway.

Gabrielle slid a twenty-dollar bill across the table as Cam entered. "To pay for your dry cleaning."

Cam shook his head. "It was just a pair of khakis. I'll throw them in the wash, and they'll be fine."

"Well, what about the rest of you?" She gave him a knowing smile. "Any permanent damage?"

"No, thankfully." He smiled back at her. "But if there was, twenty bucks wouldn't nearly cover it."

It took less than ten minutes to sign all the papers, then Cam placed the safe deposit box on the table and opened it to reveal the lead box filled with wool. He showed them where the name *Shamir* was carved in Hebrew on the box along with the Templar cross. "According to legend, the Shamir has always been kept in a lead box filled with wool. We figure this must be it."

Shelby, who had put both pieces of the ring into the jewelry box, pulled the ring out. She showed Jodi and Gabrielle how the pieces fit together and explained how the two halves of the ring had been hidden, one in a cigar cutter and the other in the latch of a leather book. "We have reason to believe this is the famous ring of King Solomon. According to the Talmud, it has magical powers."

"We've already spoken with our rabbi," Jodi said. "There is a delegation of rabbis flying in from Jerusalem tomorrow. Just as my grandfather said would occur. The great rabbis coming for it."

"Well, it's your family's decision how to handle things. There was a reason it was left to you." Shelby didn't volunteer that she and Cam had used the ring to conjure up a demon. "We're pretty sure the ring is related to the Shamir. The rabbis will know more, of course."

There didn't seem to be much more to do, and Cam guessed it had been a long day for an octogenarian. He and Shelby stood and shook hands with both women.

Gabrielle, her eyes pooling, held Shelby's hand for an extra beat. "Thank you for allowing me to be part of my family legacy."

Rivka stood in a back room, watching a video feed as Cameron and Shelby left the law office conference room. She waited a few minutes to make sure the coast was clear, then walked tentatively down the hallway. That was all she needed, Cam returning to use the men's room and bumping into her. Talk about ruining an otherwise letter-perfect operation.

Esther, her face caked in makeup and still wearing the gray wig, saw Rivka standing in the doorway and engulfed her with a hug.

"You were awesome," Rivka said, squeezing her friend. "Academy Award."

"You don't think they suspected anything?" Esther asked.

Rivka smiled. "Nope. I always said you have the personality of an eighty-year-old. And you just proved it."

Esther laughed, then leaned in. "Menachem was pissed over the soup thing. But I couldn't resist. Got him right where it counts." She grinned. "I just wish it had been even hotter."

Menachem appeared suddenly in the doorway. "Menachem still *is* pissed," he said, glaring. "It was an unnecessary risk." Then his face softened. "But I concur with Rivka." He looked at Jodi as well as Esther; Jodi was a local community theater actress, one of many Jewish-Americans nationwide who helped out the Mossad when needed. "You both did an extraordinary job, especially given the time constraints. We now have Solomon's ring. Both halves of it. And we obtained it voluntarily, as Tel Aviv demanded." He glanced around the room. "Excellent work, team."

Rivka tried to keep the smile on her face, but the truth was that this victory was bittersweet. She had been only on the periphery of the operation—for obvious reasons, she could not be "on stage" during the performance. Rivka had done some of the foundational work, such as making contact with the real Gabrielle Kahn after Esther had first intercepted Shelby's phone call to her and, with the help of Gabrielle's rabbi, convincing the old woman to cooperate with the Mossad's ruse and allow for a substitute Gabrielle. The rabbi had not gone into much detail. "You can do a great service to Israel with this one little favor." Best not to tempt her, or anyone, with visions of magic rings.

But the whole thing still felt empty for Rivka, for an obvious reason: Even a casual observer could see the sparks flying between Cam and Shelby. That they may not have consummated things yet was a mere footnote in this story. At some point, things were going to ignite.

Rivka let out a long sigh. She used to be at the center of that flame. She missed not just its heat, but its warmth.

Menachem stood in the mostly empty parking lot of the office park as dusk set in, the sound of highway traffic audible from beyond the trees. With a steady hand he lit a celebratory cigarette, his third of the year. Eyes closed, he filled his lungs, exhilarating in the feelings of pleasure and energy as the dopamine released from his brain. When he had first quit smoking, at the insistence of both his wife and his doctor, he had made himself a promise: If he lived to eighty, he would take up smoking again and gladly let it kill him.

The irony was that, at this rate, he might actually make it, something the thirty-year-old version of himself would have found ludicrous. But the thirty-year-old Menachem had no idea what field operations would become. In the past three days, his team had produced a fake paranormal conjuring—using real smoke and mirrors—and a sham theatrical performance. Sure, there had always been subterfuge. But what had happened to gun battles and car chases and back-alley brawls? The truth, of course, was that both of these ruses had been wildly successful. In less than seventy-two hours, they had secured Solomon's magic ring, and had done so without the use of force.

He took another drag of his cigarette. He couldn't exactly say he missed the violence of an earlier time; he touched the scar running down his face to remind himself of its ugliness. But he did worry that the intelligence world was passing him by. Esther, with her technological skills and creative mind, had quarterbacked both of this week's operations. He shrugged. Was it so bad if it was time for him to go out to pasture? He'd go home to Israel, run around with his grandchildren, read spy novels, and play chess in the park.

With a cigarette in his hand.

"Bullshit," he said, tossing the half-smoked butt onto the pavement and squishing it with his heel. There would be plenty of time later to play chess in the park. For now, his country needed him. He was the one, after all, who had trained Esther and Tzion and Rivka and the rest of his ace team.

Rivka. Poor kid. She was putting a brave face on, but he could tell she was hurting. Personal matters were none of Menachem's business, normally. But this was affecting Rivka's performance. And, with Thorne involved, it was affecting the mission. So it sort of was his business. And from what Menachem knew, Thorne really was being a turd. At least have the decency to break things off before moving on to the next conquest.

He felt his blood pressure rising as he recalled the pain on Rivka's face. *Asshole.* He kicked at a pebble, sending it skittering across the parking lot. Maybe there still was a time and place for an occasional back-alley brawl.

Jason stepped from the shower, flexing his stiff leg. He had spent the afternoon on his knees weeding his aunt's vegetable garden, Uncle Pomeroy having declared that his injury left him unfit for real work for the second straight day. Whatever. Yesterday, Jason had wanted to be close to the house anyway for when the package arrived. Today, he was happy to sit in the sunshine and toss out an occasional weed, pretending to be hard at work. He toweled off quickly. Even without much exertion, he had built up a healthy appetite. And Uncle Pomeroy wouldn't hold dinner for him if he was late.

He reflected on yesterday's events. The package had been a financial risk, no doubt. Jason had about two grand in the bank. He figured he needed at least twelve grand to get a decent truck and earning four hundred a week wasn't going to get the job done anytime soon. Which brought him back to his uncle's offer to chip in if Jason showed his worth. Hopefully the package would help in that regard. If not, Jason would be out almost half of his two grand.

The FedEx van had turned into the long drive late yesterday morning, around 10:30. Jason had moved quickly to intercept it. Crazy how you could sit at your computer one day and, the next, a package would arrive from London. Sure, it cost $250 in air freight charges. But, again, with some luck it would be worth it.

He had signed for the package, a rectangular box about the size of a toaster oven, hoping they had packed it well. Actually, even if it had cracked or even broke, he could still have used it. But then he would have asked for a refund. Maybe he would anyway.

Jason threw on some clean clothes, continuing to review yesterday's events. After signing for the package, he had hid it under a tarp in the garage. Then, at lunchtime, he had texted his uncle. "Taking the truck into town for a pizza." It wasn't his truck, but whatever. Rethinking it, he had added, "And I'll grab some feed while I'm there." His thought was that the errand would give him some extra time and also hopefully keep his uncle from crawling up his ass.

He had found the keys hanging by the front door and, avoiding his aunt, trotted out to the old F-150 parked in the driveway, making a quick detour to the back deck to grab a pair of grill tongs from the gas grill. He had made a quick escape and then, a hundred yards up the road, pulled onto the shoulder to open his package. Nestled deep in bubble wrap he had found a faded, six-inch clay figurine of the Phoenician goddess, Tanit. Not much to look at, to be honest. Just the vague outline of a woman draped in a hooded robe. He could have gotten one with more detail, but that would have required spending more than $600 plus the $250 shipping. And, modest as it was, this would do the trick. Jason had done his research. Took him only a few hours on the internet. The London dealer guaranteed the figurine dated to around 1,000 BC. Same time period as that historian said the Phoenicians were here.

After speeding away, he had angled onto a side road which climbed the back side of the mountain. He had parked two-thirds of the way up the ridge, grabbed a thick branch to use as a walking stick, and began the trek along his uncle's easement to the ceremonial site. Council Rocks, that lady historian had called it. Not a bad name. Every important site needed an important-sounding name. Even if the person doing the naming was a real bitch. And this site was becoming more and more important. That GoFundMe page the Indians started had raised almost $400,000. All because of some stupid rocks.

Fighting through the throbbing pain in his knee, he had followed the trail and reached the peak forty-five minutes later. Clearing the tree line, he had looked to the western horizon. The clouds had turned dark. Just his luck, he had thought: As if his life wasn't challenging enough, now even the weather was conspiring against him.

He had descended fifty feet to the cluster of boulders and stopped. This had been the hard part. He couldn't just dig a hole and bury the figurine—there would be no way to disguise the freshly disturbed earth. Instead, he had examined the boulders. He had ignored the boulder with the notch cut into it because its crevices had been fingered and its surfaces pawed-over more often than a French whore. Instead, he had focused on the split boulder, the one where the top half had slid off and rested partly on the ground, forming a crevice between the two halves. He had dropped to the ground and, using his phone, shined a light into the crevice. A few cobwebs, plus some leaves and pebbles. Not wide enough to crawl in. But wide enough for the cylindrical figurine. After rubbing dirt over the object and into its crevices, he had used the grill tongs and reached in as far as he could—almost four feet—before dropping the clay goddess statue tight against the base part of the boulder. Again using the tongs, he had partially covered the figurine with a couple of leaves, being careful not to disturb the dirt on the ground around it with fresh markings.

Now there was nothing to do but wait a few days and make a second climb. Ideally, there'd be a witness there when he made his discovery. People might doubt him at first, but once they examined the object, they would learn it was three thousand years old. Was it possible an object like that could have sat undisturbed in the crevice of the split boulder for thousands of years? He shrugged. Why not? The base of the boulder would protect it from being disturbed by runoff pouring down the mountain, the top half of the boulder which covered the figurine weighed several tons and had likely never been moved, and the figurine itself was tucked under the lip of the boulder and was invisible to any passersby.

Jason toweled off. He had overheard his uncle on the phone. He knew the plan was to drive up the price of the land and then sell. Despite his uncle's low opinion of him, Jason would prove his worth. Only a sharp eye would notice an object slightly off-color beneath the boulder. Only an inquisitive young mind would drop to the ground, dirtying himself to make a careful examination. Only a persistent inquirer would spend the time to extract the mysterious item.

Jason smiled. He knew just where to find such a sharp-eyed, inquisitive, persistent young man.

◆✝⊛

Cam and Shelby sat at a booth in a pub in West Hartford, nursing beers and listening to a guitarist sing bar ballads. They had each had a burger —no onions—and shared a piece of chocolate cake. At some point, Shelby had slipped to Cam's side of the booth so her back wasn't to the singer. Occasionally, their knees touched. Cam felt like a teenager.

"I feel light and free," she said.

"You mean because the Mossad is out of our lives?"

She nodded. "I didn't realize how much it wears on you, always wondering if you're being followed." She sipped her beer. "Do you really think they're done with us?"

"I think so, yes."

No doubt that Menachem would be furious to have lost the ring. Doubly so if Gabrielle and Jodi hesitated in turning it over to Israel. But ruthless as he was, Menachem did not resort to violence gratuitously; he would likely see the effort of exacting revenge on Cam and Shelby as wasted time and energy.

"You want another beer?" she asked.

"Not if we're driving back to Boston," he replied. But if they were spending the night in the hotel, they could take an Uber back and pick up the Toyota in the morning.

She smiled. "Who said anything about going back to Boston?" She held his eyes. "I'm enjoying our adventure. Why end it before we have to?"

He met her smile. "If we have another beer, it's going to be hard to keep me off that dance floor. Just saying."

She sighed. "God, I haven't danced in, like, decades."

"Right. Bruce doesn't even like *listening* to music." Cam immediately regretted bringing up Bruce's name, but Shelby didn't seem to flinch.

"Just so you know," she said, "I dance like Elaine in *Seinfeld*. So I can't really blame it all on Bruce."

Cam doubted, as graceful as Shelby was, that she was an awkward dancer. But he played along. "Then maybe we should have a shot of tequila with that beer."

"You do remember that I can drink you under the table, right?"

He chuckled. He did recall a Friday night at the law firm where she did shots with a bunch of young associates at the end of a late night of playing poker, then convinced a senior partner to call them all in for an "emergency" client conference at 7:30 the next morning, suits and ties mandatory. She had waltzed in at 8:00 in jeans and a t-shirt, perky as ever, and dropped a box of donuts and six coffees on the conference room table. "Fun night last night, boys and girls. How does everyone feel?"

"Like shit," one of them mumbled.

She had smiled, turned, and looked back over her shoulder as she sauntered out. "I think you mean, 'Like shit and like *fools*.'"

Now, twenty-odd years later, they ended up having that beer, plus a shot, plus another beer, interspersed with a handful of turns around the dance floor. The guitarist began to sing *Wonderful Tonight*, by Eric Clapton. In their booth, Shelby put her mouth by Cam's ear. "Can I have this dance?"

Cam swallowed. The other songs had been faster melodies; this was a slow love song. With a smile, he said, "Only because you look so wonderful tonight."

She kissed him on the cheek. "That was sweet." She took his hand. "Come on."

Bruce sat at a back table in the pub, his hat pulled low over his face, and watched the only woman he had ever loved slow dance with another man. He was not much for sentiment, and he had never suffered a broken heart before. But this felt more like broken ribs. It hurt every time he breathed. And also when he didn't.

One thing that would not help was sitting here and torturing himself. He threw a twenty on the table and, without looking back, shuffled out into the cold, dark night, leaving the music and laughter behind.

That was it, then. Time to move on. Alone. The way it used to be. The way, when he was young, he thought it always would be. The way, after he met Shelby, he thought it never would be again. He spotted his car in the parking lot and made for it, head down.

Ten steps from the car, he stopped. *No.* He was a fighter, and Shelby, more than anything else in the world, was worth fighting over. They had built a life together, filled with love and caring and support. He knew he could do better as a partner, and he would. This thing with Thorne, whatever it was, was nothing more than a temporary frolic. A lark. An itch that needed to be scratched. She was bored, and who could blame her? Because Bruce had to lie low, they rarely left the house. He was bored also. They needed to start traveling again. Have some adventures. But traveling cost money, especially when you needed to do it with fake documents and private planes.

He clenched his fists. There it was again. His money problem. Solve that and the rest of his problems, including Thorne, would most likely also disappear.

Leaning against his car, he jabbed at his phone. Pomeroy had sent him the Facebook post, the one from the historical society discussing the discovery of the Tanit figurine at the Council Rocks site. Bruce shared the post on the pages of the various Native American groups he belonged to, with the simple caption: "We must preserve this site at any cost!" He waited ten minutes, then checked the GoFundMe page—it was up another twenty-two hundred dollars.

Feeling a little better, he allowed himself a small smile. What was it that his grandfather used to say? *There's nothing to be ashamed of if you happen to do well by doing good.*

Wonderful Tonight was the classic end-of-the-night slow song, and the dance floor filled quickly as the guitarist crooned a passable rendition. Shelby rested her head on Cam's shoulder and they both quietly mouthed the lyrics as they moved slowly in a tight circle. Cam felt light, buoyed by the alcohol and the music and the floral scent of Shelby's hair. Her hand rested in his, and he could feel her pulse through his thumb on her wrist. As he pulled her closer, he imagined he felt her beat quicken. He himself felt a stirring in his groin, relieved not to feel any pain from his aloe-treated wounds. They turned slowly, his eyes half-closed, the dance floor a kaleidoscope of lights and colors and shapes…

His eyes flew open. Ten feet away, on the edge of the dance floor, stood Rivka, her lip quivering and her eyes wide with pain. Anger he could have dealt with, but pain made him want to crawl away. He stopped and gently separated himself from Shelby.

"Don't worry. I'm not going to make a scene." Rivka motioned to the slight woman standing next to her. "I think you met Esther before."

Cam nodded, not sure what to say.

"Yes, we met," Esther said boldly. She changed her voice and affected a New York accent. "You'll have to talk loud. I forgot my hearing aids."

Shelby, standing behind Cam, gasped. Cam merely blinked, stunned at the audacity of their ruse.

"That's right," Rivka said after waiting a few seconds for them to put the pieces together. "We have the ring. *Voluntarily.*"

"Shit," Shelby breathed.

"So there's no magic incantation?" Cam asked. "No family legacy?"

"No," Rivka said simply. "It was all just part of the subterfuge, part of the lie to make you believe Gabrielle—that is, Esther—was the true owner of the ring. And you handed it over like you were emptying your pocket of loose change."

Cam merely stared back at her. How could he have been so stupid?

"Goodbye, Cameron." Rivka began to walk away, then turned. "We both know that if you had been thinking straight, you never would have fallen for it. But you've been acting like a fool." She cast a dark glance at Shelby and shook her head. "I hope she was worth it."

Pomeroy walked into Jason's bedroom without knocking. Jason, lying on his bed, quickly closed the porn video on his phone and adjusted his pants.

Arms folded, his uncle said, "That feed you got yesterday was the wrong blend. And I don't see why you needed to go all the way into town just for one errand. Waste of gas."

Jason felt like replying, "It wasn't just one errand, you idiot." Instead, he said, "Right." If Jason's plan worked, his uncle could buy the entire gas station. Hell, he could buy the whole freaking town.

"There's one other thing I wanted to talk to you about."

Jason kept his eyes on his phone. "Hmm."

"There was a find at the mountain. Under one of the boulders. A clay figurine. They think it's Phoenician."

Wait, what the fuck? Jason was glad he had his chin down, so his uncle couldn't read his face. "Well, that sucks."

"Right. More busybodies snooping around my property."

Jason tried not to laugh out loud. His uncle was a shitty liar. Jason knew his uncle was secretly ecstatic at the news, since it would add to the historical value of the site. So it didn't suck at all.

But it did suck for Jason. *He* was supposed to be the one to find the figurine. What shitty luck. A few more days was all he needed. He had finally made a bold move, tried to take control of his life rather than just waiting around for something good to happen. Waiting around was for losers. He knew, because he'd been doing it basically his whole life— other than when he jumped on that fat girl, but that had been the wrong kind of bold move.

Pomeroy droned on. "You should also know I drove a Bobcat up to the site this afternoon."

"Why?"

"Just to bust their balls."

Jason knew the real reason. His uncle wanted them to think he might start clearing the site. Maybe do some strip-mining.

Pomeroy continued, "I'd like you to go up there in the morning and keep an eye on things."

"That's it? Just sit there all day?"

"Yup. Like I said, keep an eye on things. Bring a rifle. Maybe use the Bobcat to knock down a few trees. But stay away from the boulders. For now."

"Whatever." Eyes on his phone, Jason waited for his uncle to leave. What did he want, a hug or something because he had struck it rich? Jason would give him a hug as soon as his uncle shared the windfall with him. Which would have happened if Jason found the figurine. Now it was too late, and Jason was out almost a thousand dollars. *Shit.* He should have pushed that damn thing in deeper, covered it with more leaves.

Finally getting the message that Jason didn't feel like talking, Pomeroy sighed, said goodnight, and closed the door, leaving Jason to stare at the ceiling.

After a few seconds, he checked the GoFundMe page. *Holy shit.* It was up over half a million dollars. Doubled to a million, with the dollar-for-dollar match. Much of that, Jason knew, had come in after the figurine discovery. Just his luck. His plan had worked, but of course he would not get any of the credit. Instead, he got a thousand-dollar hole in his pocket.

So what was the next move? The lesson from the figurine play was that it paid to be bold. Which meant no more sitting around.

What was the stupid expression his uncle always spouted, about being patient? *You got the chicken by hatching the egg, not by smashing it.* That was fine if all you wanted out of life was a stupid clucking bird. But maybe that was a golden egg you had there, and you never bothered to crack it open. Jason was done waiting around, hoping things would work out. He understood the importance of patience. But it was one thing to go fishing. It was another to just stand there on the shore with a stick in your hand looking like a fucking idiot.

◈✝⊛

His thoughts a tumult, Cam stood on the dance floor, watching Rivka walk away. It had been a long time since he felt so … gobsmacked.

Shelby, too, stood speechless and wide-eyed. They had both been flying high. Or so they thought, until their jet smashed into a fog-shrouded mountain peak.

In a fog himself, Cam paid the bill and together they shuffled out of the noisy pub to the quiet of weeknight suburbia. He called for an Uber.

They stood near the pub entrance, waiting. "Wow," he said. "I feel like an idiot."

"Me too."

He took a deep breath. "Well, the Mossad's not the world's leading intelligence agency for nothing. We're not the first to be bested by them."

"Not just bested." She shook her head. "We got our asses kicked."

Cam knew there was nothing to do about a whupping like this besides try to learn from it. "What I don't get is, how did the Mossad know about the Kahn family? How did they know who we were planning to meet with? You were using a burner phone when you called them."

After a few seconds of silence, Shelby swallowed. "That's a good point. The only person other than me who knew the name of the person who owned that safe deposit box was Bruce."

"What about people at the French bank?"

"But they only knew the father's name. Bruce and I were the only ones who knew the *daughter's* name. And it was through Gabrielle that the Mossad set up this sting. Bruce must have ratted me out."

Cam smiled sadly. "We both left a couple of broken hearts in our wakes. But they had the last laughs."

"Well, it's not over yet."

"How so?"

"If that incantation story is fake, then that means the Shamir isn't really still in the box. You know, *waiting to be activated*."

Cam nodded. "Right. Which means it's still out there someplace."

"The one place we really haven't looked is the safe room back at my house. Maybe it fell out and is just lying there." She offered a half smile. "Waiting to be vacuumed up."

Cam nodded again. "Okay, then. Brookline it is." So much for that king-size bed. With a hand on her back, he redirected Shelby away from where the Uber would be arriving and toward the neon lights of an all-night pancake house down the block. He said, "Just give me a large cup of black coffee and a couple of hours to sober up, and I'll be good to go."

⟁✝⊕

Cam and Shelby found a booth by the window and ordered waffles. This time they sat on opposite sides. "Obviously," Shelby said, "everything the Kahns told us was made up."

"Right. So does it make sense to try to find the real Gabrielle Kahn? Maybe she could give us a clue about the Shamir. Give us the real family story."

"I think that ship has sailed. If the real Gabrielle agreed to cooperate with the Mossad's ruse, I think we need to assume that Menachem already has her in his pocket."

Cam nodded. "What do we know about the family? I mean, it would be nice to drive back to Brookline and find the Shamir under the radiator, but we need a plan B. Is there another way to pick up the trail?"

From the leather satchel, Shelby removed a stack of papers binder-clipped together. "These are all the documents from the safe deposit box.

I made digital copies and printed them out in the hotel before I handed them over."

Cam smiled. "How very lawyerly of you."

She rolled her eyes. "Yes, your Honor, I got scammed and gave away the family heirlooms. But I did keep photocopies."

"Have you read through them?"

"Just skimmed them. My French isn't very good."

He reached out a hand. "Well, we have two hours. Give me half and let's get started. I was drinking Molson. Brewed in Montreal. After three beers, I'm practically fluent."

Most of the things Cam read—he knew enough French to get by—were financial in nature involving business affairs the Kahn family had in the Philippines with a man named Levy. From the look of things, Aaron made yearly trips to the Philippines as part of this business. Apparently, Aaron Kahn and Jacob Levy were first cousins. Aaron exported pharmaceutical items—he had a background in science—to the Philippines, where Levy oversaw distribution. Many of the documents reflected this business arrangement—promissory notes, joint venture agreements, licensing arrangements. But mixed in were a few personal letters referencing some kind of research project the two cousins had embarked on.

Using his phone to translate the words he didn't know, Cam worked quickly, his knee beginning to shake as his excitement grew.

"Listen to this," Cam said. They had been working in silence for about forty-five minutes. He explained the business arrangement between the cousins. "In this letter, they are talking about a *specimen* that Aaron Kahn brought back from the Philippines. Levy is asking if it made the trip back alive. Later, Levy tells him that they have been experimenting with the specimen—they always use the same word, as if they didn't want to be more specific—and that the experiments were promising. At one point, he wrote, and I quote, 'The specimen ate through the limestone, then expelled sand out the other side as waste.'" Cam sat back. "What does that sound like to you?"

"Not only that," she replied, "but why would they keep a letter like that in the safe deposit box? It must have been important to them."

Shelby set her papers aside and picked up her phone. "You keep working on the letters. I'll see what I can find about this specimen thing they found in the Philippines."

"They found it in something called the Abatan River." He spelled it. "Maybe that'll help you."

It didn't take Shelby long. "Look at this. An article from 2019 in a newspaper out in western Massachusetts. Apparently, one of the researchers was from UMass. They discovered a rock-eating worm in the Abatan River. Or *rediscovered* it. Listen to this quote from one of the scientists." She read aloud:

> *It's the first shipworm that's ever been found that doesn't live in wood...*
> *It's taking the bedrock of this river and it's eating it and it's passing it*
> *through its system... It's basically pooping out sand.*

Cam smiled. "They call it a *shipworm*. Obviously, the scientists haven't been keeping up with their Talmudic readings. But you're right, that's it. That's the same thing Kahn and Levy found more than eighty years ago. A worm that eats through rock. Just like the Shamir."

Shelby continued to scroll through her phone. After a few seconds, she added, "As you might imagine, the religious zealots in Israel got pretty excited. Listen to this quote from one of the rabbis who's trying to rebuild the Temple: 'God sends us what we need when we need it. The Shamir was created to help build the Temple. This discovery may be a sign that the need is arising again.'"

"So the cousins aren't the only ones who thought this worm might be the Shamir. Even the rabbis agree."

"I wonder why the cousins never publicized their find," Shelby mused.

Cam held up the letter between the cousins he had been translating. "This is dated March 1940. By May, the Nazis were invading France. I'm guessing they had other things on their minds."

"Right. Like survival."

She returned to her phone while Cam continued to translate the correspondence as he downed another cup of coffee.

"Bingo," she said, five minutes later. "I found an article written by

Gabrielle about her father as part of a Holocaust remembrance project. In it, she describes him as being in the import-export business and also that, even as a young girl, she remembers that his true passion was studying the Talmud."

"Nice find. That ties it all together. Aaron reads about the Shamir in the Talmud. As a scientist, he must have wondered if there was a scientific explanation for it. Then, when he's visiting his cousin in the Philippines, they learn about this crazy stone-eating worm—"

She interjected, "That makes sense. The article said the local people along the river have known about the worm for ages."

"Okay. So he takes one of the worms back to France with him to study." He paused. "And he builds a lead box for it because that's what the Talmud says."

"And because he doesn't want the worm to eat through wood or stone."

"Right. And he carves the name *Shamir* on it, because that's what he thinks, or hopes, it might be."

"But what about the Templar cross?"

"Good question." Cam chewed his lip. "Too bad we gave the box away. I'd like to study that carving."

She held up her phone. "I don't have the box, but I have some pretty good pictures. I got some high-resolution shots of the carvings."

He smiled. "Right. The careful lawyer."

She transferred the images to her laptop, then zoomed in. Cam came around to her side of the booth and they studied the images from different angles and using different lighting settings.

"To me," Cam said, "it looks like the inscriptions were carved by different tools. The cross lines look thicker."

She nodded. "And deeper. Also, look how the Shamir name is centered both horizontally and vertically on the lid, with the cross next to it. If you were going to carve the name and the cross at the same time, you'd probably try to center the entire line, not just the name. Make it balanced."

"So, the question is, why would someone add a Templar cross to the box?" He paused. "I suppose it's possible that the cross was there first, then the Shamir name was added later, but what you said about the name being centered makes sense. The name was there, then the cross was added."

She sat back. "So, like you said, who would add the cross, and why?"

It made no sense for the observant Jew, Aaron Kahn, to add a Christian cross. Cam didn't want to say it aloud, but he could think of only one other person in the past eighty-plus years who had an opportunity to alter the inscription. As to why, Cam had no idea what Bruce was up to.

In the pancake house, Shelby sat across the booth from Cam, his question echoing in her head. *Who would add a Templar cross to the lead box, and why?*

She didn't want to admit it to herself, but she was pretty sure she knew the answer. Using her burner phone to access her email account, she scrolled back a few weeks, to when she first started corresponding with the bank in Rouen. They had sent her a few images of some of the contents of the safe deposit boxes, including one that included the lead box. She found the picture and zoomed in. The image wasn't clear on the small screen, but she could make out the Hebrew writing on the lid of the box. *Shit.* She closed her eyes and let out a long sigh. There was no cross next to the Hebrew.

That was it, then. Bruce must have done it. Which, again, if she was being honest with herself, was what she suspected. She didn't know why, but it was a classic Bruce move, no doubt part of some scam or subterfuge. But this time he had defaced an heirloom which belonged to her client. One that had both historical and religious value.

Even worse, he had lied to her. She began to tear up. She had trusted him with the safe deposit boxes, and he had violated that trust. No doubt he would try to justify and rationalize his actions. "Nobody got hurt," he would argue. But she was hurt. She felt violated. Betrayed. And foolish for trusting him. Again. Fool me twice. More like ten times…

Wiping the tears from her eyes with a napkin, she looked up to watch Cam intently translate the French letters. He seemed so energized, so vibrant. Life was a great adventure, and Cam was the kid who wouldn't get off the rollercoaster. She couldn't help but make the comparison to Bruce, who had aged into the sedentary parent, content to drop the kids off at the carnival and go home to watch a sitcom. And then lie to her during the commercials.

The past few days had driven the point home: She missed the roller-coaster. And she wouldn't mind eating fried dough and making out on the Ferris wheel, either. She was too young to be old, even if she was getting mailings from the AARP. Fuck them. They couldn't have her yet. And fuck Bruce. He didn't deserve her.

Her mind had begun to clear after the beers and tequila shot, but not so much that she necessarily trusted herself to make the best decisions. Which was okay. Rash decisions were sometimes the best kind.

And this wasn't even all that rash. She did the math in her head: She and Cam had spent fifty waking hours together over the past three days. That was the equivalent of, what, a dozen dates? Plus she had known him for more than twenty years. Until now, the only thing preventing her from taking things to the next level with Cam had been her loyalty to Bruce. She owed him that much. Or at least she had thought she did. But loyalty was a two-way street. And one of those lanes was shut down. It was time to stop traffic on the other also.

Music played over the restaurant's sound system, and her thoughts flashed back to her slow dance with Cam. The way he held her tight. His shy, eager anticipation. The stirring in his loins as their bodies rubbed together. She took a deep breath. Not believing she was actually going to do what she had in mind, she kicked off her right shoe, lifted her foot, and began to run her instep up the inside of Cam's thigh.

His head jerked.

Her stomach tight, she arched an eyebrow and smiled shyly. "You sober enough yet to drive?" Her toes, wiggling, continued their way up his thigh. "Seems a shame to let that hotel room go to waste."

Mostly sober, Cam drove the Toyota on the near-empty streets back to the Holiday Inn ten miles outside of the city. They listened to soft rock on the radio, holding hands. Cam wanted to speed in the worst way but knew better than to risk it. The digital clock on the dashboard read 1:35.

Shelby let go of his hand and rested her fingers on his thigh. "I'm hoping you're healed from the burn?"

"Put me in coach, I'm ready to play," he replied with a nervous smile.

In the hotel elevator, they came together wordlessly, their kiss light and tentative, as if not wanting to shatter the mood. After a few seconds, their mouths slowly opened to each other. They separated at the ding of the elevator, their faces only inches apart.

"I'm glad we're staying on an upper floor," he managed to say with a smile, his heart pounding.

"Any higher up and we might not have made it to the room," she replied, tugging him out.

Their room, thankfully, was near the elevator. They kissed again, this time even more passionately, just inside the door. Many times, first kisses could be awkward and even sloppy, Cam knew. But this felt natural and comfortable, like their mouths had been made to fit each other. Their breathing rhythms fell into sync, and mouths and bodies together, they glided their way toward the bed.

She pulled away. "You taste good. Human, but fresh."

He smiled. "Feel free to go back for seconds."

She did, and slowly they eased their way to a sitting position on the bed. All five of his senses rejoiced in her touch, her feel, her taste, her smell, her beauty. He closed his eyes, lest he explode. Their breathing began to quicken, and Cam moved his hand to her breasts.

She shuddered, then pulled back a few inches. "Can we take this really slow? I want to savor it." She lowered her eyes. "Plus I'm a bit nervous."

He lifted her chin and caught his breath. "I've waited more than twenty years. We can go as slow as you want."

Her eyes widened. "No you haven't."

"Well, off and on. Not when I was with Amanda. But before. And even after."

"I had no idea."

He brushed her cheek with the back of his hand. "I didn't want to lose you as a friend."

It wasn't a line, but apparently it washed away the last of any hesitation Shelby might have been feeling. She stood, took her phone from her leather satchel on the floor, and hit a play button. A piece of classical music began to play as she returned to the bed and pressed her lips to his. Drums, then a flute joined in…

"Is that *Bolero*?" he asked after ten seconds.

She grinned, pleased that he knew it. "I was a figure skater as a kid. Torvill and Dean danced to it in the 1984 Olympics. I was fourteen. I had never seen anything so … sensual … in my whole life. The way it starts so slow, then builds to this incredible crescendo. Their bodies were in such harmony, as if they were a single organism." She kissed him, her eyes moist. "Then, at the end, they collapse on the ice, exhausted."

"Wow, not much pressure."

She laughed lightly, then turned serious. "They were just playing a part." She kissed him again, this time her arms tight around him. "This," she breathed, "is real."

CHAPTER 8

Cam awoke as morning light streamed into the room through a gap in the curtains. Shelby's face rested inches away, a sweet smile on her face. He didn't know if his had been a gold medal performance, but Shelby had hit the replay button on *Bolero*, which lasted a good fifteen minutes, at least a half-dozen times. And the smile on her sleeping face said more than any medal around his neck.

She stirred as he disentangled their limbs. "Don't go," she purred.

He kissed her forehead. "Be right back."

He used the bathroom, then washed up a bit. His reflection stared back at him. No guilt in the eyes, he was pleased to see. And definitely no regret. She had chosen him over Bruce, just as he had chosen her over Rivka. Neither had broken any vows, though admittedly they both owed their ex-lovers an explanation along with some closure. He recalled a short poem he had read once on a subway wall:

Love is rare,
Life is strange,
Nothing lasts,
And people change.

Speaking of explanations, they had never resolved why it was that Bruce had added the Templar cross to the Shamir box, as Cam had suspected and Shelby confirmed. Much as he would like nothing better than to jump back into bed, he knew they needed to finish solving that mystery…

"Can you bring me some water?" Shelby called.

"Of course."

From the bedroom, he heard music begin. *Bolero.*

"And I'd like you to deliver it naked, please."

He smiled. The mystery of the cross could wait a bit.

From his sailboat bobbing in the morning light in Boston Harbor, Bruce phoned Pomeroy. He had driven back from Connecticut after watching the Shelby and Thorne slow dance, taking refuge in his Sabre. He was not sure if he would also take exile in it.

"Good morning," Pomeroy said.

"It's time."

"I thought you said we should wait."

"And we did. But no more. There's over half a million in the GoFundMe account. Plus the matching funds. If we wait, the matching funds might disappear."

"So what's our asking price? A million?"

"Two million," Bruce declared. "Once they see that Bobcat up there, the snowflakes and tree-huggers and all the other liberal types will fall all over themselves to contribute. They're cheap, so they'll only throw in ten or twenty bucks each. But there sure are a lot of them, so it adds up."

Pomeroy grunted. "You're right about that. But two million still seems steep."

"And don't forget the gun control folks. You got their attention by blasting a few rounds over the heads of the Lenape. Just the kind of thing they hate to see. Nice move, by the way. Brought good attention to the site."

"Thanks. Seems to me, the press loves stuff like that."

"Exactly. Like I said, I think we can get the two million. If not, we can always come down. But I'm pretty sure we won't have to. Agree to the price now, then give them a few weeks to raise the money and close. Let them tap into some Lebanese businessmen and foundations. Everyone loves to brag about their culture."

Pomeroy didn't seem convinced. "I say we strike while the iron is hot. Move quickly. Take the million. Originally, we said we'd be happy with eight-hundred grand."

"Yup. But greed is good."

Pomeroy let out a long breath. "No, actually it's not. Greed is a fat demon with a small mouth, and whatever you feed it is never enough."

Bruce chuckled at the odd aphorism. Pomeroy rarely questioned him, but apparently the greed thing had hit a raw nerve. "Are you getting cold feet?"

"No. Not at all. But, like you said, now is the time. If we hold out for too much, we might end up with nothing."

"It sounds like you're afraid."

"I am."

"Well, then that seals it. Warren Buffett always says to be fearful when others are greedy and greedy when others are fearful. You're afraid, so I'm going to stick to being greedy."

Bruce hung up before Pomeroy could respond. That was the problem with having partners. Either they weren't as smart as you, or they weren't as ballsy. But, overall, Bruce couldn't complain. Bruce had approached Pomeroy after Bruce heard about the land during an Indian tribal council meeting when tribal leaders had suggested trying to purchase the parcel and preserving it. "Your land is worth, what, two hundred grand?"

"A little more," Pomeroy had replied. "But I'm not interested in selling. Right away, the government will take twenty percent."

Bruce had ignored the objection. "Let's say it's worth three hundred. What if I could get you half a million above that?"

"I'd ask you if I could have a couple of bottles of whatever it was you were drinking," the farmer had said with a laugh.

"I'm serious."

"If you're serious, I'm listening."

Bruce had explained his plan. "It'll take some time, but I'm pretty sure I can get a lot of people spun up about this site. All you have to do is act ornery and obstinate, like you have no interest in selling."

"I can do that. Hell, my wife says ornery and obstinate are two of the things I do best." Pomeroy had paused. "What's the catch?"

"I get half of everything above three hundred grand."

"Half? What about my taxes?"

"Okay. Make it above three-sixty."

"How do I know you can pull it off?"

"You don't. If it turns out I'm blowing smoke up your ass, you just keep the land and I get nothing."

They had gone back and forth, eventually settling on Bruce getting half of everything above $400,000. That meant $800,000 if the parcel sold for two million.

Which, Bruce contemplated as he watched the morning mist rise off the harbor, would be a hell of a payday. Not that he didn't deserve it. Like a chess master, he had set into motion the chain of events that placed the Council Rocks site in the public eye and caused that public to view the site as an underappreciated historical treasure.

Eight hundred grand. He shook his head at the bitter irony. If only he had someone to spend it on.

Naked other than the glass of water in his hand, Cam hopped back into bed. Shelby sat up, holding the sheet over her breasts, and gulped from the glass, water dribbling down her chin.

"That was very unladylike of me," she said with a laugh.

"You did some other things last night that weren't very ladylike also."

"Yes, but those were on purpose," she replied, dropping the sheet and turning into him. They shared a long kiss, then she rolled on top of him.

Some women didn't like to banter during sex, but Cam had noticed that Shelby enjoyed keeping things light even when things got hot and heavy. "That hypnosis stuff really works," he said, kissing her neck. "I had no interest in being intimate with you, but you put me under your spell and here we are."

She playfully bit his ear. "Wait until I make you bark like a dog."

They spent an hour atop the sheets, then ordered a room service breakfast, then spent another forty-five minutes together in the Jacuzzi tub. Finally satiated, they dressed and packed their bags. Cam left a twenty for the chambermaid and looked wistfully back at the room. "Last night you said you didn't want it to go to waste."

She took his arm with a smile. "As if."

He led her out and let the door close behind them.

Taking his arm, she said with a smile, "Well, Cam, whatever happens, we'll always have Hartford."

Twenty minutes into the drive back to Boston, Cam's cell rang.

"Hi Anita," he said. "You're on speaker with my ... friend, Shelby." He smiled and Shelby shrugged. They would need to figure out where this relationship was going.

After a bit of small talk, Anita said, "Guess who's ready to sell his property?"

"No way."

"He called the Lenape chief this morning. Wants two million for it."

Cam chewed his lip. On the one hand, it was way more than the property objectively was worth. On the other hand, the history embedded on the hillside was priceless. "Honestly, I'd pay double that. But it's not my money."

"The tribe doesn't have that kind of money, of course. But that GoFundMe page is still chugging along, and lots of people have taken an interest in the site." Anita paused. "It just sucks that that son-of-a-bitch is going to get such a windfall."

Cam flexed his elbow, sharing her animosity toward Pomeroy.

"Oh," she continued, "and get this. He drove a Bobcat up there and started pushing around some dirt."

Cam sniffed. "Subtle. But it'll actually make it easier for us to raise the money. Makes it look like there's an imminent threat to the site."

"Yup. I'm sure that's why he put it there."

"Any final results on testing the figurine?"

"Nothing final yet. But it looks promising. *Real* promising."

"That's great. Please keep me in the loop. On both things."

After he hung up, Shelby asked, "So, do you still think the Shamir had anything to do with the Council Rocks site?"

"In fact, more than ever. That worm from the Philippines proves that the Shamir, or something like it, actually exists in nature."

"Right. Most legends are based in fact. And that includes the Bible."

They crossed the border into Massachusetts. Cam said, "And we know the Phoenicians sailed all around the world in ancient times. So they might have come across this worm in the Philippines, or another just like it someplace else, and figured out how to use it to cut rock." He paused. "Or King Solomon found it during *his* travels, and he gave it or traded it to the Phoenicians, who were building his Temple for him."

She nodded. "Either way, it would explain the whole worm-cutting rock at King Solomon's Temple story."

"So, to answer your question, if the Phoenicians had it, they could have brought it to Council Rocks." He turned up his palm. "We'll probably never know for sure. But it's possible."

They drove in silence for a few minutes on the Massachusetts Turnpike. Cam glanced up at a highway sign. "We've got five miles to decide where we're going."

Shelby exhaled. "I was afraid of that." She turned. "I don't suppose we can turn around and go back to that hotel in Connecticut?"

He squeezed her hand. "I think you know we need to get some answers first. And you need some closure."

She smiled sadly. "My plan sounds like more fun. But you're right." She looked out the window. "My guess is that he's on his sailboat. So head toward downtown Boston."

In the noon sunshine, Cam pulled into a lot next to a Marriott hotel not far from the USS Constitution tourist site. "The marina's over there," Shelby gestured. With a smile, she added, "Where all those boats are."

"Do you see Bruce's?"

She nodded. "I texted him and told him we were coming. He was out sailing, but he came back in."

Cam wasn't looking forward to this. But he didn't begrudge Shelby giving Bruce some closure. And getting some answers. They still had no idea why Bruce had added the cross to the Shamir box, but Shelby was convinced it was part of some ruse. Cam hoped she was right—if it turned out Bruce had a legitimate explanation, he might use that to try to worm his way back into her good graces.

They found a cement bench along the Harborwalk, the walkway winding its way along Boston's waterfront. Shelby texted Bruce the location. After a few minutes, she pointed. "There he is, walking over."

Bruce stopped ten feet away, on the other side of the walkway, and leaned against a metal railing, facing them. He wore a windbreaker and blue jeans, his dark hair blowing in the breeze and his hands in his pockets. His body language was closed and defensive, as if he sensed unpleasant business was going to be discussed. Or maybe he noticed the anger in Shelby's eyes.

Shelby turned to Cam. "Maybe you can give us a few minutes?"

"Sure."

Cam found another bench fifty feet away and pulled out his phone to catch up on emails. Out of the corner of his eye, he watched as Shelby ended a twenty-five-year relationship. Cam knew what a loner Bruce was, how he really had nobody in his life besides Shelby. Cam had never liked Bruce, but his heart ached for what he must be going through. And poor Shelby. She had to deliver the painful news to someone she, undoubtedly, still had strong feelings for. From what little she had told Cam, she was going to be simple but blunt with Bruce: *I no longer am fulfilled by being with you. I'd be willing to work on that, on our relationship, but I also no longer trust you. I trusted you with those boxes, and you betrayed that trust. You deceived me. Again. Without trust, the relationship is irreparable.*

After about twenty minutes, Shelby stepped forward and embraced Bruce. Message delivered, apparently. Both of them wiped away tears, then Shelby motioned for Cam to come over.

"Bruce has some things he wants to tell you," Shelby announced, taking Cam's hand and leading him back to the bench where they both sat. Bruce's eyes widened at seeing them hand in hand. Cam guessed he had suspected something was up. But this proved it.

Head down, not making eye contact, Bruce filled in most of the blanks from the past few days. "I added the Templar cross to the Shamir box because I knew it would cause Shelby to call you and ask for your help." Cam resisted pointing out the irony that it was actually Bruce who had pushed Shelby into Cam's arms. "I also knew you had made plans to go down to Pennsylvania to see that Council Rocks site."

Cam wasn't sure what one had to do with the other. "How did you know that?"

Bruce hesitated, his arms crossed and his body turned away. Clearly he was not happy about being forced to answer Cam's questions.

"Come on, Bruce. You promised," Shelby said sternly.

With a long sigh, he said, "I'm friendly with some people in the Lenape tribe. And I'm aware of the site and its possible historical significance. So I knew some of the local historians were planning to bring you to inspect the boulders."

"You wanted me to connect the Shamir to the site," Cam said. "To speculate that maybe the Shamir was used to cut the notch on that boulder. Which would tie the site to the Phoenicians."

Bruce nodded. "But obviously, you couldn't make that connection if you didn't know about the Shamir."

"And I'm guessing you were working with Pomeroy. Good cop, bad cop. You lured me down there, then he chased me off as soon as I swallowed the hook."

Bruce nodded again.

Cam gritted his teeth. "You know, Astarte almost died up on that mountain."

"You can't blame me for that. You guys were trespassing, and then she went off and ate wild berries."

Cam's voice rose. "Can't blame you? She ate those berries because Pomeroy, your partner, wouldn't let us use the path to get off the mountain—"

Shelby interjected, "Look, nobody wanted any harm to come to Astarte. The point is, this was all a real estate play for Bruce. He was in cahoots with the landowner to jack up the price. Obviously, the more important the site is historically, the higher the price goes."

Cam swallowed his anger. "So the Shamir box itself was authentic?" Cam asked.

"Yes," Bruce said. "I just added the cross. Then, later, I fabricated the two halves of the ring and added those. To the book clasp and cigar cutter."

"Why?" Cam asked.

"I was worried the Shamir would not be enough to get your full attention. But I figured Solomon's ring would do the trick."

"How did you know we'd even find the ring? It was pretty well hidden."

Bruce shrugged. "The two of you, together, are pretty sharp. And if you didn't find it, I was going to call Shelby and give her a hint."

"How did you know we *did* find it?" Shelby asked.

"I tracked you back to that condo in Portsmouth. Your little conjuring ceremony. I figured you wouldn't even consider trying something like that if you didn't have what you thought was a magical ring."

Cam and Shelby nodded.

Bruce, for the first time, looked up. "I'm guessing you still don't know that the Mossad set up that whole conjuring thing," he said with a smirk.

"What do you mean?" Shelby asked, her eyes wide.

"It was all smoke and mirrors. They convinced your buddy, the condo owner, to help out. Told him you were going to sell the ring to a crime syndicate."

Cam shook his head. No doubt Bruce was enjoying jabbing him about falling for the Mossad's ruse.

"How did the Mossad even know we were in Portsmouth?" Cam asked.

After a long pause, Bruce admitted, "I told them."

"And I had told Bruce," Shelby said quietly. Then she looked Bruce in the eye. "Thinking I could trust him."

Cam nodded. Once the Mossad knew to focus on Portsmouth, they could easily have connected Cam to Martin Hall-Perez through Cam's social media posts regarding Martin's black-magic music lyrics, then deduce that Cam might reach out to the occultist.

"Like I said to you before," Bruce said, looking at Shelby, "these were all harmless lies. So what if you thought you were talking to a demon and it turned out to be some actor in a studio? Nobody was hurt by it. And I knew the Mossad wasn't going to harm you guys—they just wanted the ring. Same thing with getting Cam all hot and bothered about the Shamir. No harm done."

"Um, Astarte," Cam said.

"Let it go, already. Like I said, not my fault."

Shelby again interjected. "What about all those people who gave money to the GoFundMe page? Aren't they harmed?"

Bruce shook his head. "No. They donated money to save the Council Rocks site. And that's what their money is going to do. The fact that I'm going to put a chunk of that money in my pocket isn't hurting anyone."

"It's hurting the tribe," Cam said.

"No, it's not. It's not their money. It's a bunch of foundations and private donors. The tribe is getting ceremonial land for free because of all this. They're not putting in a dime." He turned to Shelby. "You know my code. No victims. Nobody gets hurt. This is a win-win."

"*We* almost got hurt," Shelby replied. "The Mossad thought this was all real, and they were playing for keeps."

Bruce waved her comment away. "Other than Cam getting some soup spilled on him, nobody got a scratch."

Shelby spoke, her voice almost a whisper. "What about the fact that you *broke* our relationship, Bruce? Does that count as someone getting hurt?"

The question hung in the air for a few seconds, Bruce's head down. Cam moved the conversation along. "It must have been you who gave the Mossad Aaron Kahn's name," he said to Bruce.

Bruce nodded. "I was actually doing you a favor. That guy Menachem was going to get that ring from you one way or another. Shelby, I know how stubborn you can be about these things. This way, you guys handed over the ring voluntarily and nobody lost any fingernails."

Cam had to admit, Bruce had done an admirable job puppeteering things. And, to his credit, besides Astarte and Cam's injured arm, there really were no victims of his subterfuge. Other than the truth, of course.

Cam looked at Shelby. "I've heard enough."

She nodded and looked at her ex-lover. "Thank you. I think it's important that you came clean. If you ever want me back in your life, in any capacity, this was an important first step."

Bruce clenched his fists and took a deep breath. "Before you leave," he said, glaring at Cam, "I want you to know one thing: I'm not giving up on Shelby. I *will* win her back. Just so you know."

"Bruce," Shelby declared, "that's not helpful."

"I know. But I didn't want there to be any doubt in anyone's mind."

Cam didn't appreciate Bruce's tone but decided he could be magnanimous in victory. "Whatever."

Bruce took two strides forward. "No. Not *whatever*. I'm telling you what is *going* to happen. So wipe that smug look off your face or I'll wipe it off for you."

So much for magnanimous. Cam stood. "Don't threaten me, Bruce." This was the guy who set into motion events that almost killed Astarte.

"Or what?"

Bruce poked Cam in the chest with his finger as he said it. Cam reacted reflexively, knocking Bruce's hand away.

The reaction was, apparently, enough to trigger the tightly wound spurned lover. Bruce lunged, swinging his right fist toward Cam's face. Cam, who had boxed a bit in college, blocked the blow with his left arm and, without thinking, threw a punch of his own with his injured right arm. The blow connected with Bruce's jaw, sending him sprawling backward to the ground. Cam ignored the jolt of pain in his elbow and dove on top of his foe, pinning him to the ground as Bruce thrashed beneath him...

"Stop it, you two!" Shelby yelled.

Bruce didn't comply, and there was no way Cam was going to let the larger man back on his feet until he was no longer a threat. Raising a leg and pivoting a bit, Cam drove his right knee into Bruce's ribcage, stunning him. But Bruce recovered quickly, reaching up to scratch at Cam's face. Cam swung his left elbow downward, catching Bruce above the eye, opening a gash. Without hesitation, Cam followed by dropping his left forearm across Bruce's neck and pressing downward, cutting off Bruce's air supply. After ten seconds of writhing, Bruce—blood gushing down his cheek—went limp. Only then did Cam roll off and jump to his feet.

Panting, he looked at Shelby. "Sorry about that. But he'll be okay in a minute or two."

She nodded, tears in her eyes, then let out a long breath as she looked at her bloodied ex-lover. She took Cam's arm and began to lead him away. "I'm afraid it's going to take him a lot longer than that."

Jason sat in the front seat of the Bobcat, munching on a roast beef sandwich. He was bored already, and it was only lunchtime. Lots of people hiked these mountains to check out the view, supposedly. To him it was just trees and sky. Yippy shit.

He had pushed some dirt around like his uncle said, but mostly he had been thinking. He gulped some Mountain Dew, not caring that some of it splashed onto the seat, staining it. His uncle could afford to reupholster. Especially after the windfall he was getting by selling this land.

Hopping from the machine, Jason trudged to the ridgeline for better service and dialed his uncle's number on his cell. It was time to have the conversation they should have had last night.

Jason got right to it. "You said that finding that figurine was a godsend. God had nothing to do with it. I put it there."

"Wait, what?"

Jason explained how he ordered the object from an antiquities dealer in London, then hid it under the boulder. "I was going to find it myself, but someone beat me to it."

He didn't expect the reaction he got from his uncle. "Shit, Jason, this could ruin everything. If anyone finds out, people are going to think the whole site is fake. All bullshit. Nobody's going to want to put their money into it."

"Don't worry, nobody'll find out."

"How do you know that?"

"I was careful. And the statue is authentic if anyone tests it."

"Shit, Jason, I wish you would have told me. This was a pretty stupid move."

Jason shifted the phone to his other ear. "What do you mean, stupid? You just said it was a godsend. I heard you on the phone saying it would get you another half-million, maybe more."

"Yes. If it was legit."

"Well, I don't hear anyone questioning it. All I hear is the price keeps going up and that GoFundMe page keeps growing." He paused. "I think, you know, that I deserve some credit."

His uncle exhaled. "What do you want, a pat on the back?"

He steeled himself. "No. I want that truck. You can afford it. You're making a killing on this sale." Symbolically, he was standing on a ridge-line. "I want a Honda Ridgeline. Loaded."

Pomeroy chortled. "Those things cost, like, forty-five grand."

"Yup."

"Listen, Jason, I said I'd help out. I'll give you, say, five thousand bucks. I know you have some money saved of your own. That should be enough to get you something serviceable."

Jason didn't want serviceable. He wanted something flashy, impressive, luxurious. Something that made a *statement*. "I have two grand. Your five gives me seven. You can't buy shit for that."

"Look, when I was your age, I drove a freaking jalopy. You should be happy to have anything."

"But—"

His uncle cut him off. "That's all you're getting from me, Jason. Be thankful for that," he said, then hung up.

◇✝⊕

Cam and Shelby walked away from the marina, following the Harborwalk. Shelby had stayed behind long enough to make sure Bruce was okay, then joined up with Cam at the Toyota. Cam held a tissue to his cheek, dabbing at a spot where Bruce had gouged him with his fingernails. "You know," he said, "I really don't feel like getting back into that car."

"Fine with me," she replied, taking his hand. "Let's walk a bit. Maybe cross the bridge into the city."

"The Aquarium's only about a mile away." The sun was shining, and they had no place to be.

She smiled. "It's a date." She glanced sideways as they strolled. "Just so you know, I tried to convince Bruce to donate his share of the Council Rocks proceeds to charity. I wanted him to give it to the Native American tribes. Could be as much as eight hundred grand."

"No luck, huh?"

"He said he needed the money for when we got back together. He says he figures we could travel for at least a decade with a chunk of money like that. That's what we were talking about. He swears he won't spend a penny until I come back."

Cam grimaced. He didn't like Bruce. But it was sad so much had been taken from him. And scary he was holding on so fiercely.

She continued. "Putting aside the whole trust issue, which is impossible to do, of course, what he doesn't get is that traveling in and of itself isn't what I was missing. I miss *living*. He's grown old. Not physically, but in his soul. I'm not there yet."

Cam nodded. "Does that mean you think I'm a young soul?"

She smiled and leaned into him. "Still in diapers, in fact."

They ambled on. Shelby asked, "Remember when we had breakfast together, the four of us, a few years ago?"

"Concord. Right before Bruce faked his death. He wanted my opinion on the *Ghent Altarpiece* painting."

"I recall thinking how lucky Amanda was. You guys were going off hand in hand on some adventure." She scowled. "Bruce dropped me off at the train station, pecked me on the cheek, and went off to plan some heist or scam or something. At the time, I didn't think I was unhappy. I thought I was just living my life. But it stayed with me. I wanted more. I wanted what Amanda had."

Cam grinned and spread his arms. "Well, careful what you wish for."

Smiling, arm in arm, they crossed the bridge linking Charlestown to the North End and grabbed a couple of quesadillas from a food truck, then turned left to amble along Commercial Street and past the many wharfs fingering out into the harbor. Shelby pointed toward the open water. "I think that's Bruce's Sabre. I recognize the blue and yellow genoa sail."

Cam watched the boat angle out toward the mouth of the harbor. Hopefully it would just keep on going. Cam's eyes drifted past Bruce's boat, toward East Boston and the airport. Rivka was probably there, with Menachem and her team and the ring. Unless someone had already boarded a plane for Tel Aviv with it.

"I'm thinking we should tell the Mossad that the ring is fake."

Shelby sniffed. "After the way they treated us, let them figure it out themselves."

"I guess." But just as Shelby still had warm feelings for Bruce, Cam wanted the best for Rivka. "On the other hand, it never hurts to have good relations with the Mossad."

"Says the man who was sleeping with one of their agents."

He smiled. "Beyond that."

She shrugged. "I'm fine either way."

He led her away from the street and out onto one of the wharfs, then pulled out his phone and dialed Rivka's number.

"Hello," she answered curtly.

"It's Cam." Shelby had edged away to give him some privacy.

"I know. Are you calling to get your ring back?"

"Actually, I *am* calling about the ring. But not to get it back. You should know, it's not real."

"You sure thought it was real when you used it to conjure up that demon."

"I did." He almost said *we did* but figured Rivka didn't need the reminder that he had a new cohort. "But it's not. Bruce made it. And he also added the Templar cross on the box." Cam explained what he had learned about Aaron Kahn and his research on the Philippine worm. "So there is no worm, either. At least not a magical one. Bruce added the cross and planted the ring as a way to lure me in. This was all a real estate play for him." He paused. "I could give you the details, but the point is, the ring is fake."

"Why are you telling me this?"

He looked out to the east. Five thousand miles away, a team of rabbis in Israel was planning to use the ring to conjure up a demon. "Because I don't want you to go marching back to Tel Aviv like conquering heroes with a ring from a Cracker Jack box." He shifted his weight and lowered his voice. "It's bad enough the way this whole thing went down. You deserve better. A lot better. And you definitely don't deserve to have this blow up in your face."

"Okay."

He could tell she wasn't sure whether to believe him. "Just get it tested. Tell Menachem."

"Okay," she repeated.

"Okay, then. Take care, Rivka."

The line went dead.

Shelby met his eyes and moved to him. "How'd it go?"

"Well, she didn't attack me like Bruce did, so there's that. But maybe that's because I was hiding behind my phone."

Shelby smiled sadly. "This is hard." She kissed him lovingly, lingering. When she finally pulled away, she said, "Maybe we should go to a bar instead of the Aquarium. There's a nice one with water views at the hotel where our car is parked."

Cam smiled. "I can't do that to the penguins. They get so excited to see me."

She met his smile. "Okay. An hour at the Aquarium."

"Then a bar."

She took his hand. "Even better, a bar at a hotel."

Cam and Shelby stood holding hands in front of the four-story center fish tank, watching as a barracuda swam only inches from their faces on the other side of the glass.

Cam said, "I read once that most people are like fish in an aquarium. Well-fed but unable to move beyond the glass walls of their lives."

"When I said Bruce had become an old soul, that's what I was talking about. He let his life become a cage."

Cam didn't know how to respond to that, so he merely squeezed her hand.

"You're not like that." She said with a smile. "Your problem is you swim too far from home and end up with the sharks."

He smiled. "Maybe Bruce has it right after all. Some of those fish look pretty content."

"They're not content. They're bored."

He turned to look at her. "Maybe they're just waiting for the right moment to make a run for it."

The barracuda studied them for a few seconds, as if perhaps contemplating an escape, then Cam's cell rang. Anita. "I'm going to take this," he said to Shelby.

"Of course."

"I just got an interesting call," Anita declared. "We have an issue. That Tanit figurine may have been planted."

Cam closed his eyes. An artifact conclusively proving that ancient Phoenicians had come to America—it really had been too good to be true. "*May* have been?"

"*Probably* was. You remember that young workman with Pomeroy up on the ridge? The one Astarte snared?"

"Sure."

"He's the one who called me. Says he planted it. Ordered it from London. Claims his uncle didn't know."

Personally, for Cam, it was horrible news. Nobody would pay attention to all the other evidence tying the Council Rocks site to the Phoenicians; instead, they would focus on the headline, the hoax, the plant. At least for a while.

On the other hand, the news gave the historical society and the tribe

—working together to purchase the land—some significant leverage. Cam said, "Whether Pomeroy knew about the figurine or not, the price just went down. A lot."

For a transaction like this, motivated as it was by emotion, it wouldn't take much for some of the institutional money to run for the exits. The narrative used to be about Indians trying to preserve their heritage, opposed by a redneck cowboy firing a shotgun over their heads. Now it had morphed into someone planting an ancient artifact to try to scam the public.

Anita continued. "I think we're going to go on the offensive. Hold a press conference with the kid. Make Pomeroy look bad. You know, he's pissed some people off."

"Live bullets tend to do that," Cam replied.

"Right. Ideally, we'll drive the price down, then use the leftover GoFundMe money to buy some of the surrounding land and maybe even build an interpretive center. Some people will ask for their money back, but not all of them. Especially not the ones who view the site as primarily Native American."

"An interpretive center would be nice," Cam replied, looking around at the Aquarium exhibits and the scores of people interacting with them. Even putting aside the Tanit figurine, the evidence was conclusive: At a minimum, the site was almost certainly an Indian cere-monial calendar site dating back 3,000 or 4,000 years. There was also a good chance the Phoenicians helped build it. And it was even possible they did so with the aid of the Shamir. "There are very few Native American sites dating back that far, especially in the eastern part of the country."

"Right. But personally, I'm bummed about the figurine. It was a cool find."

Cam sniffed. "Tell me about it."

"Still, it might be the best thing for the site in the long run."

"And better that we found out it was a fake now instead of after the closing. That would have really sucked."

Shelby, who was listening, shrugged as Cam finished up with Anita and hung up. "Well, it was almost too good to be true." She smiled. "So much for Bruce and his mountain of money waiting for me to come back. That mountain just became a molehill."

The wind whistled through the Sabre's sails as Bruce angled toward the open mouth of the harbor. He knew he had too much sail up for such a breezy day. In fact, a nasty nor'easter was forming offshore. He looked around. He was the only boat in the harbor. And he guessed it would be even more isolated once he sailed into the open ocean. But he didn't care.

He held an icepack to his eyebrow, periodically dabbing the blood with a paper towel. He needed stitches. Again, he didn't care.

His phone rang. He ignored the first two rings, then succumbed to curiosity and yanked the device from his pants pocket. *Pomeroy.* "What?"

"Some bad news. Turns out the figurine was a fake." Pomeroy explained the situation. "They've already scheduled a press conference. And they've withdrawn their offer."

Bruce took a deep breath. Once more, he didn't care. But he needed to make it look good. "You've got to be fucking kidding me. We lost this whole deal because you cheaped-out on a new truck for your nephew?"

"The kid's a punk."

"And his uncle's an idiot."

Bruce hung up. Well, that should settle things. It would have been nice to have the $800,000. Just like it would have been nice to have Shelby. The trifecta. But the cash had been a consolation prize in the event the ultimate prize—perhaps the most monumental discovery in modern history—had evaded him. Which, thankfully, it had not.

Holding the tiller in one hand, he reached out and flipped open the lid on his cooler. Nestled inside sat a black box made of lead, custom made for the job. Bruce spun the dial on the padlock mounted on the lid's cover and the lid popped open.

"Hello, little fella," Bruce said, peering at the green, glowing, worm-like object nestled on a bed of rough white wool. "Where should we go?"

Of course, the object—Bruce called it a worm, but that was only because it had the same general shape—did not answer. Bruce had no idea what it really was or how to make it work. Even the rabbis in the Talmud seemed confused. Some called it an actual worm, some a supernatural creation, some a glowing stone. Other sources suggested it might be some kind of alien technology, perhaps radioactive. All Bruce knew for certain was that it was rare and valuable. He had put it in a lead box with a wool bed because, well, the Talmud said that was how it had always been kept. Perhaps the worm took sustenance from the wool and lead in some way. He guessed that the ring somehow activated or powered the worm, but that was only because they seemed to move through history together. He'd figure it all out. He had time.

After checking his course, Bruce focused on the ring—a chunky ring of silver with a square piece of blue-green turquoise the size of a postage stamp mounted on it. Carved into the turquoise was Solomon's magical sigil, similar to the shapes and patterns that were carved into the fake ring the Mossad now had. The ring itself was not all that impressive. Not that it needed to be—by all accounts, it was the magical sigil and incantations made by Solomon 3,000 years ago, not the ring itself, which gave the piece of jewelry its powers. Even so, Bruce had expected it to glow or something, like the worm. Or like the Ark of the Covenant. Maybe it would when he figured out how to make it conjure a demon. A demon to do Bruce's bidding.

Unleashing the powers of the ring and the worm were the last tasks remaining on Bruce's checklist. A long checklist, one that was more like a meticulous military operation. He allowed himself a wide smile as he glanced back at the Boston skyline, not sure how long it would be before he saw it again. This, no doubt, had been his masterpiece. So many moving pieces. So many variables. So many feints and dekes and deceptions. But it had come together. He had distracted Shelby, making her think this was just another real estate play, Bruce trying to scam his way to a cool $800,000. And he had bested the Mossad, stealing the worm and ring out from under their noses and—by crafting those letters about the discovery of the rock-eating worm in the Philippines—making them and also Thorne believe that the real Shamir had not been in the box in the first place. Originally, when the safe deposit boxes arrived from

France, Bruce had been sorely tempted to just pocket the worm and the ring. But that would have been too obvious. Not to mention too dangerous, with the Mossad in the game—presumably early on, probably tipped off by a contact in France. So Bruce had done what he always did—he pulled off a heist in which there was no victim. And it had worked. As far as anyone knew—Shelby, Thorne, Menachem and his team, the Kahn family, the Rabbinate—there was nothing in that safe deposit box of any real value, and there never had been.

He had been dying to tell Shelby about the worm-like object and the ring earlier today, before he took a swing at Thorne. Especially after she called him an old soul, which was one of the reasons he attacked Thorne, to show her he was still a young buck with fight in him. But it had been a foolish move. Off-script. Emotional. He deserved the thrashing Thorne had given him.

And so what if he was an old soul? An old soul with a magic ring was more like it. An old soul who boldly and brazenly just pulled off the heist of the century.

Shelby would have appreciated the complexity and subtle brilliance of Bruce's orchestration. Even as she would have resented being duped by it. But she was so love-struck—or at least she thought she was—that Bruce couldn't be sure she wouldn't rat him out. And the ring was too important. Even more important than Shelby. She'd come around, in time. And he'd be waiting.

But, in the meantime, a man only got one chance in life at harnessing the powers of a demon.

Cam and Shelby had gone from the Aquarium to the Marriott bar for a couple of drinks, and then from there up to a waterfront room overlooking the harbor where they had killed the rest of the afternoon in bed. Shelby was now in the shower, giving Cam a chance to check in with Astarte.

First, he told her about Shelby. Astarte had met her a few times and even shadowed her at her Big Sister job once for a school assignment.

"Shelby's great, Dad. The work she does with those teenagers is amazing. I liked Rivka, too, but I get that she might just have been a stage in your life."

"Well, it's only been a few days, so Shelby might only be a stage also."

"You wouldn't be telling me about her if you thought that."

"It wouldn't be *me* walking away. Maybe I'm a little nervous she'll get cold feet."

"You guys have been friends for, what, twenty-plus years? So she's heard all your bad jokes. You'll be fine."

Cam smiled. It was nice to get relationship advice from his daughter. "Thanks, honey."

He also updated her on the Council Rocks site. "Turns out that ranch hand Jason planted the Tanit figurine."

"Too bad we didn't shake it loose when we snared him," she said with a light laugh.

"Might be best the way it turned out. The tribes can use it to drive the price down."

"But won't Pomeroy just walk away? Sounds like he didn't really want to sell in the first place."

"There's a story behind that also." Cam explained how Bruce and Pomeroy had been in cahoots to drive up the value of the land. "I think the plan all along was to sell. And the tribe is still the best buyer—it's worth more to them than to anyone else. But he'll be lucky to get more than, say, a hundred grand over the assessed value."

"Still not a bad payday."

"But, literally, a million bucks away from where they were a couple of days ago, before the Tanit figurine dropped a turd into the punchbowl."

"That's a gross expression, but in this case, it sort of fits." She paused. "But it doesn't change the underlying history. That's an amazing site, even without the figurine. A calendar in stone dating back three thousand years. Lunar and solar. Indian and Phoenician. Confirmed by science. With precise alignments and also intercalations. Not to mention a mind-blowing mystery about how they carved it so precisely."

"Yup. All we need is for some of the academic types to pay attention to it. Once they do, watch out."

Astarte laughed. "The story of your life."

"Tell me about it." Cam took a deep breath. "Even more interesting is the story behind the Shamir." He told her about the letters between Aaron Kahn and his cousin discussing the rock-eating worm they had found in the Philippines and their belief that it provided a scientific explanation for the Shamir. "It, literally, eats rock and then poops out sand. Scientists just rediscovered it a few years ago, but these guys knew about it in the 1930s. But before they could publicize it, the Nazis invaded France."

Astarte was quiet for a second or two, obviously thinking. "Let me get this straight. So the magic worm wasn't magic after all?"

"Right. Turns out there was a rational explanation for it. As there usually is."

"Exactly."

Cam angled his head. "Exactly what?"

"Exactly. There's usually a rational explanation for all these stories from the Bible." She took a breath. "Okay then, so what about the magic ring that summons the demons? What's the rational explanation for that?"

"I don't know."

"But you agree there probably is one?"

Cam replied, "Sure." He guessed this discussion related back to their simulated reality conversation.

Astarte continued, "We know this: Whoever created the world— either an omnipotent God or some savvy computer programmer—also created as part of this world a rock-eating worm, right? A creature which, a few years ago, scientists would have considered a thing of fiction."

"Okay." He thought he saw where she was going with this.

"So, isn't it possible that the creator also created demons? And a magic ring which summons them? If he created one, why not the other?"

Cam chuckled. "I have to say, you make a persuasive argument."

"You didn't answer my question."

"Okay. I agree. It's possible. Demons are possible. And also a magic ring to summon them."

"Good. Now that we've settled on what I want you to get me for my birthday," she said with a laugh, "tell me more about Shelby."

They chatted for another ten minutes, then Cam hung up as Shelby sauntered out of the bathroom in a bathrobe. "I'm famished," she said. "Any chance you'll be a gentleman and take me out to a proper dinner?"

He grinned. "Anything you want."

She sat on the bed next to him. "Funny you should say that. I just got a weird text from Bruce, asking me that if I could have anything I wanted in the world, what would it be?"

"What did you say?"

"I asked him why he was asking." She read from her phone. "And he said, *Because maybe, just maybe, I can give it to you.*"

Cam made a face. "That's sort of an odd thing to say."

"I know. So I replied that that's impossible. And he said, *Is it?* And he added, like, six question marks at the end."

"And?" Cam asked.

"And nothing. Like I said, I told him it was impossible. So I never replied after that."

Cam turned to face her. He was a bit concerned, especially in light of what Astarte had just argued. What if Bruce somehow found Solomon's magic ring? He and Shelby thought they had figured things out, but Bruce was a master scammer. Maybe the ring was in the safe deposit box all along. "Do you really think it's impossible?" Cam asked.

Why else would Bruce be sending such cryptic texts? If so, would Shelby be tempted? *Anything in the world.* Bruce must have a reason for choosing those words…

"Do I really think it's impossible?" Shelby asked, interrupting his thoughts with a light laugh. She moved in for a long kiss, only pulling away to look him in the eye, put her hand on his cheek, and say, "It's impossible, silly, because I already have the one thing in all the world that I really want."

The End

DEAR READER

I love to get reader feedback, both to help me continue to write about things that you (hopefully) enjoy and also to improve on the things you don't. Please feel free to reach out to me at dsbrody@comcast.net, and/or also to leave a review at Amazon or Goodreads.

If you enjoyed *The Serpent Oracle,* you may want to read the other books featuring Cameron and Astarte in my "Templars in America" series, all of which have been Kindle Top 10 Bestsellers in their categories (see below). And if you enjoy legal thrillers, please check out the three legal thrillers in my "Boston Law" series, *Unlawful Deeds, Blood of the Tribe,* and *The Wrong Abraham:* https://www.amazon.-com/gp/product/B0753CRT9D

"Templars in America" Series

Cabal of the Westford Knight
Templars at the Newport Tower (2009)
https://www.amazon.com/gp/product/B00GWTZYLS
Set in Boston and Newport, RI, inspired by artifacts evidencing that Scottish explorers and Templar Knights traveled to New England in 1398.

Thief on the Cross
Templar Secrets in America (2011)
https://www.amazon.com/gp/product/B006OQIXCG
Set in the Catskill Mountains of New York, sparked by an ancient
Templar codex calling into question fundamental teachings of the
Catholic Church.

Powdered Gold
Templars and the American Ark of the Covenant (2013)
https://www.amazon.com/gp/product/B00GWTYJ5K
Set in Arizona, exploring the secrets and mysteries of both the Ark of the
Covenant and a manna-like powdered substance.

The Oath of Nimrod
Giants, MK-Ultra and the Smithsonian Cover-up (2014)
https://www.amazon.com/gp/product/B00NW13QTG
Set in Massachusetts and Washington, DC, triggered by the mystery of
hundreds of giant human skeletons found buried across North America.

The Isaac Question
Templars and the Secret of the Old Testament (2015)
https://www.amazon.com/gp/product/B016E3X2QK
Set in Massachusetts and Scotland, focusing on ancient stone chambers,
the mysterious Druids and a stunning reinterpretation of the biblical Isaac
story.

Echoes of Atlantis
Crones, Templars and the Lost Continent (2016)
https://www.amazon.com/gp/product/B01MXJ0BNX
Set in New England, focusing on artifacts and other evidence indicating
that the lost colony of Atlantis, featuring an advanced civilization, did
exist 12,000 years ago.

The Cult of Venus
Templars and the Ancient Goddess (2017)

https://www.amazon.com/gp/product/B0767Q4N1S
Set in New England, triggered by the discovery of a medieval journal
revealing that the Knights Templar came to America before Columbus
because they were secretly worshiping the ancient Goddess.

The Swagger Sword
Templars, Columbus and the Vatican Cover-up (2018)
https://www.amazon.com/gp/product/B07HCRNYVN
Set in Rhode Island and Ireland, inspired by the 1980s Vatican Bank
Scandal and featuring a treasure map, carved on a sword, indicating that
Christopher Columbus may have aided the Templars in secreting a trea-
sure in America.

Treasure Templari
Templars, Nazis and the Holy Grail (2019)
https://www.amazon.com/gp/product/B07XV9QJNZ
Set in New England, New York and Belgium, triggered by a 15th-century
Dutch Masterpiece which Hitler believed was a secret map to the
Templar treasure and the Holy Grail.

Watchtower of Turtle Island
Templars and the Antichrist (2020)
https://www.amazon.com/gp/product/B089QWSGM1
Set in New England and Montana, sparked by occultists who believe that
a stone tower in Newport, RI—built by the medieval Knights Templar—
is a portal through which the Antichrist will appear.

Romerica
Roman Artifacts in America (2020)
https://www.amazon.com/gp/product/B08NZ64T4N
Set in New England and the Ohio River Valley, triggered by Roman-era
artifacts—many with Jewish themes—evidencing a secret journey to
America by Roman/Jewish survivors of the Bar Kokhba uprising circa
133 AD.

The Pillars of Enoch
Templars and the Melungeon Legacy (2021)
https://www.amazon.com/gp/product/B096916H9R
Set in North Carolina and Portugal, turning on a mysterious stone tablet given to Moses by God along with the Ten Commandments, purportedly passed down to the Freemasons by the medieval Knights Templar.

Sheba's Revenge
Oak Island and the Templar Treasure (2021)
https://www.amazon.com/gp/product/B09LFK2MZD
Set in Nova Scotia and Massachusetts, sparked by the furtive pairing of the Queen of Sheba and King Solomon, an affair which even today threatens to destabilize the Middle East and which may unlock the mysterious Oak Island treasure.

The Serpent Oracle
Templars, Mormons and the Lilith Legacy (2022)
https://www.amazon.com/gp/product/B0B436C2D3
Set in New England and Ohio, triggered by a rogue group of venom-injecting, head-shaping Freemasons intent on replacing Western religions with worship of the ancient serpent alien gods.

Available at Amazon as Paperbacks and as Kindle eBooks

AUTHOR'S NOTE

It has always struck me how crazy many of the stories of the Bible are. If you hadn't been raised in a Judeo-Christian world, and someone on the street stopped to tell you about angels appearing out of burning bushes, or patriarchs parting the sea, or saviors being born from virgin mothers, you would probably drops your eyes and hurry past. And the stories of the Talmud—essentially, the teachings of Judaism's greatest rabbis—are even more outlandish. If you've read this far, you know I'm referring, in particular, to the Shamir. A rock-eating worm used by King Solomon to build his Temple? Sure, why not? There are many sources discussing the Shamir, but I found these two sites to be particularly useful as overviews:

https://www.mayimachronim.com/mystery-of-the-shamir/; http://karl shuker.blogspot.com/2014/02/the-shamir-and-stone-worm.html

I hadn't expected to find the Shamir featured in Masonic ritual, but there it was. I shouldn't have been surprised. It seems as if every time I go down a rabbit hole to research an ancient mystery, I find Freemasons waiting for me at the bottom. To paraphrase a popular saying, Freemasonry may not be a secret society, but it surely is a society with secrets.

Speaking of secrets, it seems like enigmatic stone formations and lithic arrangements scattered across this continent could be the key to unlocking mysteries involving ancient exploration of the Americas. The Council Rocks site in Wilkes-Barre, Pennsylvania is one such site. Recently discovered by researcher David Gutkowski, Council Rocks—as described in this book—seems to tell the story of ancient peoples, perhaps associated with Phoenician explorers, erecting a calendar in stone. Intriguingly, that calendar seems to incorporate both solar and lunar time passage, as explained in this story. David's research is ongoing, including some intriguing optically stimulated luminescence preliminary test results. You can read more about this site here: https://www. academia.edu/12143590/Council_Rocks_Archaeoastronomy_Re search_detail_with_photos. This research paper, along with private correspondence between David and myself, is the source for much of the information about Council Rocks in this book. Special thanks to David for all the help he gave me with writing the Council Rocks scenes and for trusting me to write about his amazing site. I can't wait to see what his continued research reveals! Please note that the Phoenician figurine as described in this story is purely fictional.

Special thanks to my friend Michael Hauptly-Pierce for walking me through the conjuring scene. MHP, as he is known, often assists me with research for books in this series, especially in matters relating to esoterica. Any mistakes or missteps during the conjuring scene are mine, not his.

As is the case with all the books in this series, if an artifact, site or object of art is pictured, it is real—except as specifically noted otherwise in this Author's Note. And if I claim the item is of a certain age or of a certain provenance or features certain characteristics, that information is correct or believed to be correct. Likewise, the historical and literary references are accurate. How I use these objects and references to weave a story is, of course, where the fiction takes root.

On the subject of fiction, the Bruce and Shelby characters were first introduced to readers in *Unlawful Deeds*, the first book in my Boston Law series. You can read more about their back-story there. The characters make periodic appearances in this Templars in America series as well.

For inquisitive readers, perhaps curious about some of the specific historical assertions made and evidence presented in this novel, more information is available here (in order of appearance in the story):

*For an explanation as to why the equinox falls a few days before March 21, see:
https://www.timeanddate.com/astronomy/equinox-not-equal.html

*Stellarium software products can be found here: https://stellarium.org/

*The source for the optically stimulated luminescence dates for the Council Rocks boulders as recounted in this story is a presentation made by Dr. James Feathers at the Spring, 2022 New England Antiquities Research Association conference, as well as from private correspondence with Mr. Gutkowski.

*For a discussion of the fourteen supernatural things created by God on the night of the sixth day, see:
https://www.setaria.org/English_Explanation_of_Pirkei_Avot.5.5.9?lang=bi&with=all&lang2=en , at section 5:6.

*The source for the Masonic historian Finch's assertion that Hiram Abiff was killed by ruffians in order to obtain the Shamir, as well as the direct quote asserting such, can be found here: https://www.academia.edu/43129202/Who_is_Asmodeus_King_of_Demons_A_Study_of_King_Solomons_Master_Craftsman?email_work_card=view-paper   ,   at page 21.

*For the assertion that the Templars may have used the Shamir to aid them in erecting the massive Gothic cathedrals—including Notre Dame and Chartres—of medieval Europe, see *The Templar Papers*, by Oddvar Olson at p. 19 (Career Press, 2006), with a link to the online version here: https://www.academia.edu/36146056/2746_The_Templar_Papers_pdf?email_work_card=view-paper

*For the assertion that the Shamir was a glowing, jade-colored stone able to cut like a laser, perhaps because it was radioactive, see: https://general ist.academy/2021/02/04/solomons-laser/

*For information on the 1683 German book asserting that a rock-eating worm had been discovered in a monastery in Normandy, see: http://karl shuker.blogspot.com/2014/02/the-shamir-and-stone-worm.html

*The quote from the architectural historians regarding the Pumapunku wall can be found here: https://en.wikipedia.org/wiki/Pumapunku#Engi neering (edited for clarity and brevity)

*For the story of how Asmodeus cloned himself and took Solomon's throne, see: https://muse.jhu.edu/article/639595

*For the details of the "tyrannical" things Asmodeus did while on Solomon's throne, see: https://en.wikisource.org/wiki/Translation: The_Story_of_King_Solomon_and_Ashmedai

*For details of the *Arabian Nights* story of a fisherman who finds a genie named Asmodeus locked in a copper jar with the seal of Solomon on it, see https://en.wikipedia.org/wiki/The_Fisherman_and_the_Jinni

*For information about the ancient Copper Culture in the Great Lakes region, including the Cornwall arrowhead and Uluburun shipwreck, as well as the specific assertions that 1) oral history of the tribes in the Great Lakes region spoke of mining conducted by "fair-haired marine men" and that carbon-dating of artifacts found in the ancient Great Lakes copper mines dated back to the Phoenician era, and that 2) Phoenicians would have made the long trip to America because of the abundance of American copper, its purity, and the fact that other supplies had dried up, see: https://bookofmormonevidence.org/michigan-copper-in-the-mediterranean/

*The quote about the Cusco wall in Peru, attributed to Pizarro, can be found here: https://en.wikipedia.org/wiki/Sacsayhuam%C3%A1n

*The quote about the quality of stonework in the Cusco wall in Peru can be found here: https://www.peruforless.com/blog/twelve-angle-stone/

*The quote about the quality of stonework in the Machu Picchu wall can be found here: https://artsandculture.google.com/story/8-unsolved-mysteries-of-machu-picchu/0AKy0UOme0vAJA

*For the assertion that an Austrian professor who wrote a book about the ancient history of Brazil and a Dutch scholar considered the father of Brazilian archeology both asserted that Phoenician explorers crossed the Atlantic to Brazil, see: https://gnosticwarrior.com/the-paraiba-inscription.html

*The quote regarding the eight serpents writhing at the foot of the Apprentice Pillar enshrining the legend of the Shamir can be found in *The Secret Scroll,* by Andrew Sinclair, online version: https://www.electricscotland.com/history/kt7-12.htm , at Part 1.

*The lyrics from the song, "Babes in the Abyss," are from a song written by musician Michael Hauptly-Pierce of the band, Jam Tomorrow.

*The magical incantations spoken during the Asmodeus conjuring scene are taken from (sometimes after being paraphrased) these two books: *The Al Ghoul Compendium,* by Diablito Ordo Al Ghoul and Arundell Overman (CreateSpace 2018); also, *Modern Magick: Eleven Lessons in the High Magickal Arts,* by Donald Michael Kraig (Llewellyn 1988).

*For the assertion that the god Baal was depicted by ancient Phoenicians in their artwork with large round eyes, an open mouth, and curly hair, see:
   Phoenician funerary masks and pendant/head beads: A feature

analysis and catalogue, by Alexandria Miller, at p. 5 (2020) https://commons.emich.edu/cgi/viewcontent.cgi?article=1675&context=honors

*For more information about the *Key of Solomon* book of magic, see: https://en.wikipedia.org/wiki/Key_of_Solomon

*For the quote about the rock-eating worm found in the Philippine's Abatan River, see: https://www.gazettenet.com/UMass-Amherst-scientist-helped-identify-new-genus-and-species-of-shipworm-26410711#:~:text=UMass%20researcher%20helps%20identify%20new%20genus%20of%20rock%2Deating%20mollusk,-Microscopy%20image%20of&text=AMHERST%20%E2%80%94%20A%20worm%2Dlike%20freshwater,sand%20out%20the%20other%20end

*For the quote from the rabbi about the discovery of the worm indicating it was time to rebuild the Temple, see: https://www.israel365news.com/132404/recently-discovered-rock-eating-worm-key-third-temple/

So, do I believe in a magic worm which can cut stone, or that Solomon's magic ring can summon demons? No. But, as I alluded to earlier, are supernatural worms and magic rings really any more outlandish than other things considered gospel in modern religions? The point is, one person's religion is another's quackery. People are free to believe what they want, of course. But let's not make the mistake of believing that our particular beliefs are any more "valid" than anyone else's. Unless, of course, your beliefs happen to enable you to conjure up a demon to grant you three wishes...

As always, thanks for reading and coming on this journey with me.

David S. Brody, November, 2022
Newburyport, Massachusetts

ACKNOWLEDGMENTS

Research is a key part of putting these books together, and I was the beneficiary of some invaluable research assistance for this book. As mentioned in the Author's Note, special thanks go to David Gutkowski and Michael Hauptly-Pierce, without whom this book could not have been written. Thanks also go to Richard Kretz, Michael Yannetti and Dr. Michael Sandberg for sharing their valuable knowledge, insights and guidance with me.

I am grateful aw well to my dedicated team of Beta Readers. Some are newbies, while others have been with me for as many as a dozen books. They provide an invaluable service, helping me polish and improve the story before releasing it publicly. I offer my heartfelt thanks —for their astute insights, observations and comments—to the following individuals (in alphabetical order):

Adam Aquilante
Mary Baier
Paul Barnett II
Eileen Briesch
Carol A. Bye-MacLeod
Scott Clarke
Travis Collins
Edmund Correa
Darlene Crouthamel
Tim Culhane
Randy Dickey

David Gutkowski
Michael Hauptly-Pierce
Mark Hickox
Jim Ingalls
Edward Kdonian
Lisa Klee
Richard Kretz
Penny Lacroix
Paul McNamee
Damon Merrylees
Scott Eric Miller
Liz Perrella
Szilveszter Poczik
David Runge
Ruth Sanderson
Scott Selig
Ryan Shaw
Wario Suarez
George Tournas
Carolos Varin
Ted Vaught
Terry Anne Wildman
Sheila Williams
Mary Yannetti
Michael Yannetti

Any mistakes in the story are mine, not theirs. And the fact that they may have assisted me does not mean they endorse or support any of the things written.

I seem to write the same words at the end of every book, but they are true now more than ever: I owe a huge debt of gratitude to my wife Kim. She spends hours reading the early drafts of my stories, sometimes slogging through them three or even four times. As the singer Prince said, "I like constructive criticism from smart people." A gifted writer herself,

Kim is incredibly smart and does her best to offer comments and feedback in a constructive, positive manner. I couldn't ask for a better writing partner—or life partner, either. Thanks, honey.

PHOTO CREDITS

Hamsa Hand, Alabama Burial Mound, credit:
https://en.m.wikipedia.org/wiki/Moundville_Archaeological_Site

Cusco Stone Wall, Peru, credit:
Diego Delso, CC BY-SA 4.0:
https://commons.wikimedia.org/w/index.php?curid=43175184

Cusco Twelve Angle Stone, Peru, credit:
https://www.peruforless.com/blog/twelve-angle-stone/

Machu Picchu Wall, Peru, credit:
https://www.annees-de-pelerinage.com/machu-picchu-architecture-explained/

Made in the USA
Middletown, DE
05 May 2023

30093172R00166